P9-DWT-047

THE BABY-SITTERS CLUB

CLAUDIA AND MEAN JANINE

DON'T MISS THE OTHER BABY-SITTERS CLUB GRAPHIC NOVELS!

KRISTY'S GREAT IDEA

THE TRUTH ABOUT STACEY

MARY ANNE SAVES THE DAY

DAWN AND THE IMPOSSIBLE THREE

ANN M. MARTIN

THE BABY-SITTERS CLUB®

CLAUDIA AND MEAN JANINE

A GRAPHIC NOVEL BY

RAINA TELGEMEIER

WITH COLOR BY BRADEN LAMB

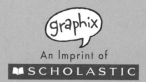

graphix

An Imprint of

■SCHOLASTIC

All rights reserved. Published by Graphix, an imprint of
Scholastic Inc., *Publishers since 1920.* SCHOLASTIC, GRAPHIX,
THE BABY-SITTERS CLUB, and associated logos are trademarks
and/or registered trademarks of Scholastic Inc.

Library of Congress Control Number: 2015935840

ISBN 978-0-545-88623-9 (hardcover)
ISBN 978-0-545-88622-2 (paperback)

10 9 8 7 6   18 19 20

Printed in Malaysia   108
First color edition printing, February 2016

Lettering by John Green
Edited by David Levithan, Sheila Keenan, and Cassandra Pelham
Book design by Phil Falco
Creative Director: David Saylor

For Aunt Adele and Uncle Paul
A. M. M.

Thanks to everyone who has helped make this project a
reality! Dave Roman, Marion Vitus, John Green, Ashley Button,
Janna Morishima, David Saylor, David Levithan, Cassandra Pelham,
Ellie Berger, Sheila Keenan, Kristina Albertson, Phil Falco, Vera Brosgol,
Dr. Laurie Kane, the Green family: Bill, Martha, and MarMar,
and most especially, Ann M. Martin.
R. T.

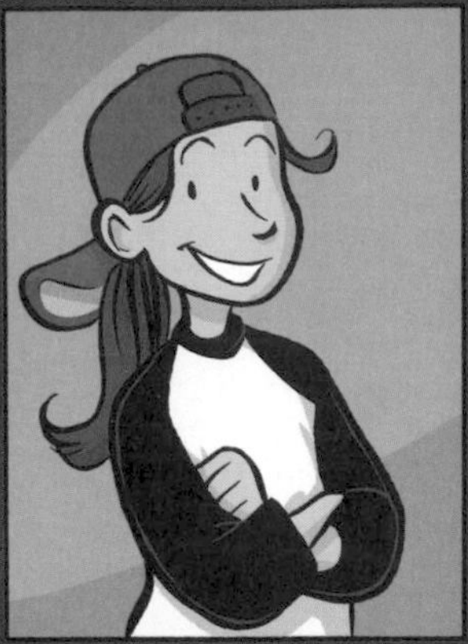

KRISTY THOMAS
PRESIDENT

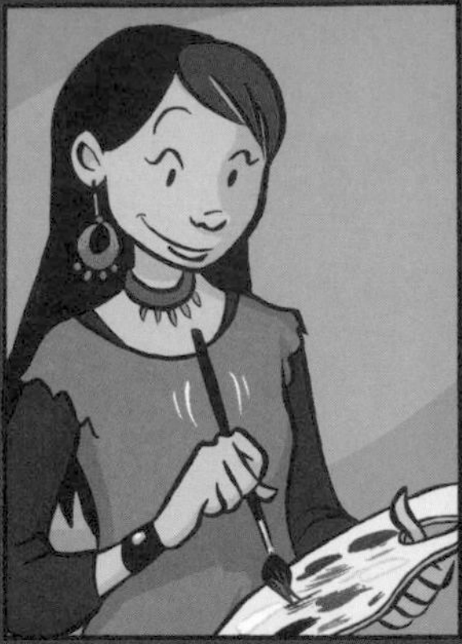

CLAUDIA KISHI
VICE PRESIDENT

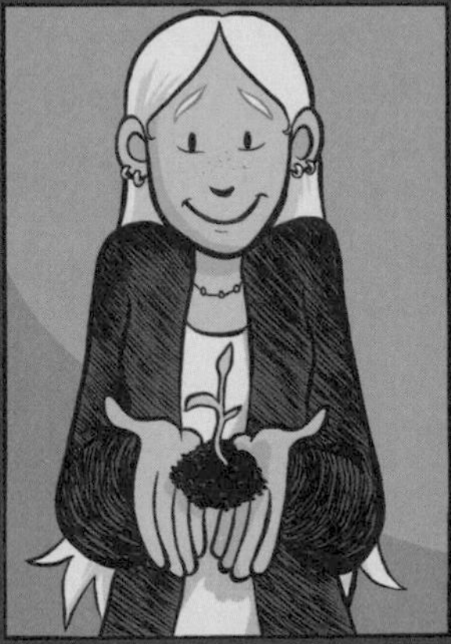

DAWN SCHAFER

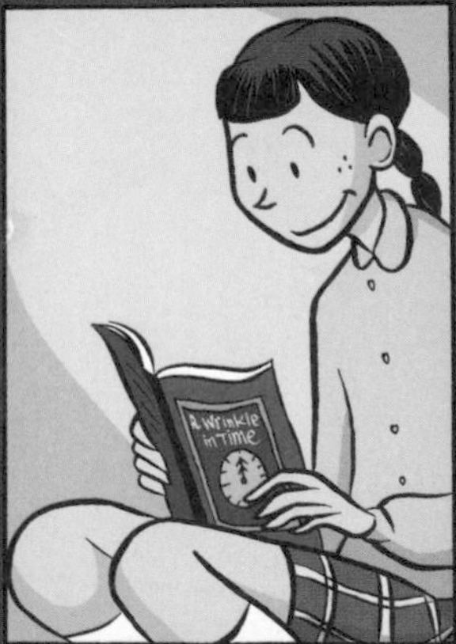
A Wrinkle in Time

MARY ANNE SPIER
SECRETARY

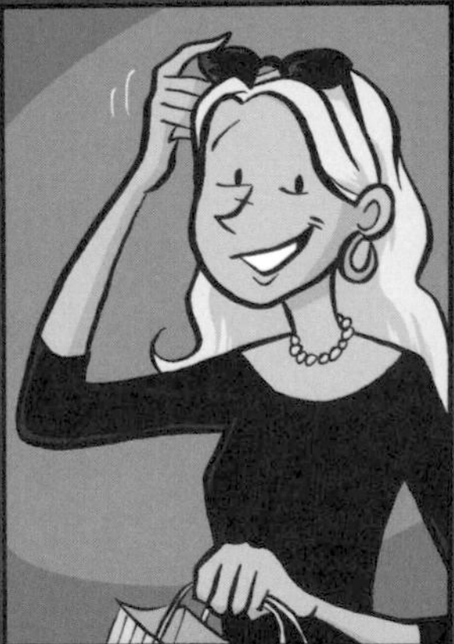

STACEY MCGILL
TREASURER

CHAPTER 1

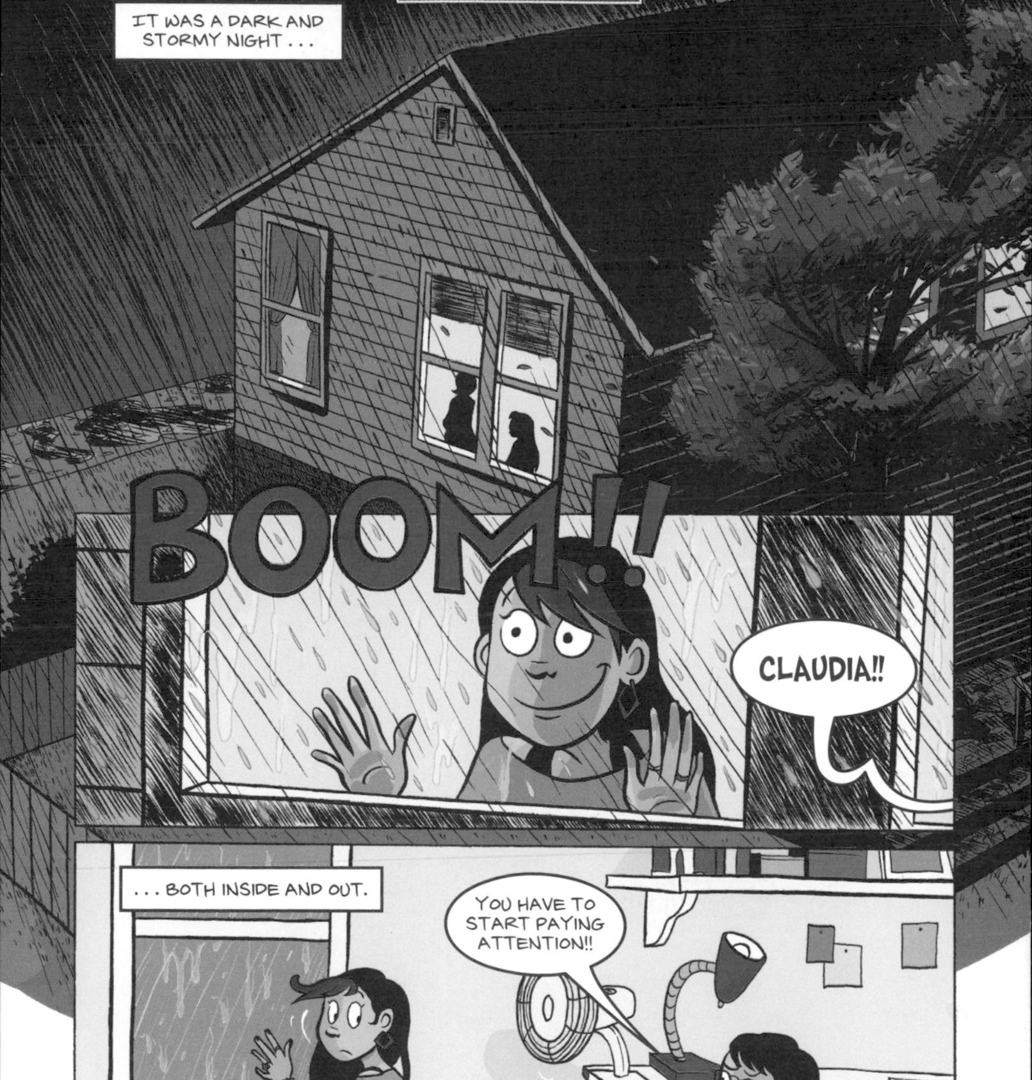

IT WAS A DARK AND STORMY NIGHT . . .
BOOM!!
CLAUDIA!!
. . . BOTH INSIDE AND OUT.
YOU HAVE TO START PAYING ATTENTION!!

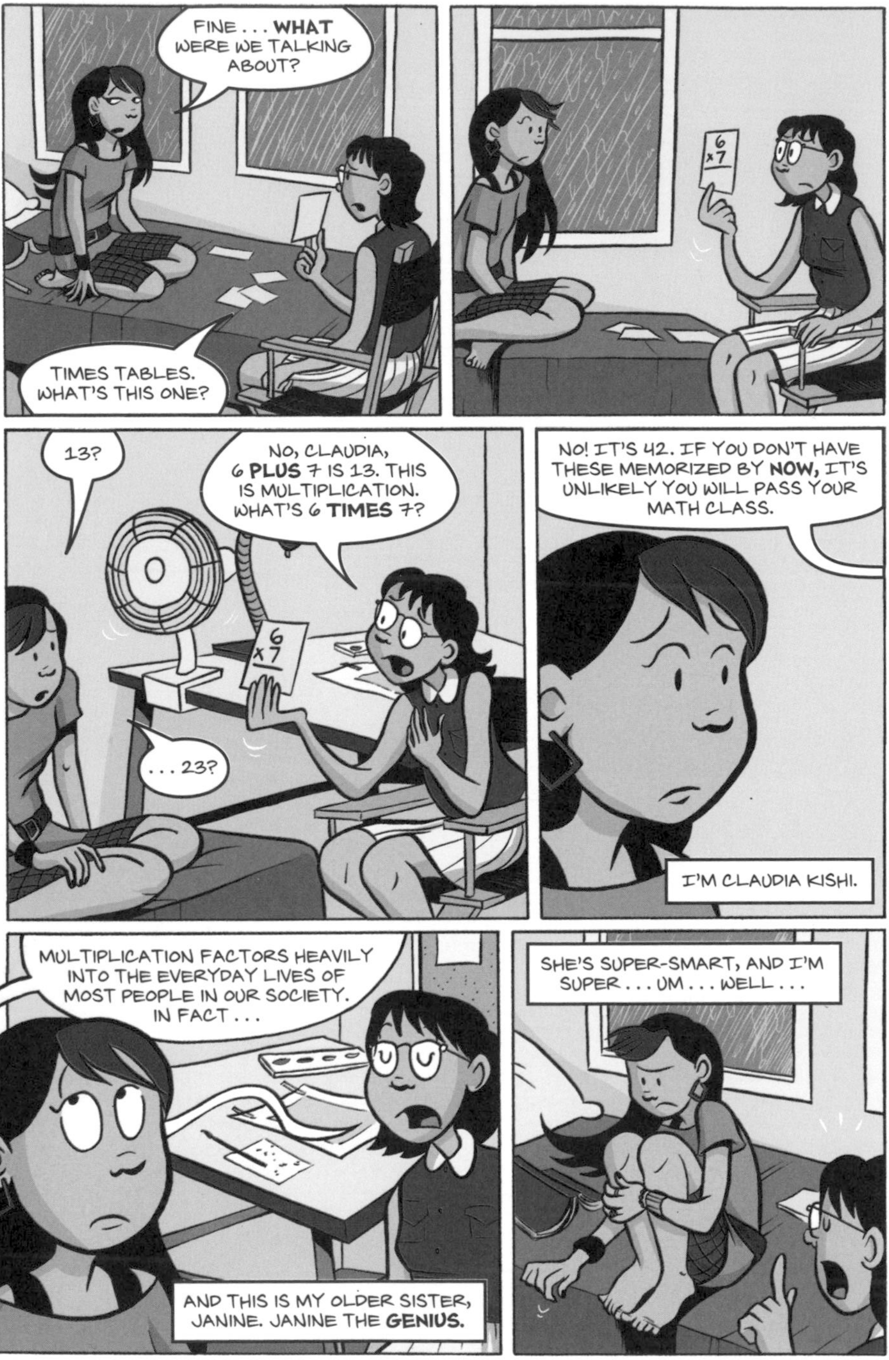
FINE . . . WHAT WERE WE TALKING ABOUT?
TIMES TABLES. WHAT'S THIS ONE?
6 x 7
13?
NO, CLAUDIA, 6 PLUS 7 IS 13. THIS IS MULTIPLICATION. WHAT'S 6 TIMES 7?
6 x 7
. . . 23?
NO! IT'S 42. IF YOU DON'T HAVE THESE MEMORIZED BY NOW, IT'S UNLIKELY YOU WILL PASS YOUR MATH CLASS.
I'M CLAUDIA KISHI.
MULTIPLICATION FACTORS HEAVILY INTO THE EVERYDAY LIVES OF MOST PEOPLE IN OUR SOCIETY. IN FACT . . .
AND THIS IS MY OLDER SISTER, JANINE. JANINE THE GENIUS.
SHE'S SUPER-SMART, AND I'M SUPER . . . UM . . . WELL . . .

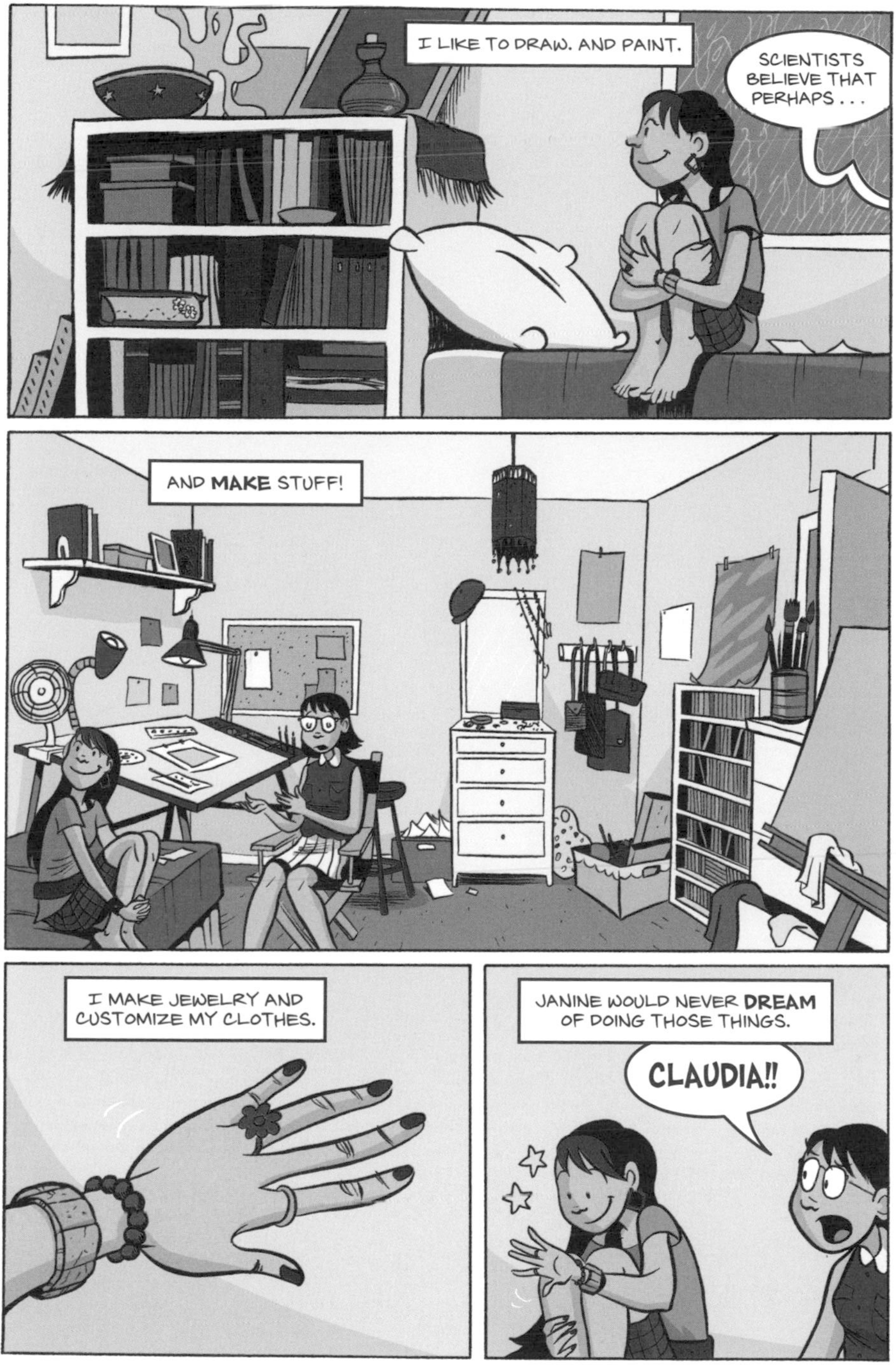
I LIKE TO DRAW. AND PAINT.
SCIENTISTS BELIEVE THAT PERHAPS . . .
AND MAKE STUFF!
I MAKE JEWELRY AND CUSTOMIZE MY CLOTHES.
JANINE WOULD NEVER DREAM OF DOING THOSE THINGS.
CLAUDIA!!

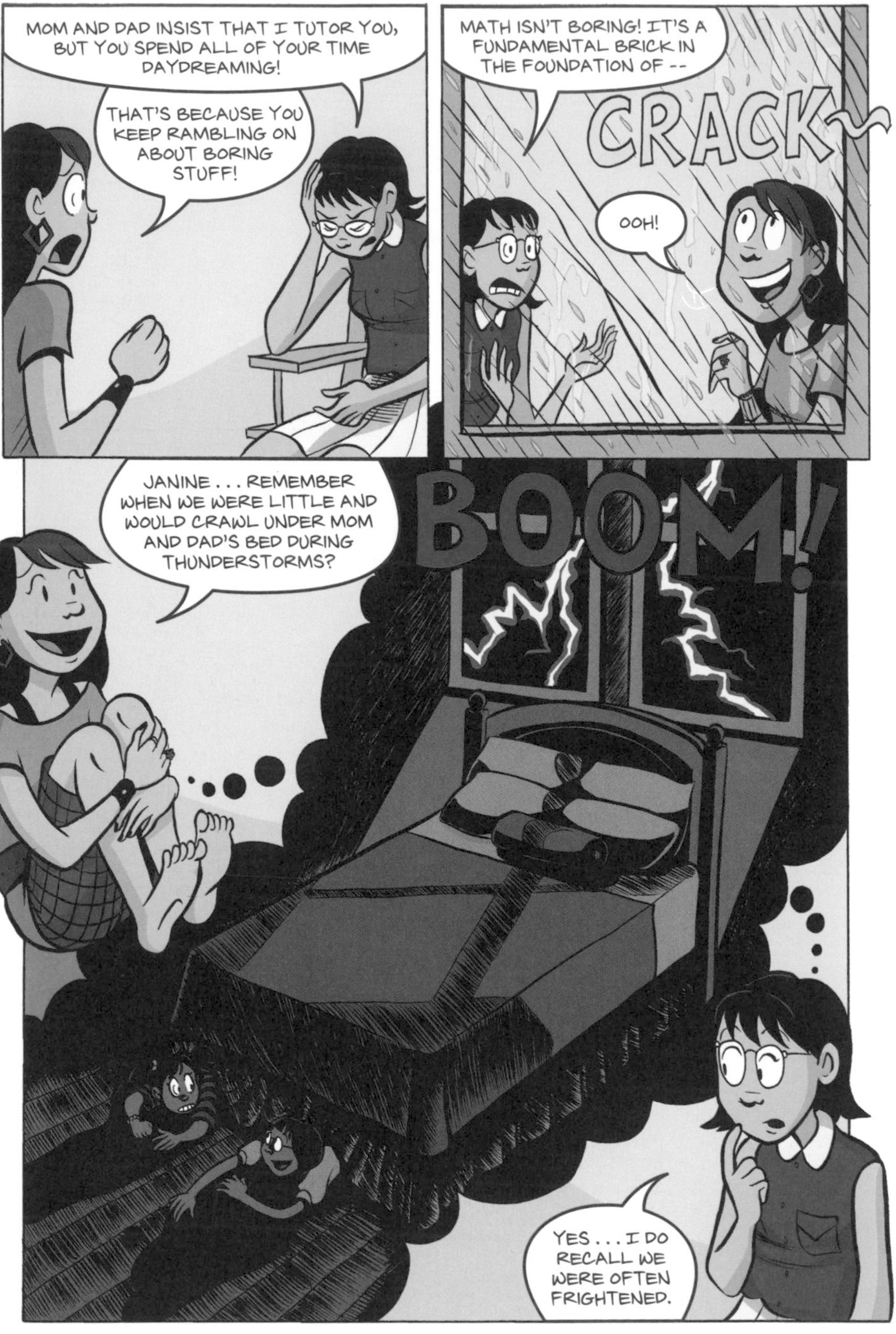
MOM AND DAD INSIST THAT I TUTOR YOU, BUT YOU SPEND ALL OF YOUR TIME DAYDREAMING!
THAT'S BECAUSE YOU KEEP RAMBLING ON ABOUT BORING STUFF!
MATH ISN'T BORING! IT'S A FUNDAMENTAL BRICK IN THE FOUNDATION OF --
CRACK
OOH!
JANINE . . . REMEMBER WHEN WE WERE LITTLE AND WOULD CRAWL UNDER MOM AND DAD'S BED DURING THUNDERSTORMS?
BOOM!
YES . . . I DO RECALL WE WERE OFTEN FRIGHTENED.

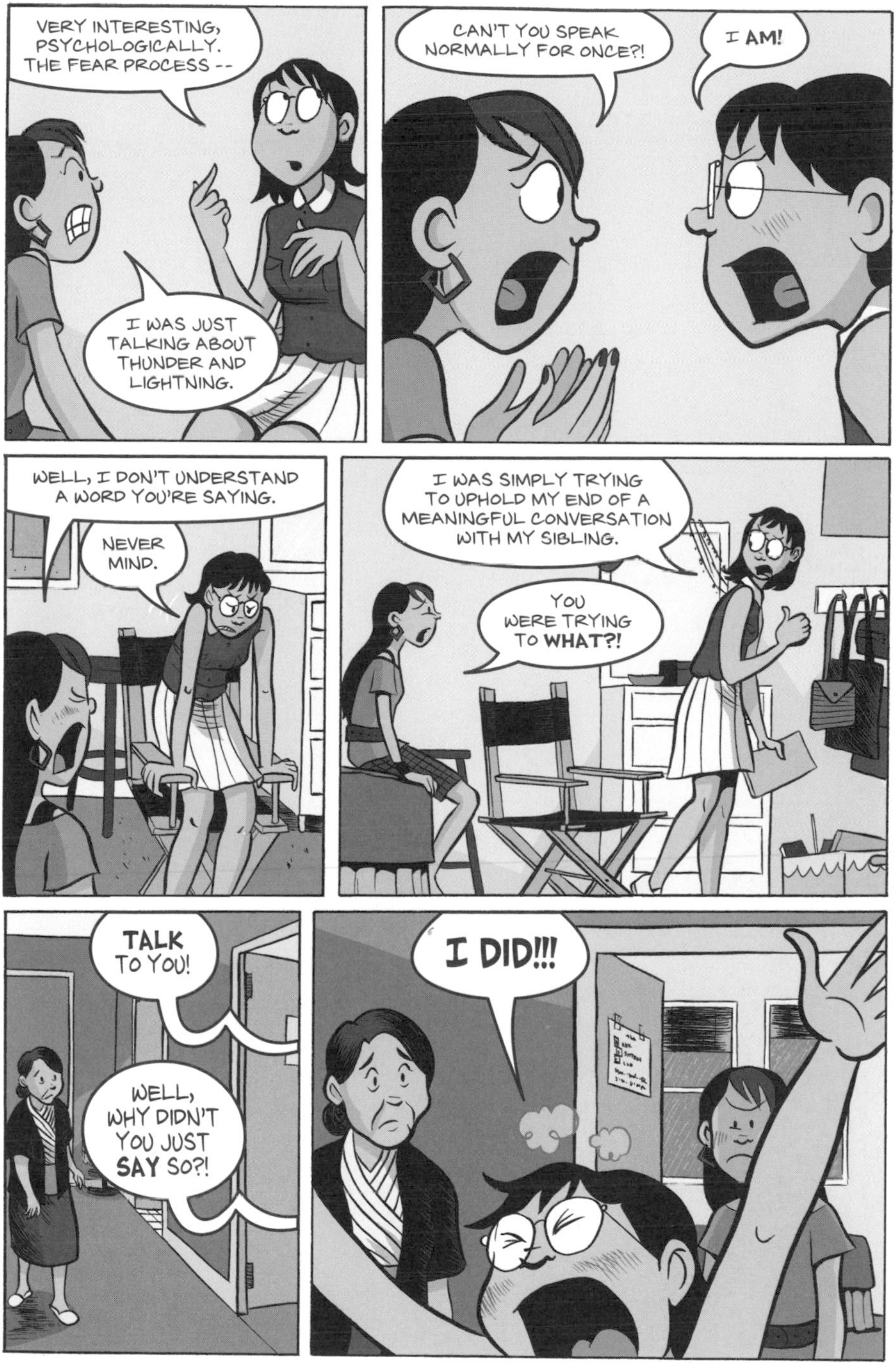
VERY INTERESTING, PSYCHOLOGICALLY. THE FEAR PROCESS --
I WAS JUST TALKING ABOUT THUNDER AND LIGHTNING.
CAN'T YOU SPEAK NORMALLY FOR ONCE?!
I AM!
WELL, I DON'T UNDERSTAND A WORD YOU'RE SAYING.
NEVER MIND.
I WAS SIMPLY TRYING TO UPHOLD MY END OF A MEANINGFUL CONVERSATION WITH MY SIBLING.
YOU WERE TRYING TO WHAT?!
TALK TO YOU!
WELL, WHY DIDN'T YOU JUST SAY SO?!
I DID!!!

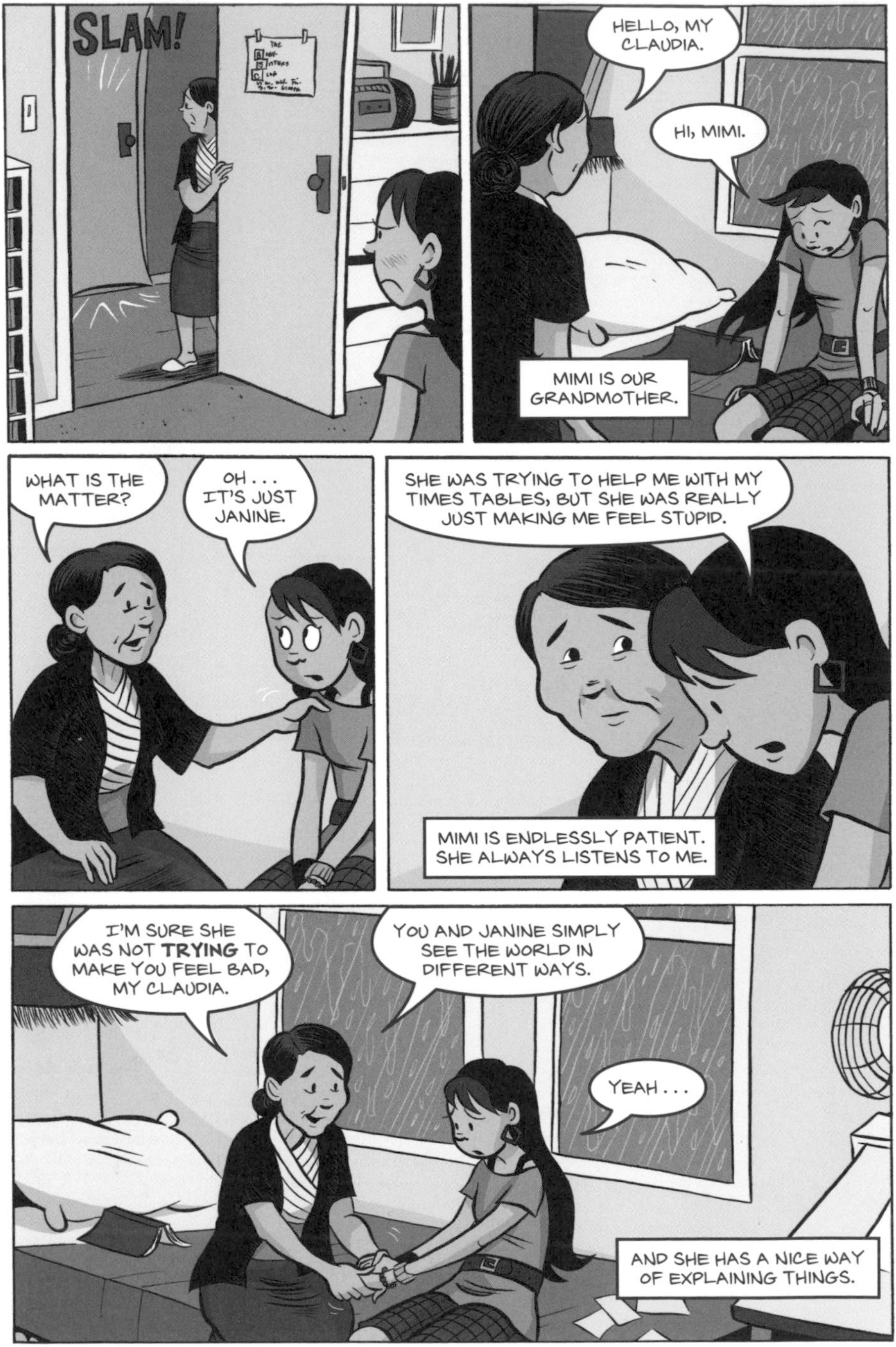
SLAM!
HELLO, MY CLAUDIA.
HI, MIMI.
MIMI IS OUR GRANDMOTHER.
WHAT IS THE MATTER?
OH . . . IT'S JUST JANINE.
SHE WAS TRYING TO HELP ME WITH MY TIMES TABLES, BUT SHE WAS REALLY JUST MAKING ME FEEL STUPID.
MIMI IS ENDLESSLY PATIENT. SHE ALWAYS LISTENS TO ME.
I'M SURE SHE WAS NOT TRYING TO MAKE YOU FEEL BAD, MY CLAUDIA.
YOU AND JANINE SIMPLY SEE THE WORLD IN DIFFERENT WAYS.
YEAH . . .
AND SHE HAS A NICE WAY OF EXPLAINING THINGS.

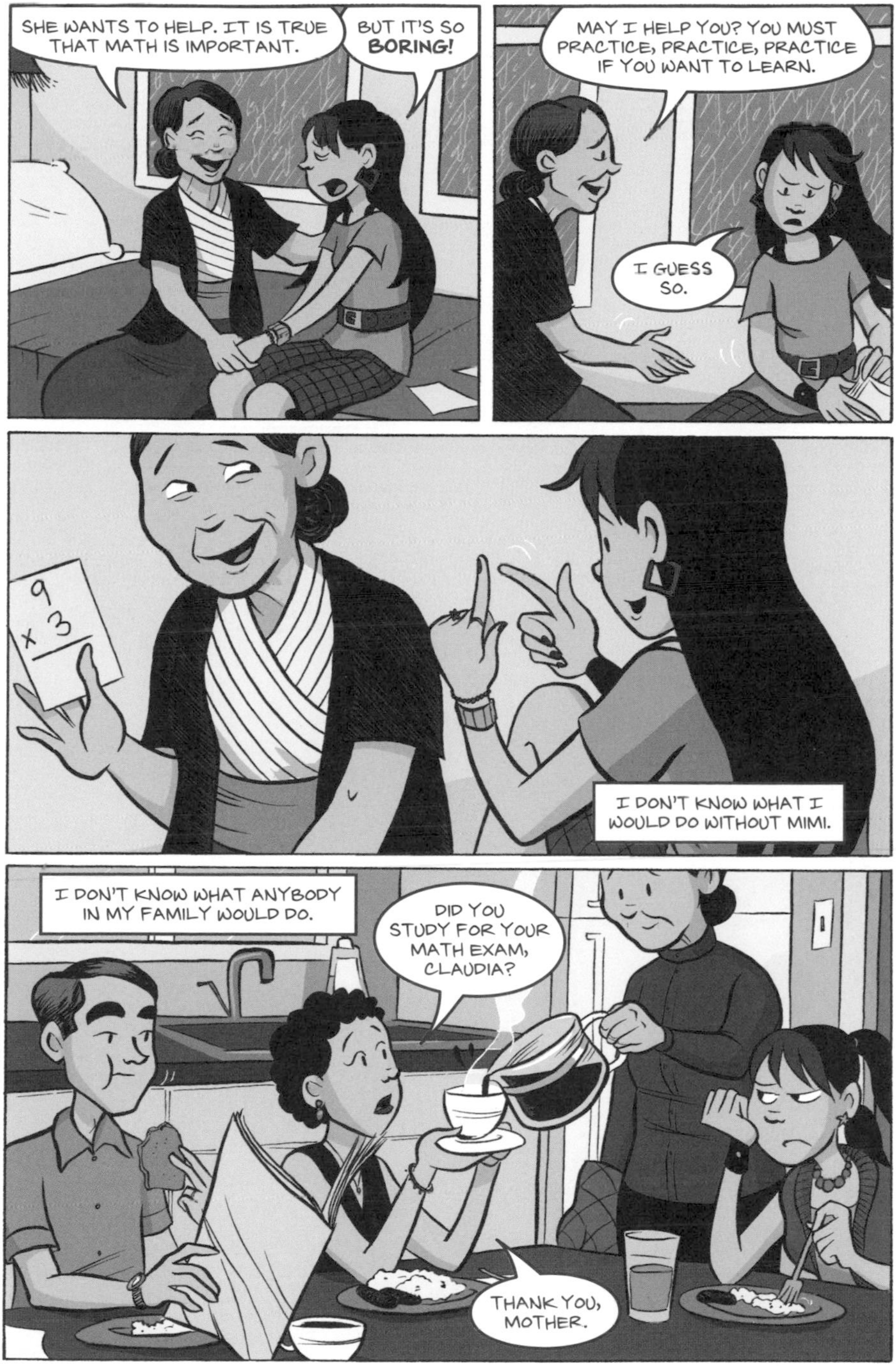
SHE WANTS TO HELP. IT IS TRUE THAT MATH IS IMPORTANT.
BUT IT'S SO **BORING!**
MAY I HELP YOU? YOU MUST PRACTICE, PRACTICE, PRACTICE IF YOU WANT TO LEARN.
I GUESS SO.
9 x 3
I DON'T KNOW WHAT I WOULD DO WITHOUT MIMI.
I DON'T KNOW WHAT ANYBODY IN MY FAMILY WOULD DO.
DID YOU STUDY FOR YOUR MATH EXAM, CLAUDIA?
THANK YOU, MOTHER.

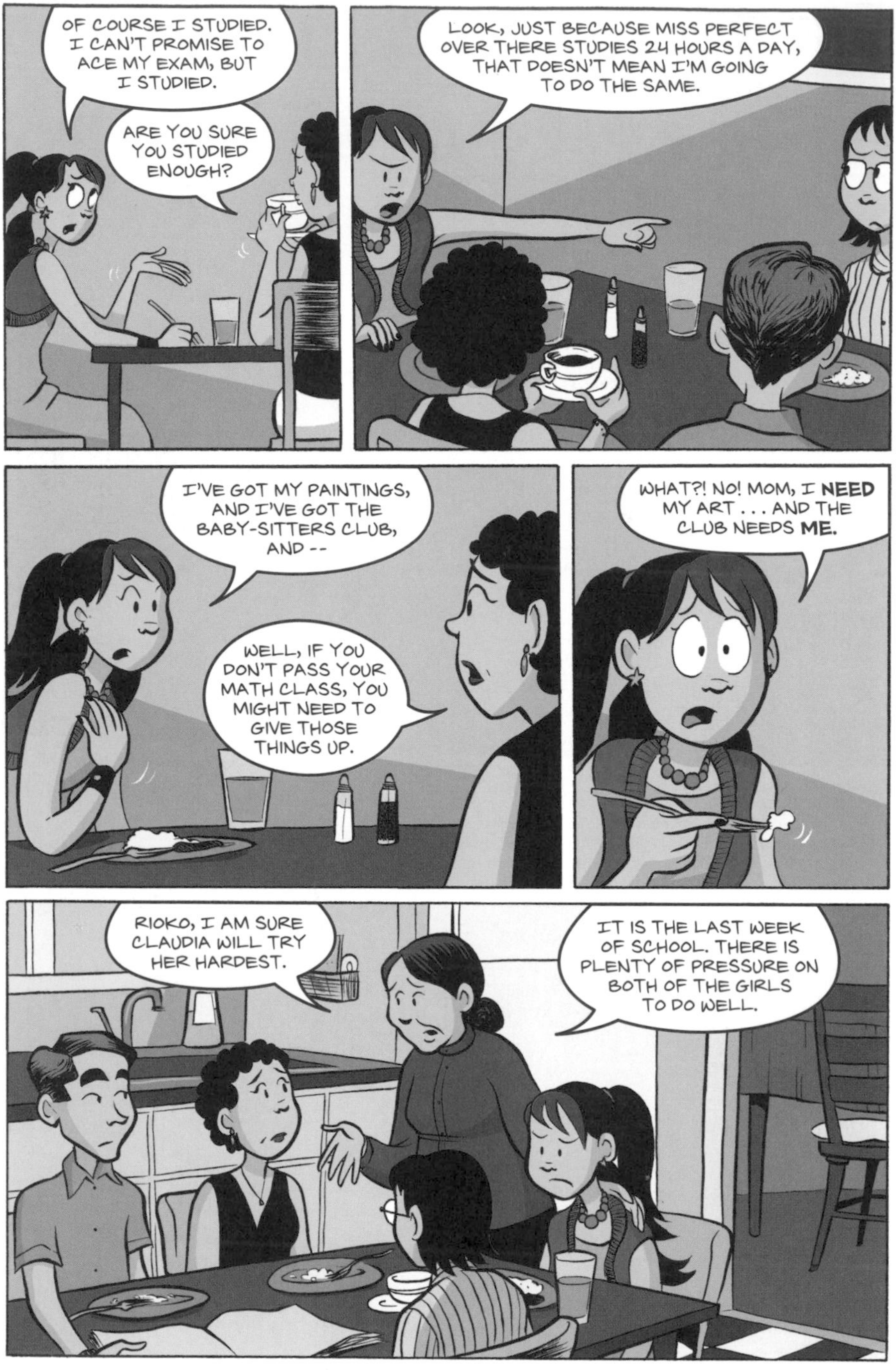
OF COURSE I STUDIED. I CAN'T PROMISE TO ACE MY EXAM, BUT I STUDIED.
ARE YOU SURE YOU STUDIED ENOUGH?
LOOK, JUST BECAUSE MISS PERFECT OVER THERE STUDIES 24 HOURS A DAY, THAT DOESN'T MEAN I'M GOING TO DO THE SAME.
I'VE GOT MY PAINTINGS, AND I'VE GOT THE BABY-SITTERS CLUB, AND --
WELL, IF YOU DON'T PASS YOUR MATH CLASS, YOU MIGHT NEED TO GIVE THOSE THINGS UP.
WHAT?! NO! MOM, I **NEED** MY ART . . . AND THE CLUB NEEDS **ME.**
RIOKO, I AM SURE CLAUDIA WILL TRY HER HARDEST.
IT IS THE LAST WEEK OF SCHOOL. THERE IS PLENTY OF PRESSURE ON BOTH OF THE GIRLS TO DO WELL.

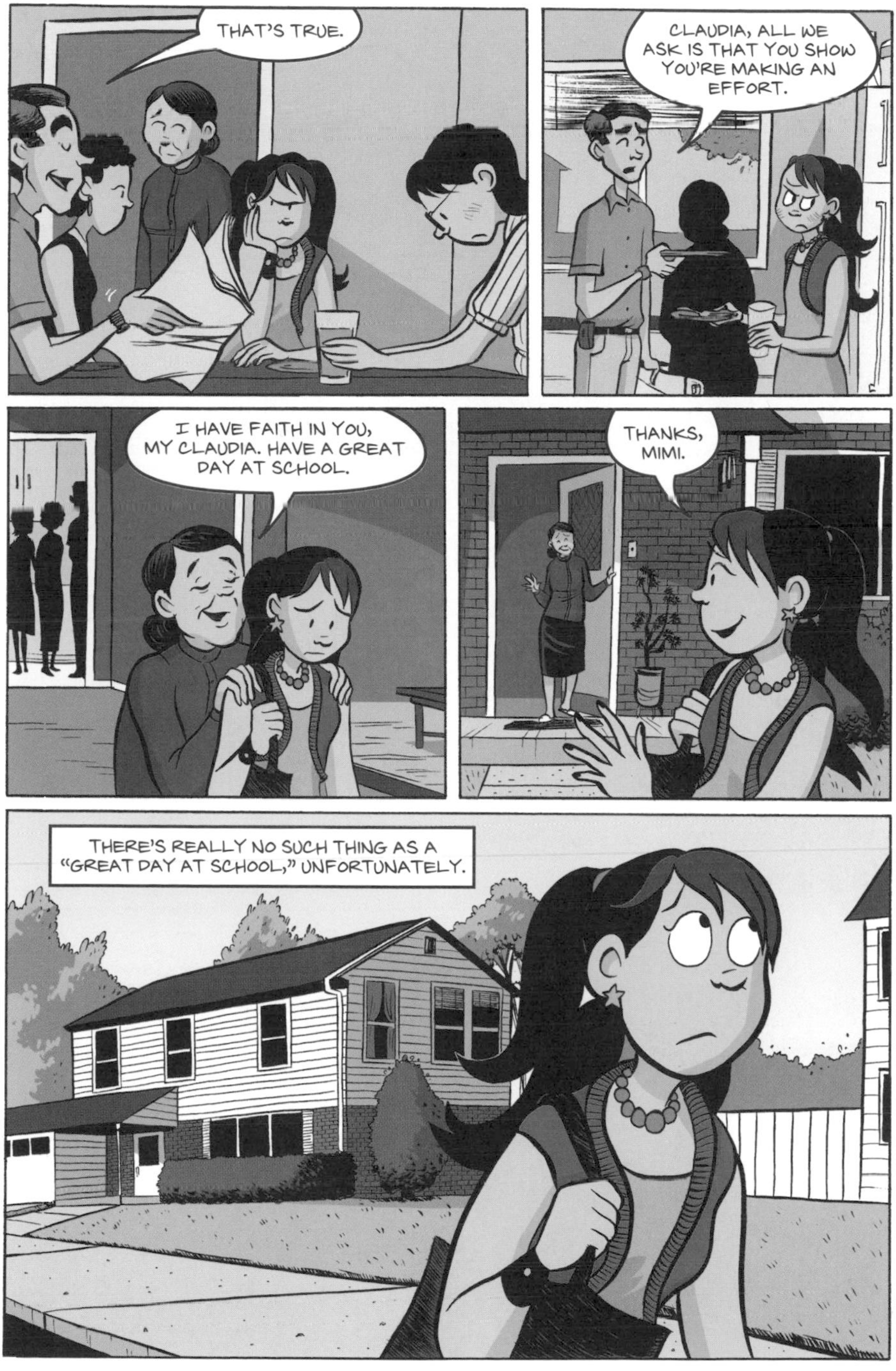
THAT'S TRUE.
CLAUDIA, ALL WE ASK IS THAT YOU SHOW YOU'RE MAKING AN EFFORT.
I HAVE FAITH IN YOU, MY CLAUDIA. HAVE A GREAT DAY AT SCHOOL.
THANKS, MIMI.
THERE'S REALLY NO SUCH THING AS A "GREAT DAY AT SCHOOL," UNFORTUNATELY.

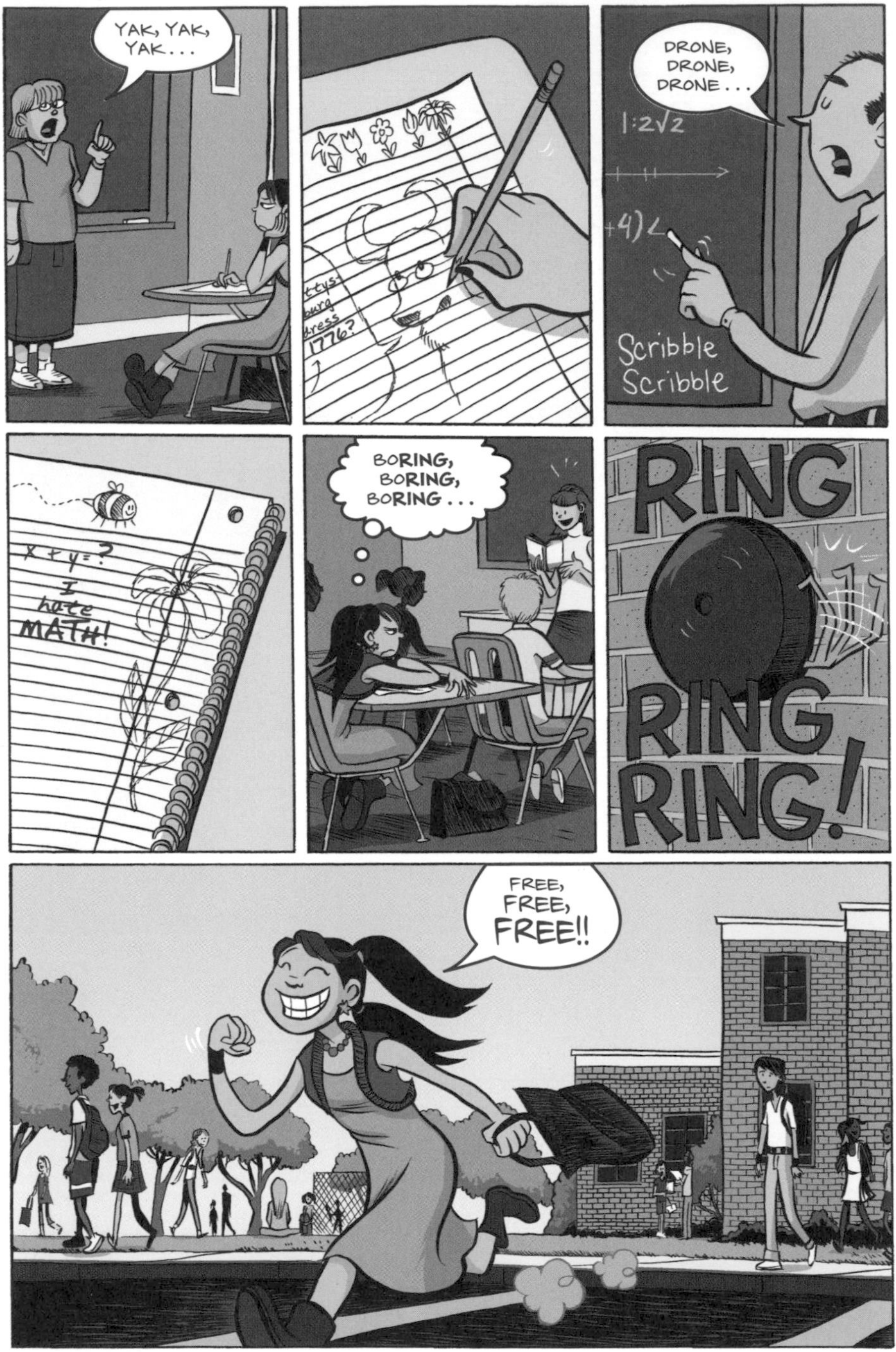
YAK, YAK, YAK . . .
DRONE, DRONE, DRONE . . .
1:2√2
Scribble Scribble
x + y = ?
I hate MATH!
BORING, BORING, BORING . . .
RING RING RING!
FREE, FREE, FREE!!

CHAPTER 2

AFTER SCHOOL, I RETURNED TO MY ROOM ... MY SANCTUARY!

LET'S SEE ... M&MS ... COOKIES ...

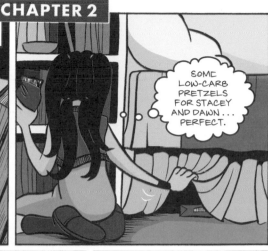

SOME LOW-CARB PRETZELS FOR STACEY AND DAWN ... PERFECT.

IT WAS TIME FOR ANOTHER MEETING OF THE BABY-SITTERS CLUB. AS THE CLUB'S VICE PRESIDENT, IT'S MY JOB TO PROVIDE SNACKS!

HEY, CLAUD!

HEY, STACEY -- YOU'RE EARLY! C'MON IN, I WANT TO SHOW YOU THE NEW EARRINGS I --

AUGH!

YOUR HAIR! IT'S SO SHORT! YOU LOOK SO ... MATURE!

STACEY MCGILL IS MY BEST FRIEND. SHE'S THE BSC TREASURER, A JOB I WOULD NEVER WANT TO DO. TOO MUCH MATH!

SHE'S SOPHISTICATED AND FASHION-CONSCIOUS, LIKE ME. SHE GREW UP IN NEW YORK CITY -- LUCKY!

SOOO ... ANY NEWS ABOUT PETE BLACK?

HE HELD MY HAND ON THE WAY HOME FROM SCHOOL TODAY!

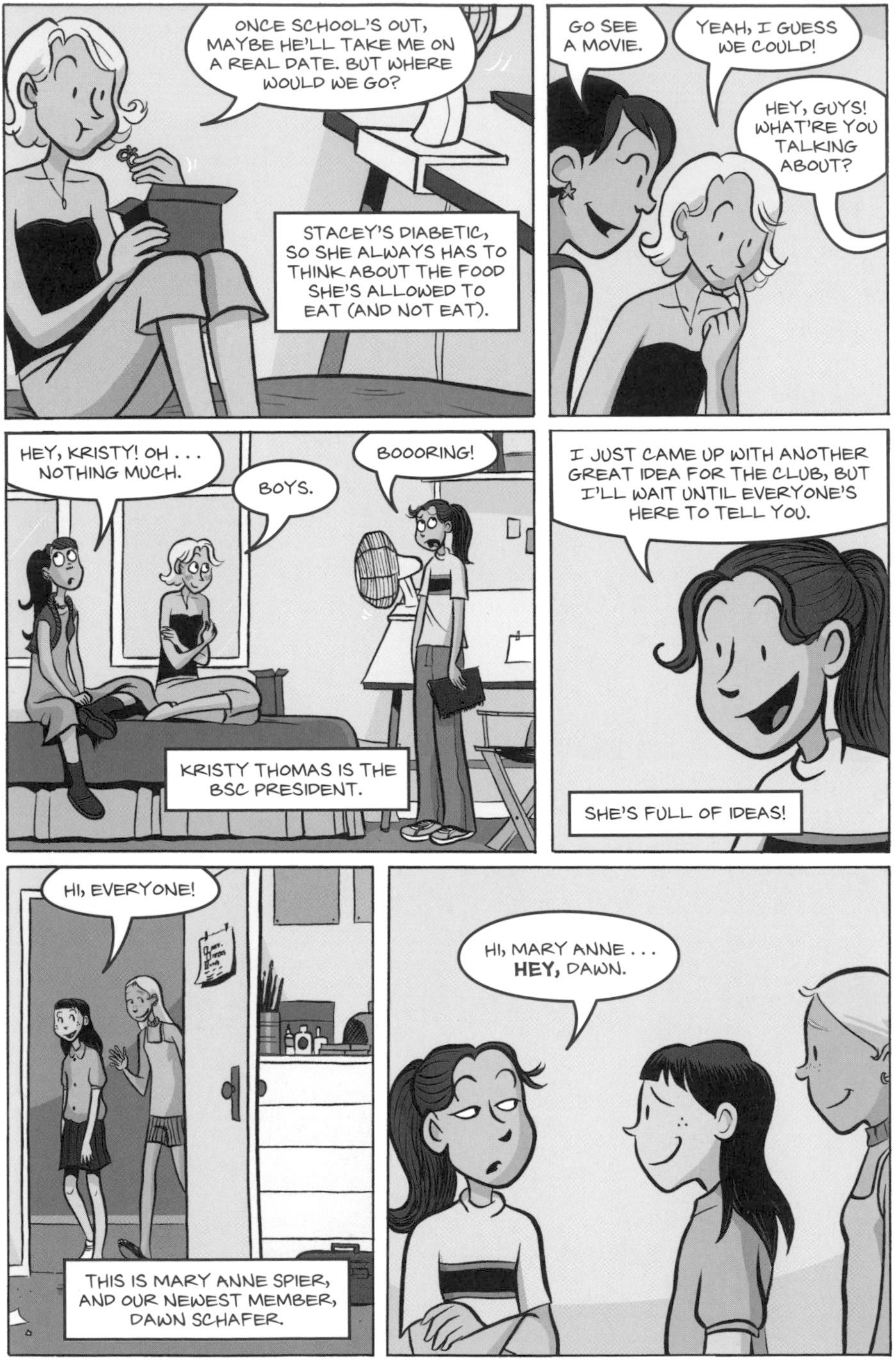
ONCE SCHOOL'S OUT, MAYBE HE'LL TAKE ME ON A REAL DATE. BUT WHERE WOULD WE GO?
STACEY'S DIABETIC, SO SHE ALWAYS HAS TO THINK ABOUT THE FOOD SHE'S ALLOWED TO EAT (AND NOT EAT).
GO SEE A MOVIE.
YEAH, I GUESS WE COULD!
HEY, GUYS! WHAT'RE YOU TALKING ABOUT?
HEY, KRISTY! OH . . . NOTHING MUCH.
BOYS.
BOOORING!
KRISTY THOMAS IS THE BSC PRESIDENT.
I JUST CAME UP WITH ANOTHER GREAT IDEA FOR THE CLUB, BUT I'LL WAIT UNTIL EVERYONE'S HERE TO TELL YOU.
SHE'S FULL OF IDEAS!
HI, EVERYONE!
THIS IS MARY ANNE SPIER, AND OUR NEWEST MEMBER, DAWN SCHAFER.
HI, MARY ANNE . . . **HEY,** DAWN.

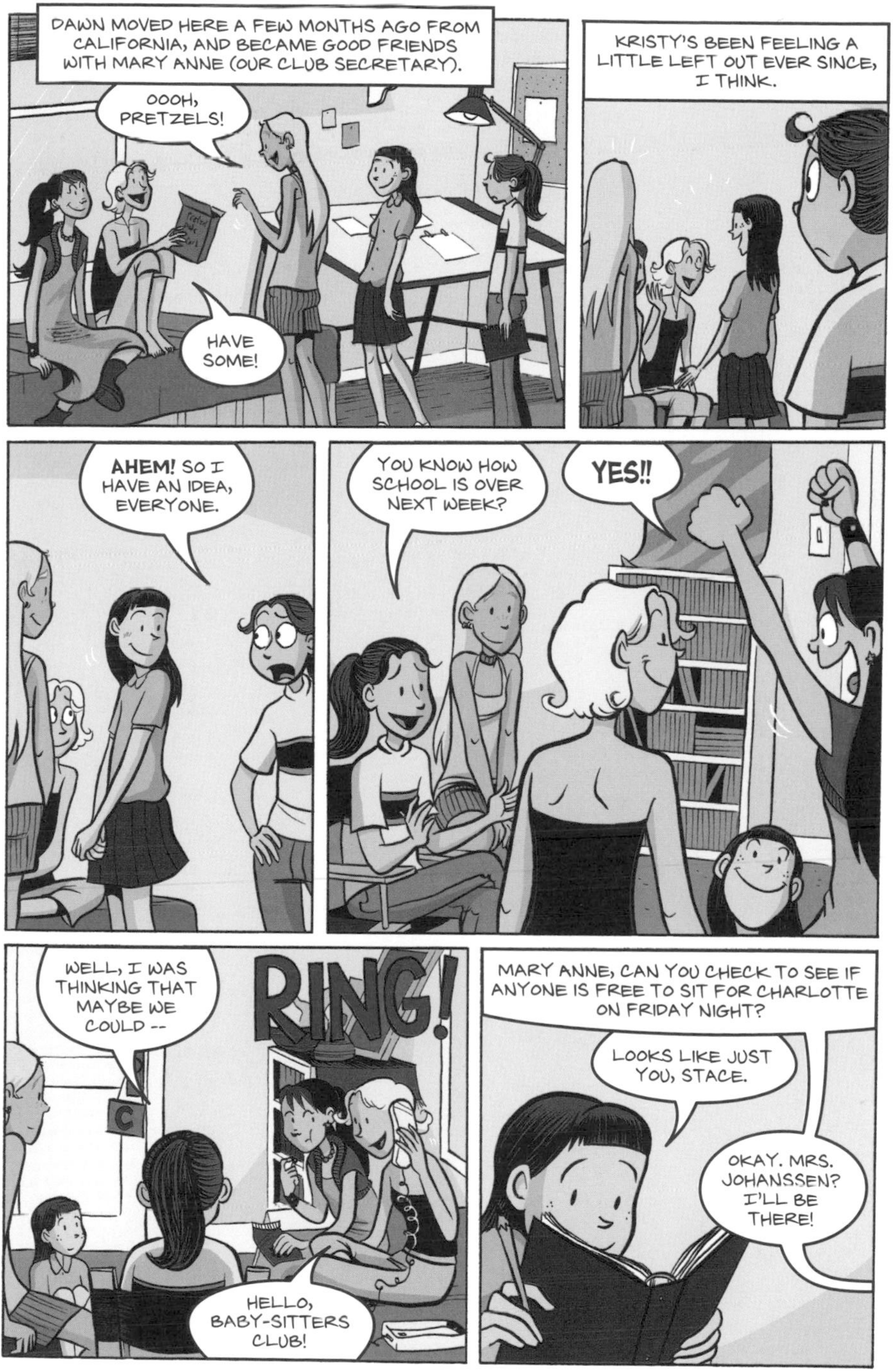
DAWN MOVED HERE A FEW MONTHS AGO FROM CALIFORNIA, AND BECAME GOOD FRIENDS WITH MARY ANNE (OUR CLUB SECRETARY).
OOOH, PRETZELS!
HAVE SOME!
KRISTY'S BEEN FEELING A LITTLE LEFT OUT EVER SINCE, I THINK.
AHEM! SO I HAVE AN IDEA, EVERYONE.
YOU KNOW HOW SCHOOL IS OVER NEXT WEEK?
YES!!
WELL, I WAS THINKING THAT MAYBE WE COULD --
RING!
HELLO, BABY-SITTERS CLUB!
MARY ANNE, CAN YOU CHECK TO SEE IF ANYONE IS FREE TO SIT FOR CHARLOTTE ON FRIDAY NIGHT?
LOOKS LIKE JUST YOU, STACE.
OKAY. MRS. JOHANSSEN? I'LL BE THERE!

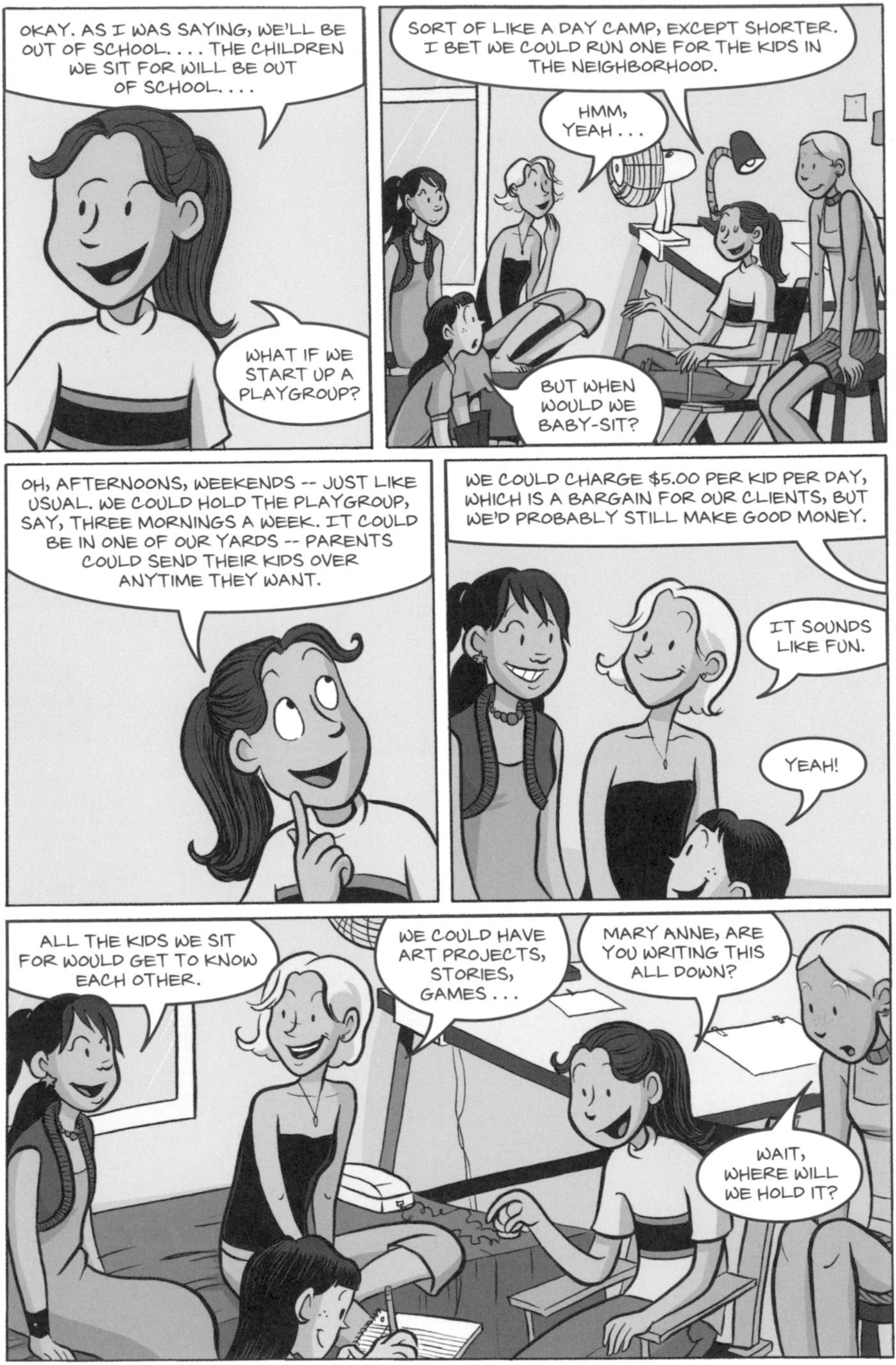
OKAY. AS I WAS SAYING, WE'LL BE OUT OF SCHOOL. . . . THE CHILDREN WE SIT FOR WILL BE OUT OF SCHOOL. . . .
WHAT IF WE START UP A PLAYGROUP?
SORT OF LIKE A DAY CAMP, EXCEPT SHORTER. I BET WE COULD RUN ONE FOR THE KIDS IN THE NEIGHBORHOOD.
HMM, YEAH . . .
BUT WHEN WOULD WE BABY-SIT?
OH, AFTERNOONS, WEEKENDS -- JUST LIKE USUAL. WE COULD HOLD THE PLAYGROUP, SAY, THREE MORNINGS A WEEK. IT COULD BE IN ONE OF OUR YARDS -- PARENTS COULD SEND THEIR KIDS OVER ANYTIME THEY WANT.
WE COULD CHARGE $5.00 PER KID PER DAY, WHICH IS A BARGAIN FOR OUR CLIENTS, BUT WE'D PROBABLY STILL MAKE GOOD MONEY.
IT SOUNDS LIKE FUN.
YEAH!
ALL THE KIDS WE SIT FOR WOULD GET TO KNOW EACH OTHER.
WE COULD HAVE ART PROJECTS, STORIES, GAMES . . .
MARY ANNE, ARE YOU WRITING THIS ALL DOWN?
WAIT, WHERE WILL WE HOLD IT?

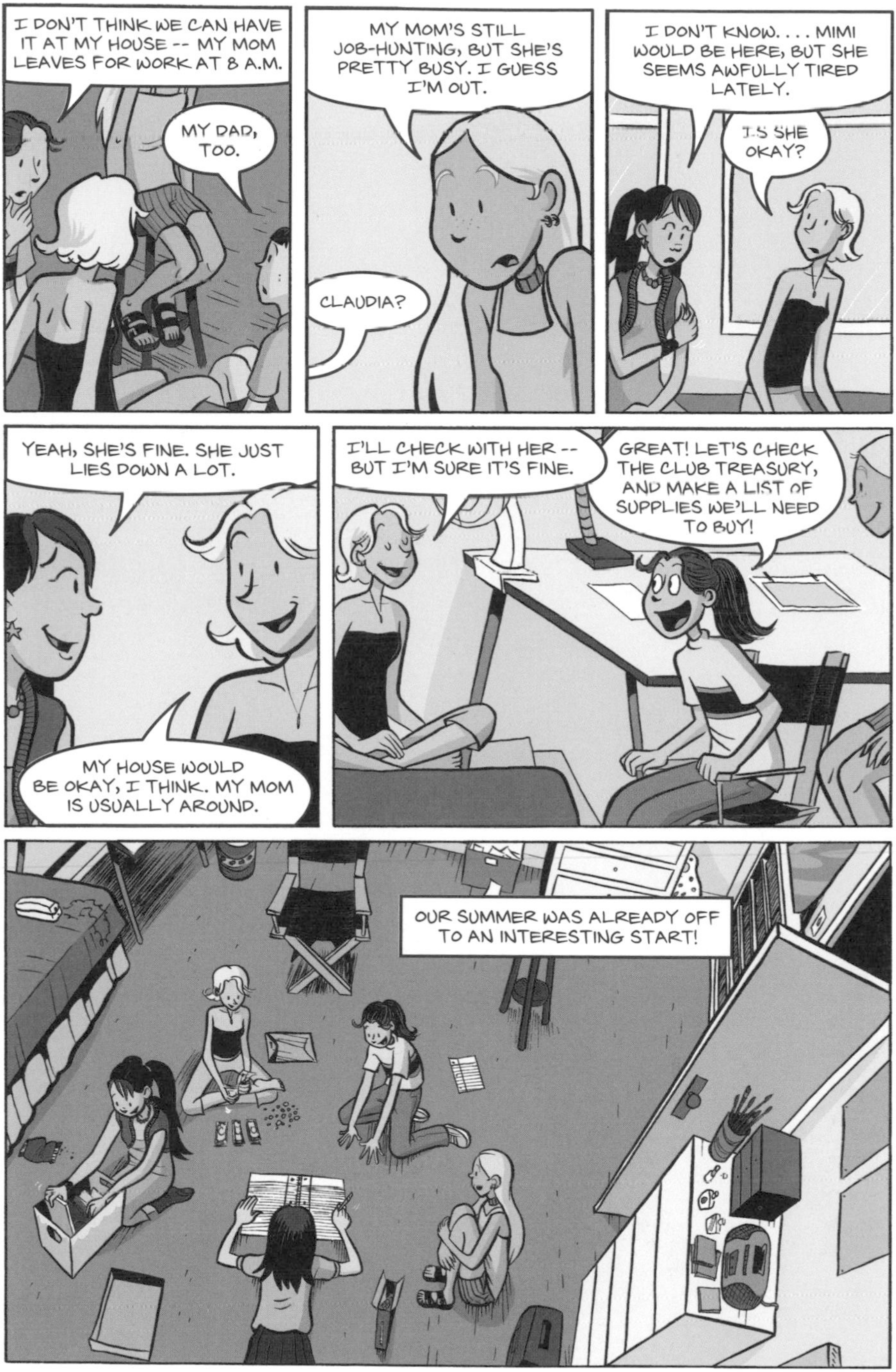
I DON'T THINK WE CAN HAVE IT AT MY HOUSE -- MY MOM LEAVES FOR WORK AT 8 A.M.
MY DAD, TOO.
MY MOM'S STILL JOB-HUNTING, BUT SHE'S PRETTY BUSY. I GUESS I'M OUT.
CLAUDIA?
I DON'T KNOW. . . . MIMI WOULD BE HERE, BUT SHE SEEMS AWFULLY TIRED LATELY.
IS SHE OKAY?
YEAH, SHE'S FINE. SHE JUST LIES DOWN A LOT.
MY HOUSE WOULD BE OKAY, I THINK. MY MOM IS USUALLY AROUND.
I'LL CHECK WITH HER -- BUT I'M SURE IT'S FINE.
GREAT! LET'S CHECK THE CLUB TREASURY, AND MAKE A LIST OF SUPPLIES WE'LL NEED TO BUY!
OUR SUMMER WAS ALREADY OFF TO AN INTERESTING START!

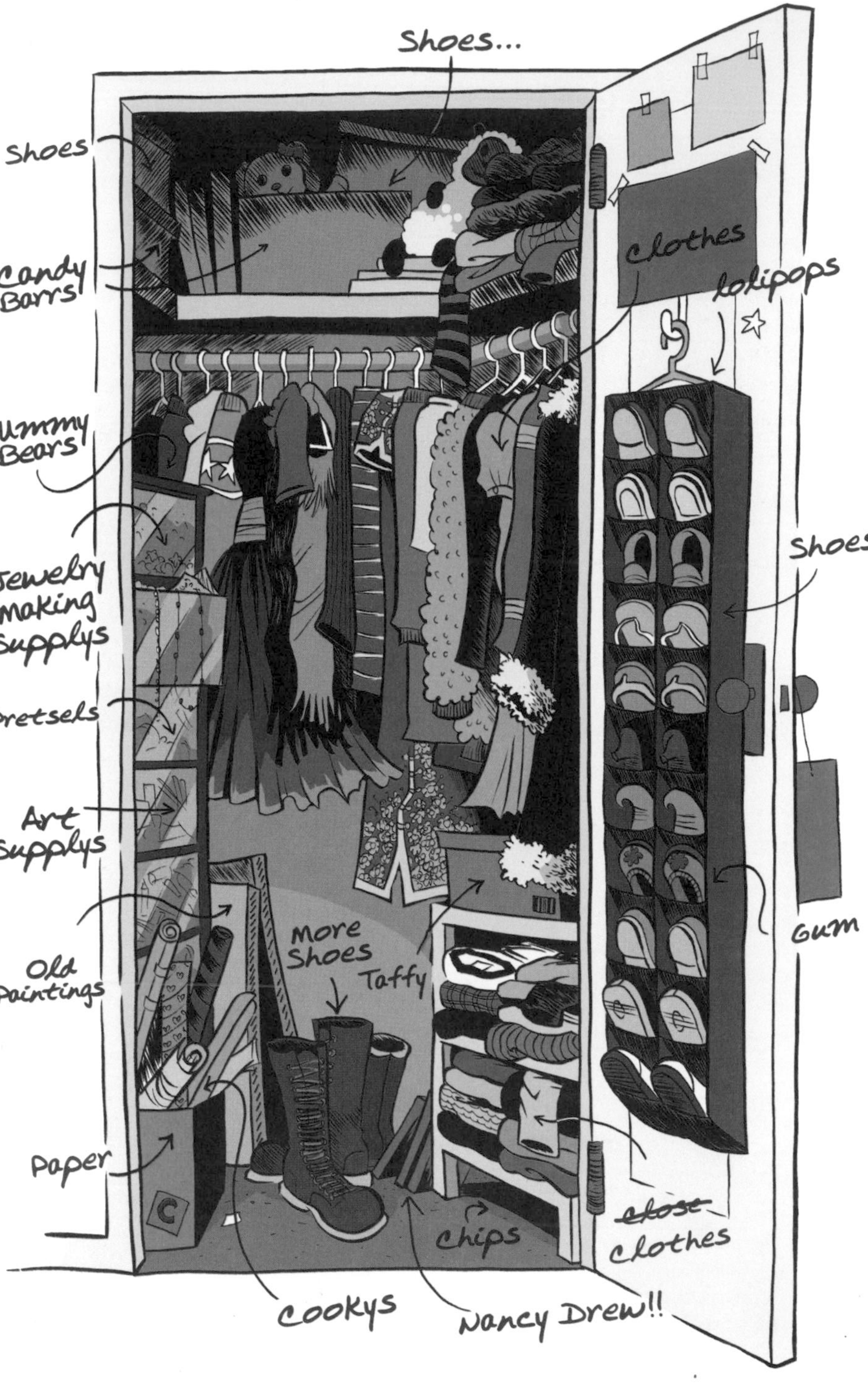

Shoes...
Shoes
Candy Barrs
Clothes
Lolipops
Gummy Bears
Jewelry Making Supplys
Shoes
Pretsels
Art Supplys
Gum
Old Paintings
More Shoes
Taffy
Paper
~~Clost~~ Clothes
Chips
Cookys
Nancy Drew!!

CHAPTER 3

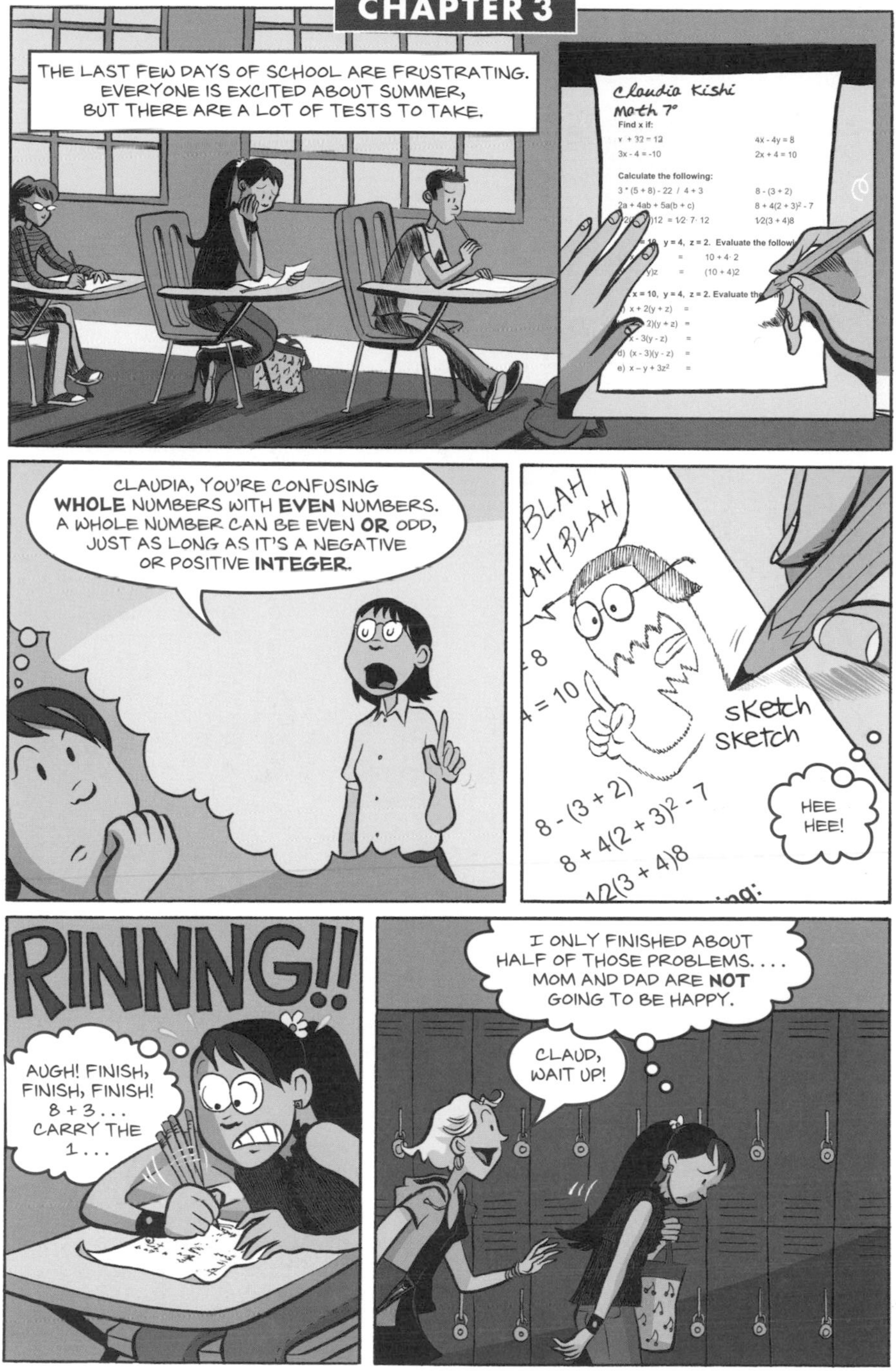
THE LAST FEW DAYS OF SCHOOL ARE FRUSTRATING. EVERYONE IS EXCITED ABOUT SUMMER, BUT THERE ARE A LOT OF TESTS TO TAKE.
Claudia Kishi
Math 7°
Find x if:
Calculate the following:
CLAUDIA, YOU'RE CONFUSING **WHOLE** NUMBERS WITH **EVEN** NUMBERS. A WHOLE NUMBER CAN BE EVEN **OR** ODD, JUST AS LONG AS IT'S A NEGATIVE OR POSITIVE **INTEGER**.
BLAH BLAH BLAH
SKETCH SKETCH
8 - (3 + 2)
8 + 4(2 + 3)2 - 7
HEE HEE!
RINNNG!!
AUGH! FINISH, FINISH, FINISH! 8 + 3 . . . CARRY THE 1 . . .
I ONLY FINISHED ABOUT HALF OF THOSE PROBLEMS. . . . MOM AND DAD ARE **NOT** GOING TO BE HAPPY.
CLAUD, WAIT UP!

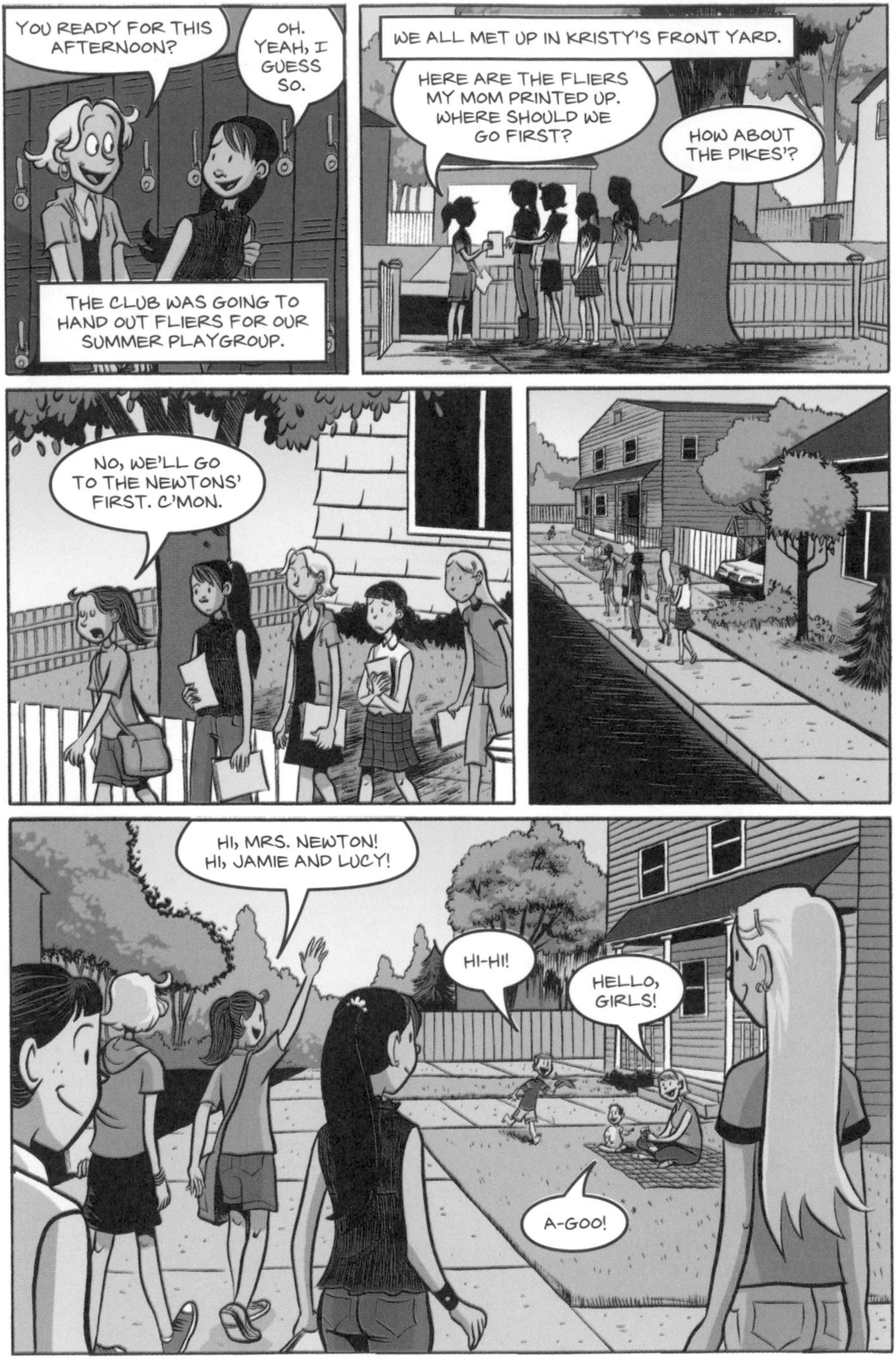
YOU READY FOR THIS AFTERNOON?
OH. YEAH, I GUESS SO.
THE CLUB WAS GOING TO HAND OUT FLIERS FOR OUR SUMMER PLAYGROUP.
WE ALL MET UP IN KRISTY'S FRONT YARD.
HERE ARE THE FLIERS MY MOM PRINTED UP. WHERE SHOULD WE GO FIRST?
HOW ABOUT THE PIKES'?
NO, WE'LL GO TO THE NEWTONS' FIRST. C'MON.
HI, MRS. NEWTON! HI, JAMIE AND LUCY!
HI-HI!
HELLO, GIRLS!
A-GOO!

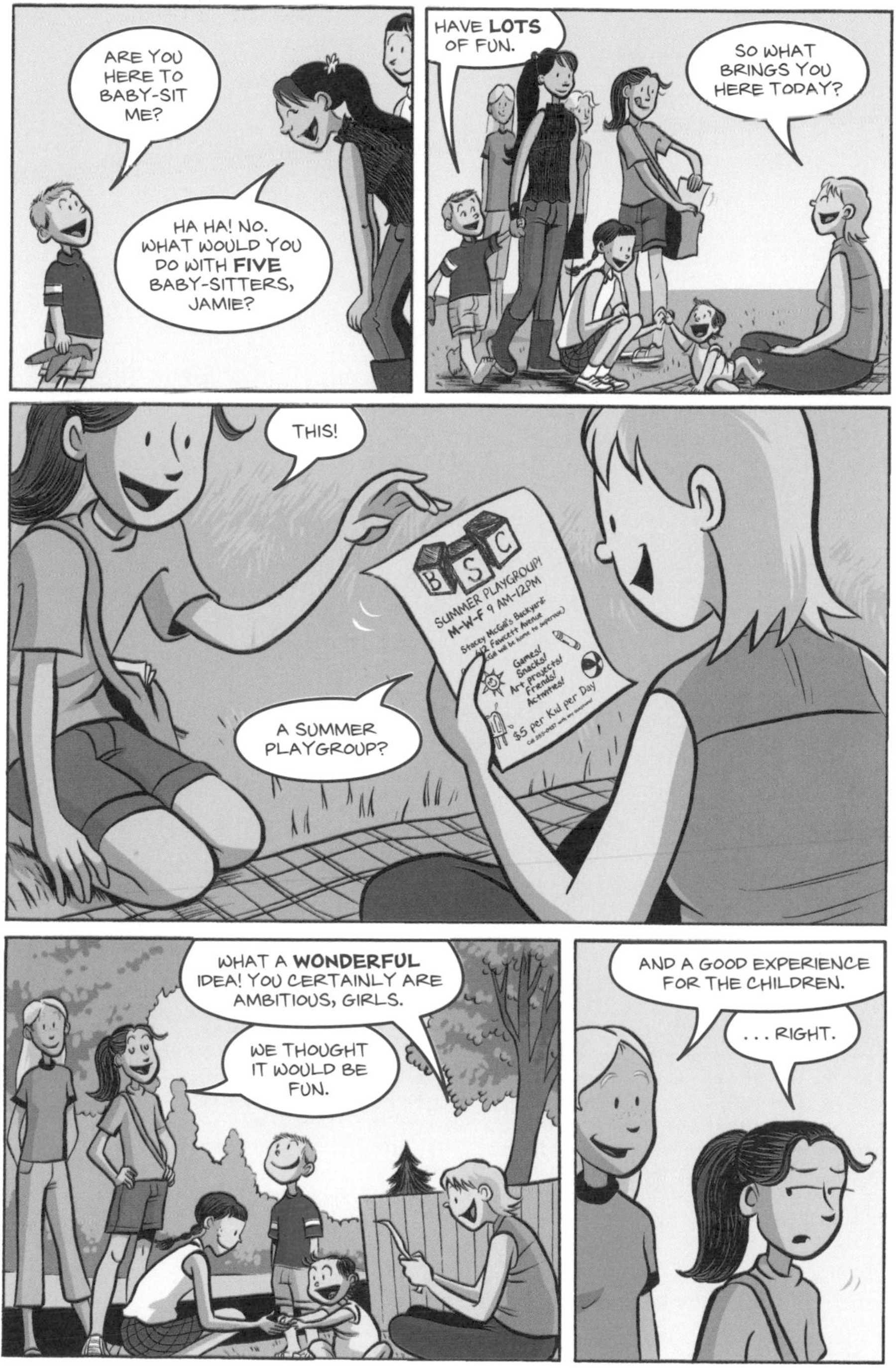
ARE YOU HERE TO BABY-SIT ME?
HA HA! NO. WHAT WOULD YOU DO WITH **FIVE** BABY-SITTERS, JAMIE?
HAVE **LOTS** OF FUN.
SO WHAT BRINGS YOU HERE TODAY?
THIS!
B S C
SUMMER PLAYGROUP! 9 AM-12PM
M-W-F
Stacey McGill's Backyard
112 Fawcett Avenue
Games!
Snacks!
Art projects!
Friends!
Activities!
$5 per Kid per Day
A SUMMER PLAYGROUP?
WHAT A **WONDERFUL** IDEA! YOU CERTAINLY ARE AMBITIOUS, GIRLS.
WE THOUGHT IT WOULD BE FUN.
AND A GOOD EXPERIENCE FOR THE CHILDREN.
. . . RIGHT.

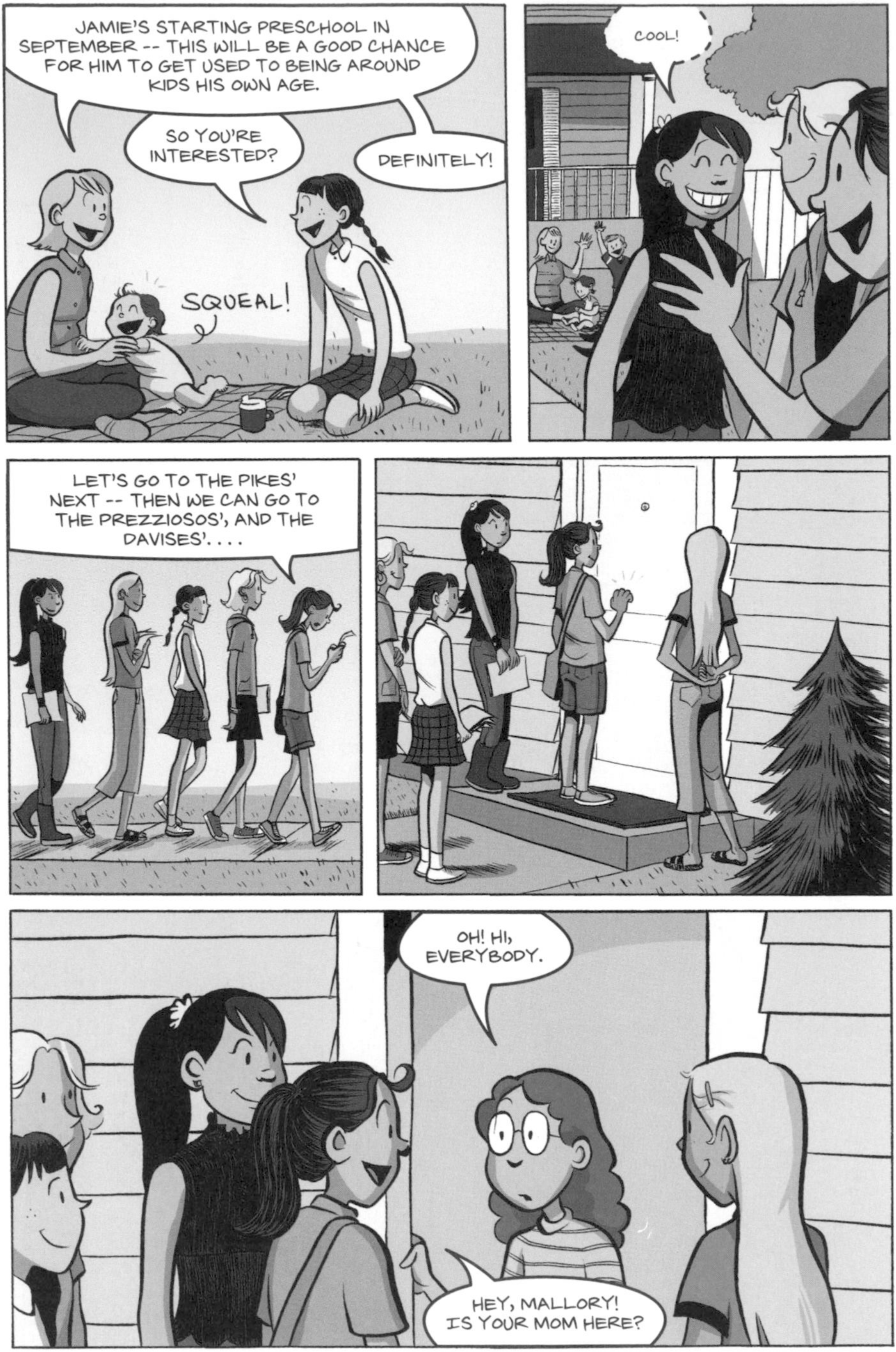
JAMIE'S STARTING PRESCHOOL IN SEPTEMBER -- THIS WILL BE A GOOD CHANCE FOR HIM TO GET USED TO BEING AROUND KIDS HIS OWN AGE.
SO YOU'RE INTERESTED?
DEFINITELY!
SQUEAL!
COOL!
LET'S GO TO THE PIKES' NEXT -- THEN WE CAN GO TO THE PREZZIOSOS', AND THE DAVISES'. . . .
OH! HI, EVERYBODY.
HEY, MALLORY! IS YOUR MOM HERE?

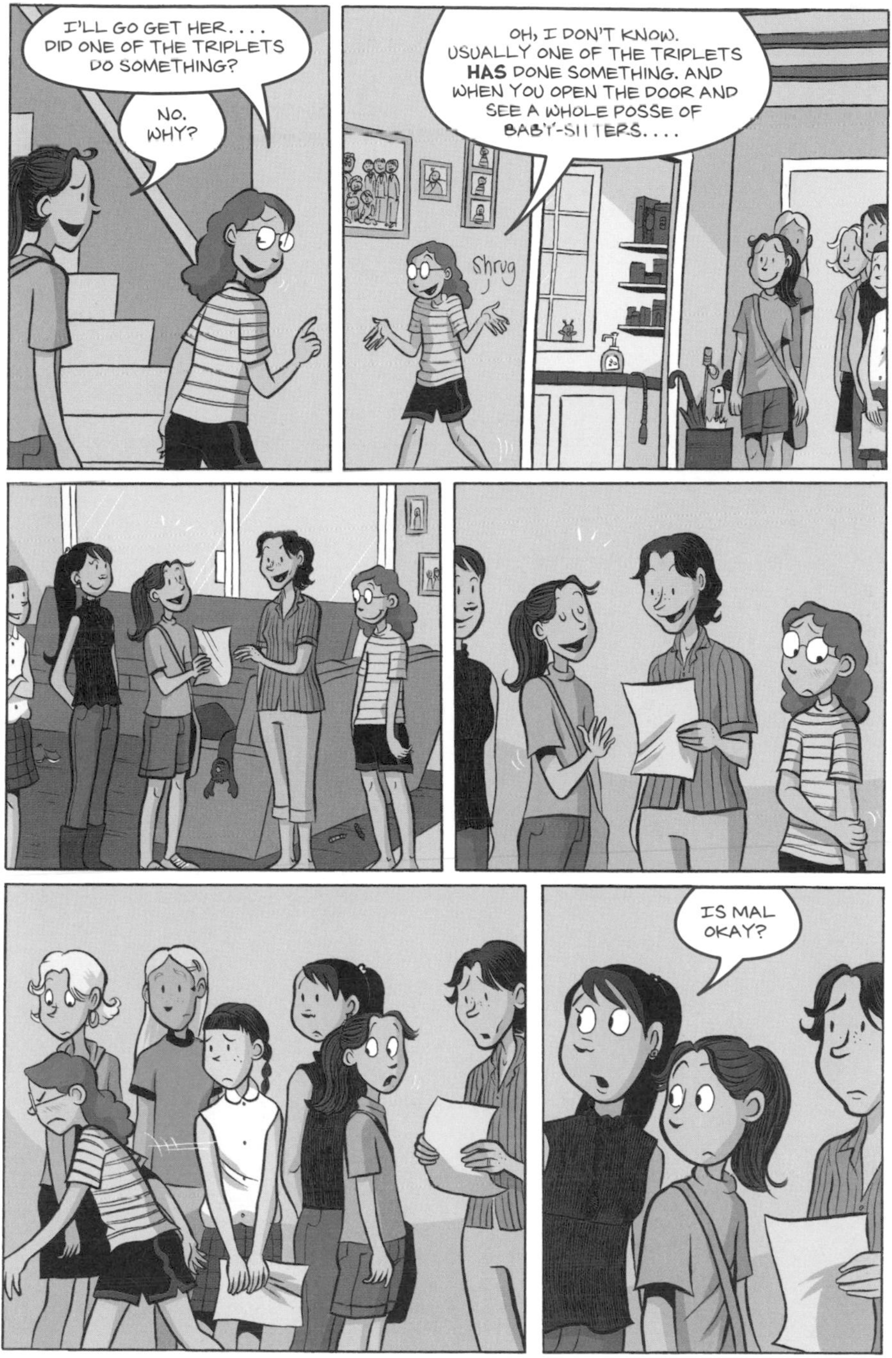
I'LL GO GET HER.... DID ONE OF THE TRIPLETS DO SOMETHING?
NO. WHY?
OH, I DON'T KNOW. USUALLY ONE OF THE TRIPLETS **HAS** DONE SOMETHING. AND WHEN YOU OPEN THE DOOR AND SEE A WHOLE POSSE OF BABY-SITTERS....
Shrug
IS MAL OKAY?

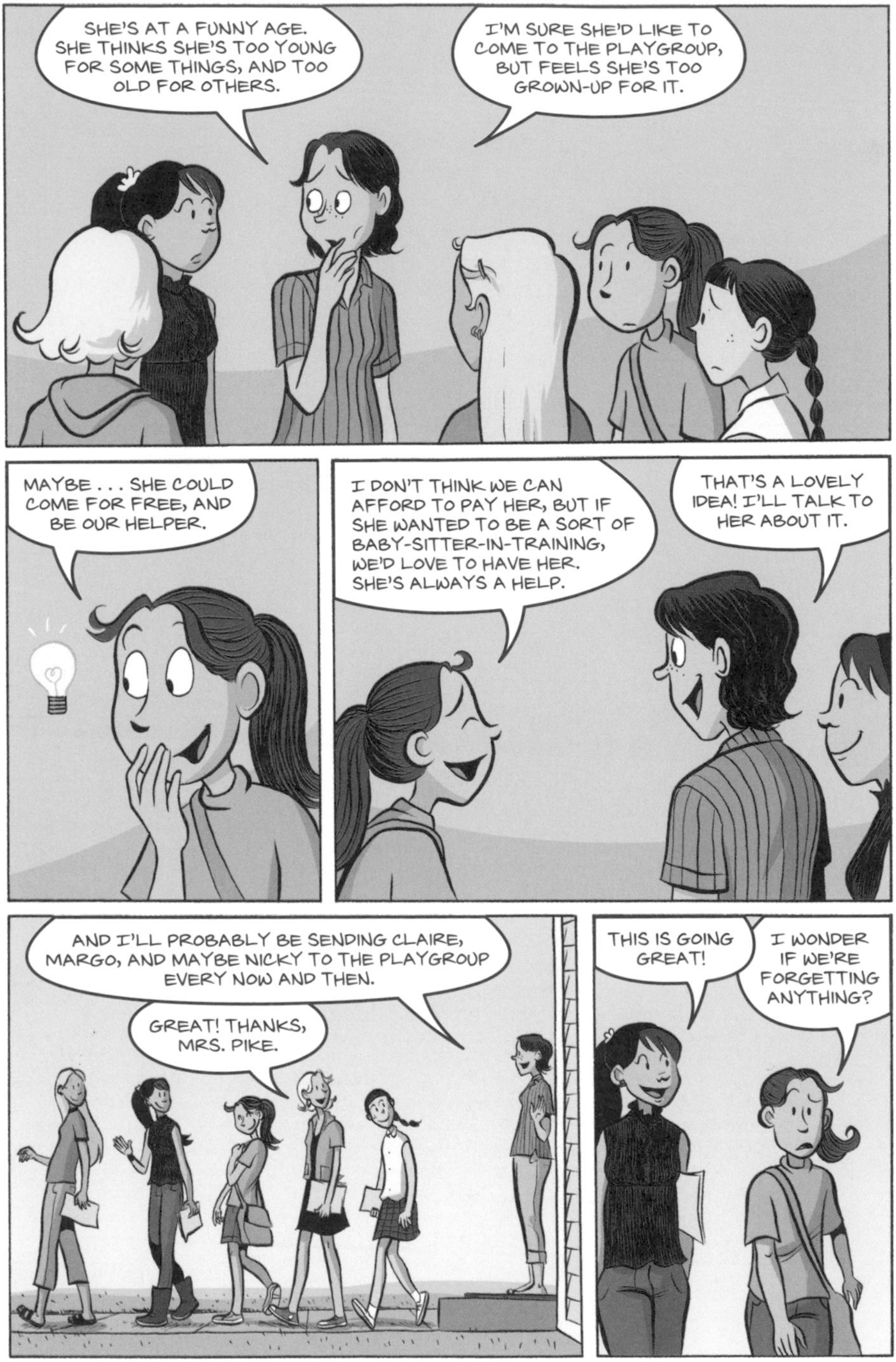
SHE'S AT A FUNNY AGE. SHE THINKS SHE'S TOO YOUNG FOR SOME THINGS, AND TOO OLD FOR OTHERS.
I'M SURE SHE'D LIKE TO COME TO THE PLAYGROUP, BUT FEELS SHE'S TOO GROWN-UP FOR IT.
MAYBE . . . SHE COULD COME FOR FREE, AND BE OUR HELPER.
I DON'T THINK WE CAN AFFORD TO PAY HER, BUT IF SHE WANTED TO BE A SORT OF BABY-SITTER-IN-TRAINING, WE'D LOVE TO HAVE HER. SHE'S ALWAYS A HELP.
THAT'S A LOVELY IDEA! I'LL TALK TO HER ABOUT IT.
AND I'LL PROBABLY BE SENDING CLAIRE, MARGO, AND MAYBE NICKY TO THE PLAYGROUP EVERY NOW AND THEN.
GREAT! THANKS, MRS. PIKE.
THIS IS GOING GREAT!
I WONDER IF WE'RE FORGETTING ANYTHING?

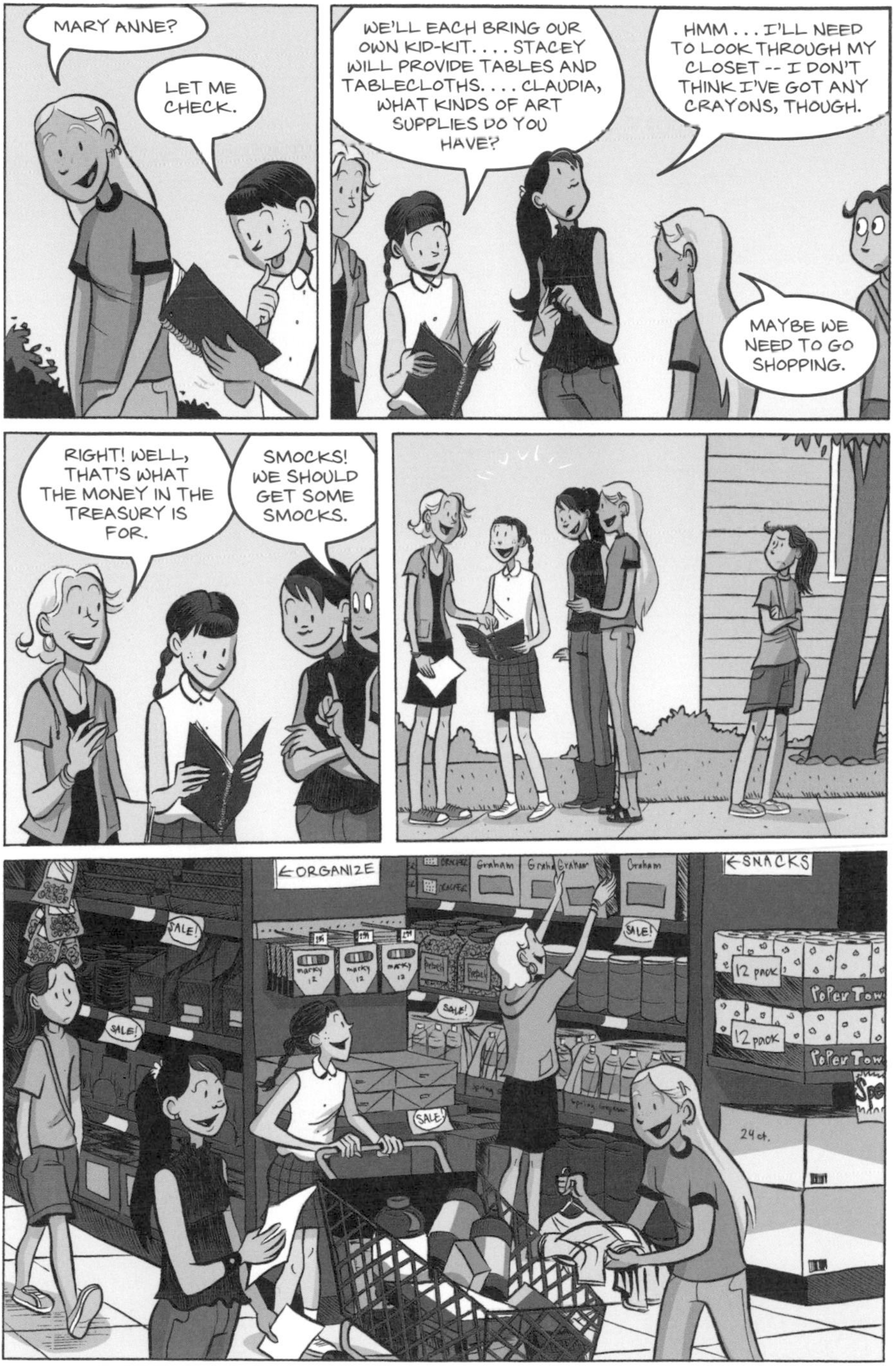

MARY ANNE?
LET ME CHECK.
WE'LL EACH BRING OUR OWN KID-KIT. . . . STACEY WILL PROVIDE TABLES AND TABLECLOTHS. . . . CLAUDIA, WHAT KINDS OF ART SUPPLIES DO YOU HAVE?
HMM . . . I'LL NEED TO LOOK THROUGH MY CLOSET -- I DON'T THINK I'VE GOT ANY CRAYONS, THOUGH.
MAYBE WE NEED TO GO SHOPPING.
RIGHT! WELL, THAT'S WHAT THE MONEY IN THE TREASURY IS FOR.
SMOCKS! WE SHOULD GET SOME SMOCKS.
←ORGANIZE
←SNACKS
SALE!
12 pack
Paper Towels

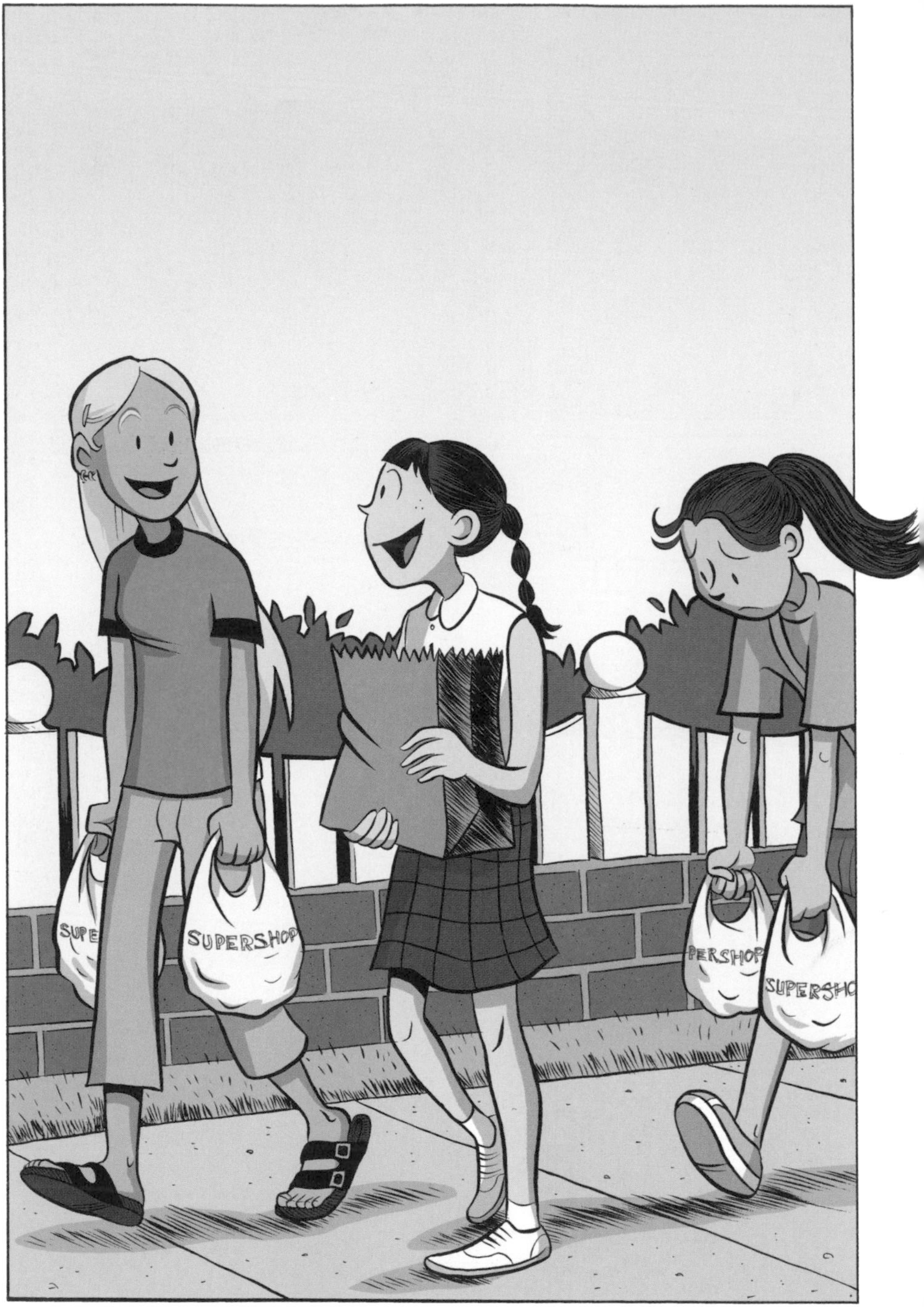
SUPE
SUPERSHOP
PERSHOP
SUPERSHO

CHAPTER 4

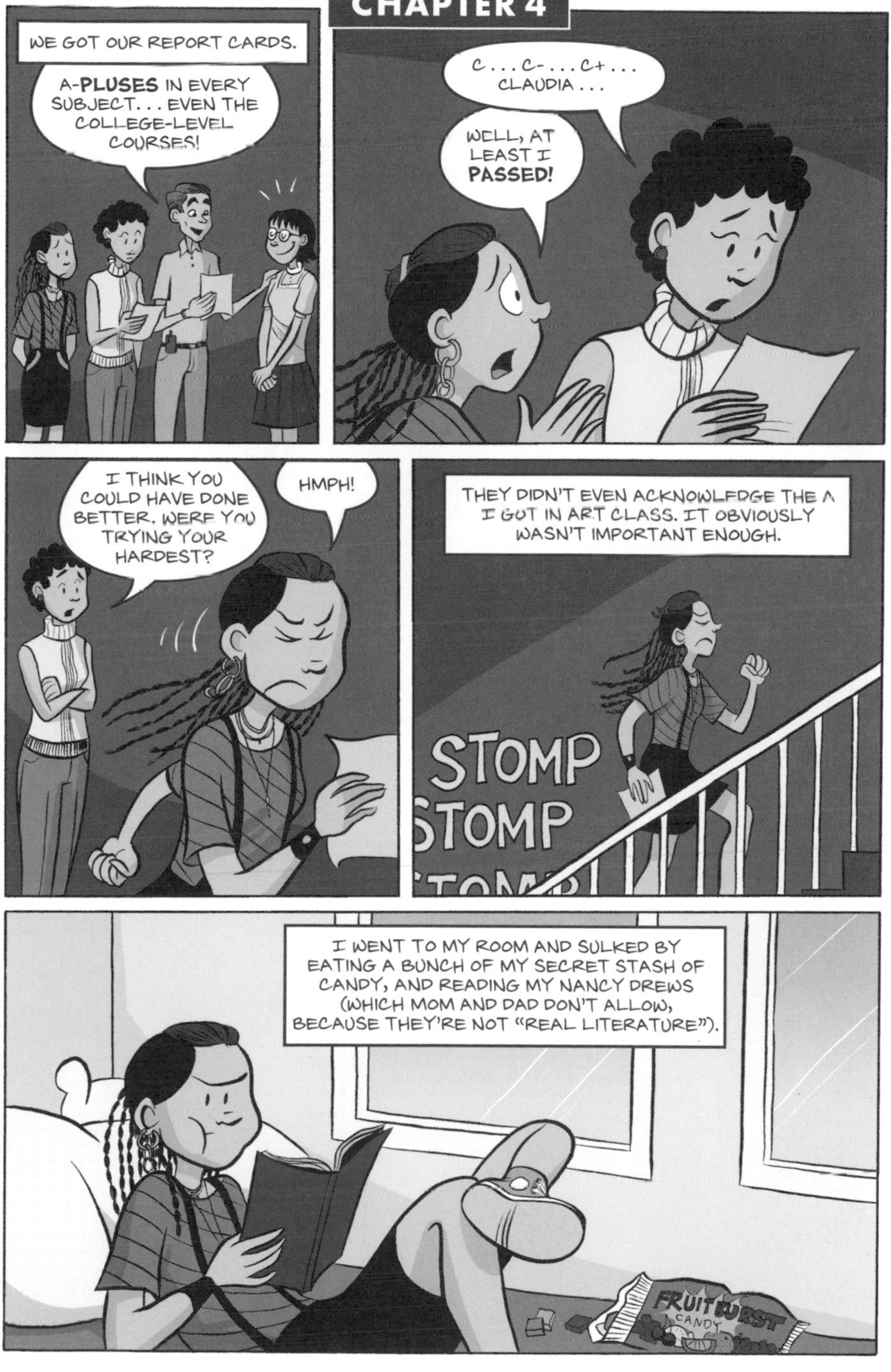

WE GOT OUR REPORT CARDS.
A-PLUSES IN EVERY SUBJECT. . . EVEN THE COLLEGE-LEVEL COURSES!
C . . . C- . . . C+ . . . CLAUDIA . . .
WELL, AT LEAST I PASSED!
I THINK YOU COULD HAVE DONE BETTER. WERE YOU TRYING YOUR HARDEST?
HMPH!
THEY DIDN'T EVEN ACKNOWLEDGE THE A I GOT IN ART CLASS. IT OBVIOUSLY WASN'T IMPORTANT ENOUGH.
STOMP
STOMP
I WENT TO MY ROOM AND SULKED BY EATING A BUNCH OF MY SECRET STASH OF CANDY, AND READING MY NANCY DREWS (WHICH MOM AND DAD DON'T ALLOW, BECAUSE THEY'RE NOT "REAL LITERATURE").
FRUITBURST CANDY

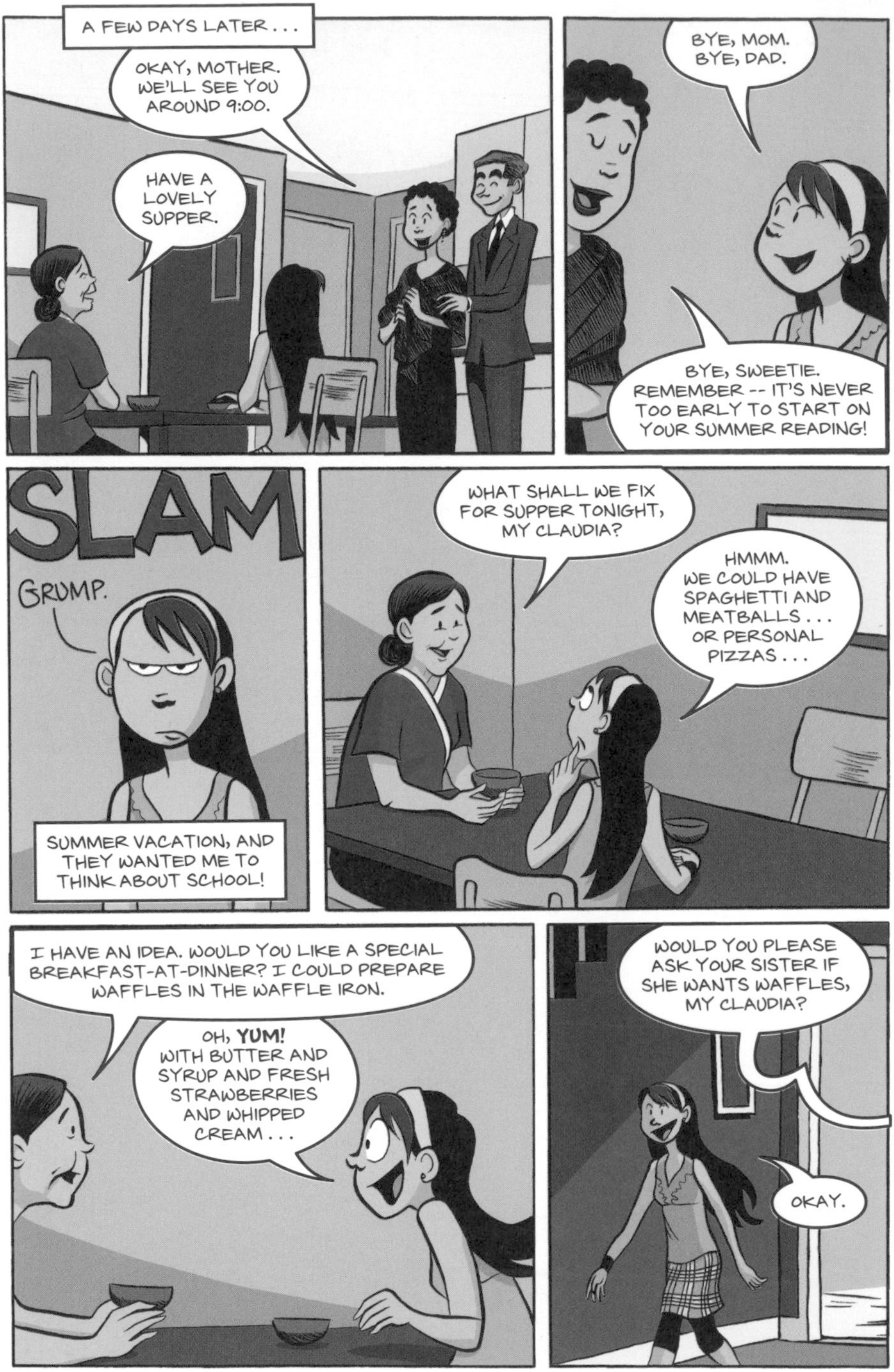
A FEW DAYS LATER . . .
OKAY, MOTHER. WE'LL SEE YOU AROUND 9:00.
HAVE A LOVELY SUPPER.
BYE, MOM. BYE, DAD.
BYE, SWEETIE. REMEMBER -- IT'S NEVER TOO EARLY TO START ON YOUR SUMMER READING!
SLAM
GRUMP.
SUMMER VACATION, AND THEY WANTED ME TO THINK ABOUT SCHOOL!
WHAT SHALL WE FIX FOR SUPPER TONIGHT, MY CLAUDIA?
HMMM. WE COULD HAVE SPAGHETTI AND MEATBALLS . . . OR PERSONAL PIZZAS . . .
I HAVE AN IDEA. WOULD YOU LIKE A SPECIAL BREAKFAST-AT-DINNER? I COULD PREPARE WAFFLES IN THE WAFFLE IRON.
OH, **YUM!** WITH BUTTER AND SYRUP AND FRESH STRAWBERRIES AND WHIPPED CREAM . . .
WOULD YOU PLEASE ASK YOUR SISTER IF SHE WANTS WAFFLES, MY CLAUDIA?
OKAY.

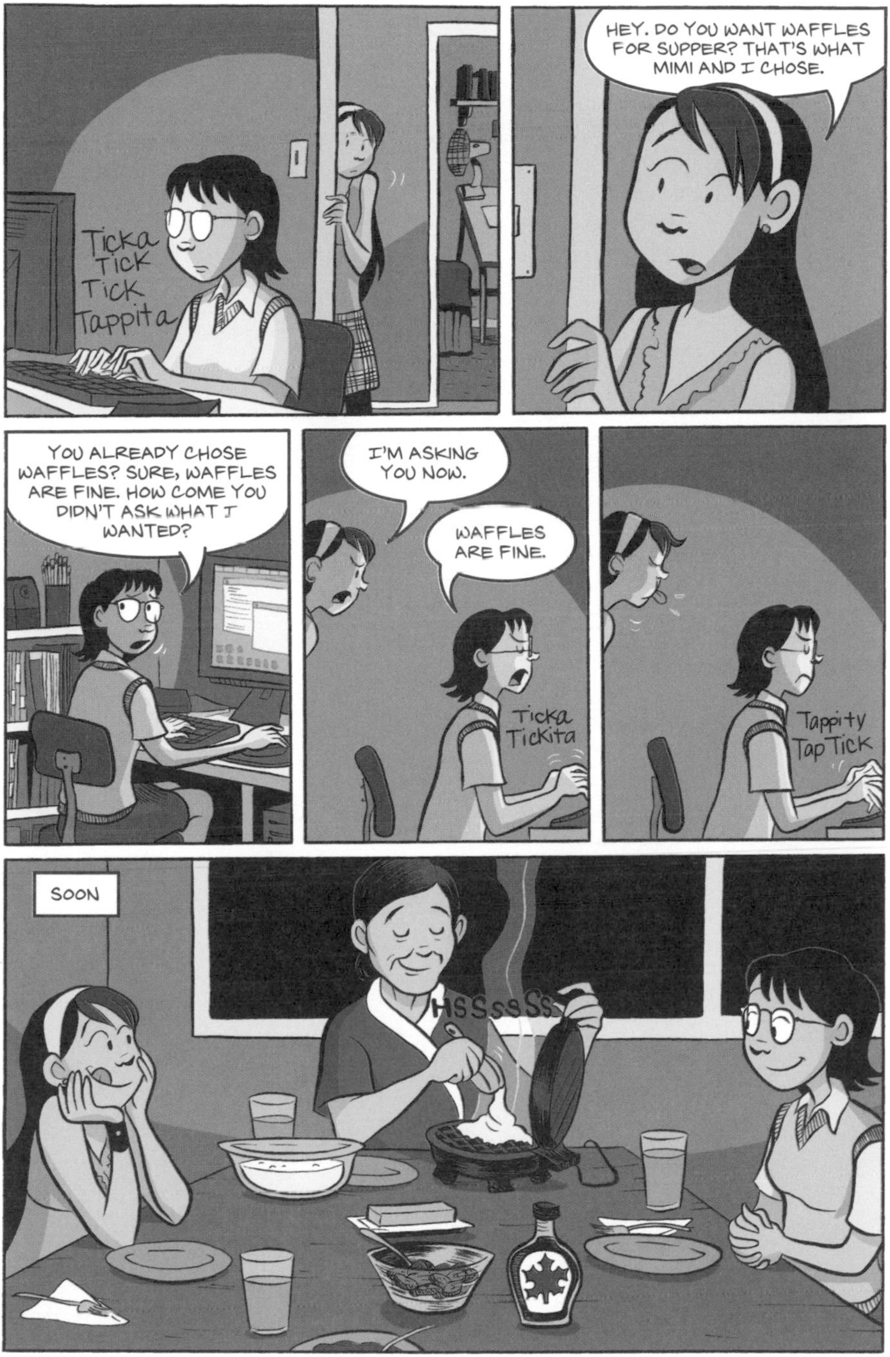
Ticka Tick Tick Tappita
HEY. DO YOU WANT WAFFLES FOR SUPPER? THAT'S WHAT MIMI AND I CHOSE.
YOU ALREADY CHOSE WAFFLES? SURE, WAFFLES ARE FINE. HOW COME YOU DIDN'T ASK WHAT I WANTED?
I'M ASKING YOU NOW.
WAFFLES ARE FINE.
Ticka Tickita
Tappity Tap Tick
SOON
HSSssSs

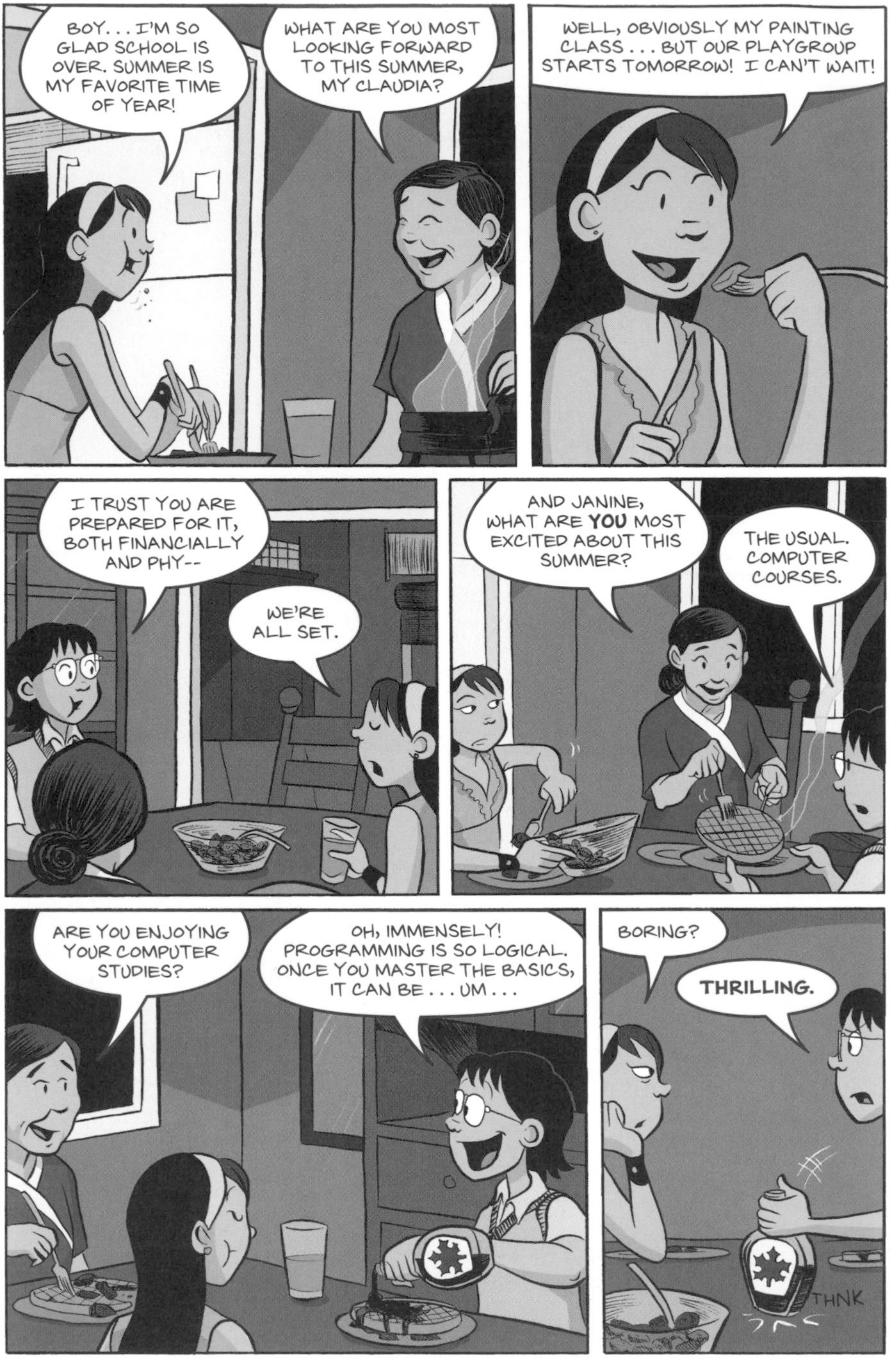
BOY. . . I'M SO GLAD SCHOOL IS OVER. SUMMER IS MY FAVORITE TIME OF YEAR!
WHAT ARE YOU MOST LOOKING FORWARD TO THIS SUMMER, MY CLAUDIA?
WELL, OBVIOUSLY MY PAINTING CLASS . . . BUT OUR PLAYGROUP STARTS TOMORROW! I CAN'T WAIT!
I TRUST YOU ARE PREPARED FOR IT, BOTH FINANCIALLY AND PHY--
WE'RE ALL SET.
AND JANINE, WHAT ARE YOU MOST EXCITED ABOUT THIS SUMMER?
THE USUAL. COMPUTER COURSES.
ARE YOU ENJOYING YOUR COMPUTER STUDIES?
OH, IMMENSELY! PROGRAMMING IS SO LOGICAL. ONCE YOU MASTER THE BASICS, IT CAN BE . . . UM . . .
BORING?
THRILLING.
THNK

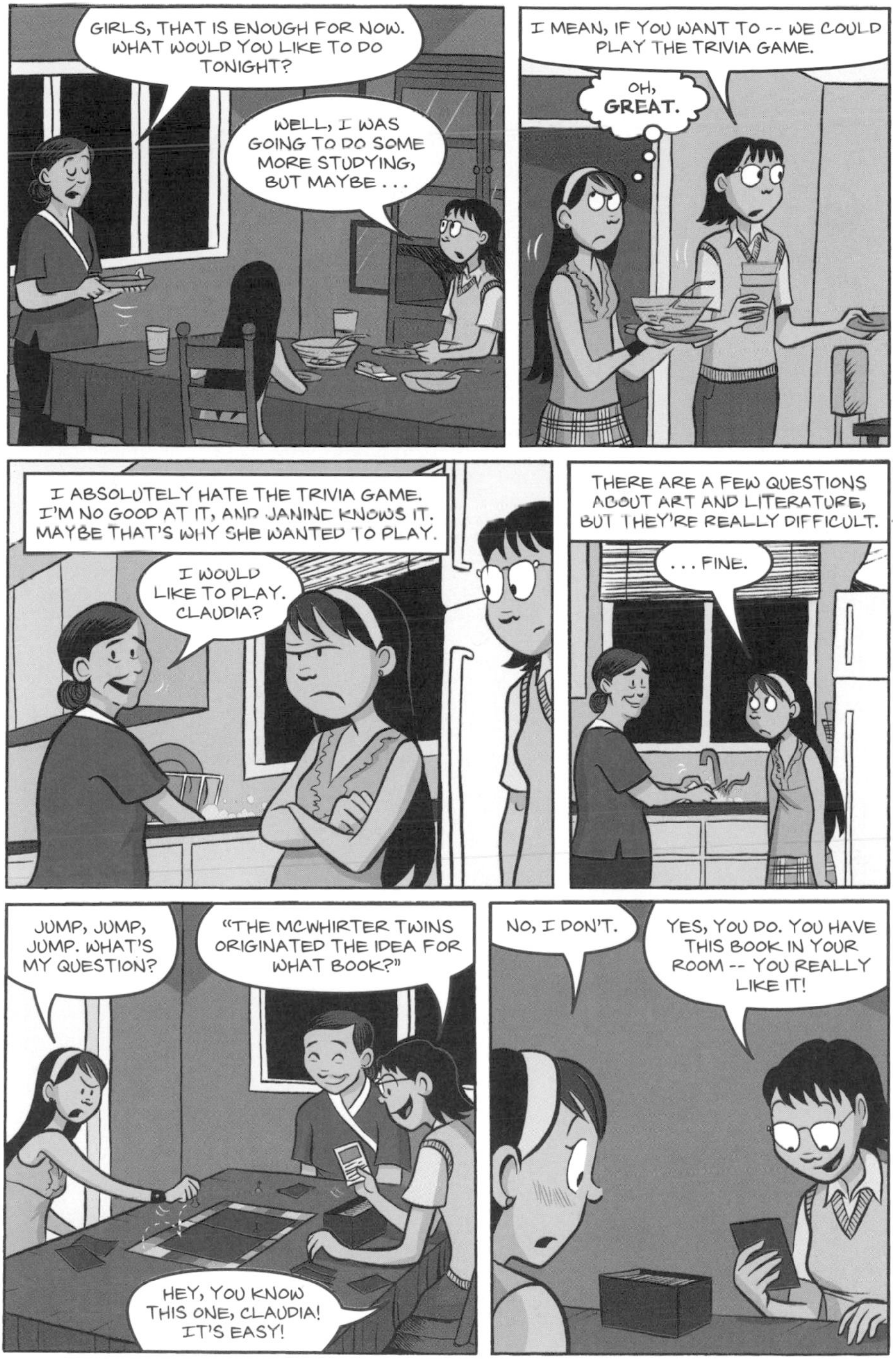
GIRLS, THAT IS ENOUGH FOR NOW. WHAT WOULD YOU LIKE TO DO TONIGHT?
WELL, I WAS GOING TO DO SOME MORE STUDYING, BUT MAYBE . . .
I MEAN, IF YOU WANT TO -- WE COULD PLAY THE TRIVIA GAME.
OH, GREAT.
I ABSOLUTELY HATE THE TRIVIA GAME. I'M NO GOOD AT IT, AND JANINE KNOWS IT. MAYBE THAT'S WHY SHE WANTED TO PLAY.
I WOULD LIKE TO PLAY. CLAUDIA?
THERE ARE A FEW QUESTIONS ABOUT ART AND LITERATURE, BUT THEY'RE REALLY DIFFICULT.
. . . FINE.
JUMP, JUMP, JUMP. WHAT'S MY QUESTION?
"THE MCWHIRTER TWINS ORIGINATED THE IDEA FOR WHAT BOOK?"
HEY, YOU KNOW THIS ONE, CLAUDIA! IT'S EASY!
NO, I DON'T.
YES, YOU DO. YOU HAVE THIS BOOK IN YOUR ROOM -- YOU REALLY LIKE IT!

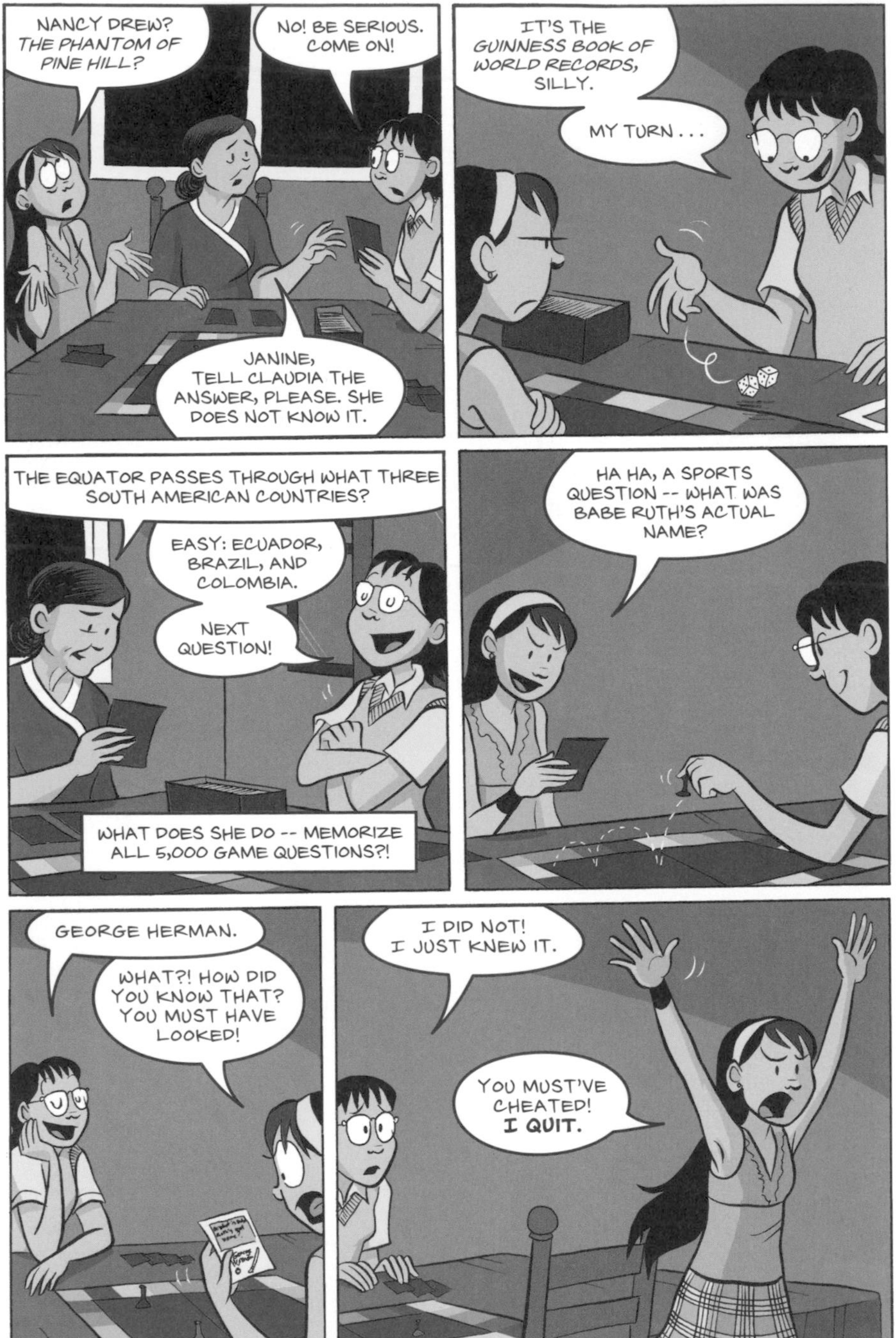
NANCY DREW? THE PHANTOM OF PINE HILL?
NO! BE SERIOUS. COME ON!
JANINE, TELL CLAUDIA THE ANSWER, PLEASE. SHE DOES NOT KNOW IT.
IT'S THE GUINNESS BOOK OF WORLD RECORDS, SILLY.
MY TURN . . .
THE EQUATOR PASSES THROUGH WHAT THREE SOUTH AMERICAN COUNTRIES?
EASY: ECUADOR, BRAZIL, AND COLOMBIA.
NEXT QUESTION!
WHAT DOES SHE DO -- MEMORIZE ALL 5,000 GAME QUESTIONS?!
HA HA, A SPORTS QUESTION -- WHAT WAS BABE RUTH'S ACTUAL NAME?
GEORGE HERMAN.
WHAT?! HOW DID YOU KNOW THAT? YOU MUST HAVE LOOKED!
I DID NOT! I JUST KNEW IT.
YOU MUST'VE CHEATED! **I QUIT.**

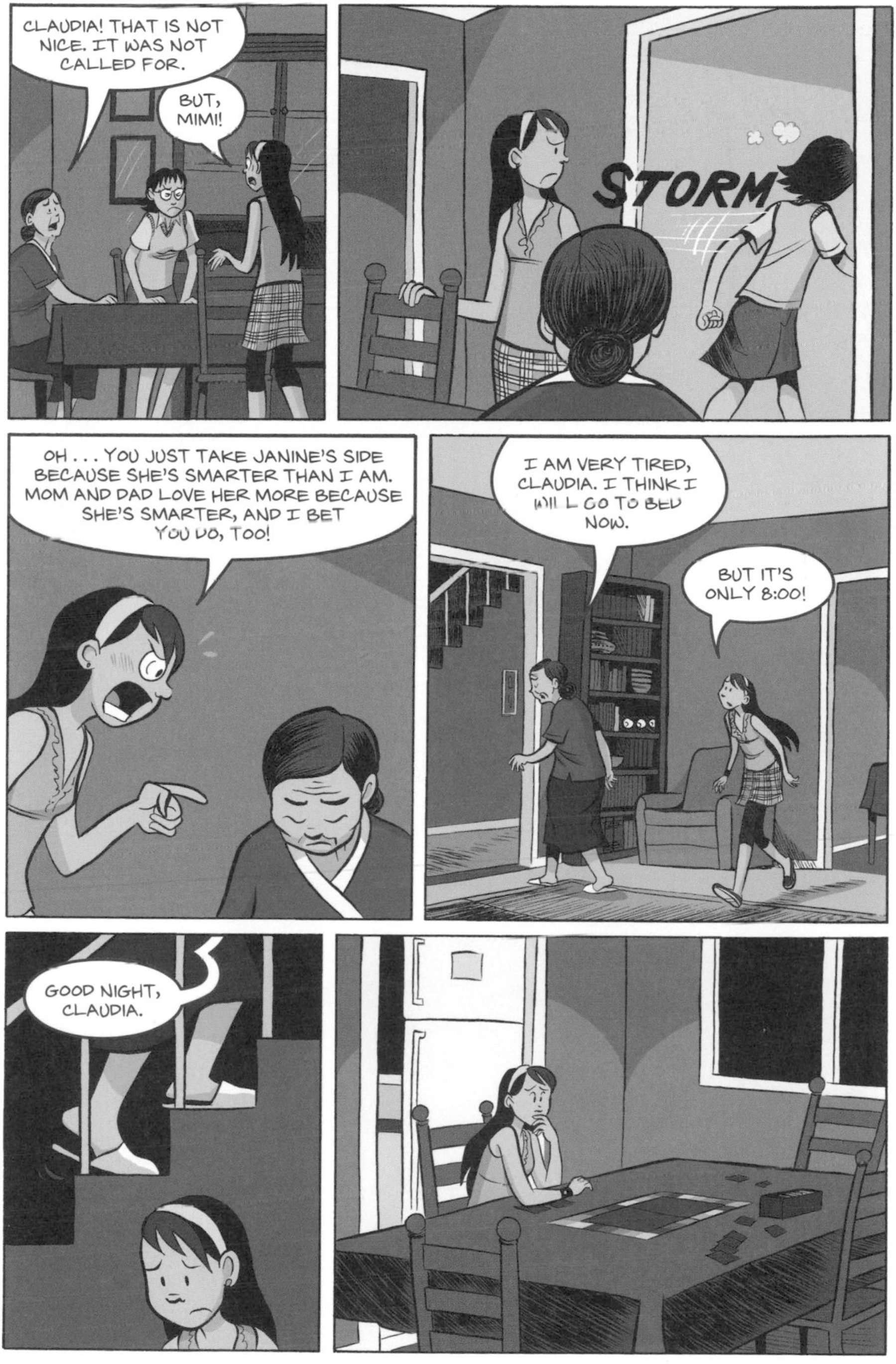
CLAUDIA! THAT IS NOT NICE. IT WAS NOT CALLED FOR.
BUT, MIMI!
STORM
OH . . . YOU JUST TAKE JANINE'S SIDE BECAUSE SHE'S SMARTER THAN I AM. MOM AND DAD LOVE HER MORE BECAUSE SHE'S SMARTER, AND I BET YOU DO, TOO!
I AM VERY TIRED, CLAUDIA. I THINK I WILL GO TO BED NOW.
BUT IT'S ONLY 8:00!
GOOD NIGHT, CLAUDIA.

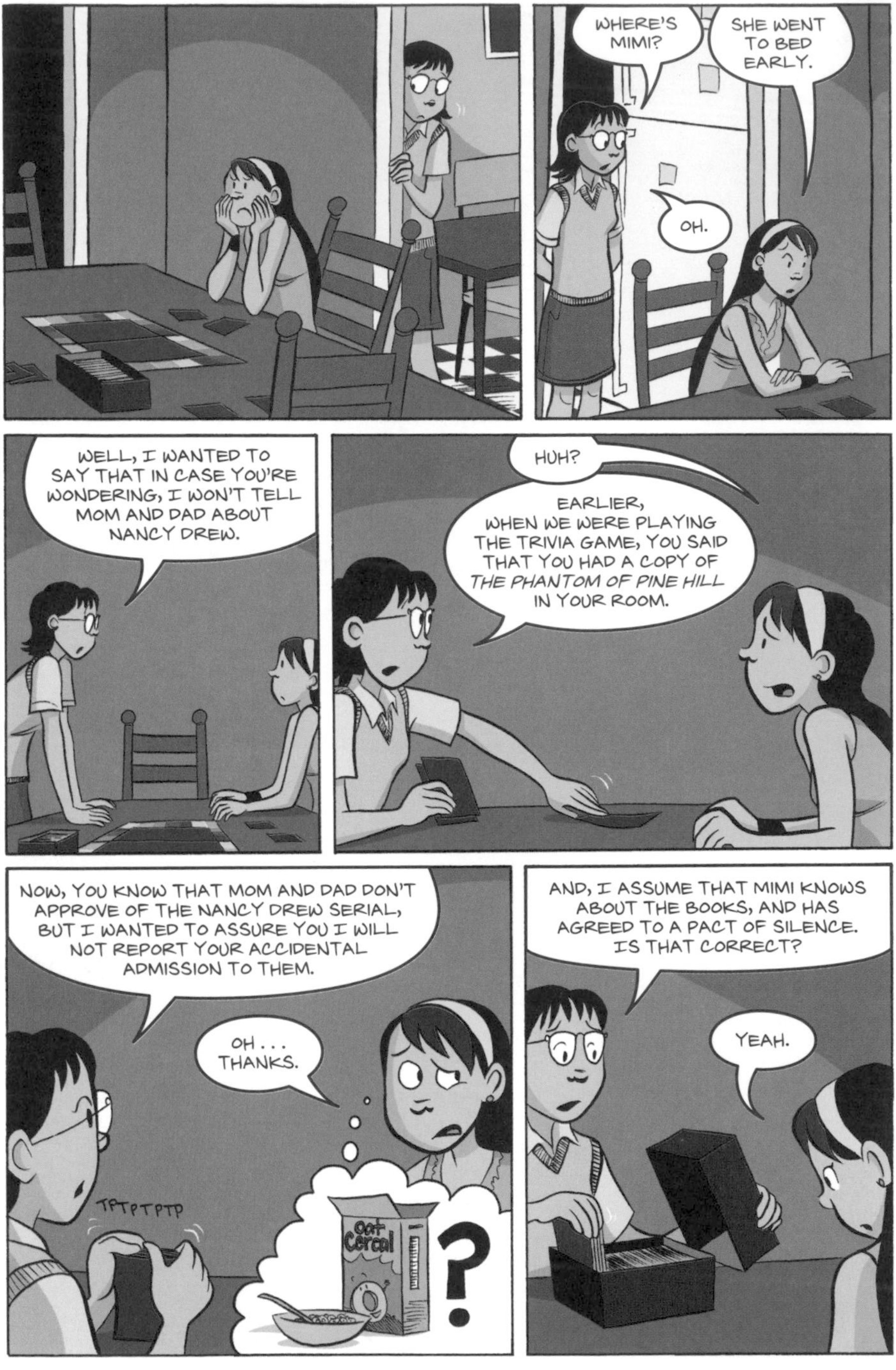
WHERE'S MIMI?
SHE WENT TO BED EARLY.
OH.
WELL, I WANTED TO SAY THAT IN CASE YOU'RE WONDERING, I WON'T TELL MOM AND DAD ABOUT NANCY DREW.
HUH?
EARLIER, WHEN WE WERE PLAYING THE TRIVIA GAME, YOU SAID THAT YOU HAD A COPY OF *THE PHANTOM OF PINE HILL* IN YOUR ROOM.
NOW, YOU KNOW THAT MOM AND DAD DON'T APPROVE OF THE NANCY DREW SERIAL, BUT I WANTED TO ASSURE YOU I WILL NOT REPORT YOUR ACCIDENTAL ADMISSION TO THEM.
OH . . . THANKS.
TPTPTPTP
Oat Cereal
?
AND, I ASSUME THAT MIMI KNOWS ABOUT THE BOOKS, AND HAS AGREED TO A PACT OF SILENCE. IS THAT CORRECT?
YEAH.

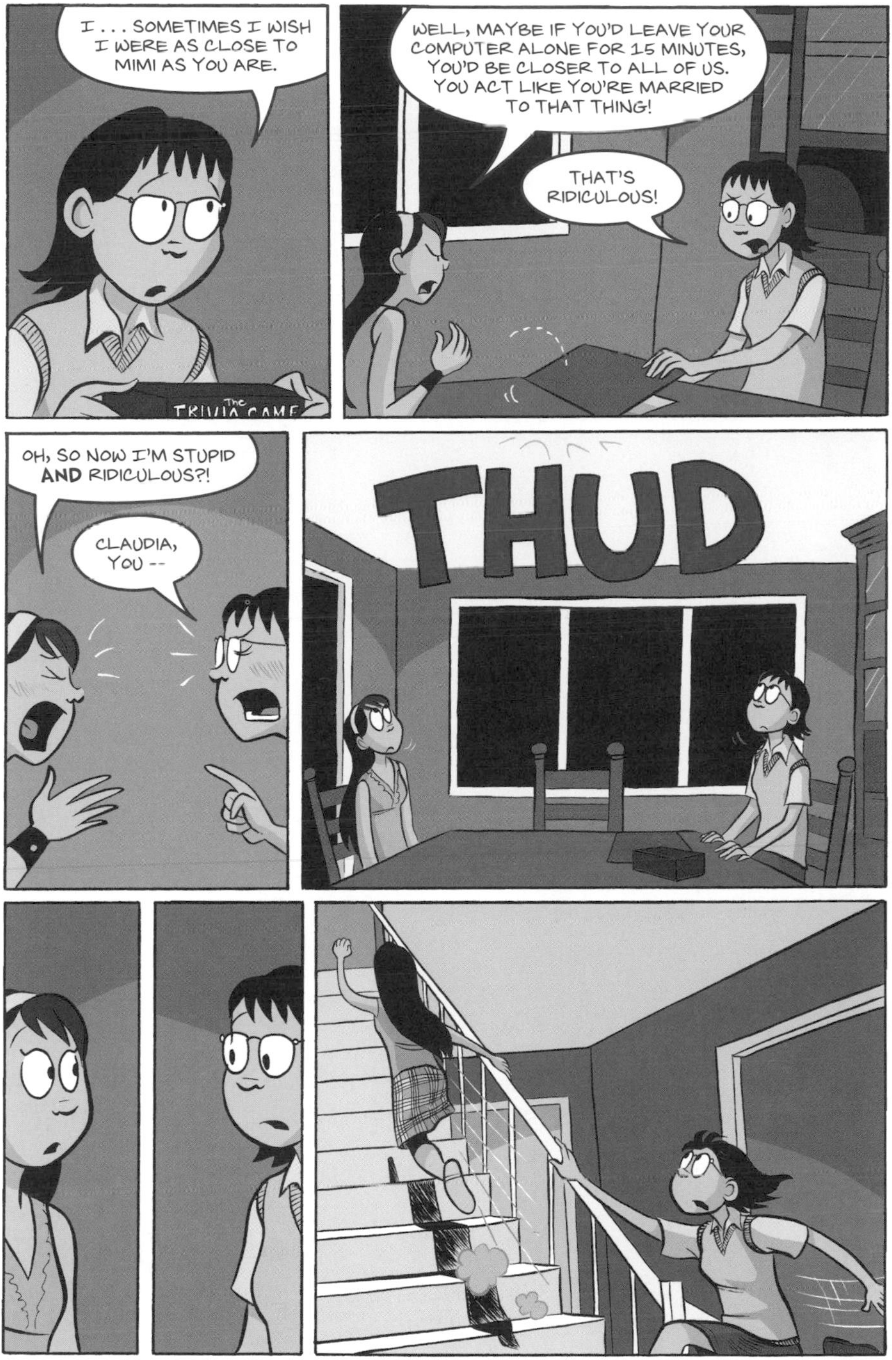
I . . . SOMETIMES I WISH I WERE AS CLOSE TO MIMI AS YOU ARE.
The TRIVIA GAME
WELL, MAYBE IF YOU'D LEAVE YOUR COMPUTER ALONE FOR 15 MINUTES, YOU'D BE CLOSER TO ALL OF US. YOU ACT LIKE YOU'RE MARRIED TO THAT THING!
THAT'S RIDICULOUS!
OH, SO NOW I'M STUPID **AND** RIDICULOUS?!
CLAUDIA, YOU --
THUD

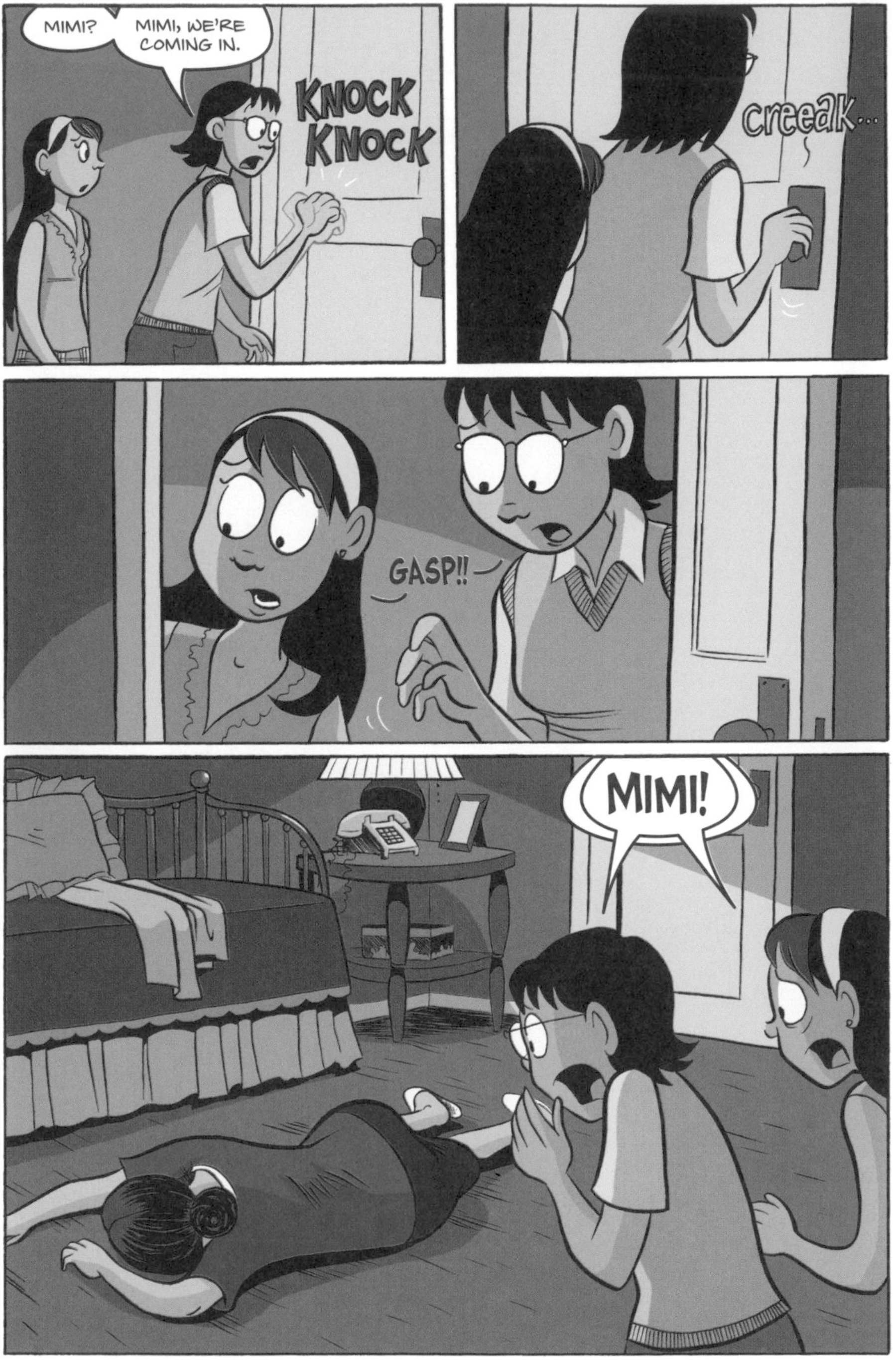
MIMI?
MIMI, WE'RE COMING IN.
KNOCK KNOCK
creeak...
GASP!!
MIMI!

CHAPTER 5

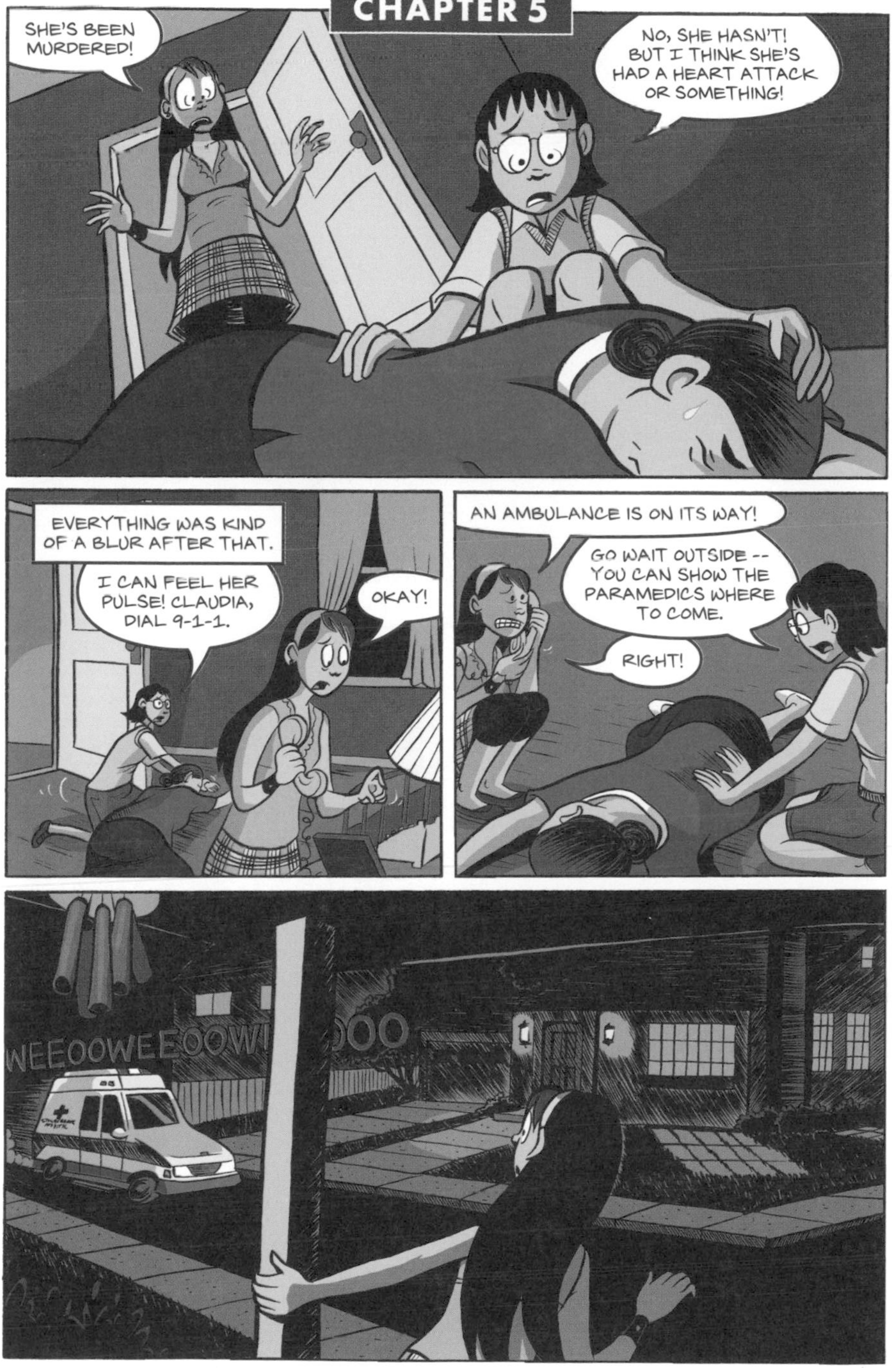
SHE'S BEEN MURDERED!
NO, SHE HASN'T! BUT I THINK SHE'S HAD A HEART ATTACK OR SOMETHING!
EVERYTHING WAS KIND OF A BLUR AFTER THAT.
I CAN FEEL HER PULSE! CLAUDIA, DIAL 9-1-1.
OKAY!
AN AMBULANCE IS ON ITS WAY!
GO WAIT OUTSIDE -- YOU CAN SHOW THE PARAMEDICS WHERE TO COME.
RIGHT!
WEEOOWEEOOWI OOO

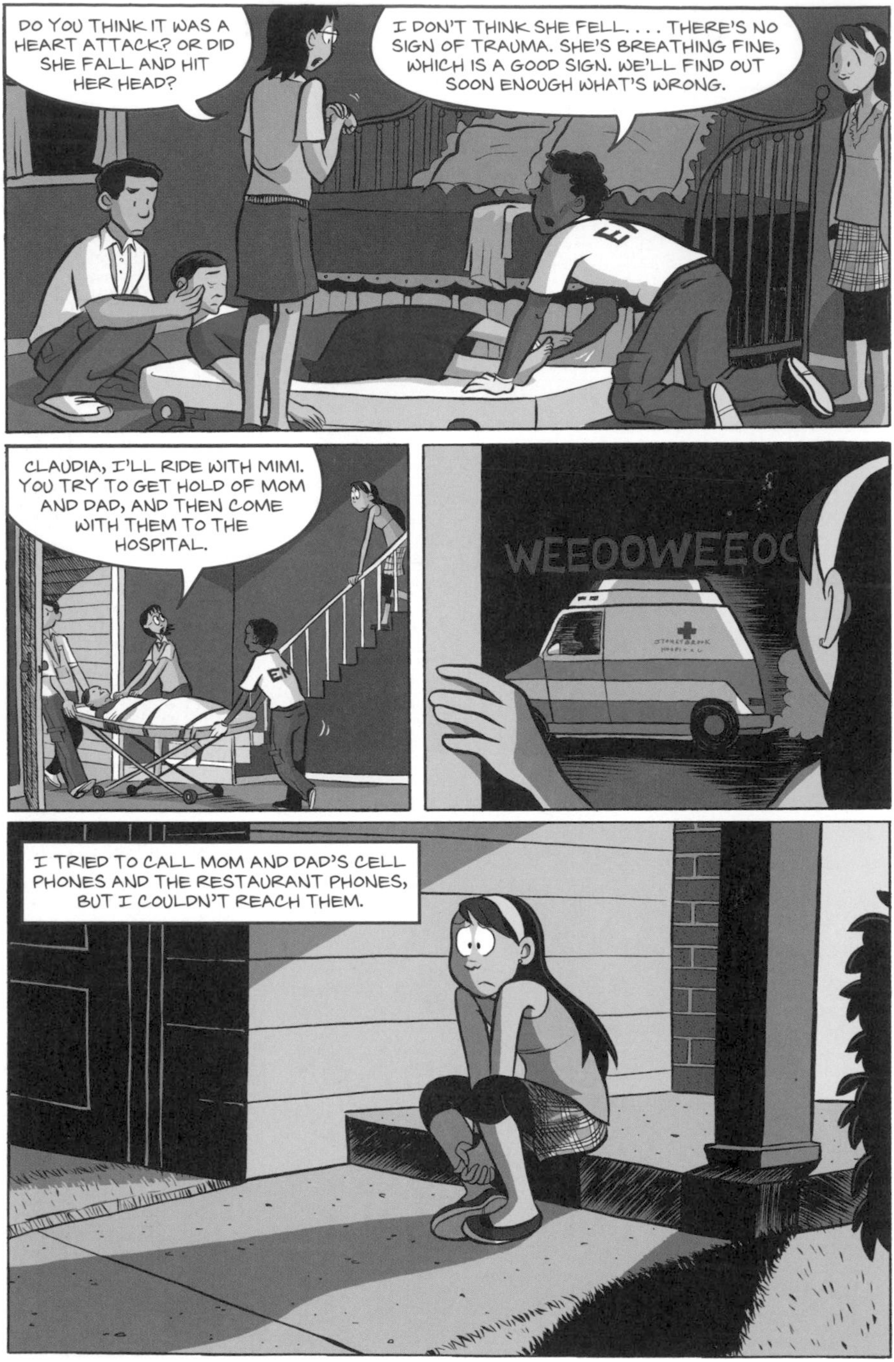
DO YOU THINK IT WAS A HEART ATTACK? OR DID SHE FALL AND HIT HER HEAD?
I DON'T THINK SHE FELL. . . . THERE'S NO SIGN OF TRAUMA. SHE'S BREATHING FINE, WHICH IS A GOOD SIGN. WE'LL FIND OUT SOON ENOUGH WHAT'S WRONG.
CLAUDIA, I'LL RIDE WITH MIMI. YOU TRY TO GET HOLD OF MOM AND DAD, AND THEN COME WITH THEM TO THE HOSPITAL.
WEEOOWEEOO
I TRIED TO CALL MOM AND DAD'S CELL PHONES AND THE RESTAURANT PHONES, BUT I COULDN'T REACH THEM.

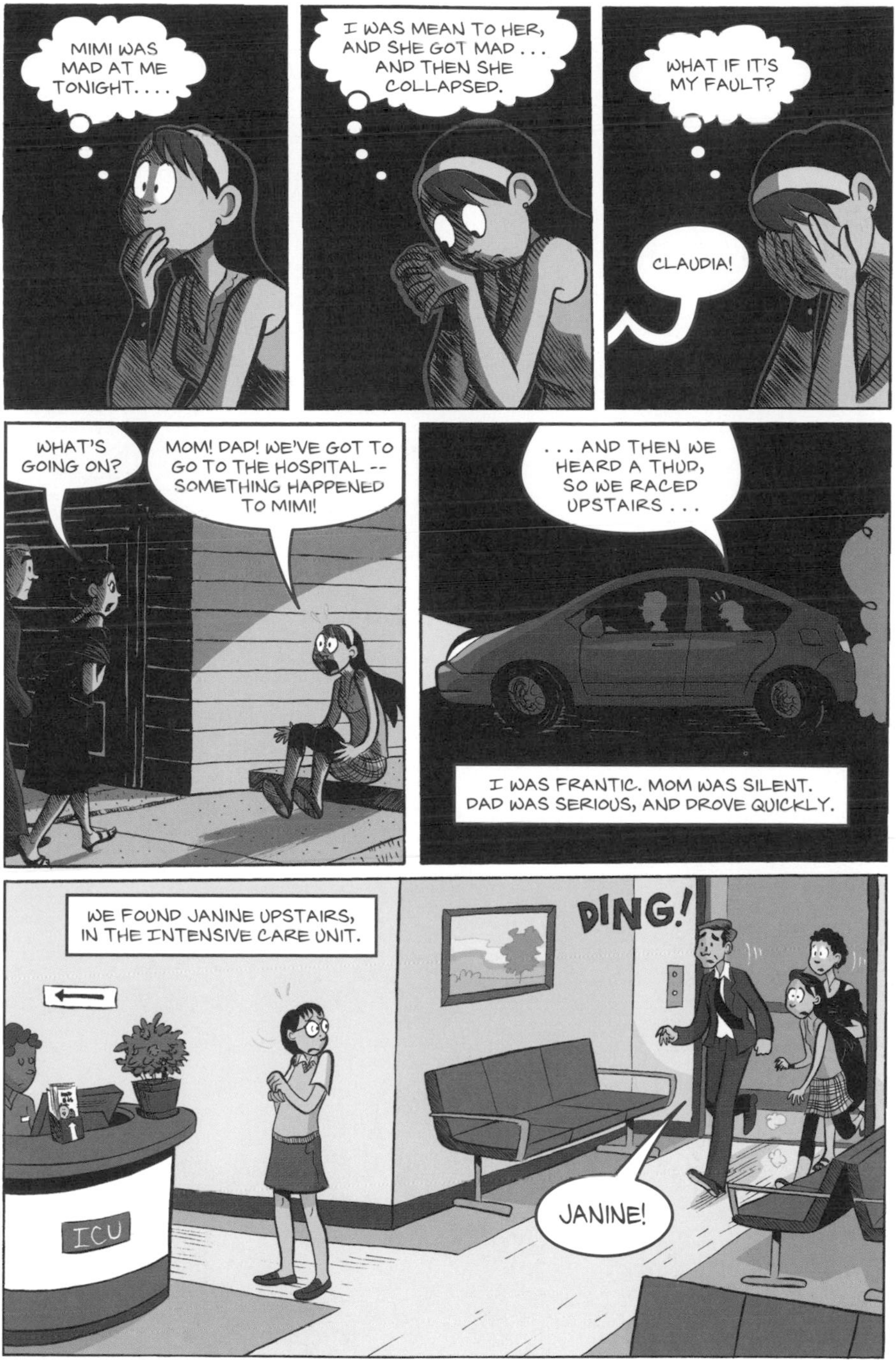

MIMI WAS MAD AT ME TONIGHT. . . .
I WAS MEAN TO HER, AND SHE GOT MAD . . . AND THEN SHE COLLAPSED.
WHAT IF IT'S MY FAULT?
CLAUDIA!
WHAT'S GOING ON?
MOM! DAD! WE'VE GOT TO GO TO THE HOSPITAL -- SOMETHING HAPPENED TO MIMI!
. . . AND THEN WE HEARD A THUD, SO WE RACED UPSTAIRS . . .
I WAS FRANTIC. MOM WAS SILENT. DAD WAS SERIOUS, AND DROVE QUICKLY.
WE FOUND JANINE UPSTAIRS, IN THE INTENSIVE CARE UNIT.
DING!
ICU
JANINE!

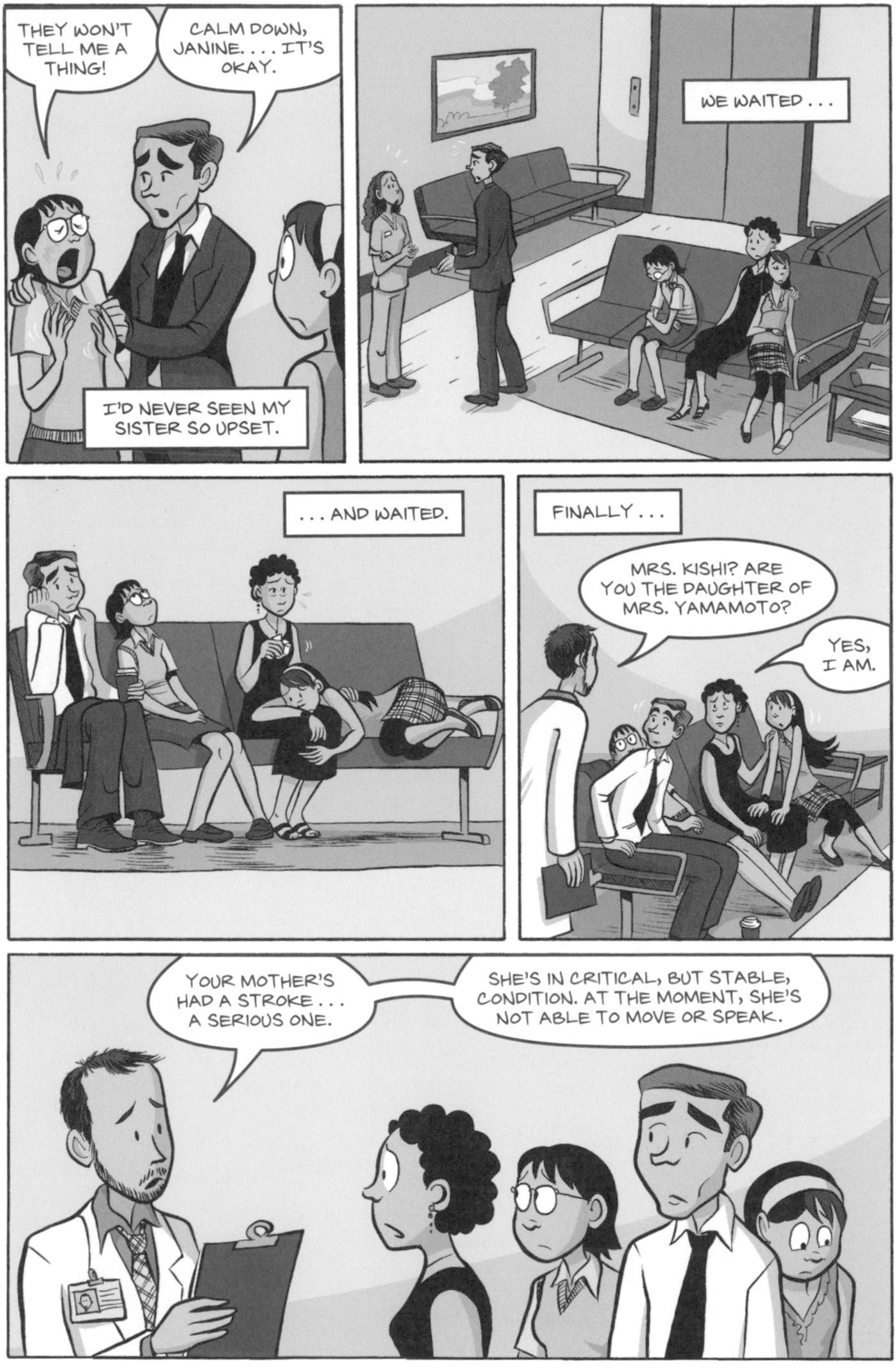
THEY WON'T TELL ME A THING!
CALM DOWN, JANINE. . . . IT'S OKAY.
I'D NEVER SEEN MY SISTER SO UPSET.
WE WAITED . . .
. . . AND WAITED.
FINALLY . . .
MRS. KISHI? ARE YOU THE DAUGHTER OF MRS. YAMAMOTO?
YES, I AM.
YOUR MOTHER'S HAD A STROKE . . . A SERIOUS ONE.
SHE'S IN CRITICAL, BUT STABLE, CONDITION. AT THE MOMENT, SHE'S NOT ABLE TO MOVE OR SPEAK.

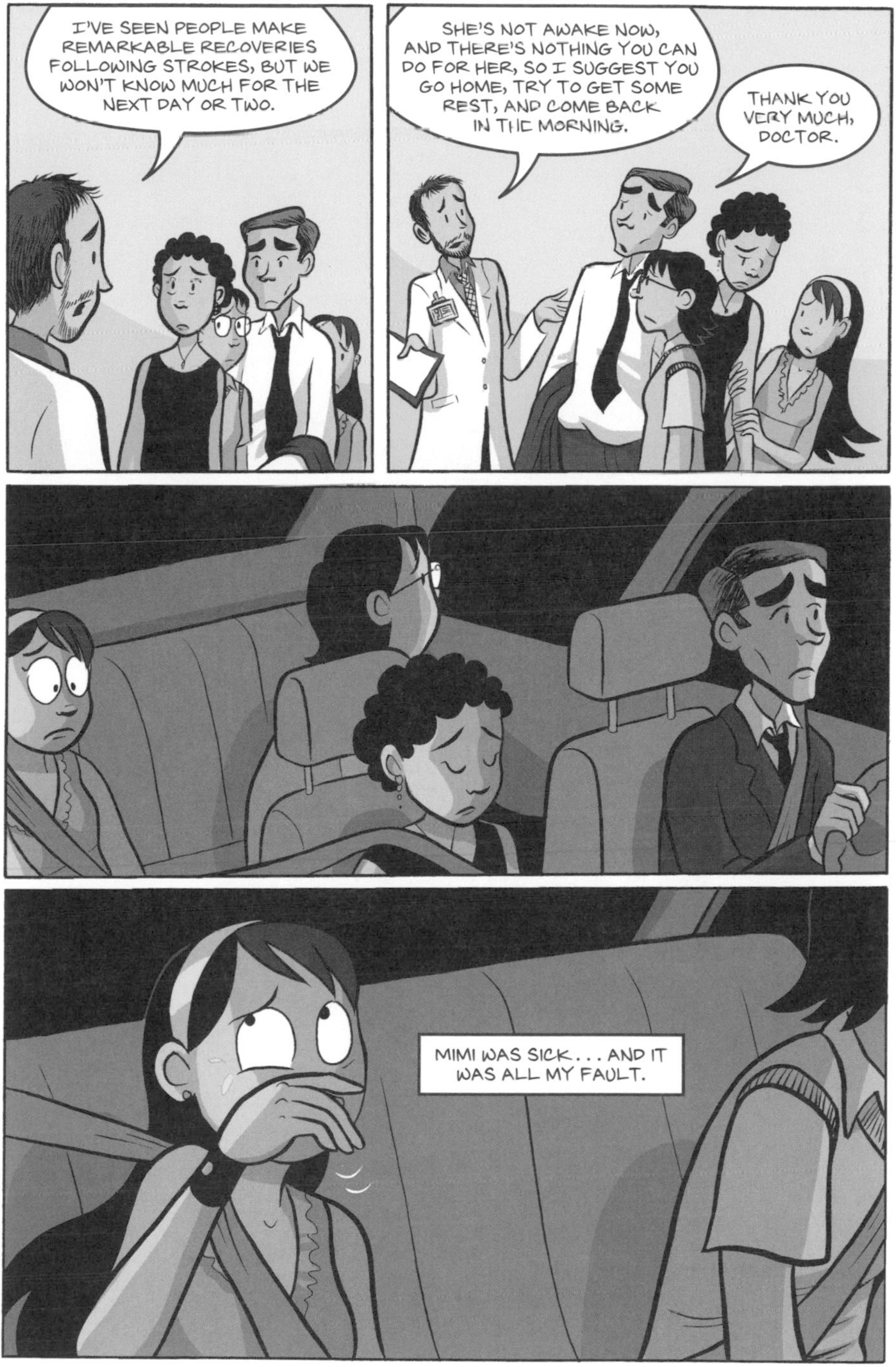
I'VE SEEN PEOPLE MAKE REMARKABLE RECOVERIES FOLLOWING STROKES, BUT WE WON'T KNOW MUCH FOR THE NEXT DAY OR TWO.
SHE'S NOT AWAKE NOW, AND THERE'S NOTHING YOU CAN DO FOR HER, SO I SUGGEST YOU GO HOME, TRY TO GET SOME REST, AND COME BACK IN THE MORNING.
THANK YOU VERY MUCH, DOCTOR.
MIMI WAS SICK . . . AND IT WAS ALL MY FAULT.

MONDAY, JUNE 16

TODAY WAS A GOOD NEWS - BAD NEWS DAY FOR US
BABY-SITTERS. THE GOOD NEWS WAS THAT NINE CHILDREN
CAME TO THE FIRST SESSION OF OUR PLAYGROUP AND
IT WENT REALLY WELL. DAVID MICHAEL, NICKY, AND
MARCUS ARE KIND OF WILD WHEN THEY GET TOGETHER,
BUT THEY'RE MANAGEABLE. AND WE'RE GOING TO HAVE
TO DO SOMETHING ABOUT JENNY PREZZIOSO... SHE'S
A PAIN. GOT ANY IDEAS, MARY ANNE?

THE BAD NEWS WAS ABOUT CLAUDIA'S GRANDMOTHER, MIMI.
IT TURNS OUT THAT SHE HAD A STROKE LAST NIGHT AND
IS IN THE HOSPITAL. THE NEWS KIND OF UPSET US, BUT
WE WERE ABLE TO PUT OUR WORRIES ASIDE AND RUN
THE PLAYGROUP OKAY, WHICH I GUESS PROVES
WE'RE PROFESSIONALS.
                    -DAWN

CHAPTER 6

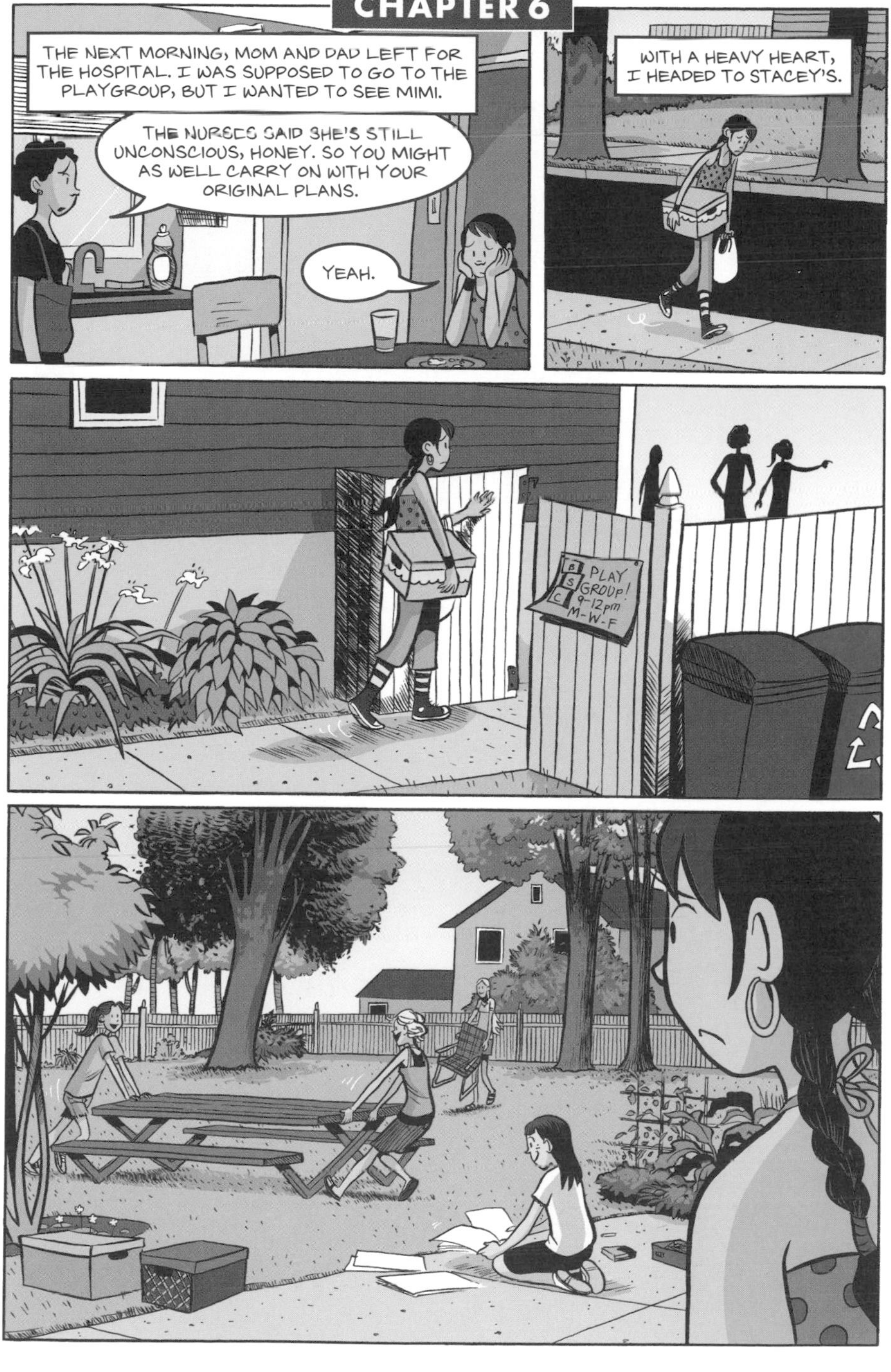
THE NEXT MORNING, MOM AND DAD LEFT FOR THE HOSPITAL. I WAS SUPPOSED TO GO TO THE PLAYGROUP, BUT I WANTED TO SEE MIMI.
THE NURSES SAID SHE'S STILL UNCONSCIOUS, HONEY. SO YOU MIGHT AS WELL CARRY ON WITH YOUR ORIGINAL PLANS.
YEAH.
WITH A HEAVY HEART, I HEADED TO STACEY'S.
B S C
PLAY GROUP! 9-12pm M-W-F

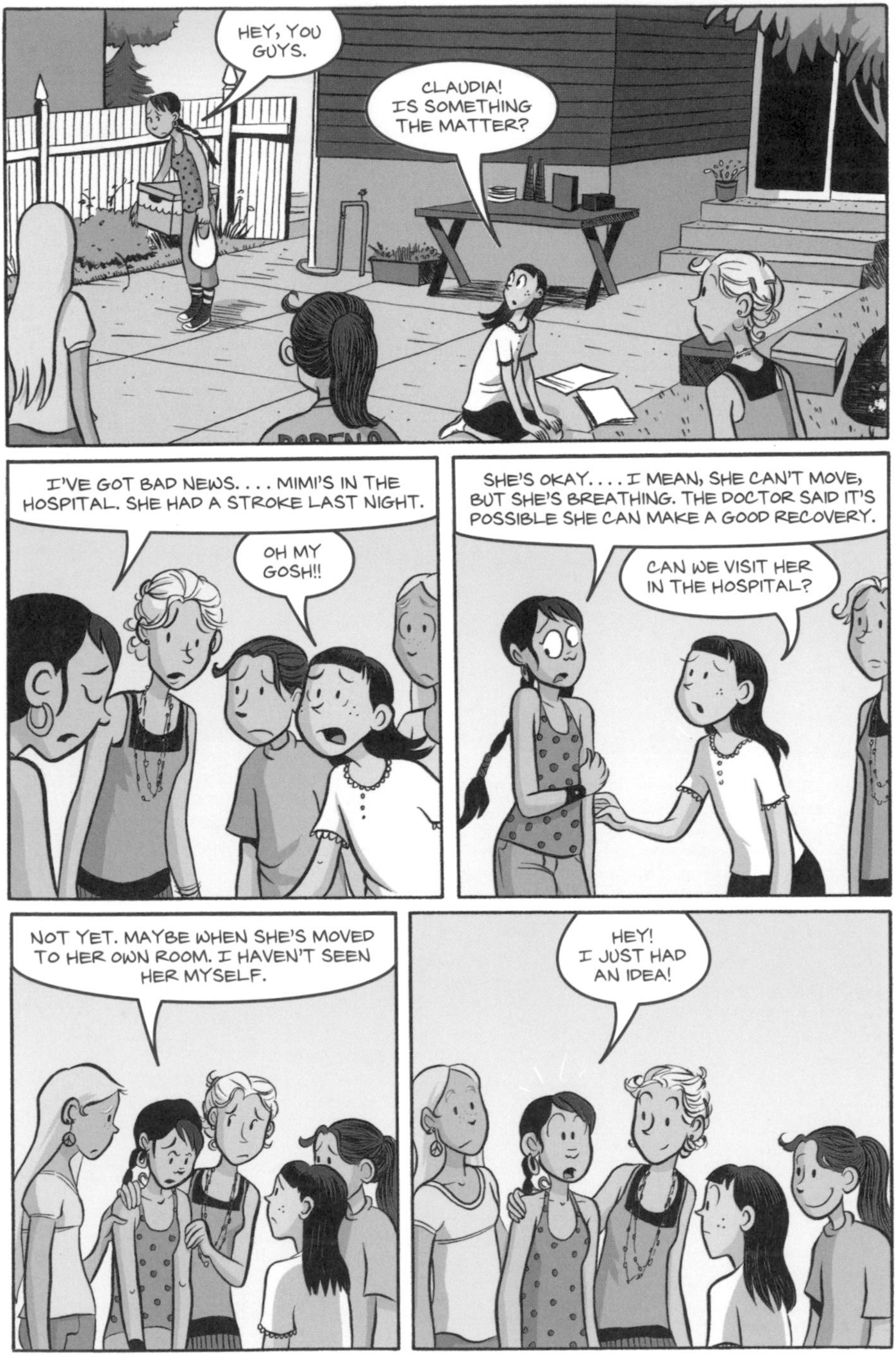

HEY, YOU GUYS.
CLAUDIA! IS SOMETHING THE MATTER?
I'VE GOT BAD NEWS. . . . MIMI'S IN THE HOSPITAL. SHE HAD A STROKE LAST NIGHT.
OH MY GOSH!!
SHE'S OKAY. . . . I MEAN, SHE CAN'T MOVE, BUT SHE'S BREATHING. THE DOCTOR SAID IT'S POSSIBLE SHE CAN MAKE A GOOD RECOVERY.
CAN WE VISIT HER IN THE HOSPITAL?
NOT YET. MAYBE WHEN SHE'S MOVED TO HER OWN ROOM. I HAVEN'T SEEN HER MYSELF.
HEY! I JUST HAD AN IDEA!

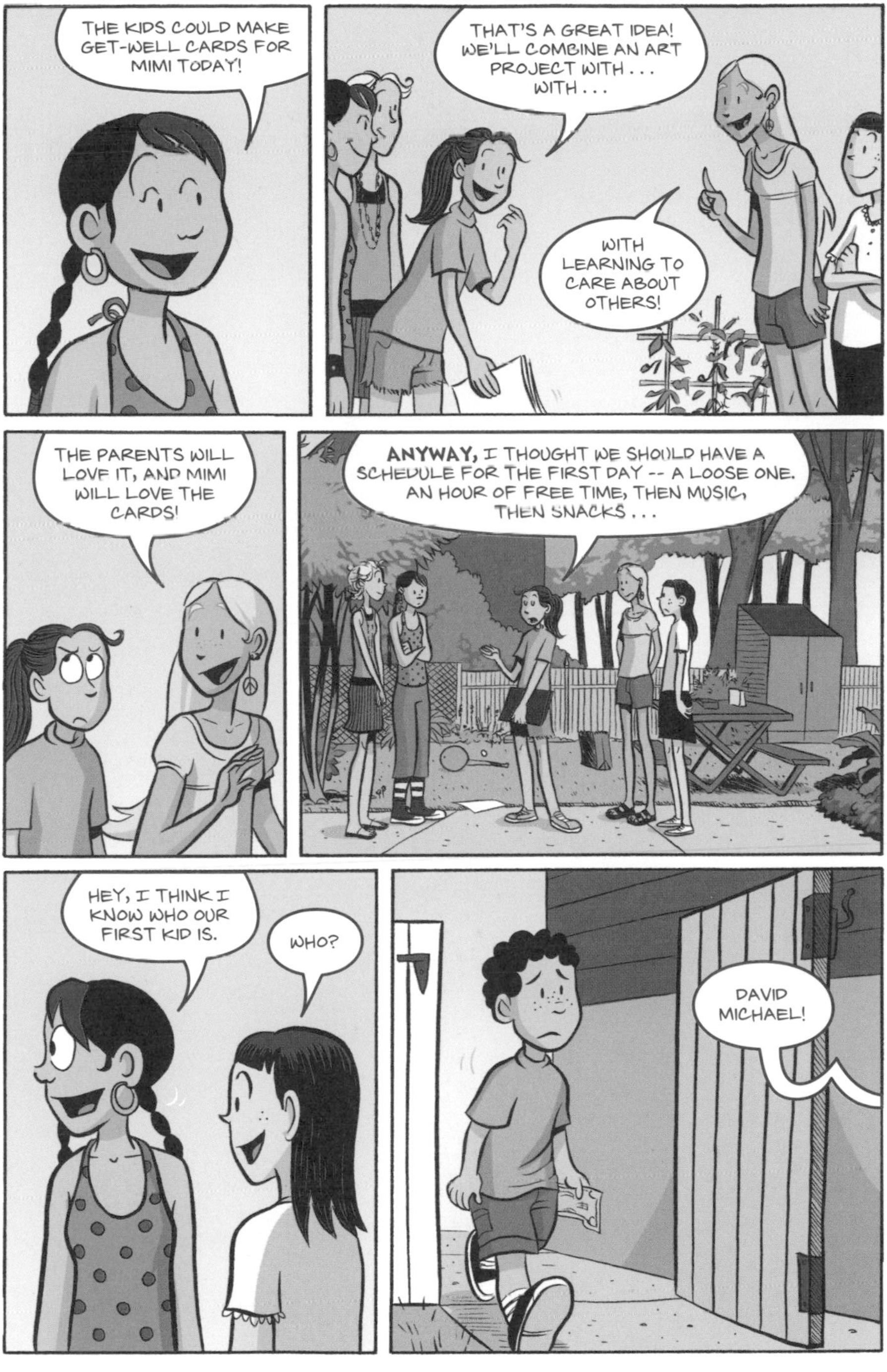
THE KIDS COULD MAKE GET-WELL CARDS FOR MIMI TODAY!
THAT'S A GREAT IDEA! WE'LL COMBINE AN ART PROJECT WITH . . . WITH . . .
WITH LEARNING TO CARE ABOUT OTHERS!
THE PARENTS WILL LOVE IT, AND MIMI WILL LOVE THE CARDS!
ANYWAY, I THOUGHT WE SHOULD HAVE A SCHEDULE FOR THE FIRST DAY -- A LOOSE ONE. AN HOUR OF FREE TIME, THEN MUSIC, THEN SNACKS . . .
HEY, I THINK I KNOW WHO OUR FIRST KID IS.
WHO?
DAVID MICHAEL!

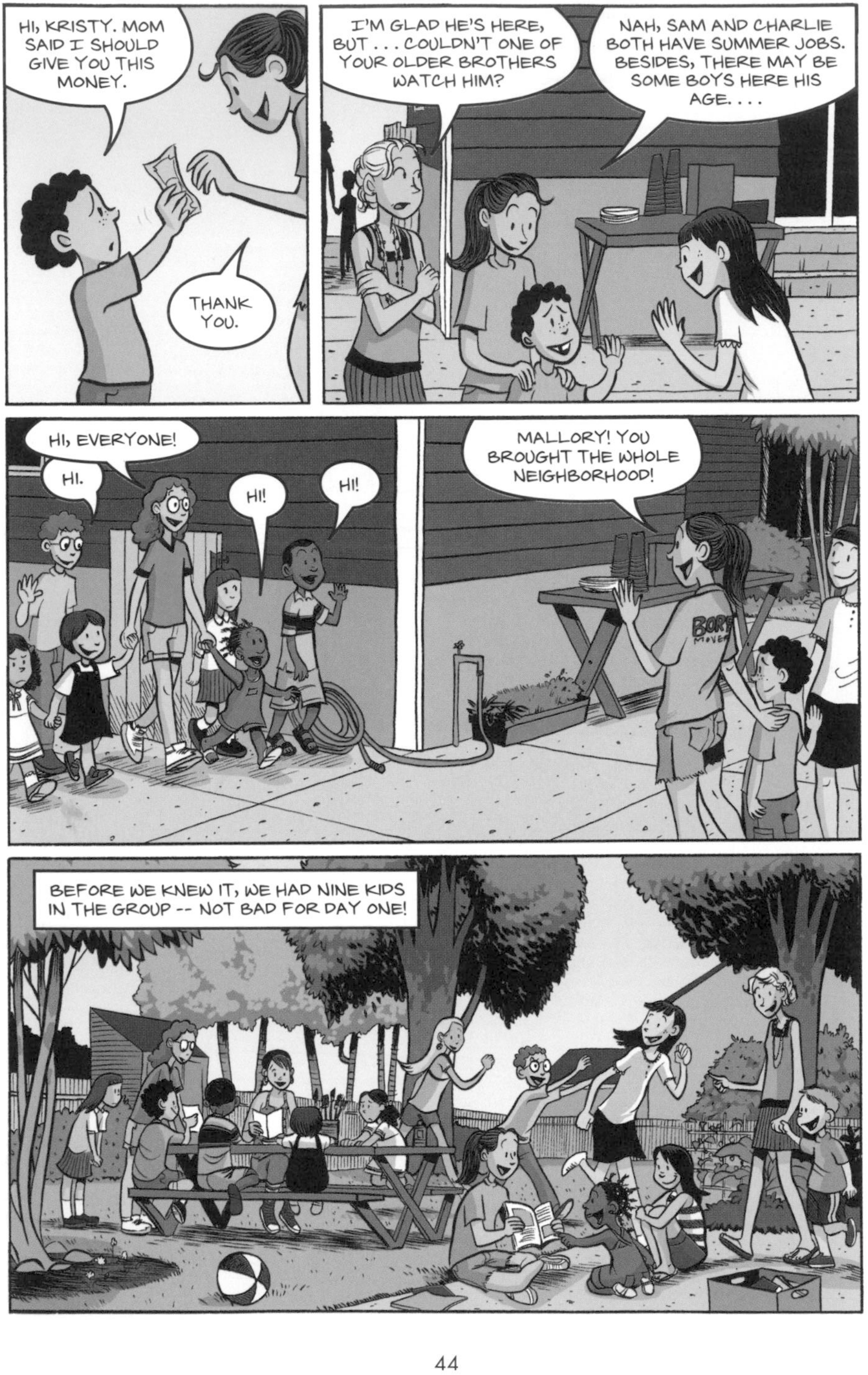
HI, KRISTY. MOM SAID I SHOULD GIVE YOU THIS MONEY.
THANK YOU.
I'M GLAD HE'S HERE, BUT . . . COULDN'T ONE OF YOUR OLDER BROTHERS WATCH HIM?
NAH, SAM AND CHARLIE BOTH HAVE SUMMER JOBS. BESIDES, THERE MAY BE SOME BOYS HERE HIS AGE. . . .
HI, EVERYONE!
HI.
HI!
HI!
MALLORY! YOU BROUGHT THE WHOLE NEIGHBORHOOD!
BEFORE WE KNEW IT, WE HAD NINE KIDS IN THE GROUP -- NOT BAD FOR DAY ONE!

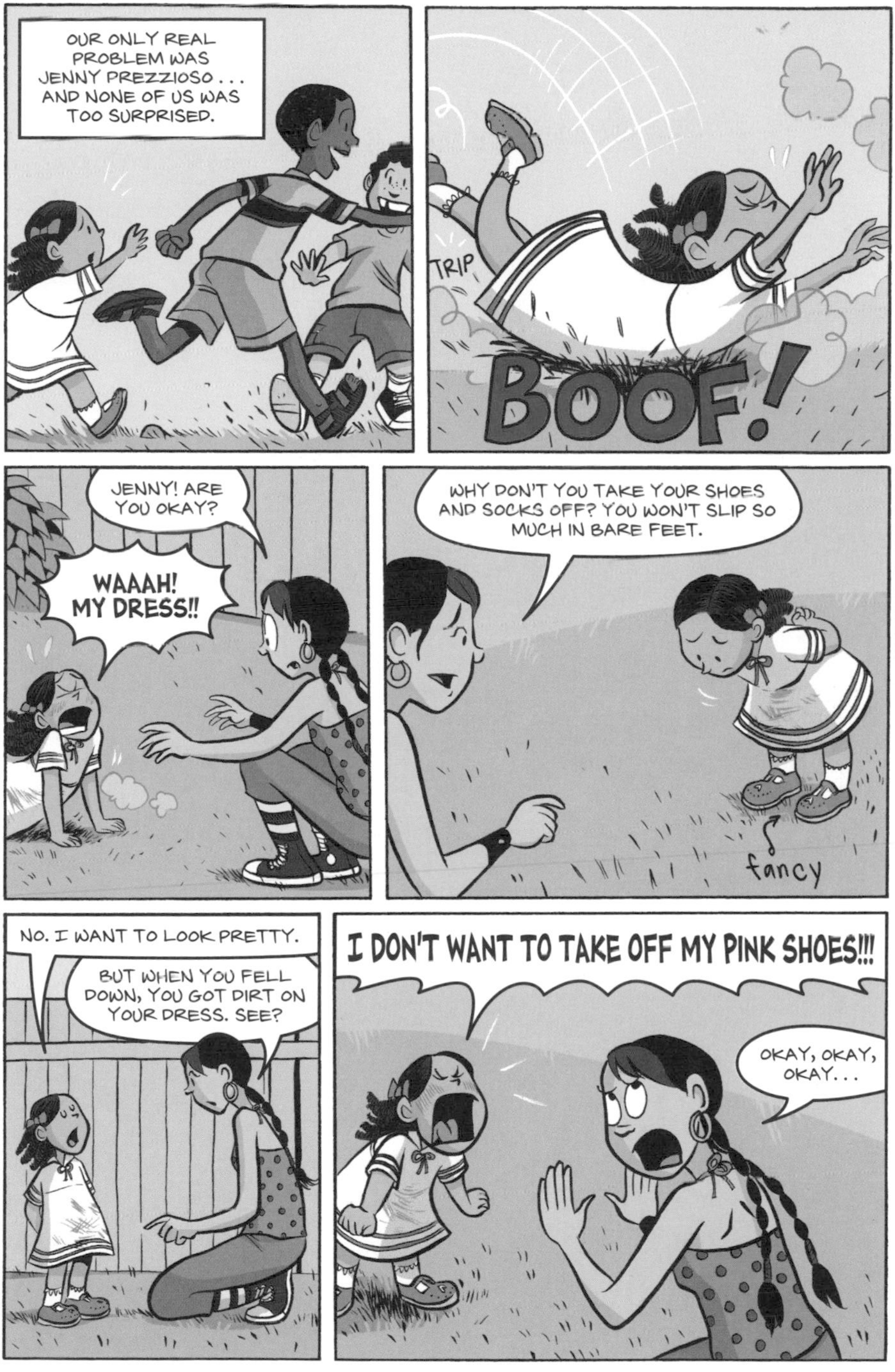
OUR ONLY REAL PROBLEM WAS JENNY PREZZIOSO . . . AND NONE OF US WAS TOO SURPRISED.
TRIP
BOOF!
JENNY! ARE YOU OKAY?
WAAAH! MY DRESS!!
WHY DON'T YOU TAKE YOUR SHOES AND SOCKS OFF? YOU WON'T SLIP SO MUCH IN BARE FEET.
fancy
NO. I WANT TO LOOK PRETTY.
BUT WHEN YOU FELL DOWN, YOU GOT DIRT ON YOUR DRESS. SEE?
I DON'T WANT TO TAKE OFF MY PINK SHOES!!!
OKAY, OKAY, OKAY...

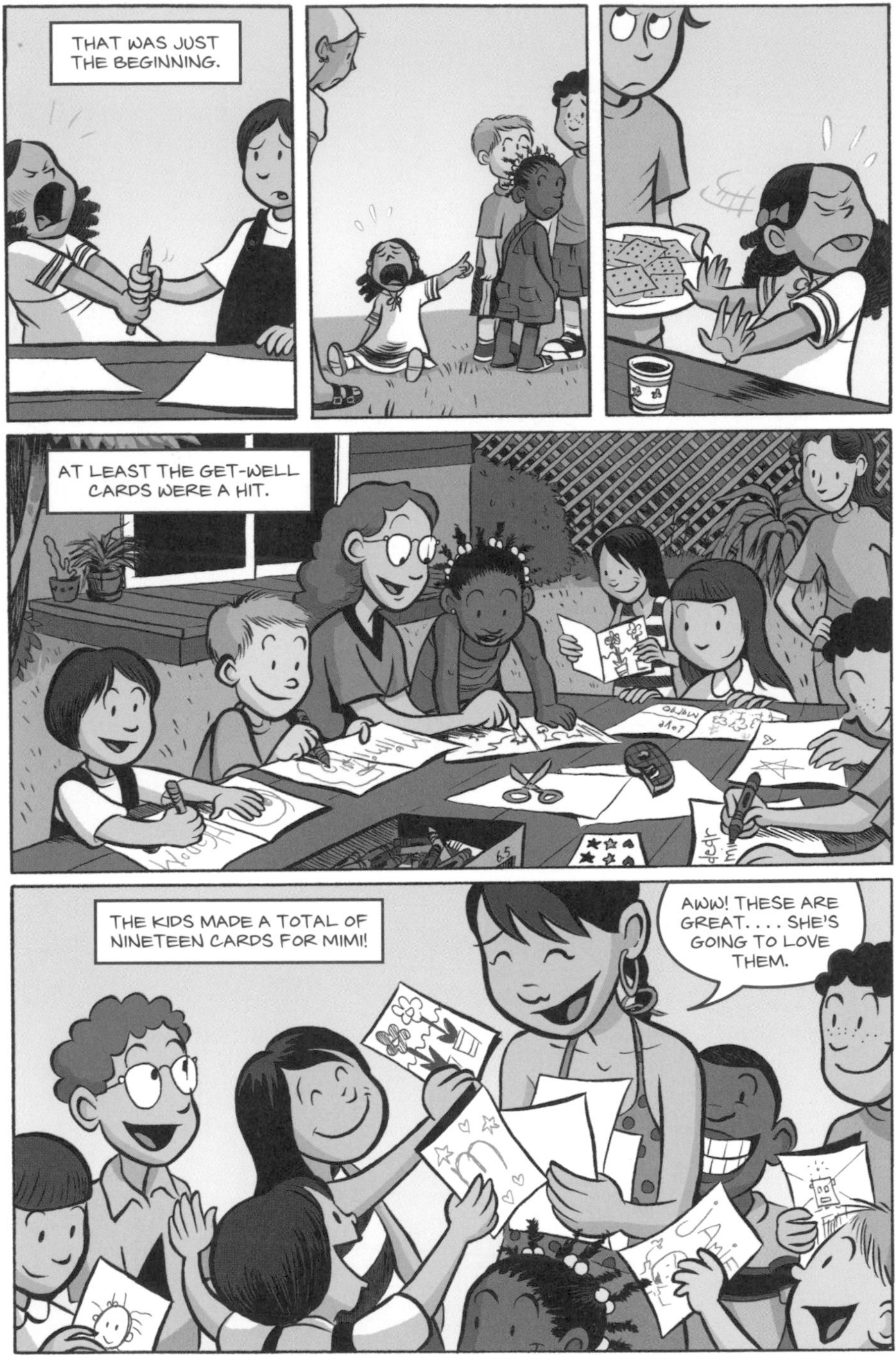
THAT WAS JUST THE BEGINNING.
AT LEAST THE GET-WELL CARDS WERE A HIT.
THE KIDS MADE A TOTAL OF NINETEEN CARDS FOR MIMI!
AWW! THESE ARE GREAT. . . . SHE'S GOING TO LOVE THEM.

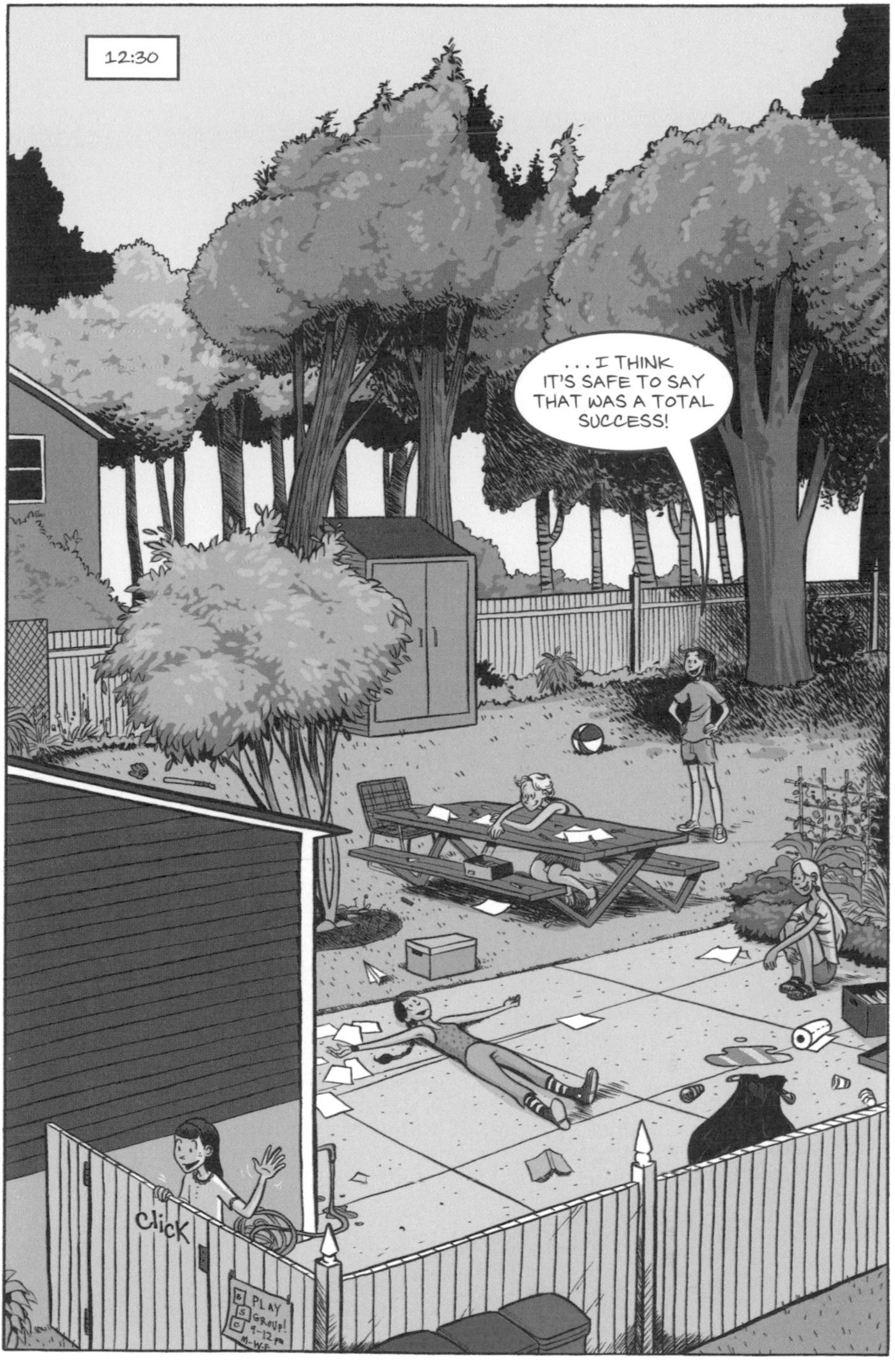
12:30
. . . I THINK IT'S SAFE TO SAY THAT WAS A TOTAL SUCCESS!
CLICK
PLAY GROUP! 9-12 PM M-W-F

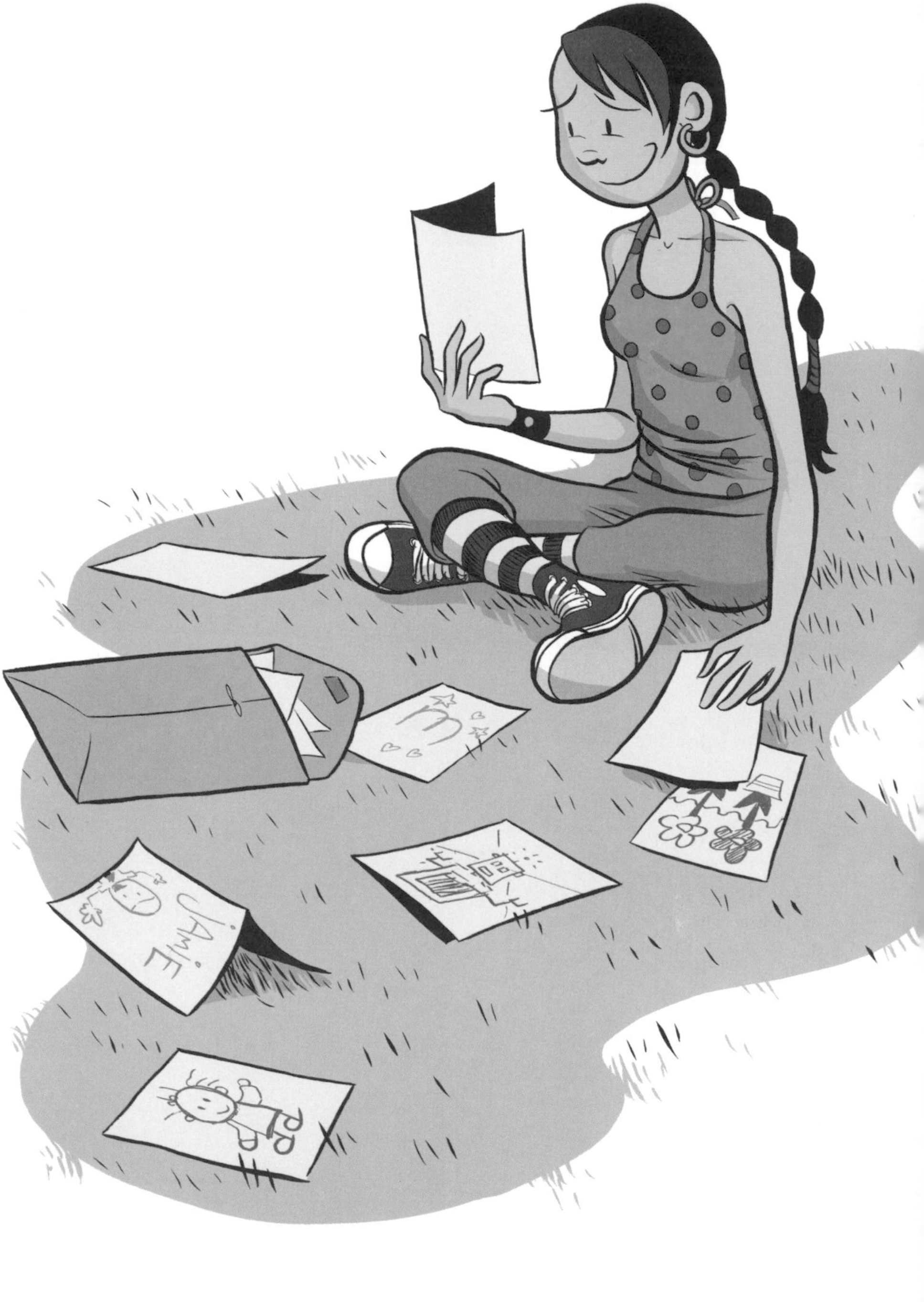
JAMIE

CHAPTER 7

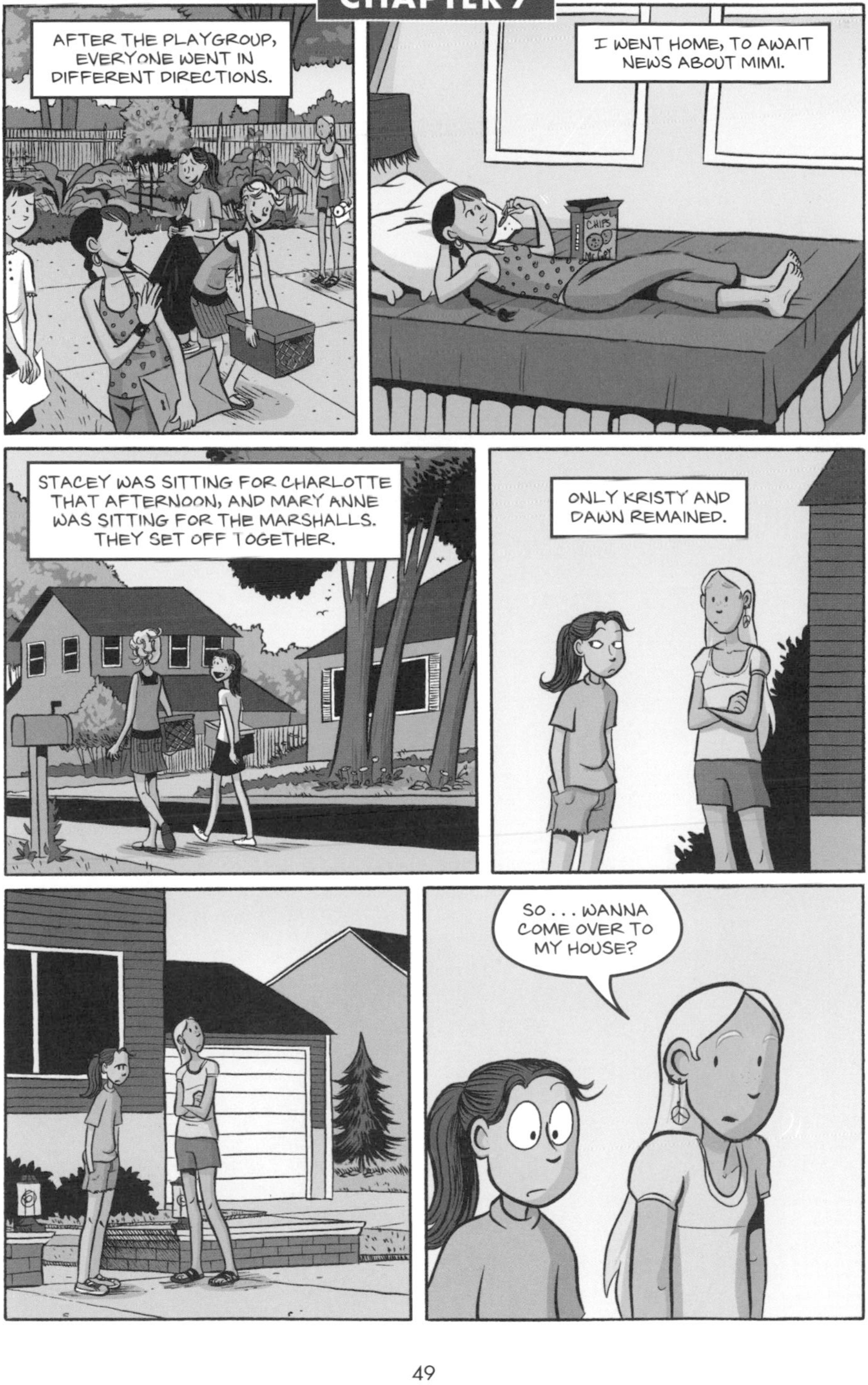
AFTER THE PLAYGROUP, EVERYONE WENT IN DIFFERENT DIRECTIONS.
I WENT HOME, TO AWAIT NEWS ABOUT MIMI.
STACEY WAS SITTING FOR CHARLOTTE THAT AFTERNOON, AND MARY ANNE WAS SITTING FOR THE MARSHALLS. THEY SET OFF TOGETHER.
ONLY KRISTY AND DAWN REMAINED.
SO . . . WANNA COME OVER TO MY HOUSE?

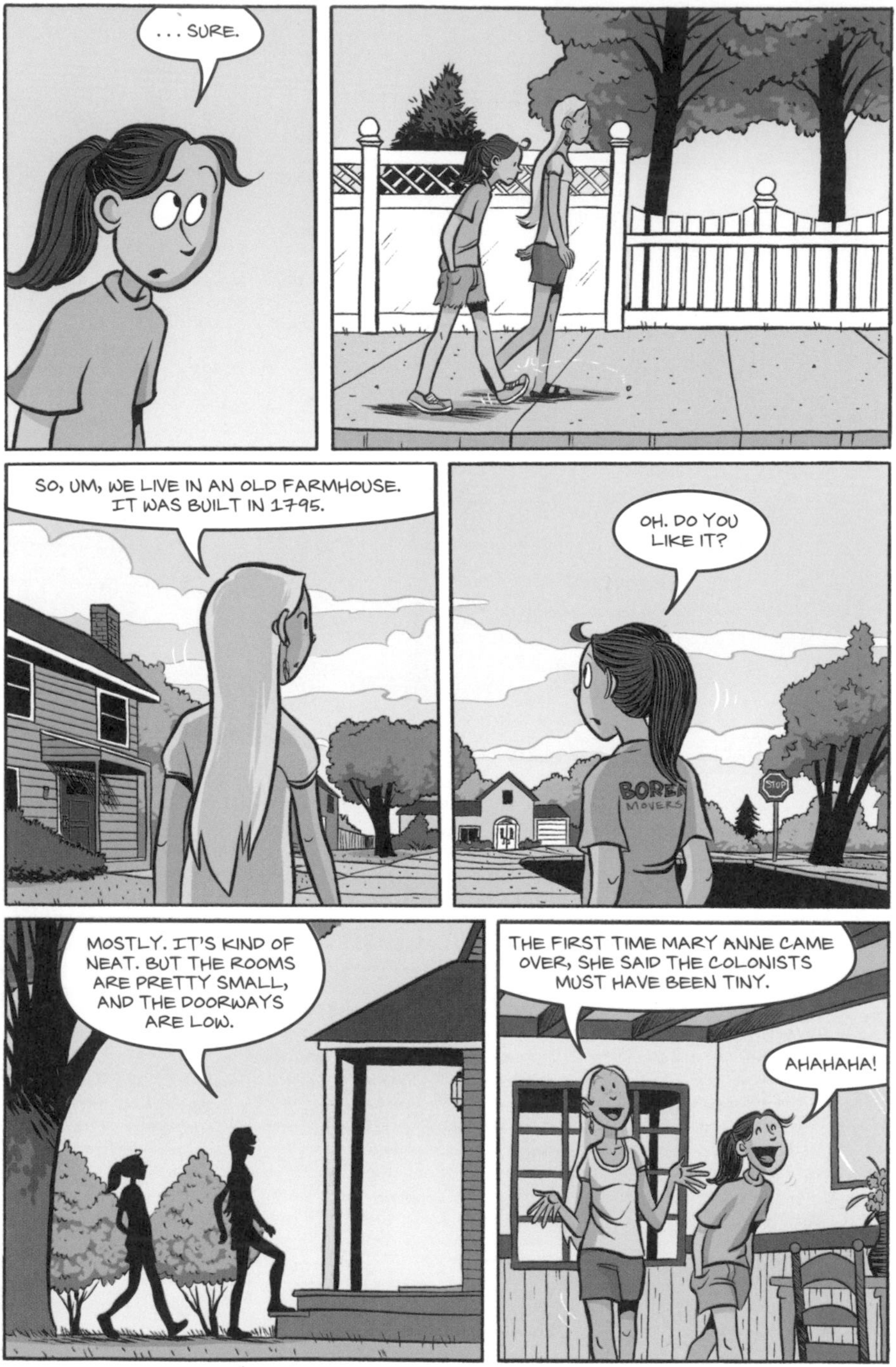
. . . SURE.
SO, UM, WE LIVE IN AN OLD FARMHOUSE. IT WAS BUILT IN 1795.
OH. DO YOU LIKE IT?
BOREN MOVERS
STOP
MOSTLY. IT'S KIND OF NEAT. BUT THE ROOMS ARE PRETTY SMALL, AND THE DOORWAYS ARE LOW.
THE FIRST TIME MARY ANNE CAME OVER, SHE SAID THE COLONISTS MUST HAVE BEEN TINY.
AHAHAHA!

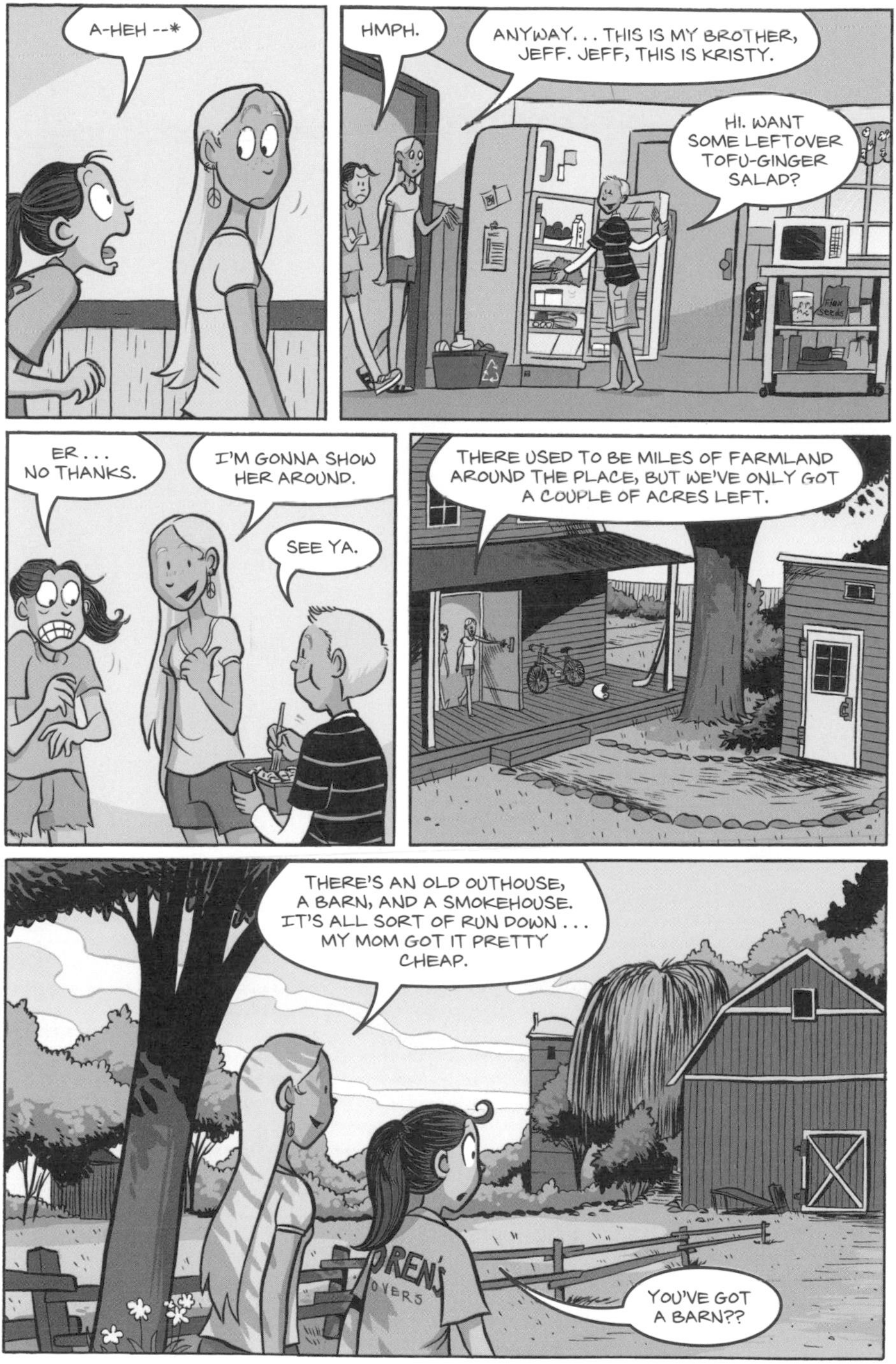
A-HEH --*
HMPH.
ANYWAY. . . THIS IS MY BROTHER, JEFF. JEFF, THIS IS KRISTY.
HI. WANT SOME LEFTOVER TOFU-GINGER SALAD?
ER . . . NO THANKS.
I'M GONNA SHOW HER AROUND.
SEE YA.
THERE USED TO BE MILES OF FARMLAND AROUND THE PLACE, BUT WE'VE ONLY GOT A COUPLE OF ACRES LEFT.
THERE'S AN OLD OUTHOUSE, A BARN, AND A SMOKEHOUSE. IT'S ALL SORT OF RUN DOWN . . . MY MOM GOT IT PRETTY CHEAP.
YOU'VE GOT A BARN??

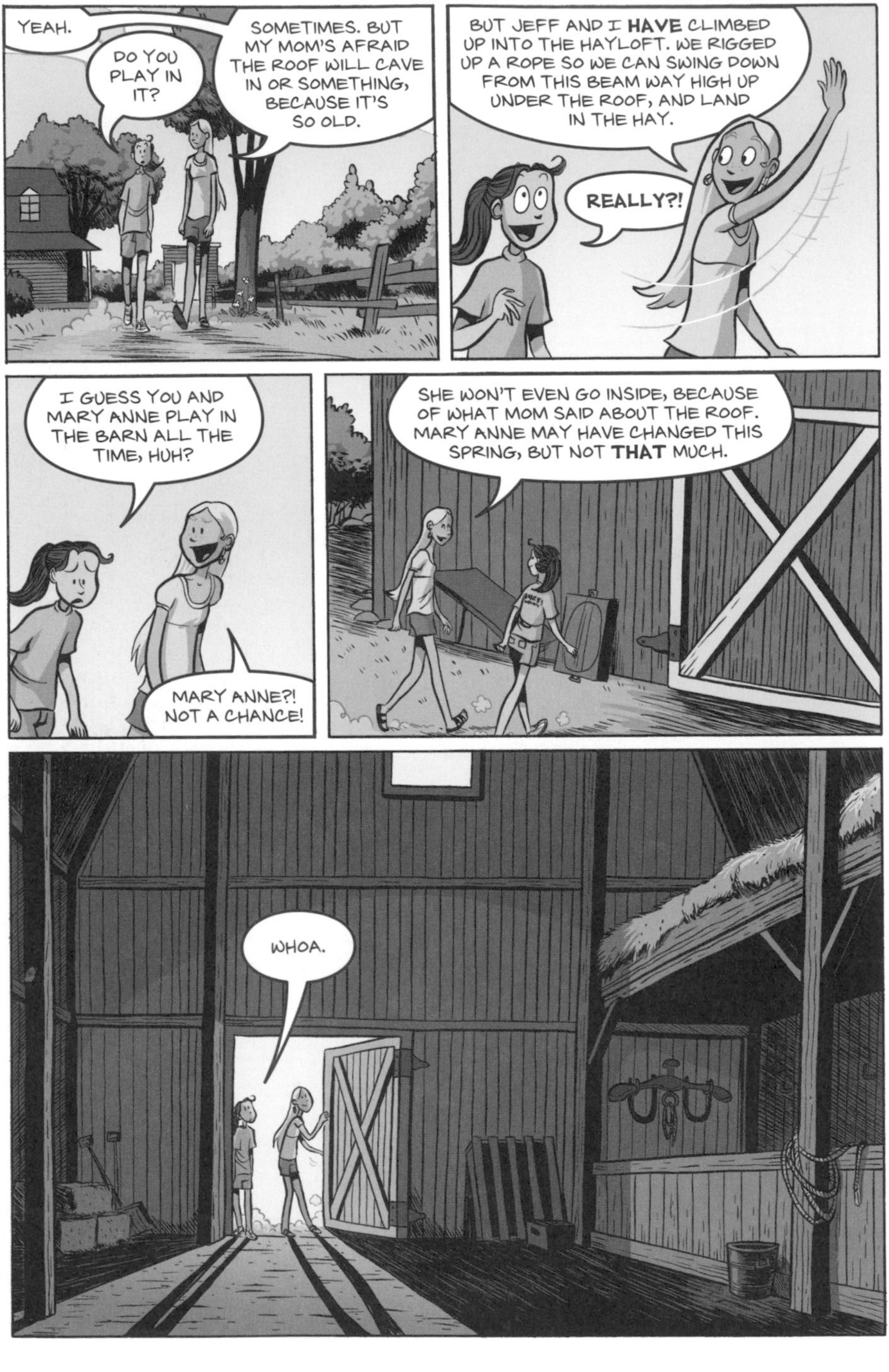
YEAH.
DO YOU PLAY IN IT?
SOMETIMES. BUT MY MOM'S AFRAID THE ROOF WILL CAVE IN OR SOMETHING, BECAUSE IT'S SO OLD.
BUT JEFF AND I HAVE CLIMBED UP INTO THE HAYLOFT. WE RIGGED UP A ROPE SO WE CAN SWING DOWN FROM THIS BEAM WAY HIGH UP UNDER THE ROOF, AND LAND IN THE HAY.
REALLY?!
I GUESS YOU AND MARY ANNE PLAY IN THE BARN ALL THE TIME, HUH?
MARY ANNE?! NOT A CHANCE!
SHE WON'T EVEN GO INSIDE, BECAUSE OF WHAT MOM SAID ABOUT THE ROOF. MARY ANNE MAY HAVE CHANGED THIS SPRING, BUT NOT THAT MUCH.
WHOA.

HOW DO YOU GET TO THE HAYLOFT?
THIS WAY.
NEAT.
IT'S SO QUIET UP HERE.
DO YOU WANT TO SWING FROM THE ROPE?
SURE . . . I THINK!

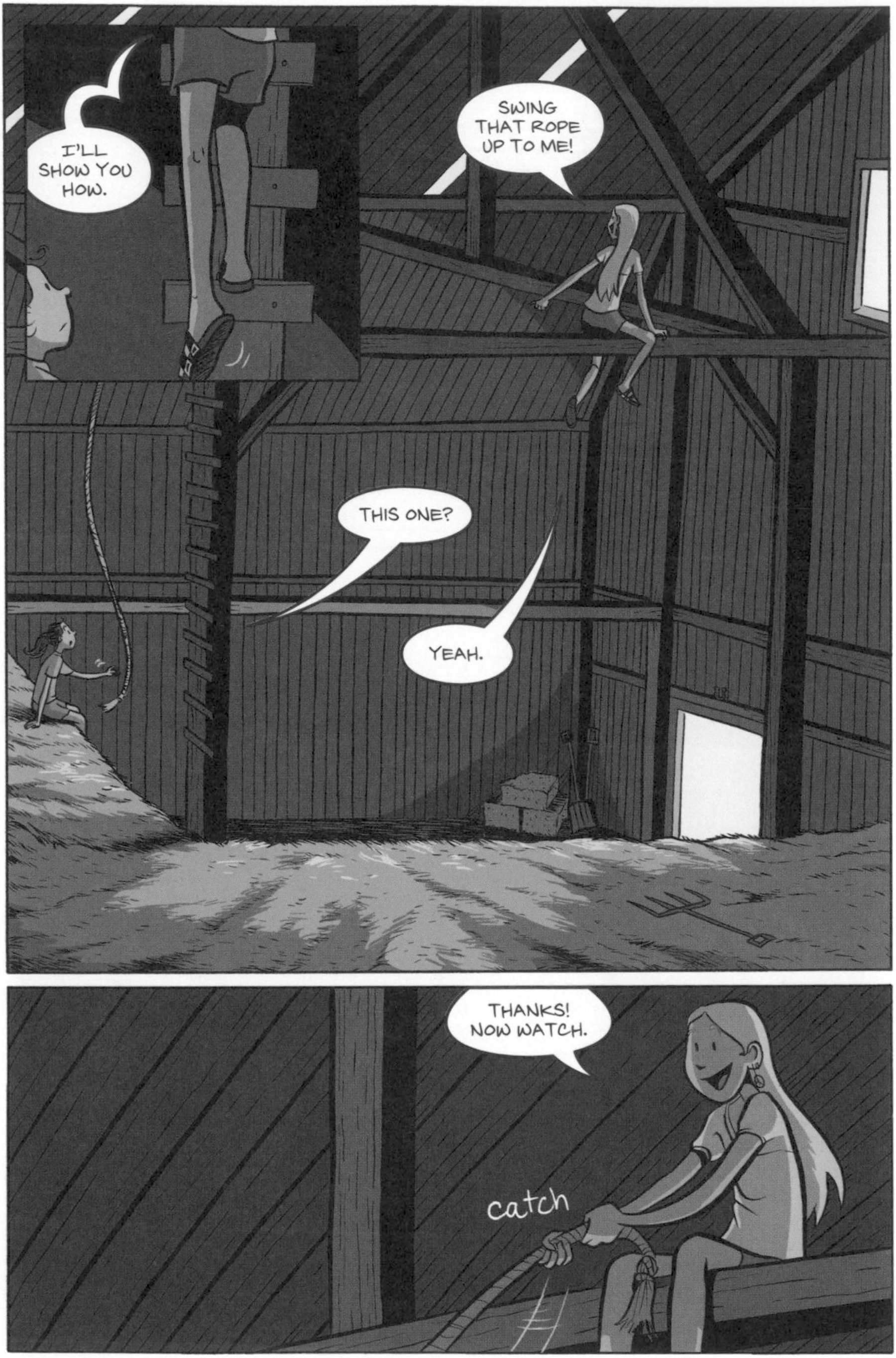

I'LL SHOW YOU HOW.
SWING THAT ROPE UP TO ME!
THIS ONE?
YEAH.
THANKS! NOW WATCH.
catch

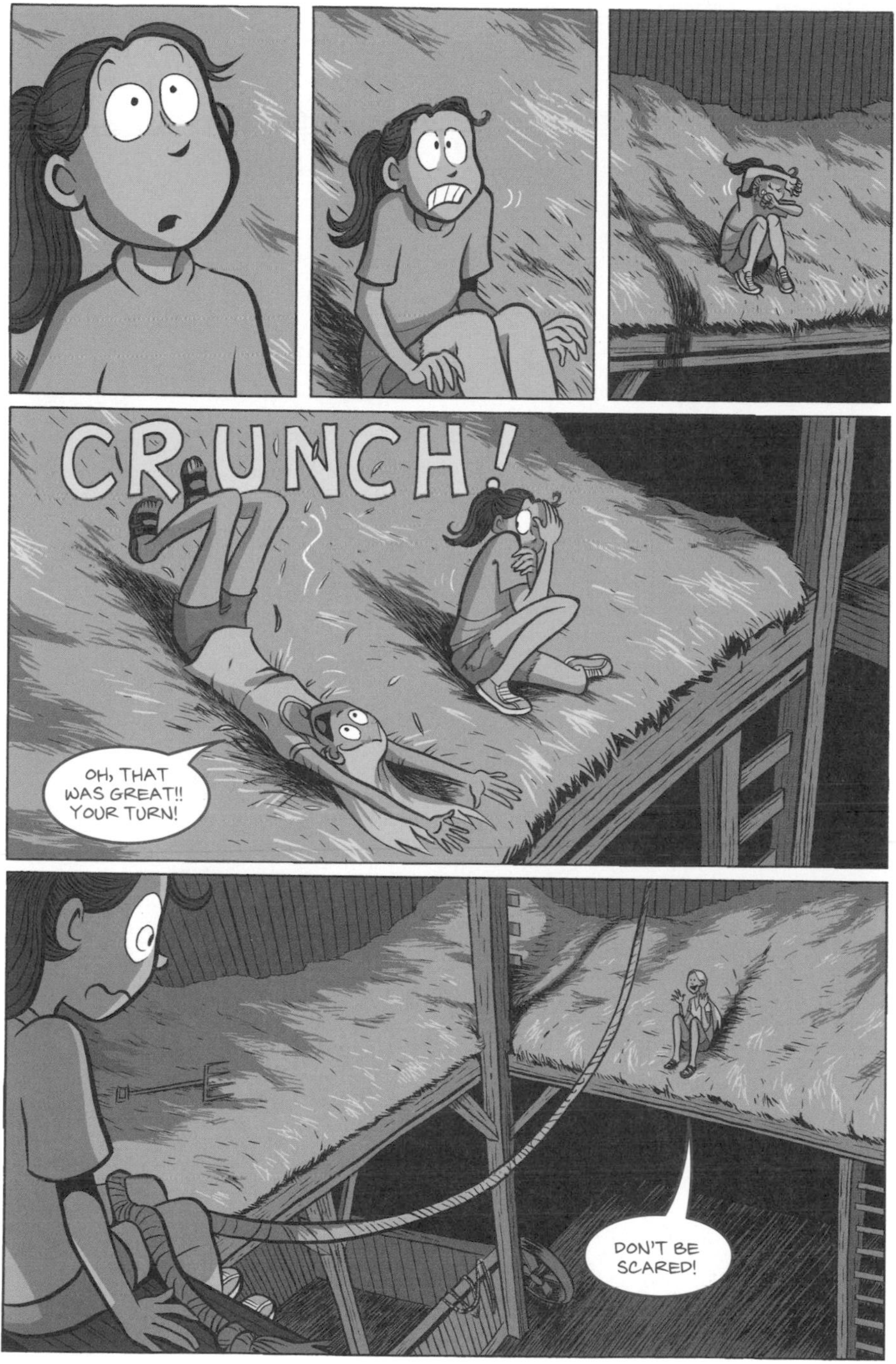
CRUNCH!
OH, THAT WAS GREAT!! YOUR TURN!
DON'T BE SCARED!

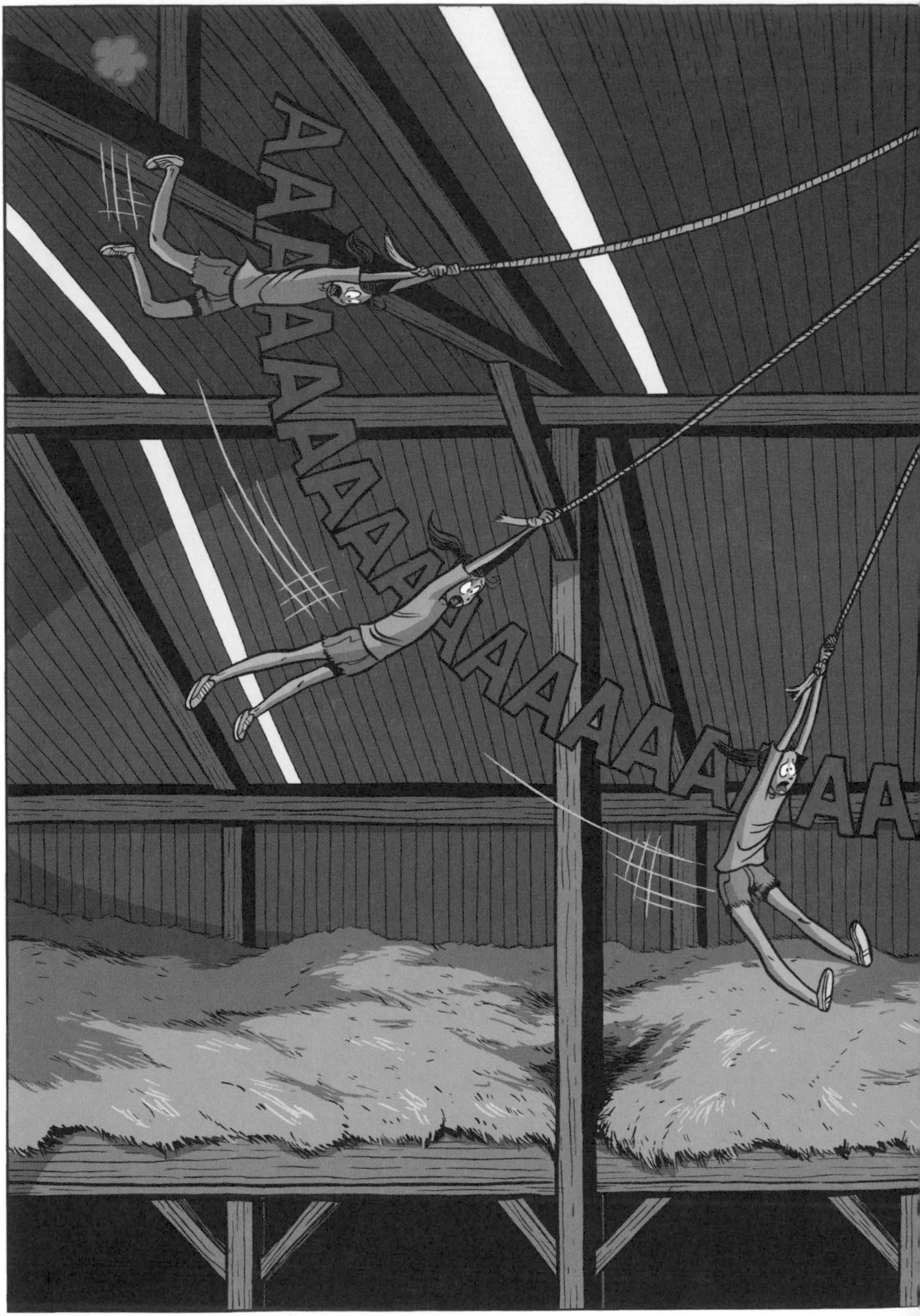
AAAAAAAAAAAAAAAAAAAA

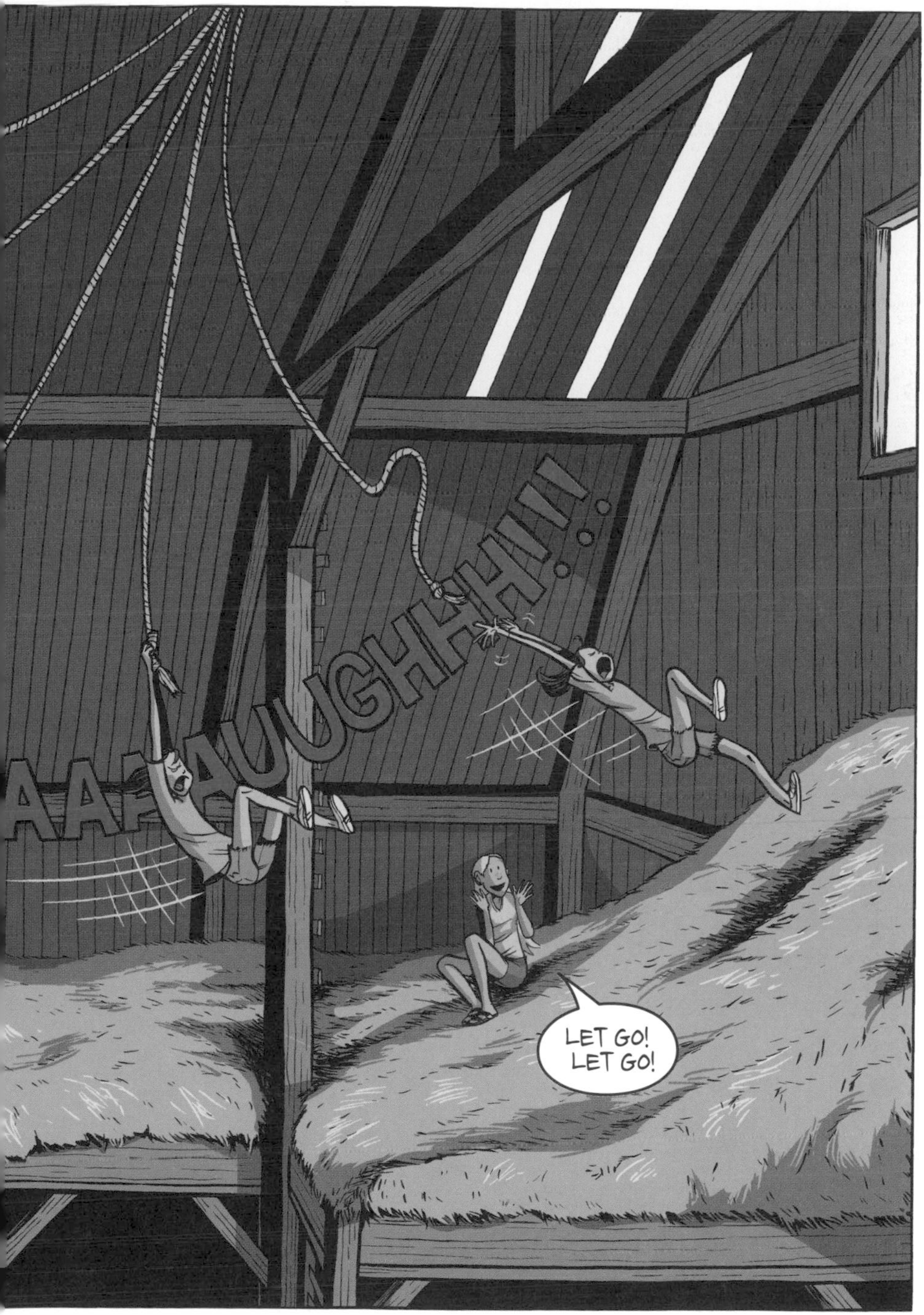
AAAAUUGHHH!!!...
LET GO! LET GO!

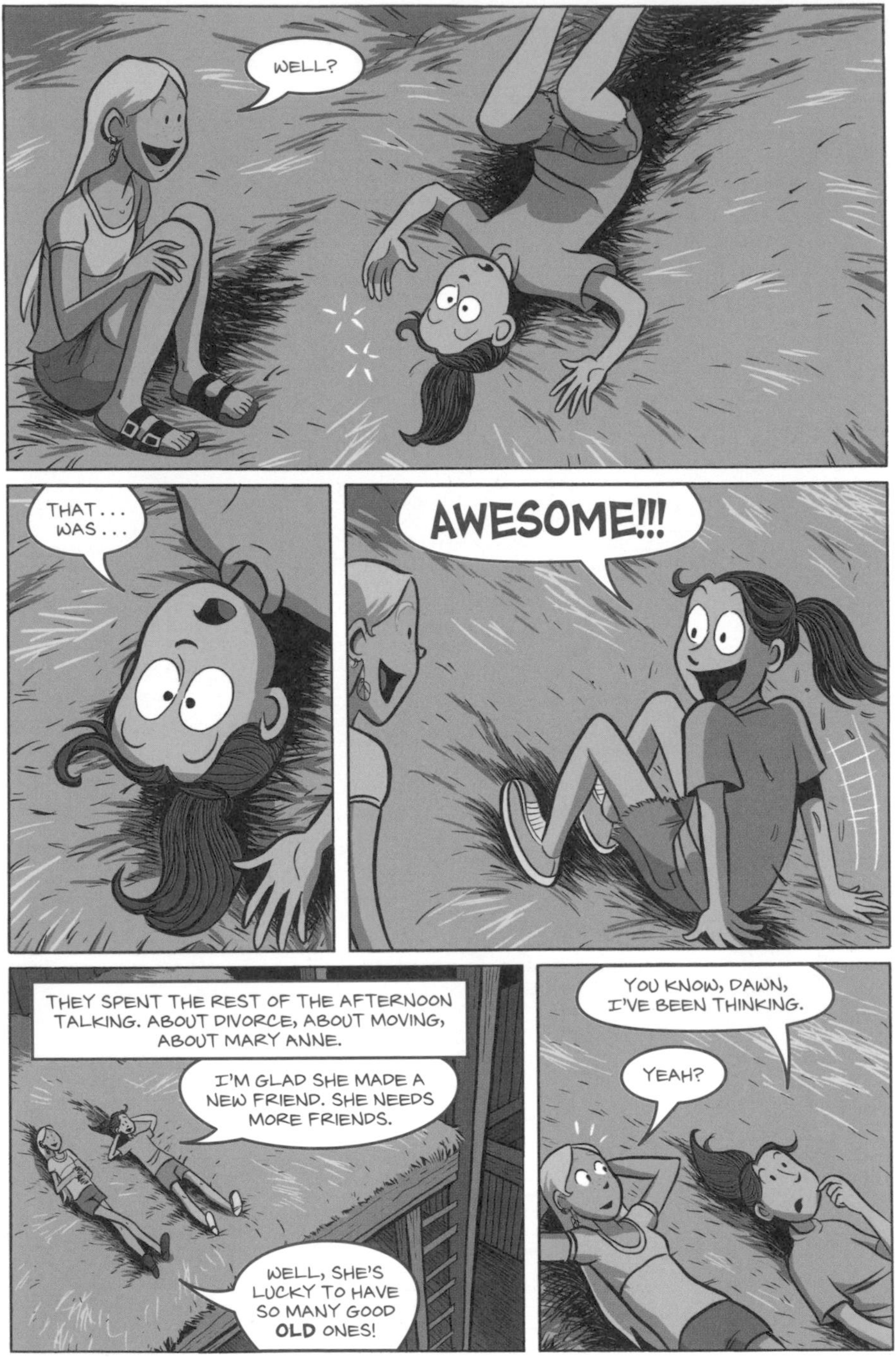
WELL?
THAT... WAS...
AWESOME!!!
THEY SPENT THE REST OF THE AFTERNOON TALKING. ABOUT DIVORCE, ABOUT MOVING, ABOUT MARY ANNE.
I'M GLAD SHE MADE A NEW FRIEND. SHE NEEDS MORE FRIENDS.
WELL, SHE'S LUCKY TO HAVE SO MANY GOOD **OLD** ONES!
YOU KNOW, DAWN, I'VE BEEN THINKING.
YEAH?

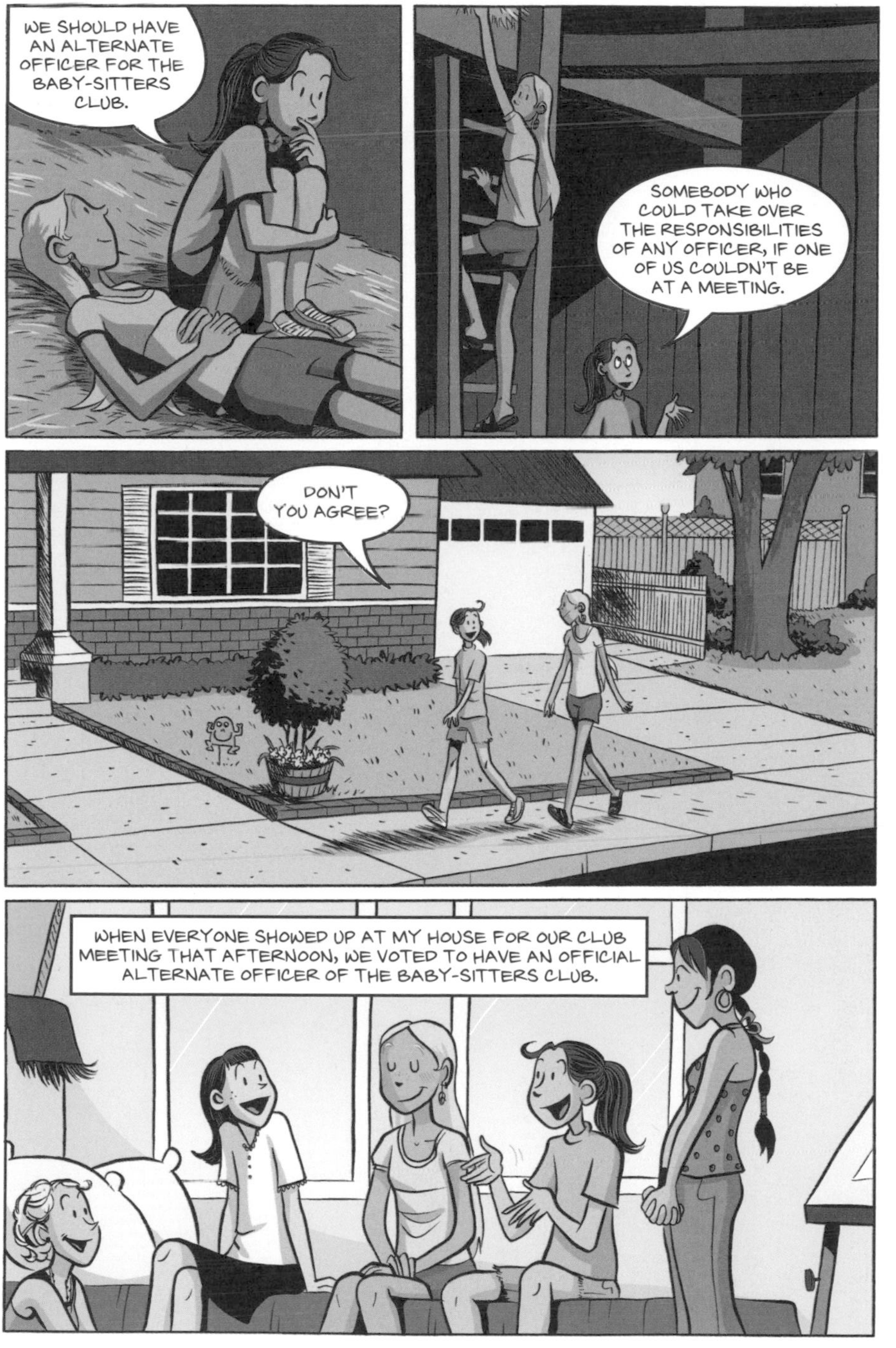
WE SHOULD HAVE AN ALTERNATE OFFICER FOR THE BABY-SITTERS CLUB.
SOMEBODY WHO COULD TAKE OVER THE RESPONSIBILITIES OF ANY OFFICER, IF ONE OF US COULDN'T BE AT A MEETING.
DON'T YOU AGREE?
WHEN EVERYONE SHOWED UP AT MY HOUSE FOR OUR CLUB MEETING THAT AFTERNOON, WE VOTED TO HAVE AN OFFICIAL ALTERNATE OFFICER OF THE BABY-SITTERS CLUB.

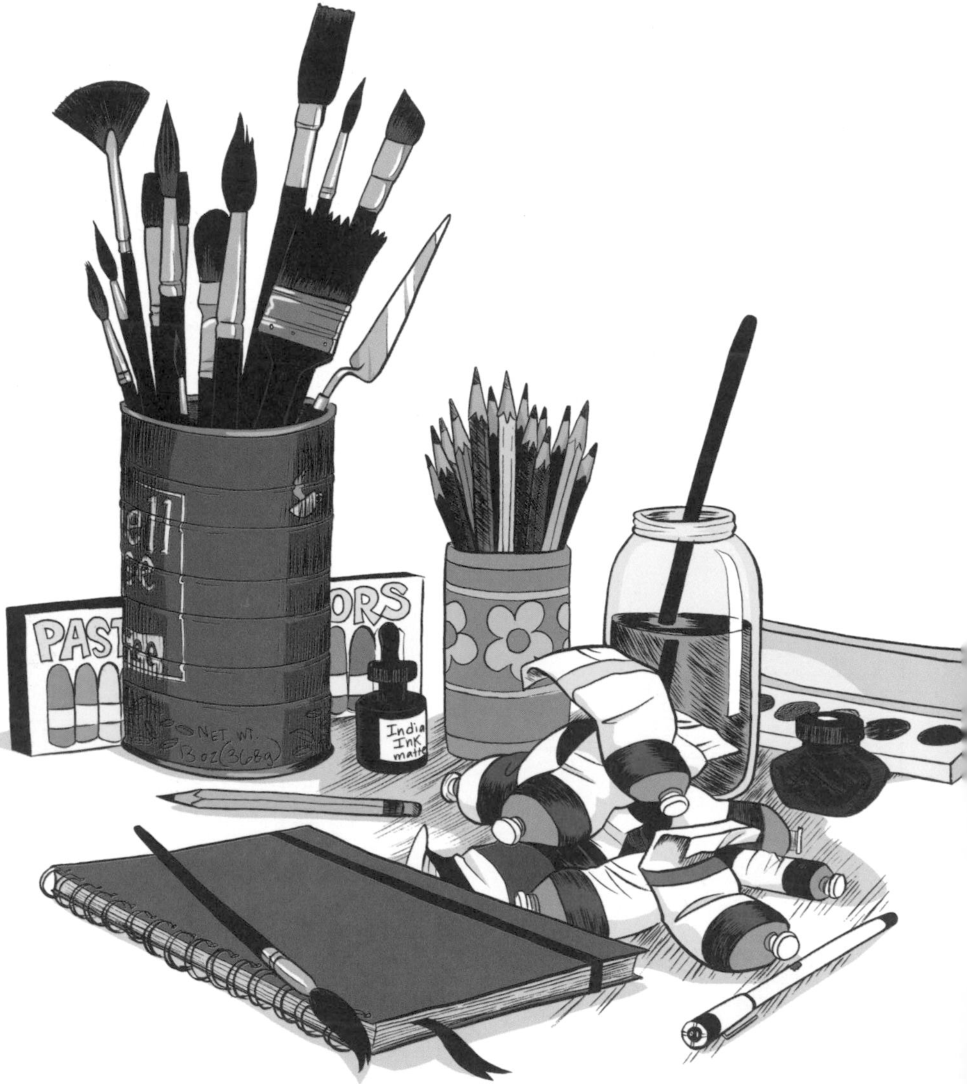
PAST
ORS
India
Ink
NET. WT.
13 oz (368g)

CHAPTER 8

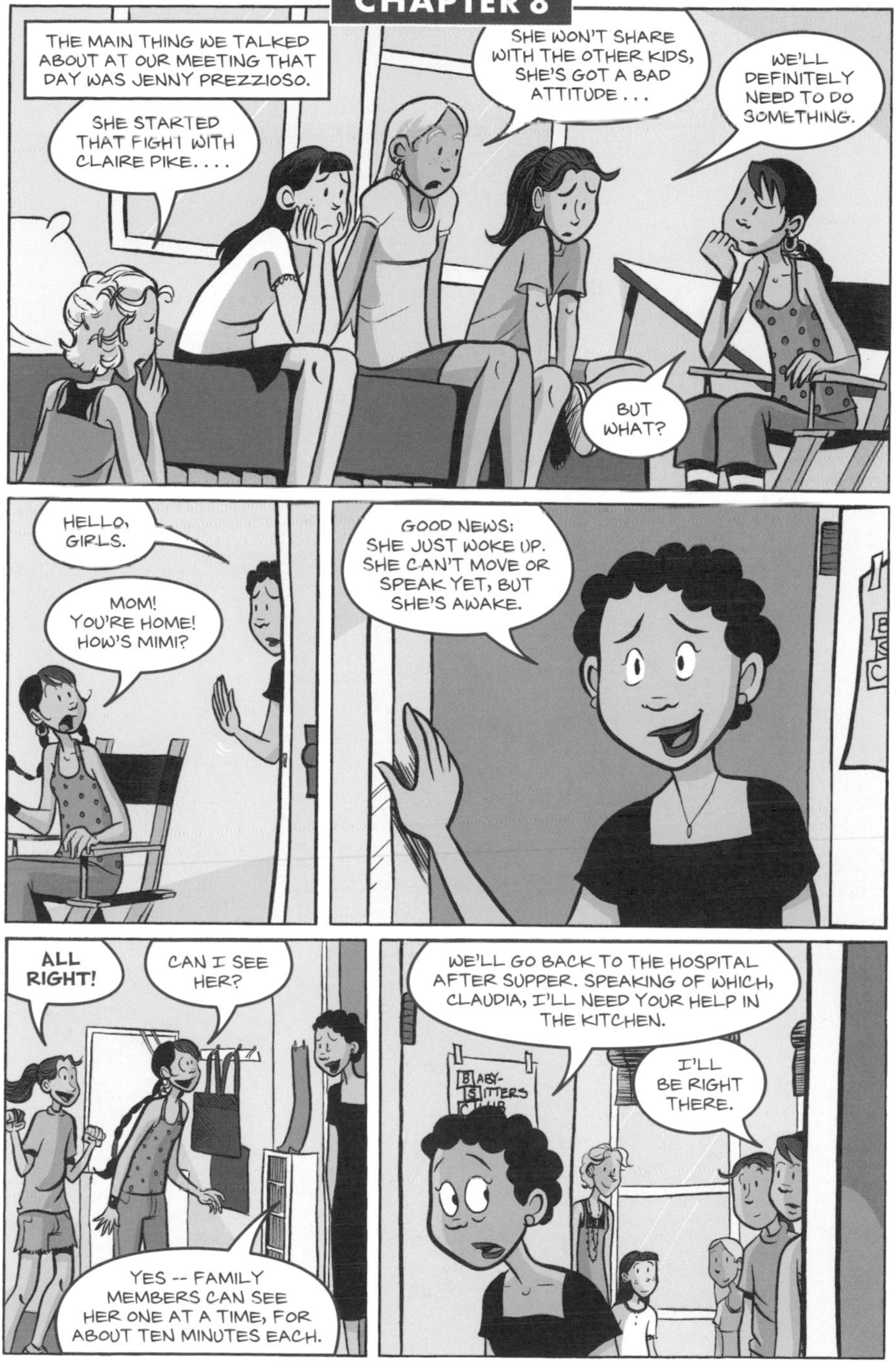

THE MAIN THING WE TALKED ABOUT AT OUR MEETING THAT DAY WAS JENNY PREZZIOSO.
SHE STARTED THAT FIGHT WITH CLAIRE PIKE. . . .
SHE WON'T SHARE WITH THE OTHER KIDS, SHE'S GOT A BAD ATTITUDE . . .
WE'LL DEFINITELY NEED TO DO SOMETHING.
BUT WHAT?
HELLO, GIRLS.
MOM! YOU'RE HOME! HOW'S MIMI?
GOOD NEWS: SHE JUST WOKE UP. SHE CAN'T MOVE OR SPEAK YET, BUT SHE'S AWAKE.
ALL RIGHT!
CAN I SEE HER?
YES -- FAMILY MEMBERS CAN SEE HER ONE AT A TIME, FOR ABOUT TEN MINUTES EACH.
WE'LL GO BACK TO THE HOSPITAL AFTER SUPPER. SPEAKING OF WHICH, CLAUDIA, I'LL NEED YOUR HELP IN THE KITCHEN.
I'LL BE RIGHT THERE.

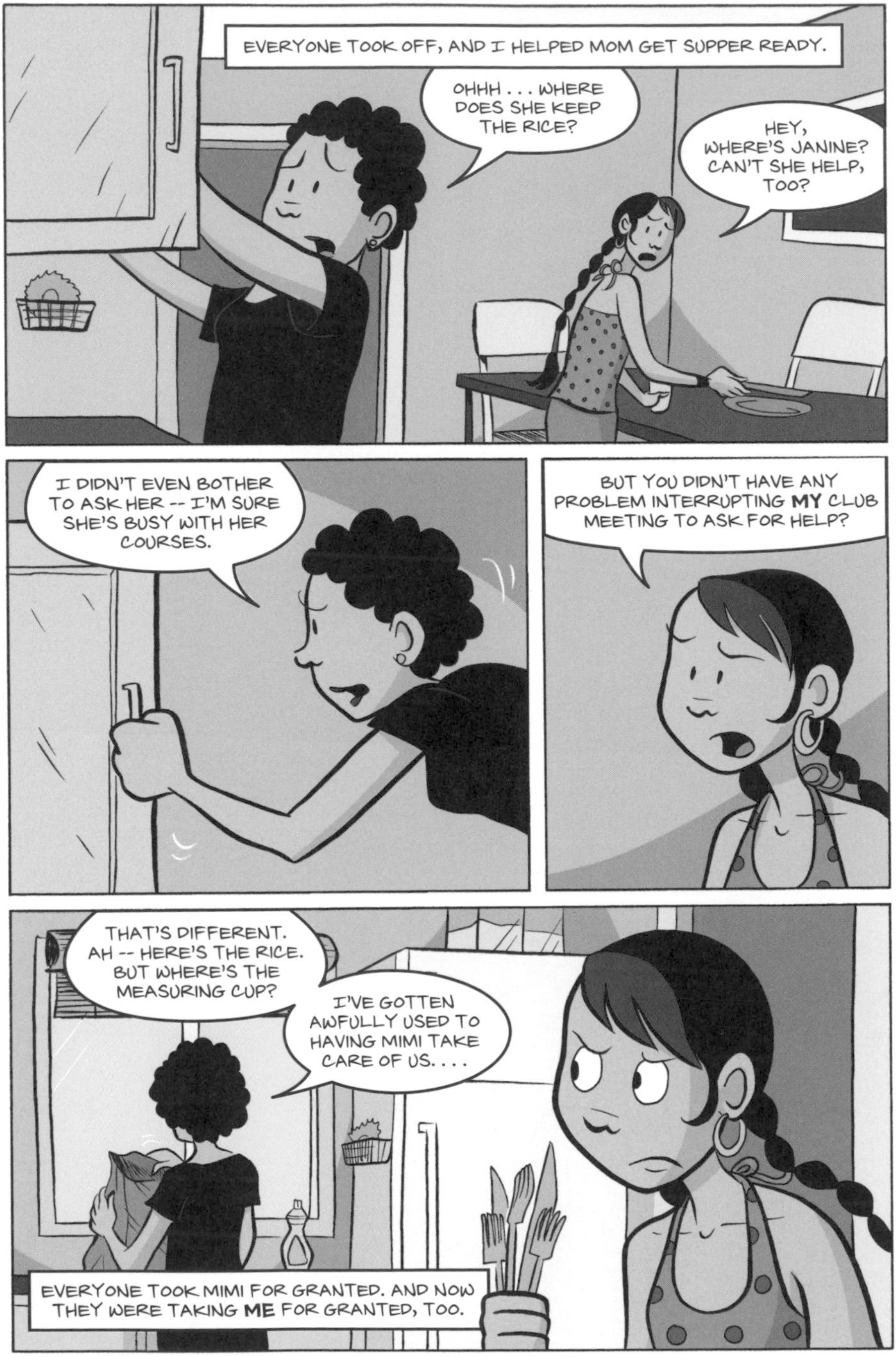
EVERYONE TOOK OFF, AND I HELPED MOM GET SUPPER READY.
OHHH . . . WHERE DOES SHE KEEP THE RICE?
HEY, WHERE'S JANINE? CAN'T SHE HELP, TOO?
I DIDN'T EVEN BOTHER TO ASK HER -- I'M SURE SHE'S BUSY WITH HER COURSES.
BUT YOU DIDN'T HAVE ANY PROBLEM INTERRUPTING **MY** CLUB MEETING TO ASK FOR HELP?
THAT'S DIFFERENT. AH -- HERE'S THE RICE. BUT WHERE'S THE MEASURING CUP?
I'VE GOTTEN AWFULLY USED TO HAVING MIMI TAKE CARE OF US. . . .
EVERYONE TOOK MIMI FOR GRANTED. AND NOW THEY WERE TAKING **ME** FOR GRANTED, TOO.

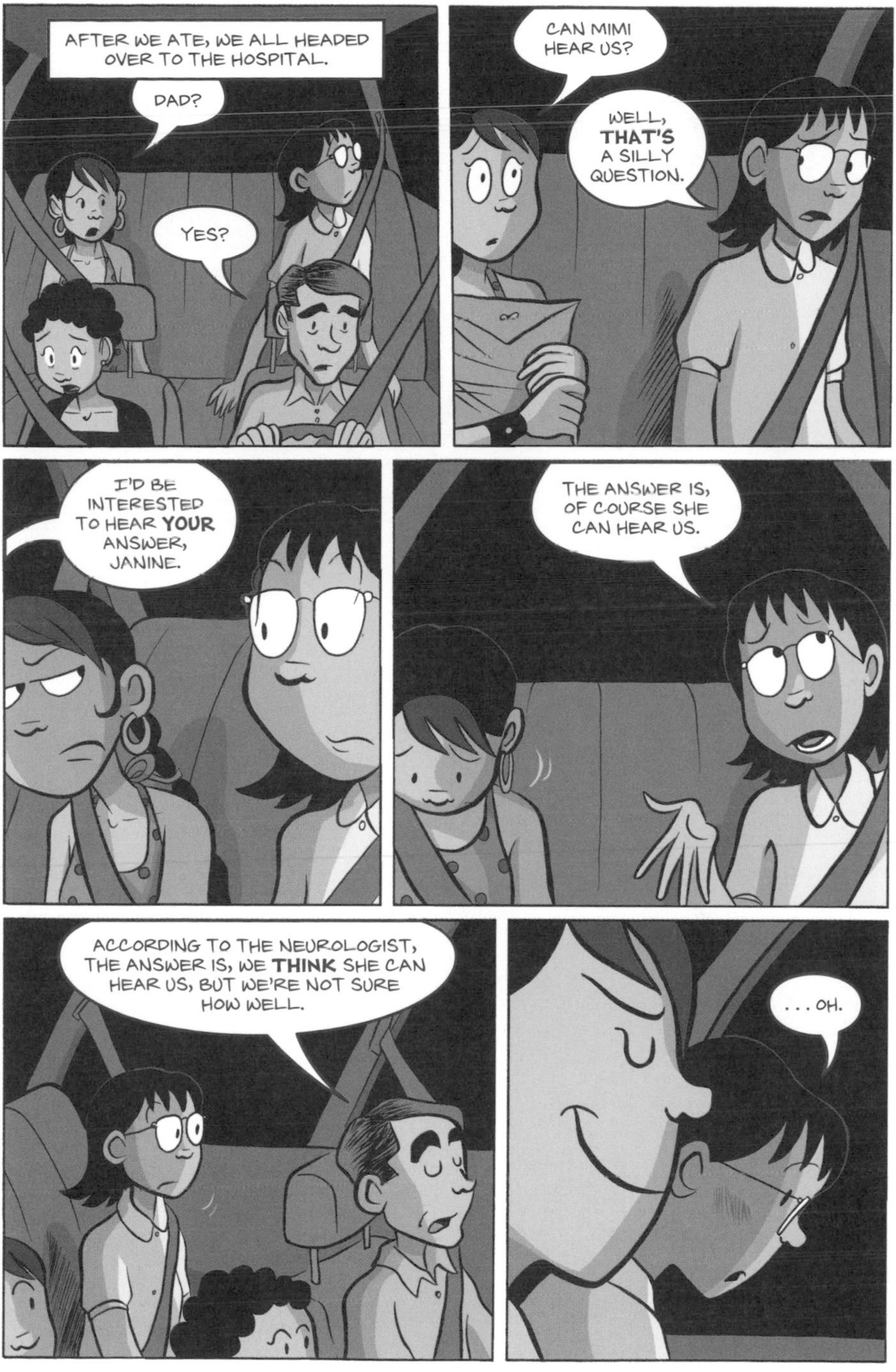

AFTER WE ATE, WE ALL HEADED OVER TO THE HOSPITAL.
DAD?
YES?
CAN MIMI HEAR US?
WELL, **THAT'S** A SILLY QUESTION.
I'D BE INTERESTED TO HEAR **YOUR** ANSWER, JANINE.
THE ANSWER IS, OF COURSE SHE CAN HEAR US.
ACCORDING TO THE NEUROLOGIST, THE ANSWER IS, WE **THINK** SHE CAN HEAR US, BUT WE'RE NOT SURE HOW WELL.
. . . OH.

CAN I SEE HER FIRST?

SURE -- JUST KEEP TRACK OF THE TIME.

Yamamoto

307

AND DON'T BE FRIGHTENED . . . THERE'S A LOT OF EQUIPMENT IN THE ROOM. JUST REMEMBER THAT IT'S THERE TO HELP MIMI.

OKAY.

Beep... Beep... Beep...

drip

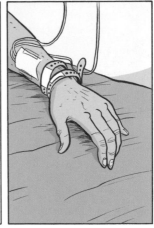

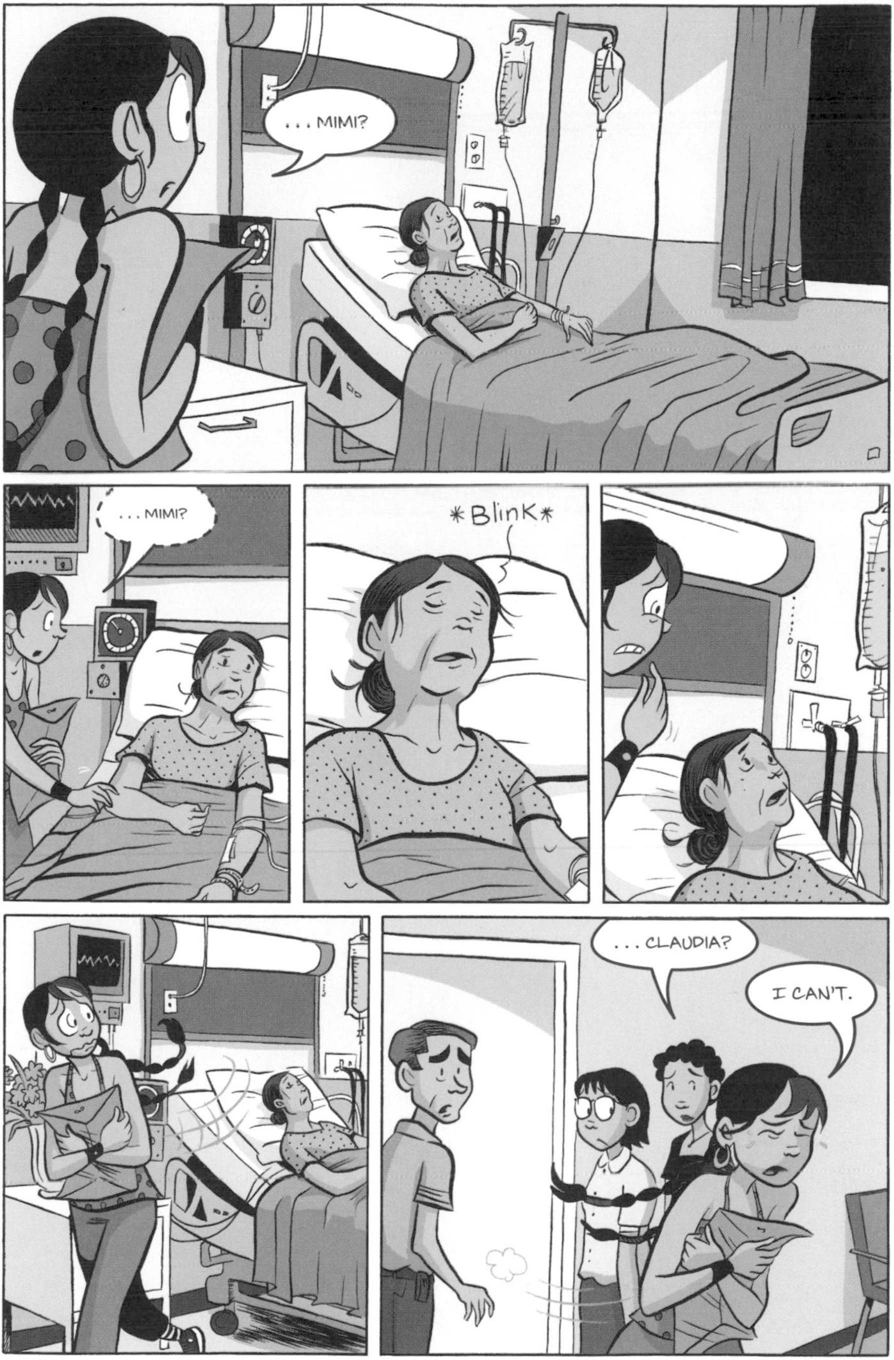
. . . MIMI?
. . . MIMI?
Blink
. . . CLAUDIA?
I CAN'T.

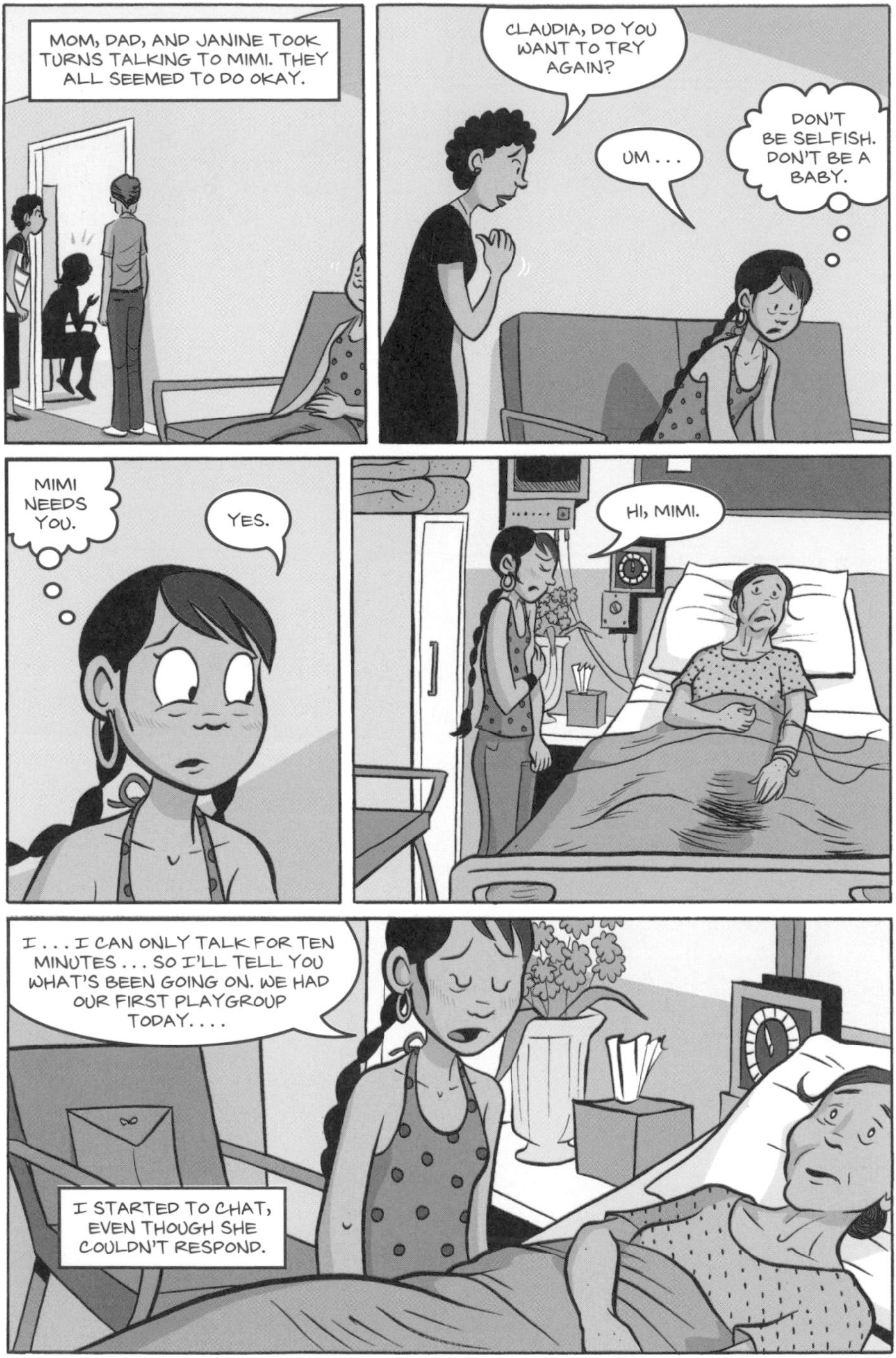
MOM, DAD, AND JANINE TOOK TURNS TALKING TO MIMI. THEY ALL SEEMED TO DO OKAY.
CLAUDIA, DO YOU WANT TO TRY AGAIN?
UM . . .
DON'T BE SELFISH. DON'T BE A BABY.
MIMI NEEDS YOU.
YES.
HI, MIMI.
I . . . I CAN ONLY TALK FOR TEN MINUTES . . . SO I'LL TELL YOU WHAT'S BEEN GOING ON. WE HAD OUR FIRST PLAYGROUP TODAY. . . .
I STARTED TO CHAT, EVEN THOUGH SHE COULDN'T RESPOND.

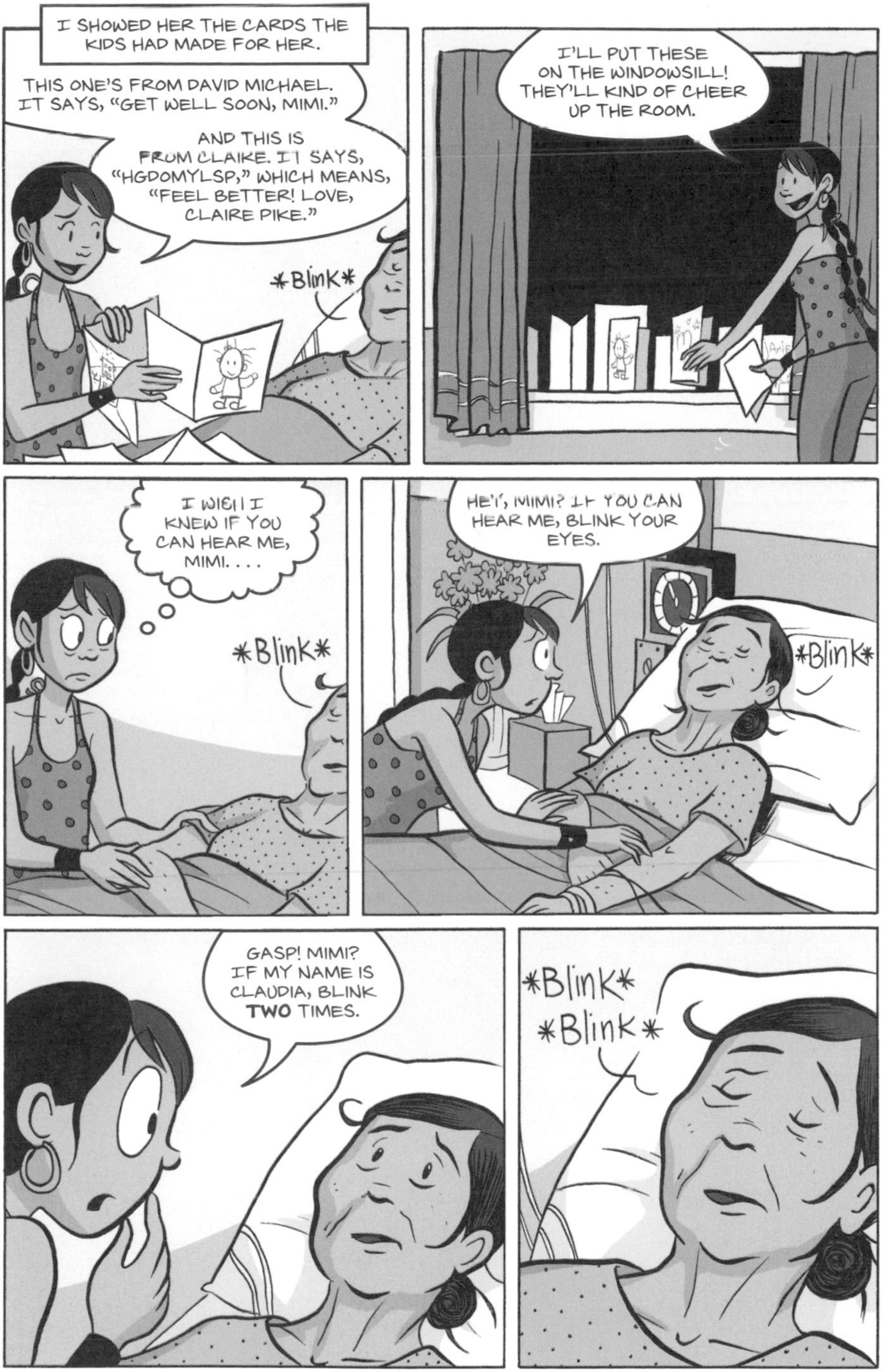
I SHOWED HER THE CARDS THE KIDS HAD MADE FOR HER.
THIS ONE'S FROM DAVID MICHAEL. IT SAYS, "GET WELL SOON, MIMI."
AND THIS IS FROM CLAIRE. IT SAYS, "HGDOMYLSP," WHICH MEANS, "FEEL BETTER! LOVE, CLAIRE PIKE."
Blink
I'LL PUT THESE ON THE WINDOWSILL! THEY'LL KIND OF CHEER UP THE ROOM.
I WISH I KNEW IF YOU CAN HEAR ME, MIMI. . . .
Blink
HEY, MIMI? IF YOU CAN HEAR ME, BLINK YOUR EYES.
Blink
GASP! MIMI? IF MY NAME IS CLAUDIA, BLINK **TWO** TIMES.
Blink
Blink

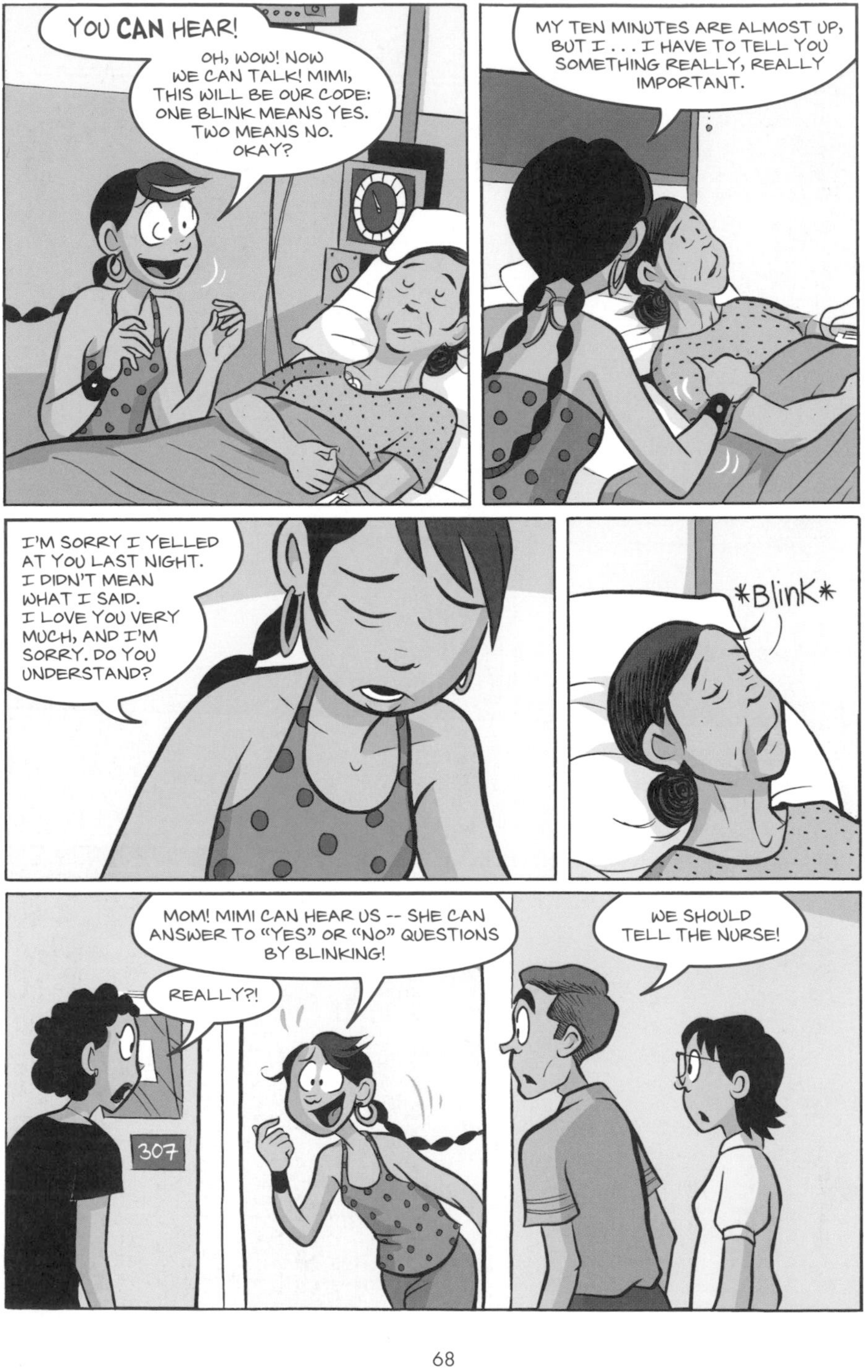
YOU CAN HEAR!
OH, WOW! NOW WE CAN TALK! MIMI, THIS WILL BE OUR CODE: ONE BLINK MEANS YES. TWO MEANS NO. OKAY?
MY TEN MINUTES ARE ALMOST UP, BUT I . . . I HAVE TO TELL YOU SOMETHING REALLY, REALLY IMPORTANT.
I'M SORRY I YELLED AT YOU LAST NIGHT. I DIDN'T MEAN WHAT I SAID. I LOVE YOU VERY MUCH, AND I'M SORRY. DO YOU UNDERSTAND?
Blink
MOM! MIMI CAN HEAR US -- SHE CAN ANSWER TO "YES" OR "NO" QUESTIONS BY BLINKING!
REALLY?!
307
WE SHOULD TELL THE NURSE!

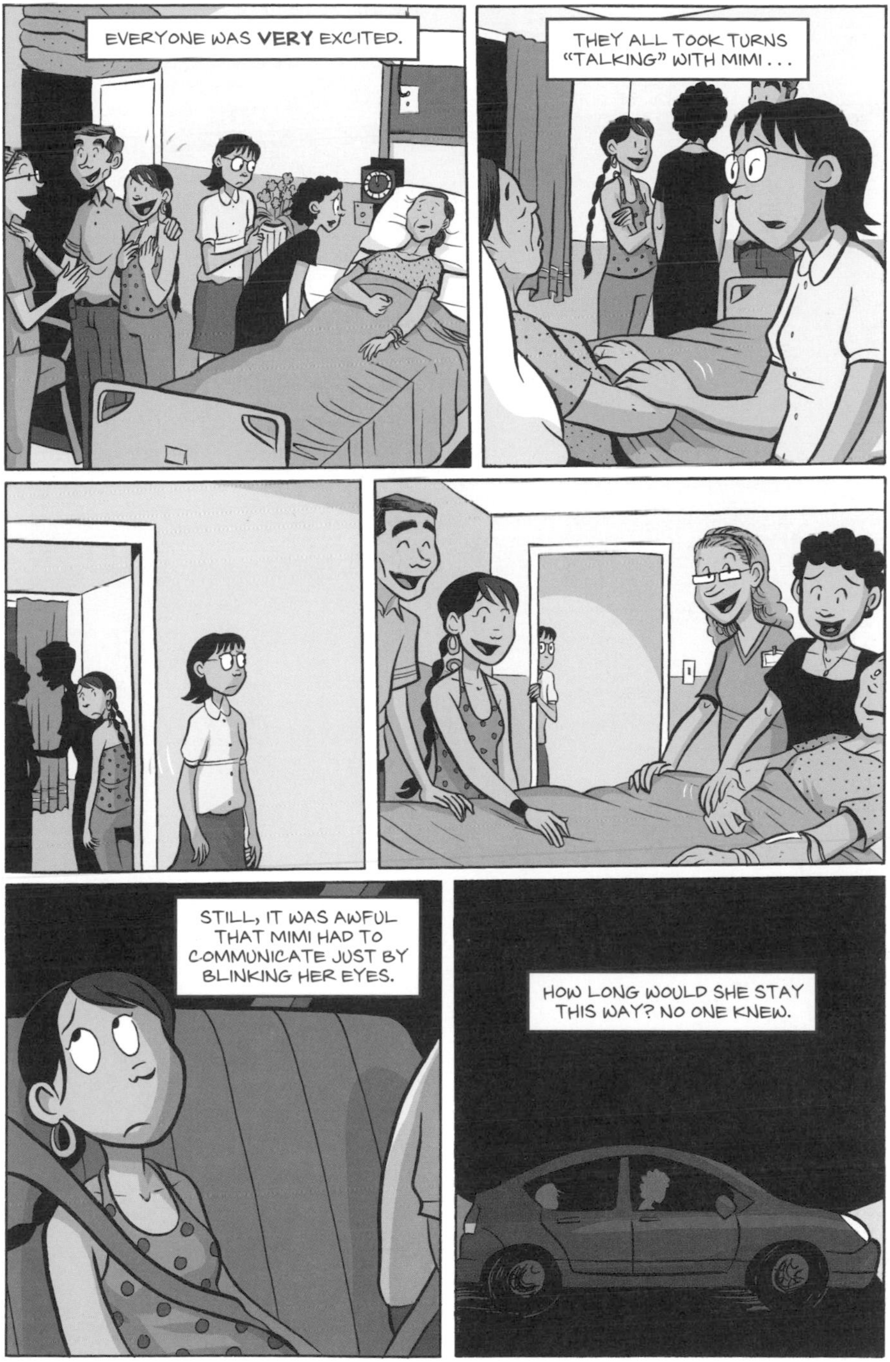
EVERYONE WAS **VERY** EXCITED.
THEY ALL TOOK TURNS "TALKING" WITH MIMI . . .
STILL, IT WAS AWFUL THAT MIMI HAD TO COMMUNICATE JUST BY BLINKING HER EYES.
HOW LONG WOULD SHE STAY THIS WAY? NO ONE KNEW.

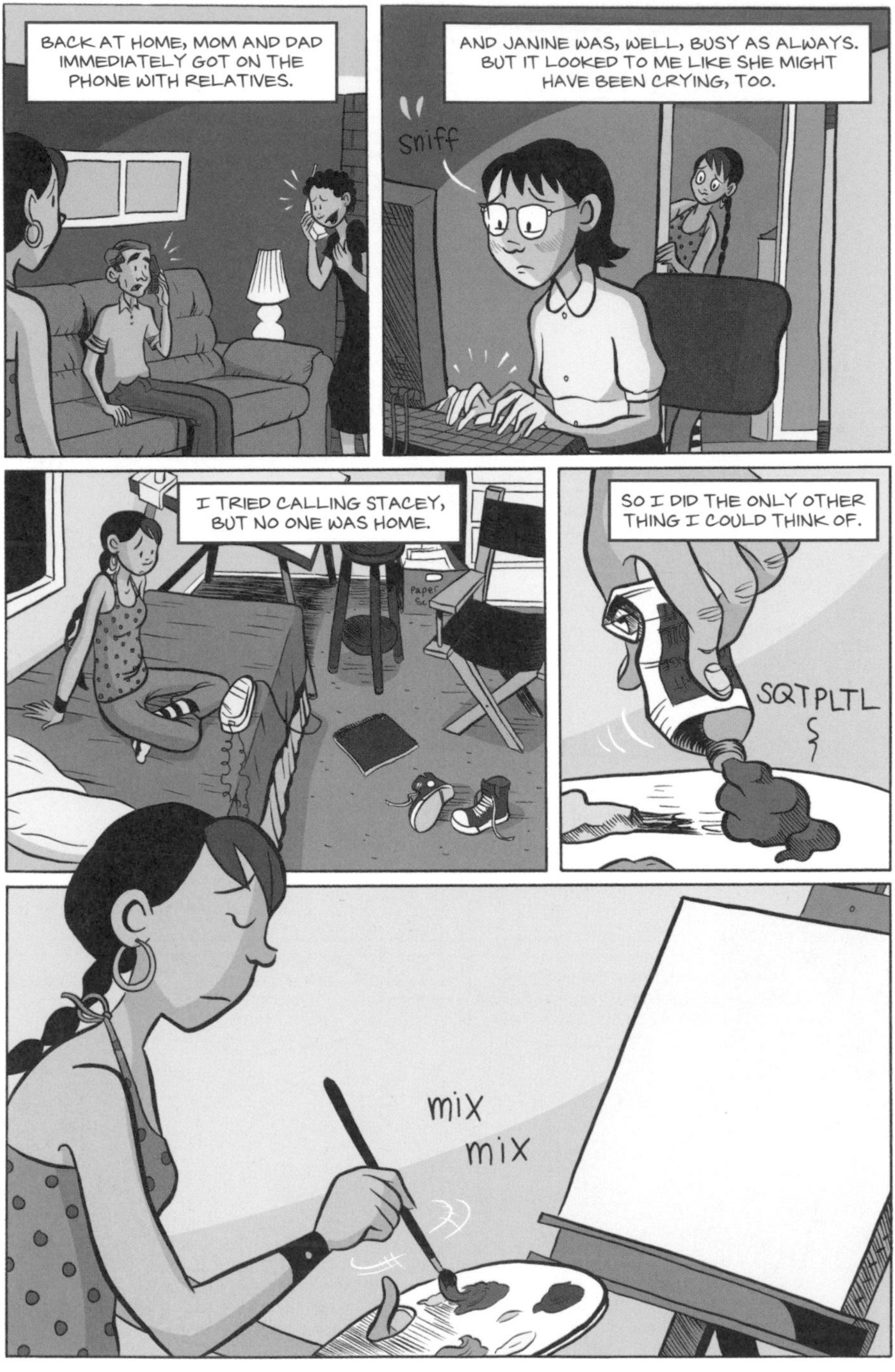

BACK AT HOME, MOM AND DAD IMMEDIATELY GOT ON THE PHONE WITH RELATIVES.
AND JANINE WAS, WELL, BUSY AS ALWAYS. BUT IT LOOKED TO ME LIKE SHE MIGHT HAVE BEEN CRYING, TOO.
sniff
I TRIED CALLING STACEY, BUT NO ONE WAS HOME.
SO I DID THE ONLY OTHER THING I COULD THINK OF.
SQTPLTL
mix
mix

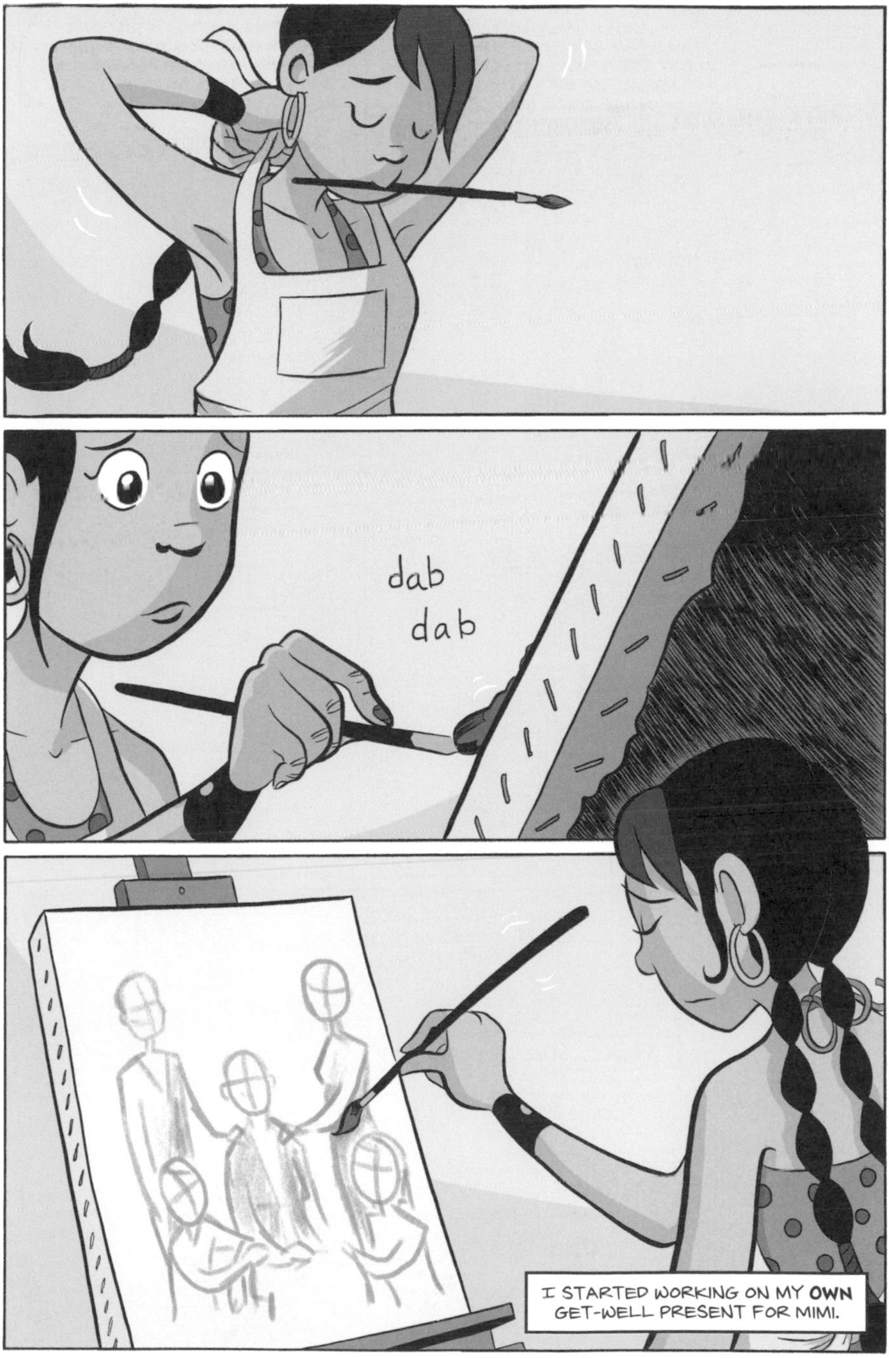
dab
dab
I STARTED WORKING ON MY OWN GET-WELL PRESENT FOR MIMI.

Wednesday, June 18

Well, Karen Brewer strikes again. When she's around, things are never dull. Today was the second session of our playgroup and Andrew and Karen came to it. Watson's ex-wife needed a last-minute sitter for them, so she called Watson and he decided to drop them off at Stacey's.

In the past, Karen has scared other kids with stories of witches, ghosts, and Martians. Today, she had a new one — a monster tale. But it was a monster tale with a twist, as you guys know. I'm not sure there's anything we can do about Karen. The thing is, she usually doesn't mean to scare people. She just has a wild imagination.

But, oh boy, when Karen and Jenny got together . . .

— Kristy

CHAPTER 9

THE SECOND SESSION OF OUR PLAYGROUP WAS ON A WEDNESDAY MORNING. THE KIDS WERE FULL OF ENERGY....

AND GUESS WHAT US BABY-SITTERS WERE DOING?

NO, NO, NO, NO!!

COME ON, JENNY, JUST PUT THE SMOCK ON. PLEASE?

NO!

JENNY WAS CAUSING TROUBLE AGAIN.

ENTER KAREN AND ANDREW: KRISTY'S SOON-TO-BE STEPSISTER AND STEPBROTHER.

...HERE WE ARE!!

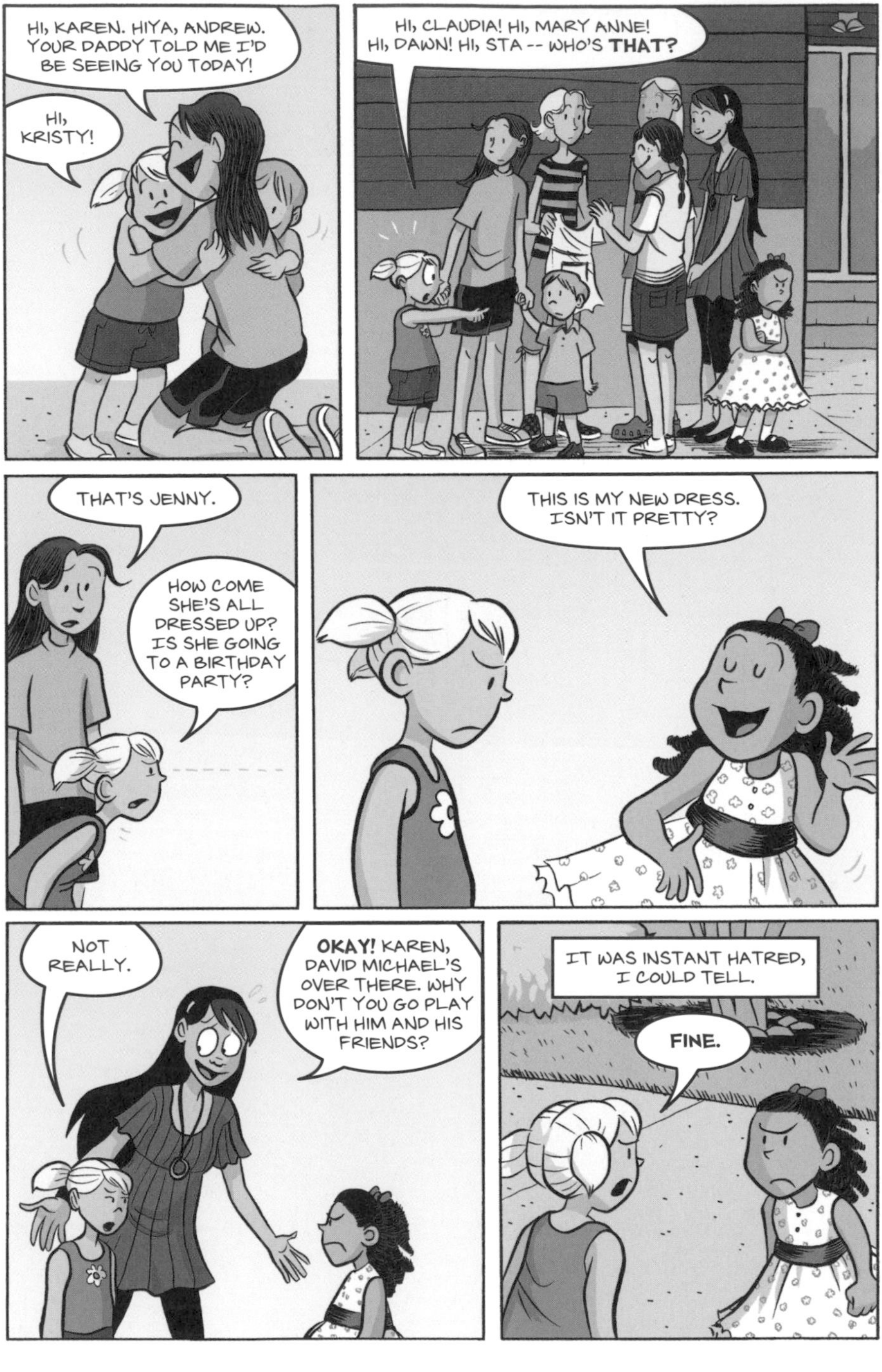
HI, KAREN. HIYA, ANDREW. YOUR DADDY TOLD ME I'D BE SEEING YOU TODAY!
HI, KRISTY!
HI, CLAUDIA! HI, MARY ANNE! HI, DAWN! HI, STA -- WHO'S **THAT?**
THAT'S JENNY.
HOW COME SHE'S ALL DRESSED UP? IS SHE GOING TO A BIRTHDAY PARTY?
THIS IS MY NEW DRESS. ISN'T IT PRETTY?
NOT REALLY.
OKAY! KAREN, DAVID MICHAEL'S OVER THERE. WHY DON'T YOU GO PLAY WITH HIM AND HIS FRIENDS?
IT WAS INSTANT HATRED, I COULD TELL.
FINE.

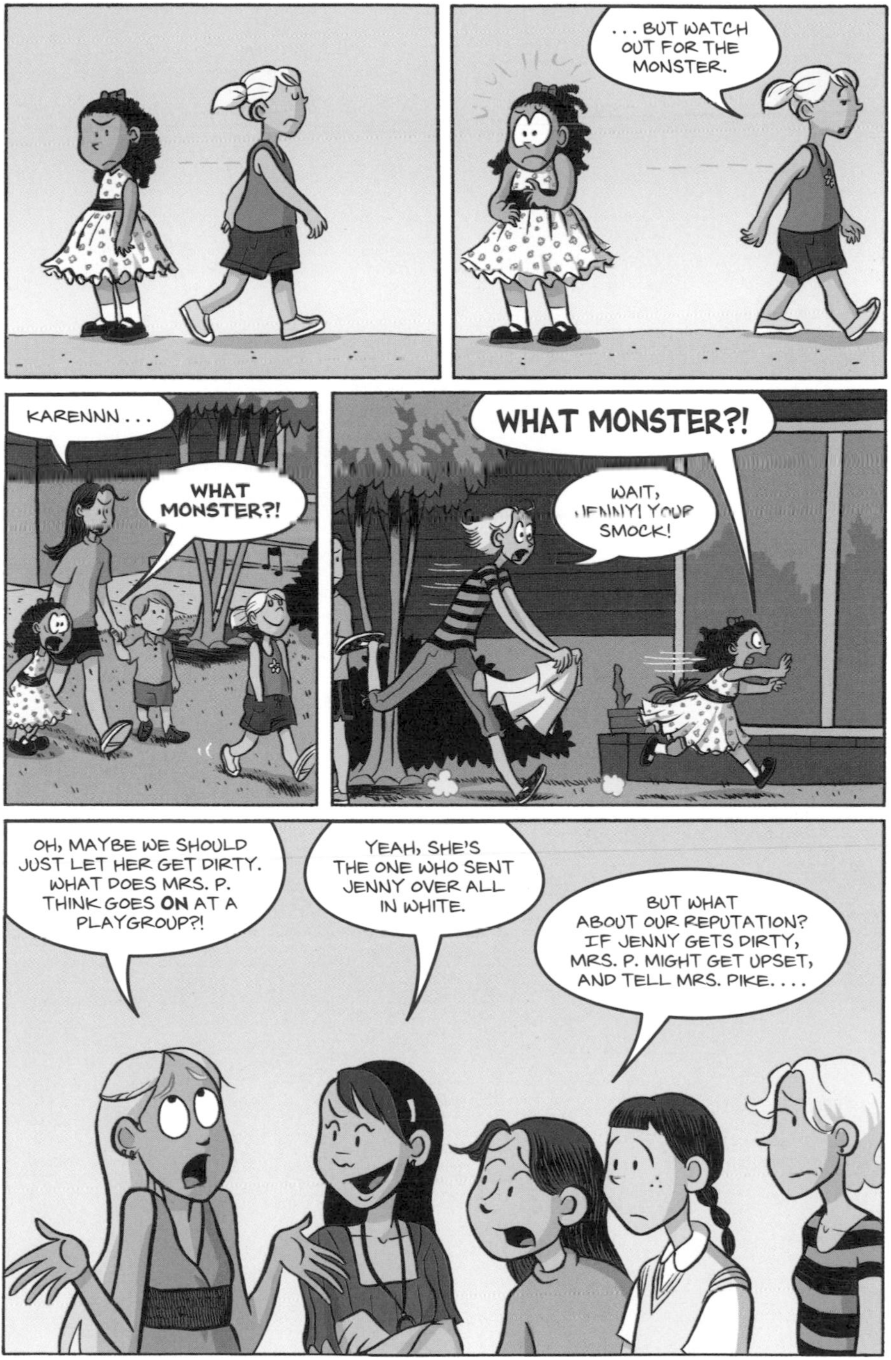
. . . BUT WATCH OUT FOR THE MONSTER.
KARENNN . . .
WHAT MONSTER?!
WHAT MONSTER?!
WAIT, JENNY! YOUR SMOCK!
OH, MAYBE WE SHOULD JUST LET HER GET DIRTY. WHAT DOES MRS. P. THINK GOES **ON** AT A PLAYGROUP?!
YEAH, SHE'S THE ONE WHO SENT JENNY OVER ALL IN WHITE.
BUT WHAT ABOUT OUR REPUTATION? IF JENNY GETS DIRTY, MRS. P. MIGHT GET UPSET, AND TELL MRS. PIKE. . . .

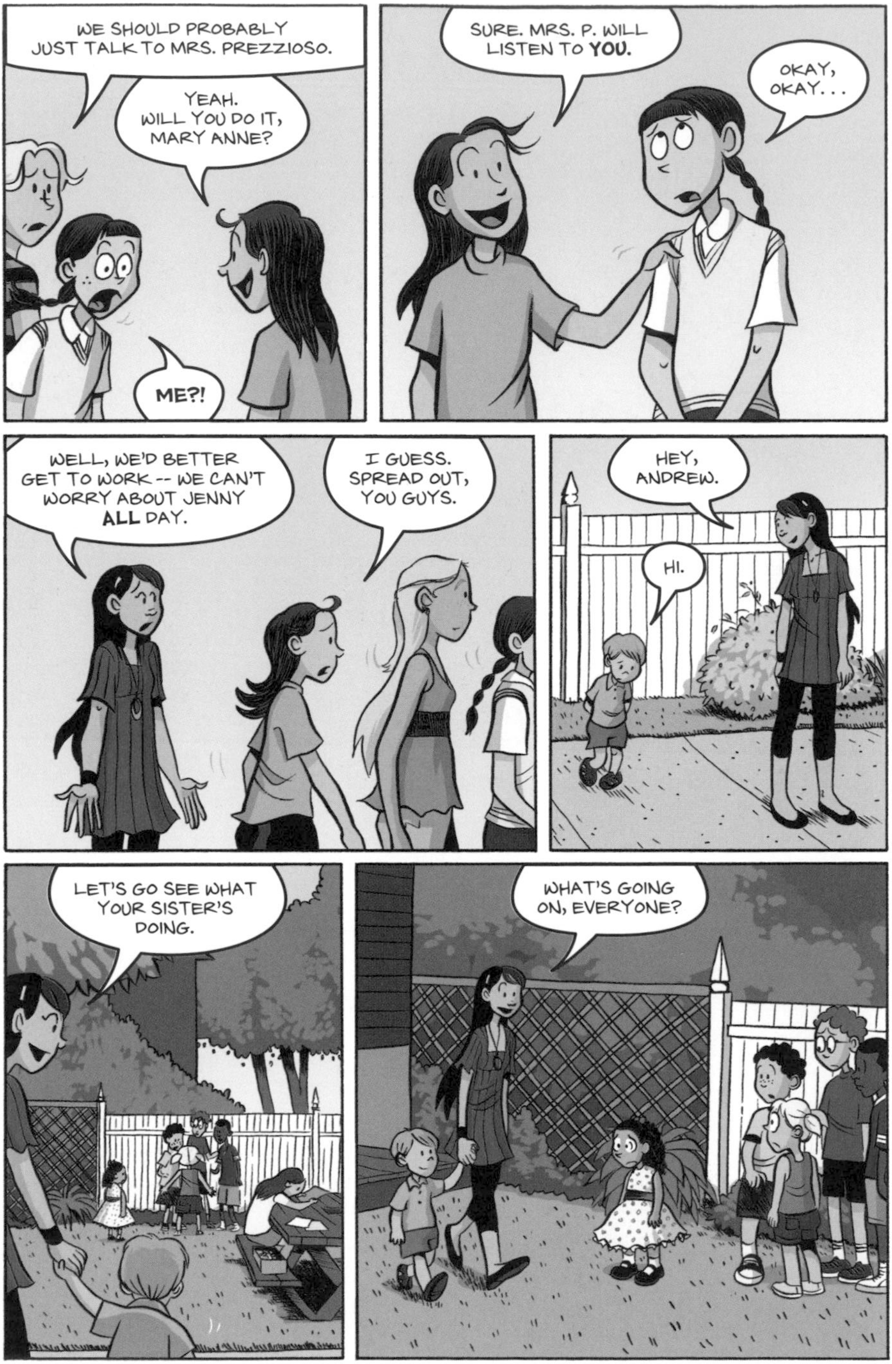

WE SHOULD PROBABLY JUST TALK TO MRS. PREZZIOSO.
YEAH. WILL YOU DO IT, MARY ANNE?
ME?!
SURE. MRS. P. WILL LISTEN TO **YOU.**
OKAY, OKAY...
WELL, WE'D BETTER GET TO WORK -- WE CAN'T WORRY ABOUT JENNY **ALL** DAY.
I GUESS. SPREAD OUT, YOU GUYS.
HEY, ANDREW.
HI.
LET'S GO SEE WHAT YOUR SISTER'S DOING.
WHAT'S GOING ON, EVERYONE?

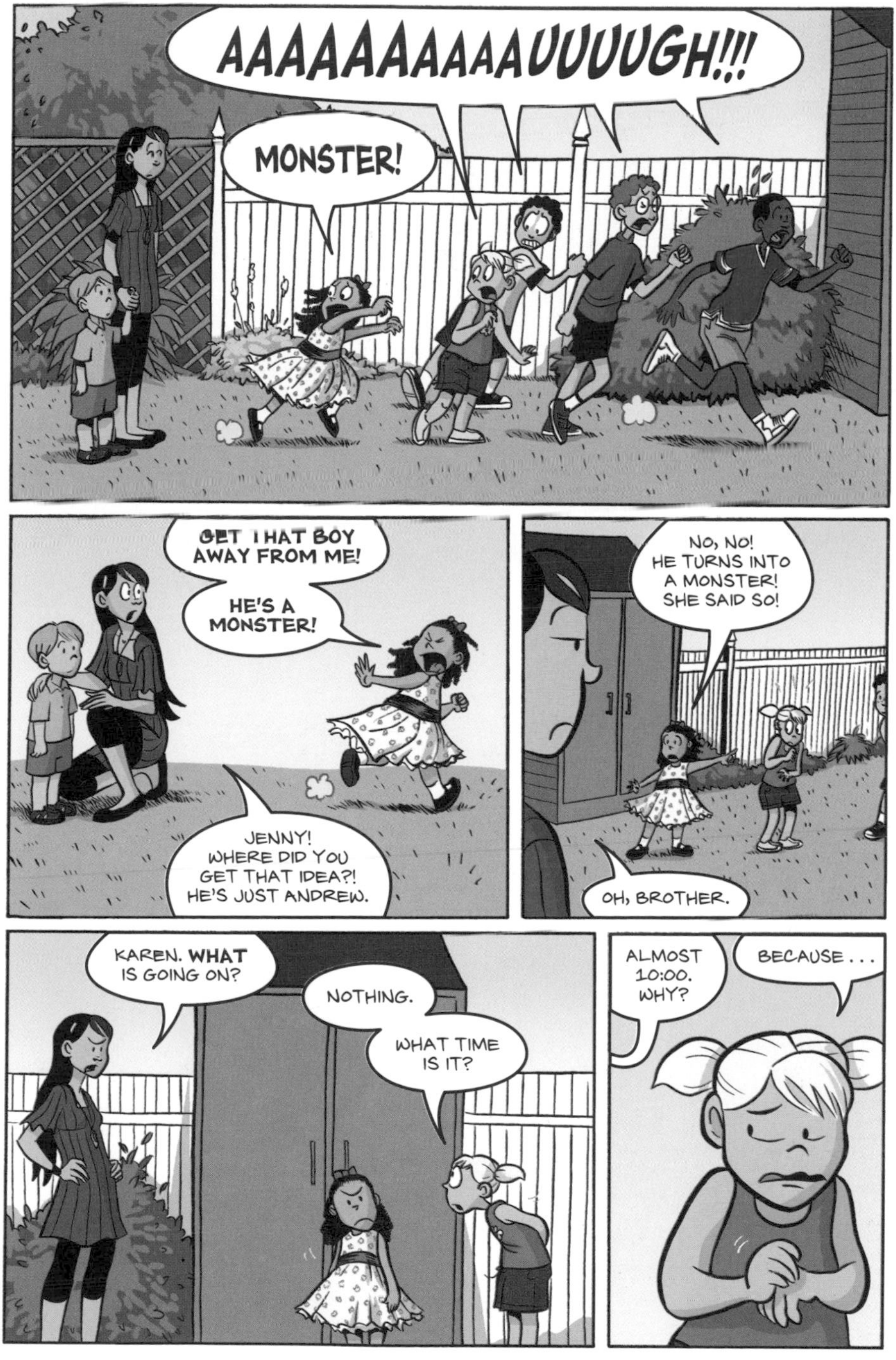
AAAAAAAAAAUUUUGH!!!
MONSTER!
GET THAT BOY AWAY FROM ME!
HE'S A MONSTER!
JENNY! WHERE DID YOU GET THAT IDEA?! HE'S JUST ANDREW.
NO, NO! HE TURNS INTO A MONSTER! SHE SAID SO!
OH, BROTHER.
KAREN. WHAT IS GOING ON?
NOTHING.
WHAT TIME IS IT?
ALMOST 10:00. WHY?
BECAUSE . . .

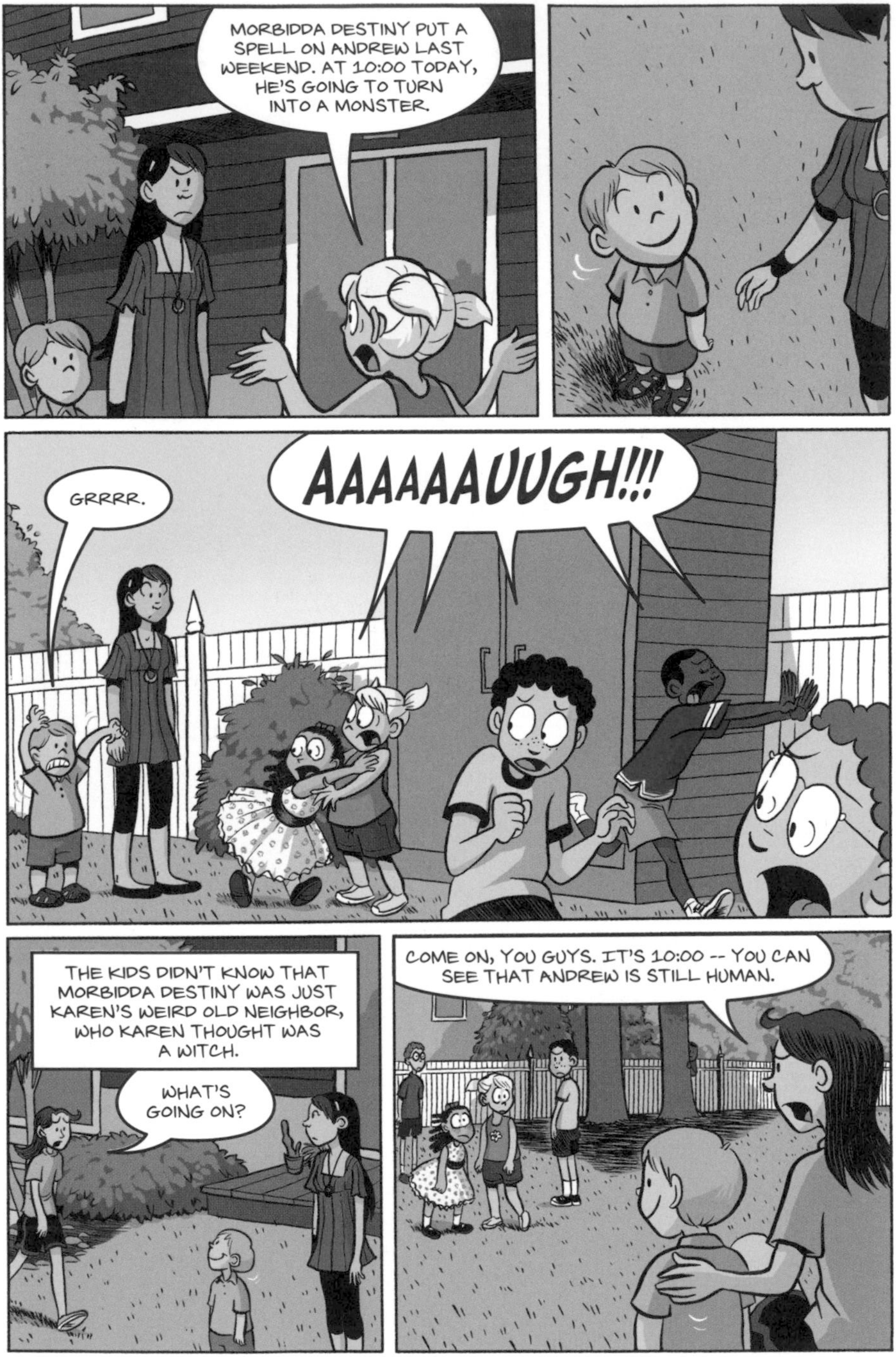

MORBIDDA DESTINY PUT A SPELL ON ANDREW LAST WEEKEND. AT 10:00 TODAY, HE'S GOING TO TURN INTO A MONSTER.
GRRRR.
AAAAAAUUGH!!!
THE KIDS DIDN'T KNOW THAT MORBIDDA DESTINY WAS JUST KAREN'S WEIRD OLD NEIGHBOR, WHO KAREN THOUGHT WAS A WITCH.
WHAT'S GOING ON?
COME ON, YOU GUYS. IT'S 10:00 -- YOU CAN SEE THAT ANDREW IS STILL HUMAN.

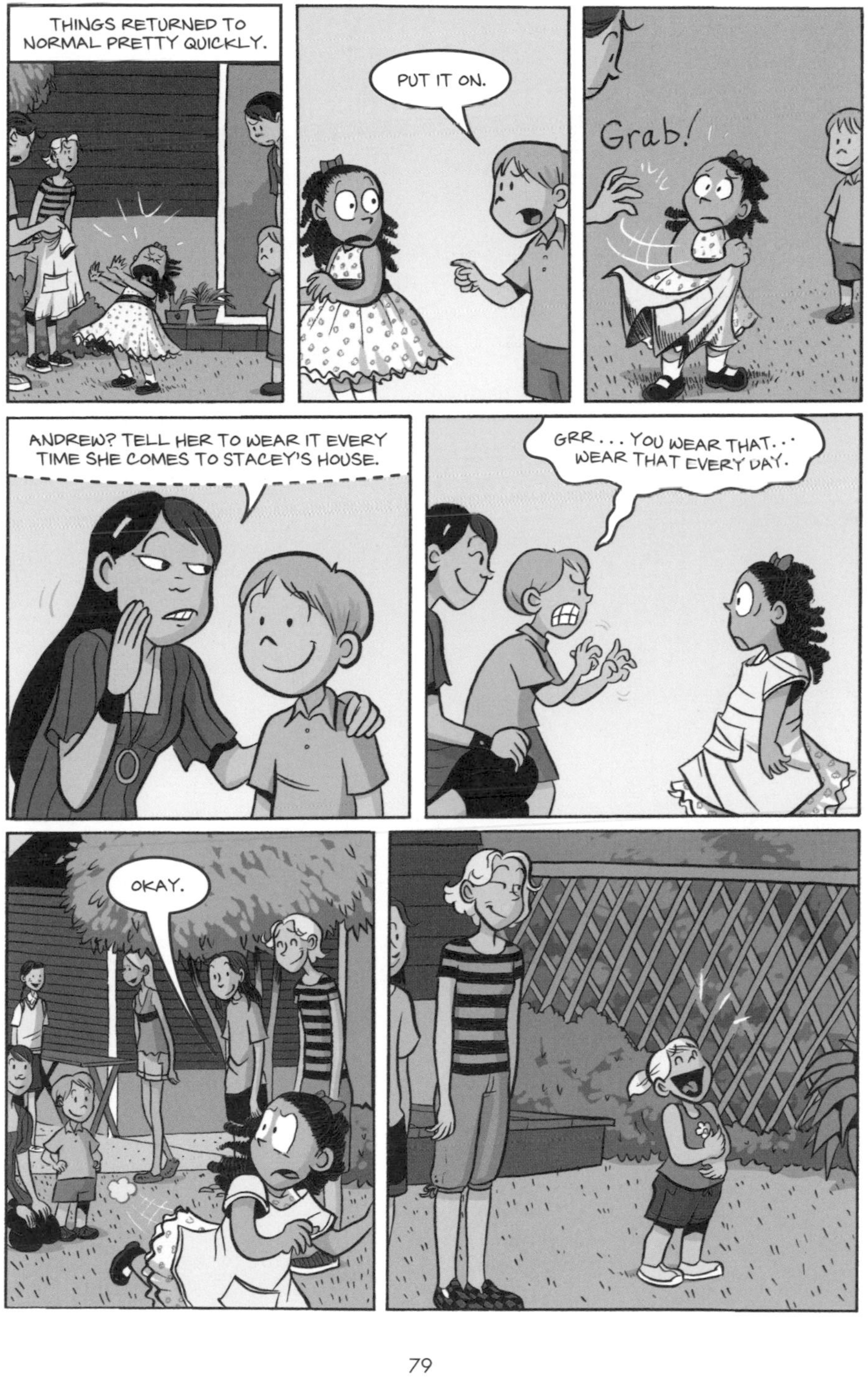
THINGS RETURNED TO NORMAL PRETTY QUICKLY.
PUT IT ON.
Grab!
ANDREW? TELL HER TO WEAR IT EVERY TIME SHE COMES TO STACEY'S HOUSE.
GRR . . . YOU WEAR THAT. . . WEAR THAT EVERY DAY.
OKAY.

CHAPTER 10

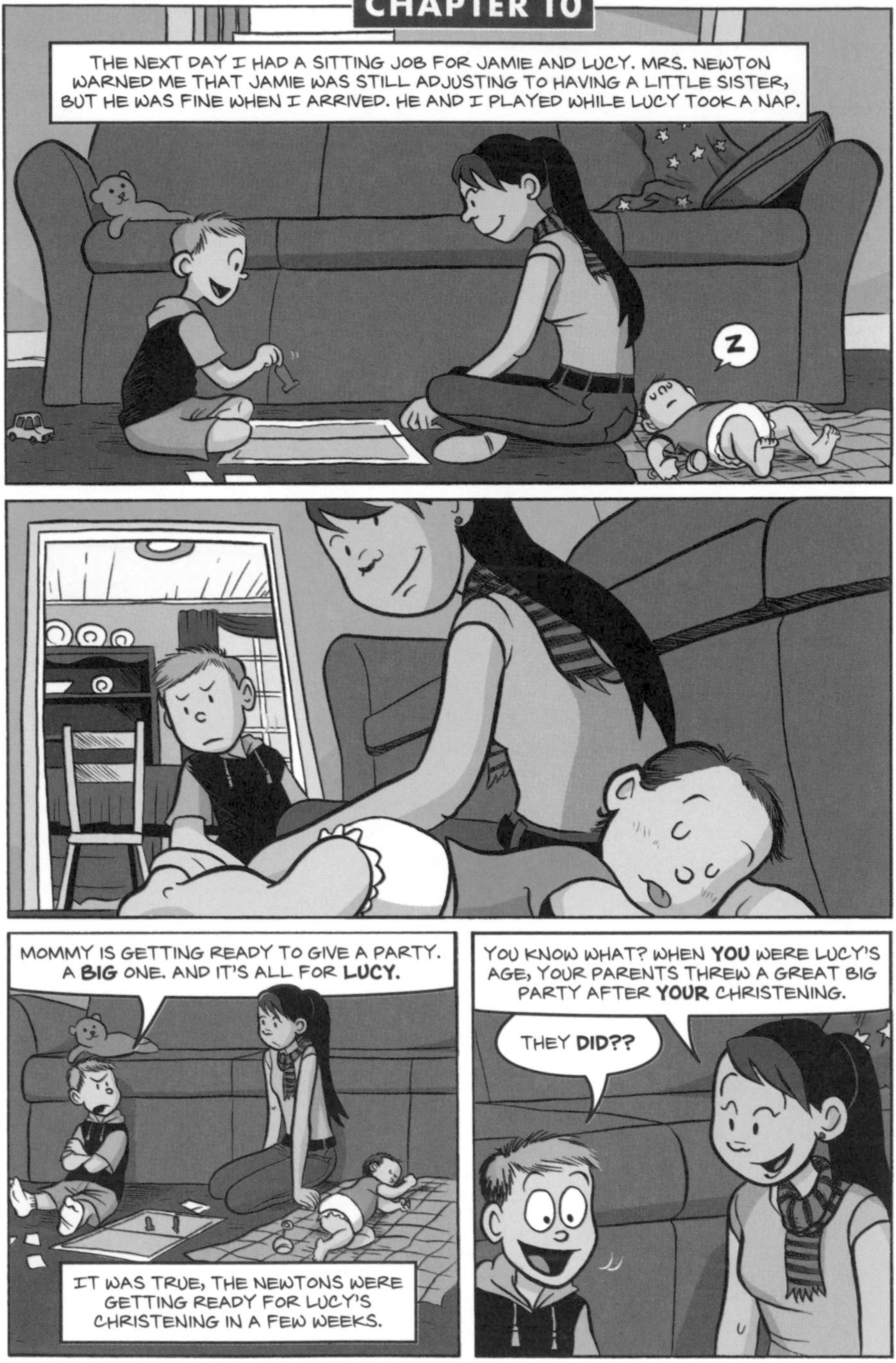
THE NEXT DAY I HAD A SITTING JOB FOR JAMIE AND LUCY. MRS. NEWTON WARNED ME THAT JAMIE WAS STILL ADJUSTING TO HAVING A LITTLE SISTER, BUT HE WAS FINE WHEN I ARRIVED. HE AND I PLAYED WHILE LUCY TOOK A NAP.
Z
MOMMY IS GETTING READY TO GIVE A PARTY. A **BIG** ONE. AND IT'S ALL FOR **LUCY.**
IT WAS TRUE, THE NEWTONS WERE GETTING READY FOR LUCY'S CHRISTENING IN A FEW WEEKS.
YOU KNOW WHAT? WHEN **YOU** WERE LUCY'S AGE, YOUR PARENTS THREW A GREAT BIG PARTY AFTER **YOUR** CHRISTENING.
THEY **DID??**

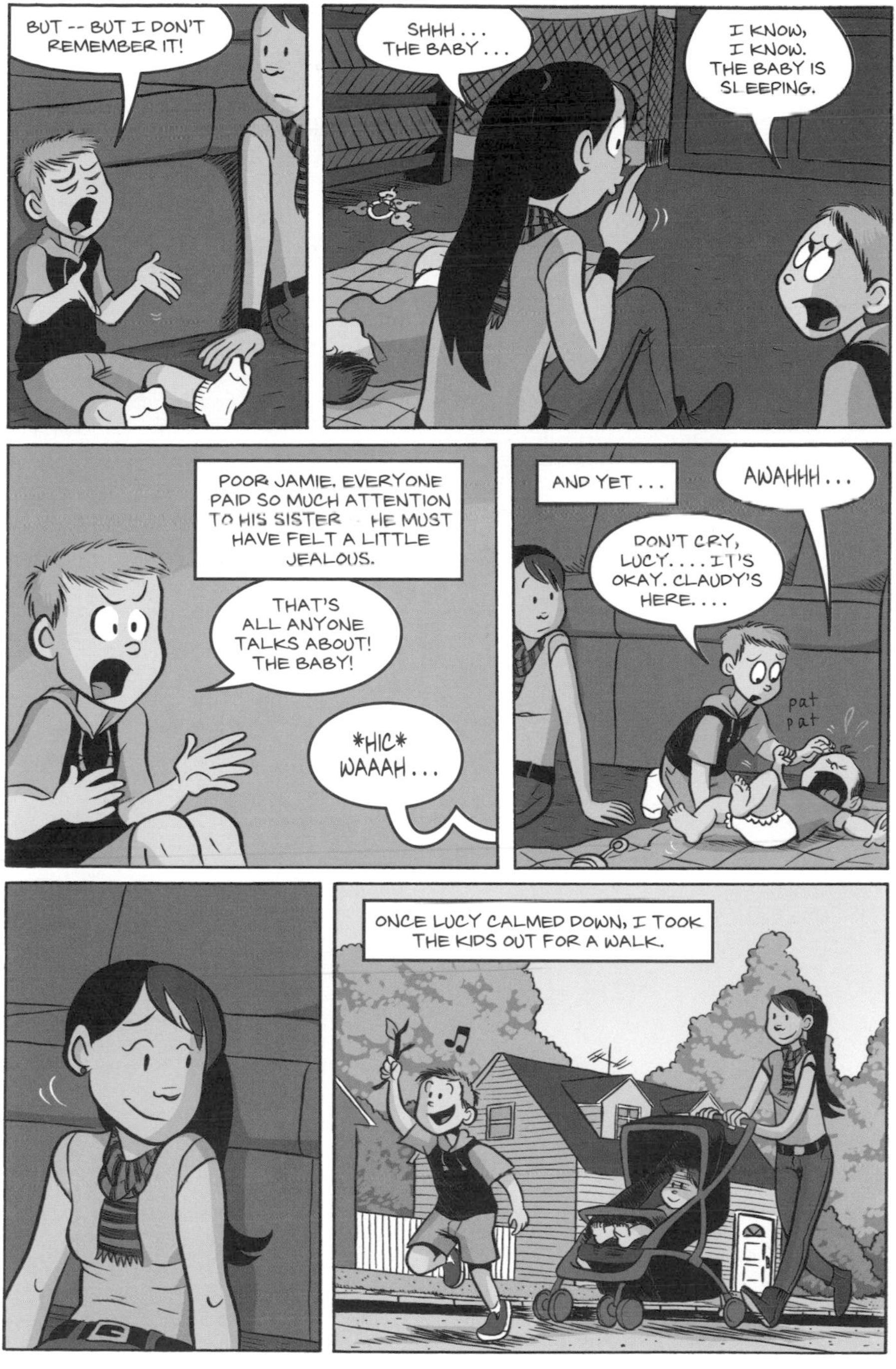
BUT -- BUT I DON'T REMEMBER IT!
SHHH . . . THE BABY . . .
I KNOW, I KNOW. THE BABY IS SLEEPING.
POOR JAMIE. EVERYONE PAID SO MUCH ATTENTION TO HIS SISTER -- HE MUST HAVE FELT A LITTLE JEALOUS.
THAT'S ALL ANYONE TALKS ABOUT! THE BABY!
HIC WAAAH . . .
AND YET . . .
AWAHHH . . .
DON'T CRY, LUCY. . . . IT'S OKAY. CLAUDY'S HERE. . . .
pat pat
ONCE LUCY CALMED DOWN, I TOOK THE KIDS OUT FOR A WALK.

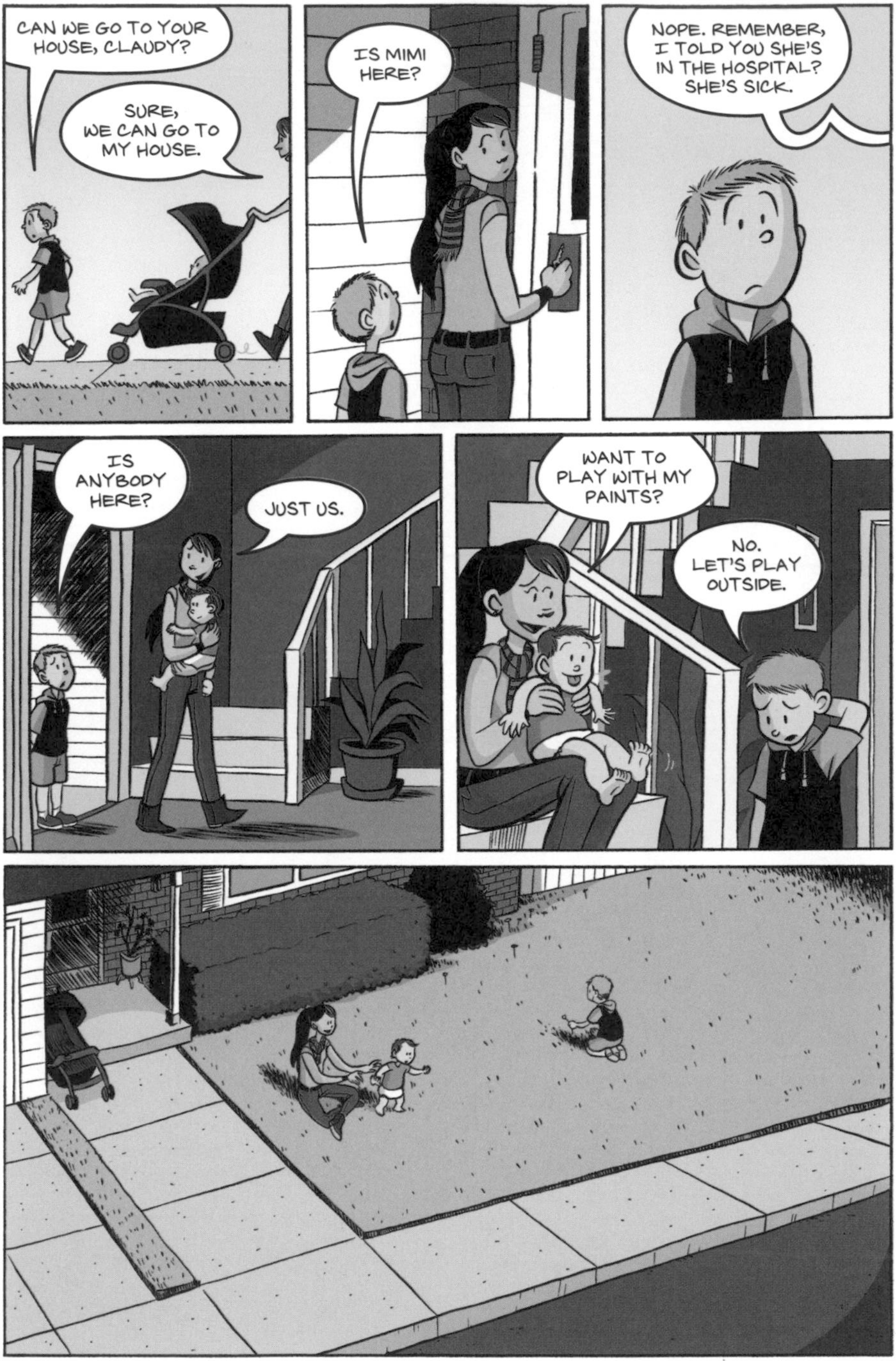
CAN WE GO TO YOUR HOUSE, CLAUDY?
SURE, WE CAN GO TO MY HOUSE.
IS MIMI HERE?
NOPE. REMEMBER, I TOLD YOU SHE'S IN THE HOSPITAL? SHE'S SICK.
IS ANYBODY HERE?
JUST US.
WANT TO PLAY WITH MY PAINTS?
NO. LET'S PLAY OUTSIDE.

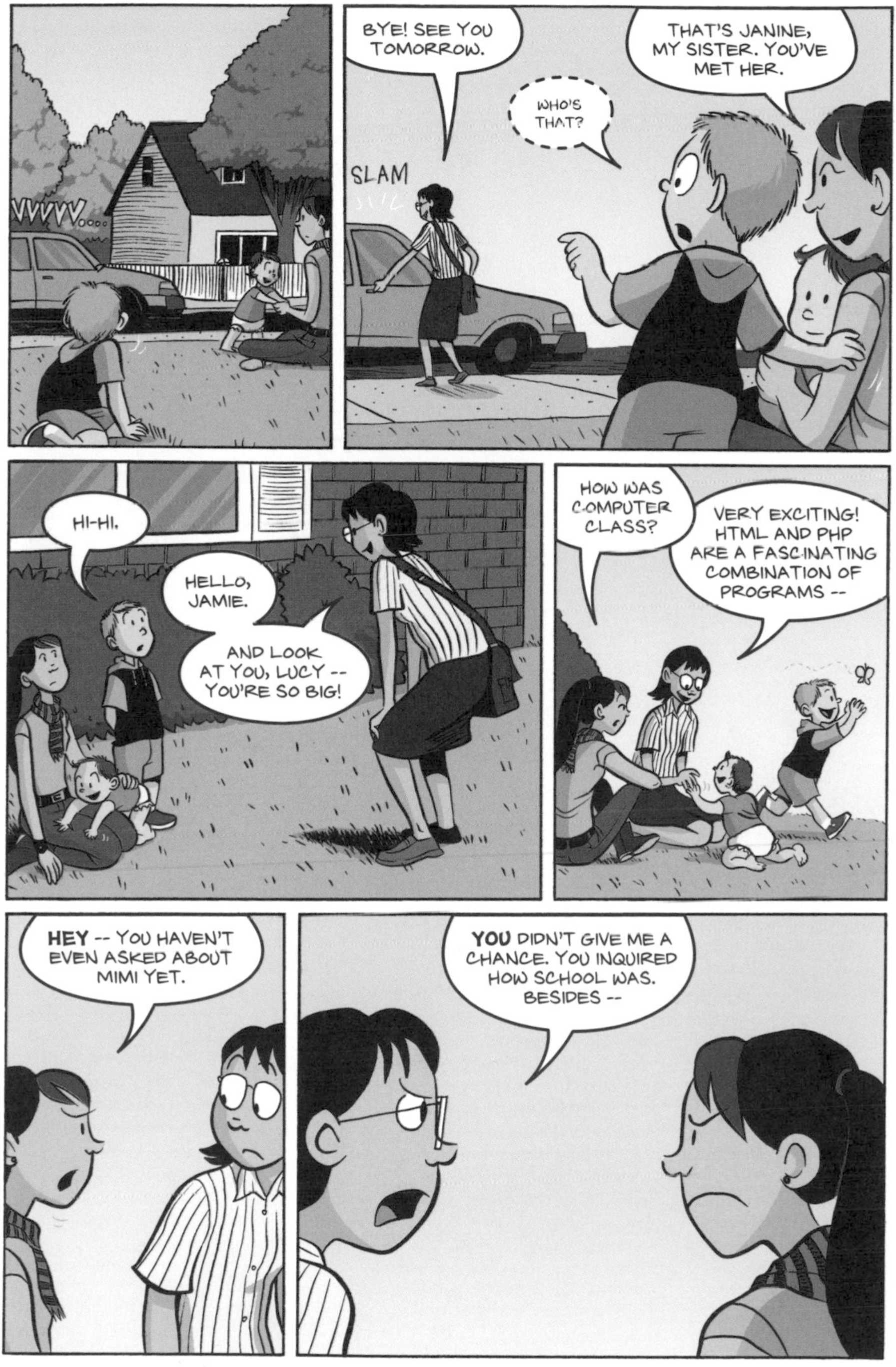
VVVVV....
BYE! SEE YOU TOMORROW.
SLAM
WHO'S THAT?
THAT'S JANINE, MY SISTER. YOU'VE MET HER.
HI-HI.
HELLO, JAMIE.
AND LOOK AT YOU, LUCY -- YOU'RE SO BIG!
HOW WAS COMPUTER CLASS?
VERY EXCITING! HTML AND PHP ARE A FASCINATING COMBINATION OF PROGRAMS --
HEY -- YOU HAVEN'T EVEN ASKED ABOUT MIMI YET.
YOU DIDN'T GIVE ME A CHANCE. YOU INQUIRED HOW SCHOOL WAS. BESIDES --

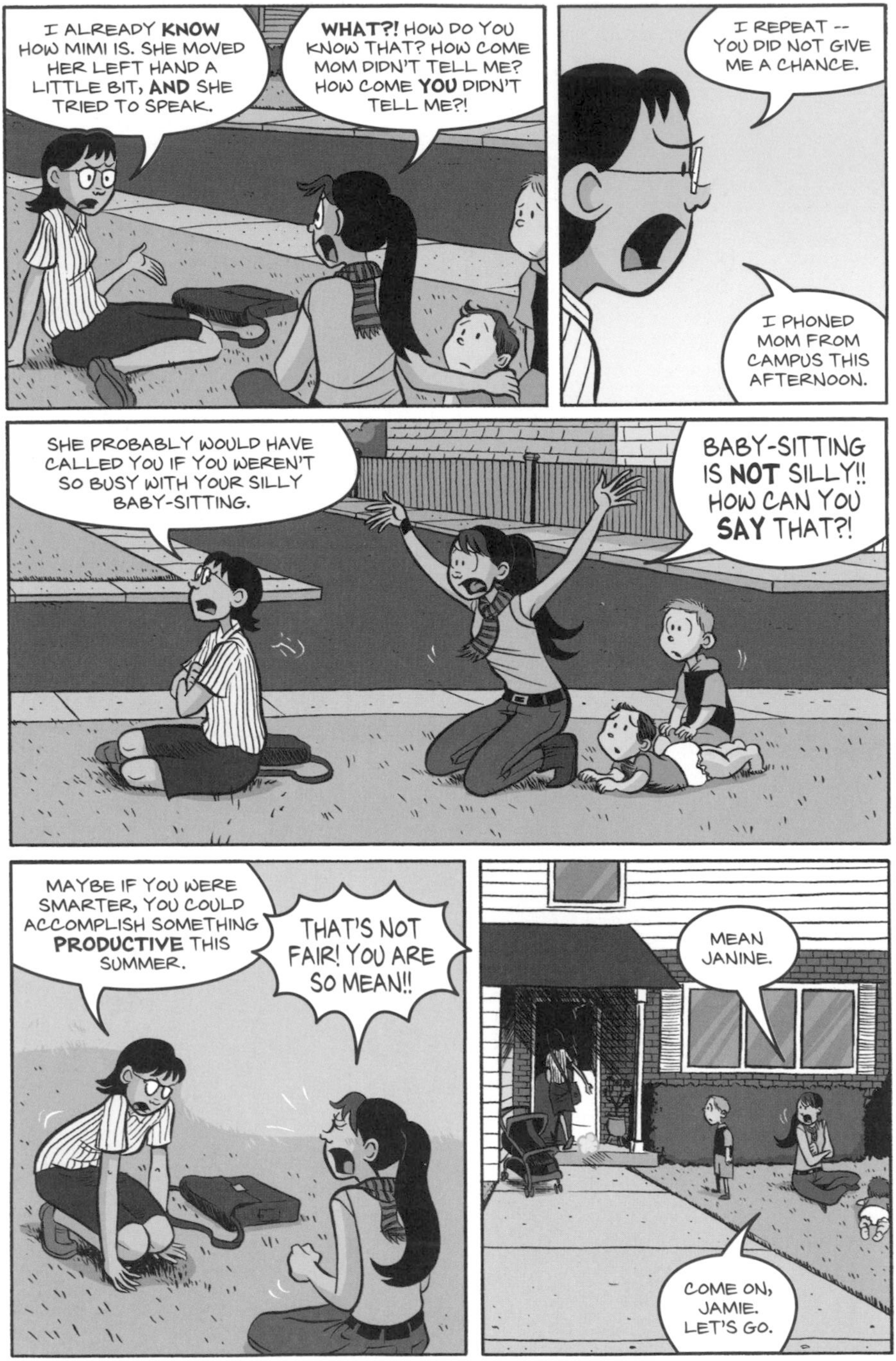
I ALREADY KNOW HOW MIMI IS. SHE MOVED HER LEFT HAND A LITTLE BIT, AND SHE TRIED TO SPEAK.
WHAT?! HOW DO YOU KNOW THAT? HOW COME MOM DIDN'T TELL ME? HOW COME YOU DIDN'T TELL ME?!
I REPEAT -- YOU DID NOT GIVE ME A CHANCE.
I PHONED MOM FROM CAMPUS THIS AFTERNOON.
SHE PROBABLY WOULD HAVE CALLED YOU IF YOU WEREN'T SO BUSY WITH YOUR SILLY BABY-SITTING.
BABY-SITTING IS NOT SILLY!! HOW CAN YOU SAY THAT?!
MAYBE IF YOU WERE SMARTER, YOU COULD ACCOMPLISH SOMETHING PRODUCTIVE THIS SUMMER.
THAT'S NOT FAIR! YOU ARE SO MEAN!!
MEAN JANINE.
COME ON, JAMIE. LET'S GO.

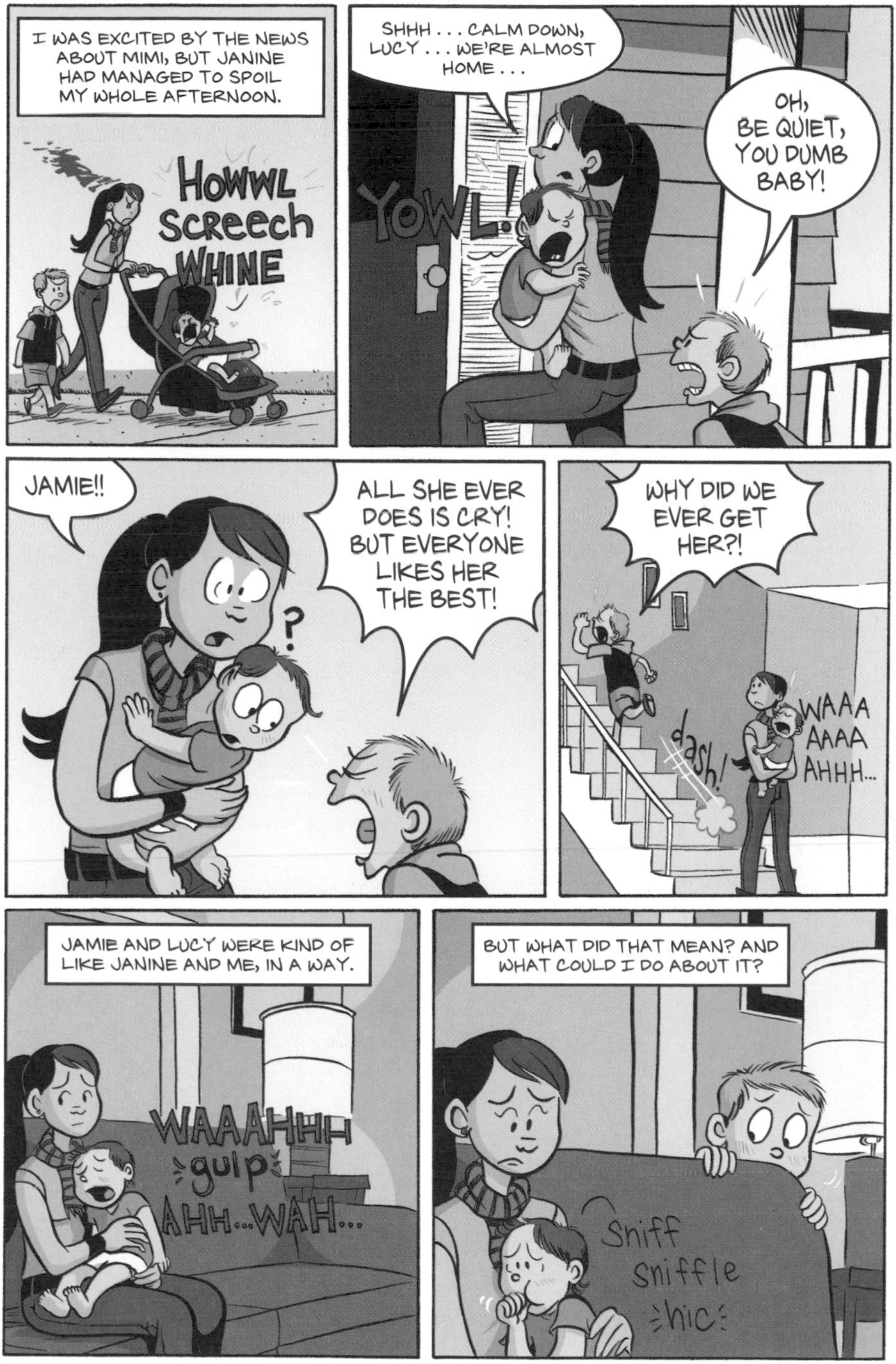
I WAS EXCITED BY THE NEWS ABOUT MIMI, BUT JANINE HAD MANAGED TO SPOIL MY WHOLE AFTERNOON.
HOWWL
SCREECH
WHINE
SHHH . . . CALM DOWN, LUCY . . . WE'RE ALMOST HOME . . .
YOWL!
OH, BE QUIET, YOU DUMB BABY!
JAMIE!!
ALL SHE EVER DOES IS CRY! BUT EVERYONE LIKES HER THE BEST!
?
WHY DID WE EVER GET HER?!
dash!
WAAA AAAA AHHH...
JAMIE AND LUCY WERE KIND OF LIKE JANINE AND ME, IN A WAY.
WAAAHHH
gulp
AHH...WAH...
BUT WHAT DID THAT MEAN? AND WHAT COULD I DO ABOUT IT?
sniff
sniffle
hic

CHAPTER 11

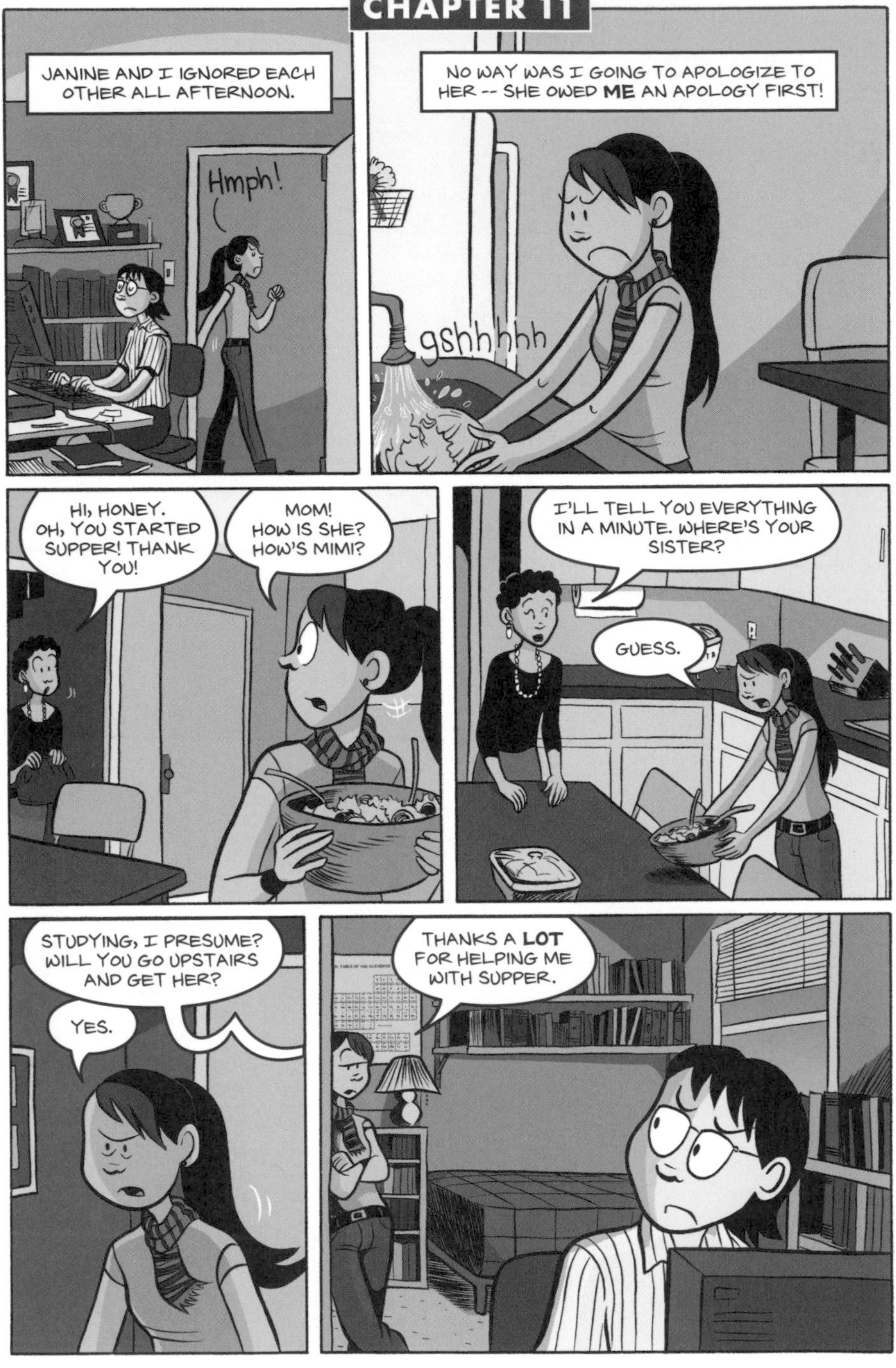

JANINE AND I IGNORED EACH OTHER ALL AFTERNOON.
Hmph!
NO WAY WAS I GOING TO APOLOGIZE TO HER -- SHE OWED **ME** AN APOLOGY FIRST!
gshhhhh
HI, HONEY. OH, YOU STARTED SUPPER! THANK YOU!
MOM! HOW IS SHE? HOW'S MIMI?
I'LL TELL YOU EVERYTHING IN A MINUTE. WHERE'S YOUR SISTER?
GUESS.
STUDYING, I PRESUME? WILL YOU GO UPSTAIRS AND GET HER?
YES.
THANKS A **LOT** FOR HELPING ME WITH SUPPER.

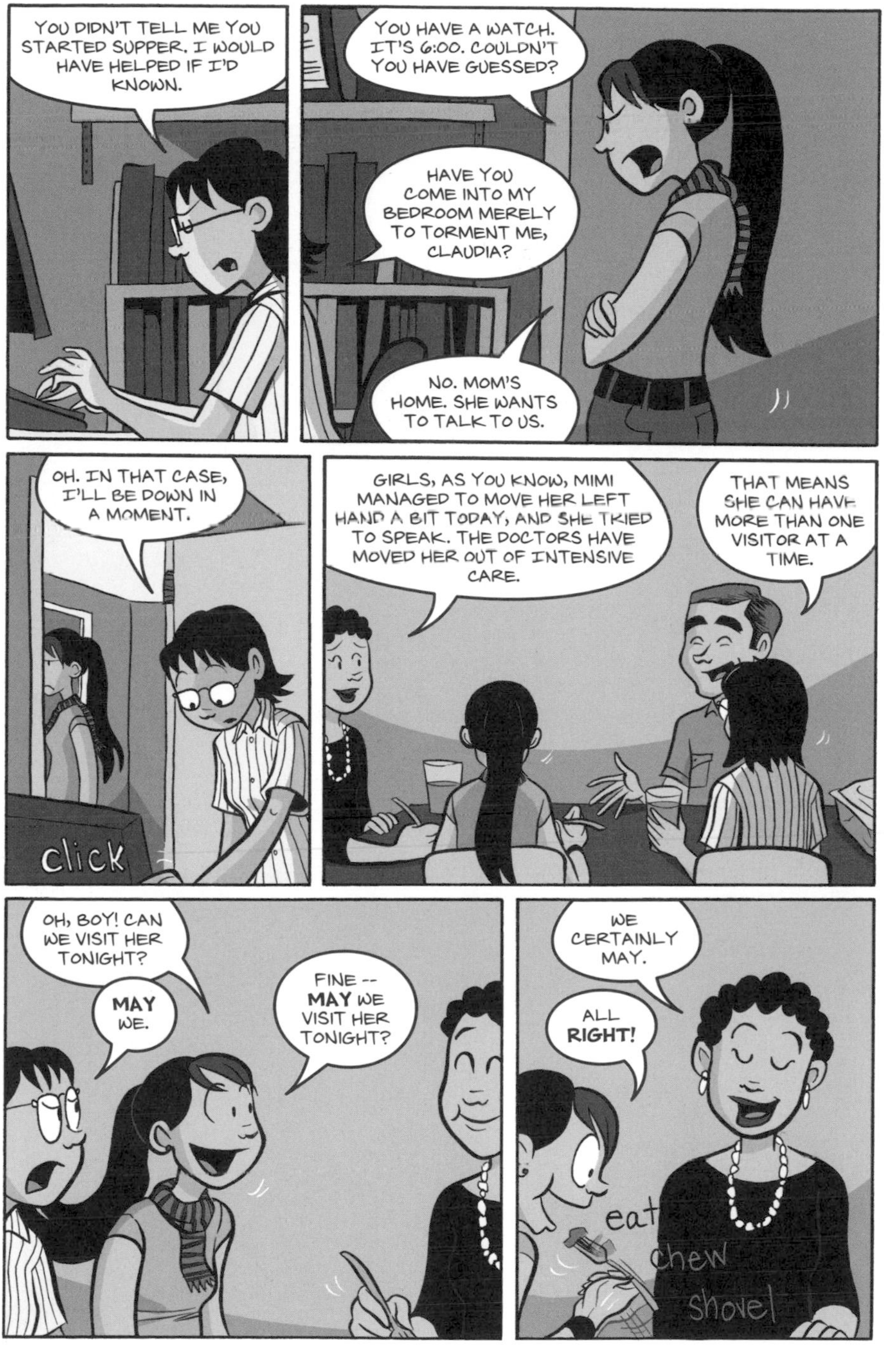
YOU DIDN'T TELL ME YOU STARTED SUPPER. I WOULD HAVE HELPED IF I'D KNOWN.
YOU HAVE A WATCH. IT'S 6:00. COULDN'T YOU HAVE GUESSED?
HAVE YOU COME INTO MY BEDROOM MERELY TO TORMENT ME, CLAUDIA?
NO. MOM'S HOME. SHE WANTS TO TALK TO US.
OH. IN THAT CASE, I'LL BE DOWN IN A MOMENT.
click
GIRLS, AS YOU KNOW, MIMI MANAGED TO MOVE HER LEFT HAND A BIT TODAY, AND SHE TRIED TO SPEAK. THE DOCTORS HAVE MOVED HER OUT OF INTENSIVE CARE.
THAT MEANS SHE CAN HAVE MORE THAN ONE VISITOR AT A TIME.
OH, BOY! CAN WE VISIT HER TONIGHT?
MAY WE.
FINE -- **MAY** WE VISIT HER TONIGHT?
WE CERTAINLY MAY.
ALL **RIGHT**!
eat
chew
shovel

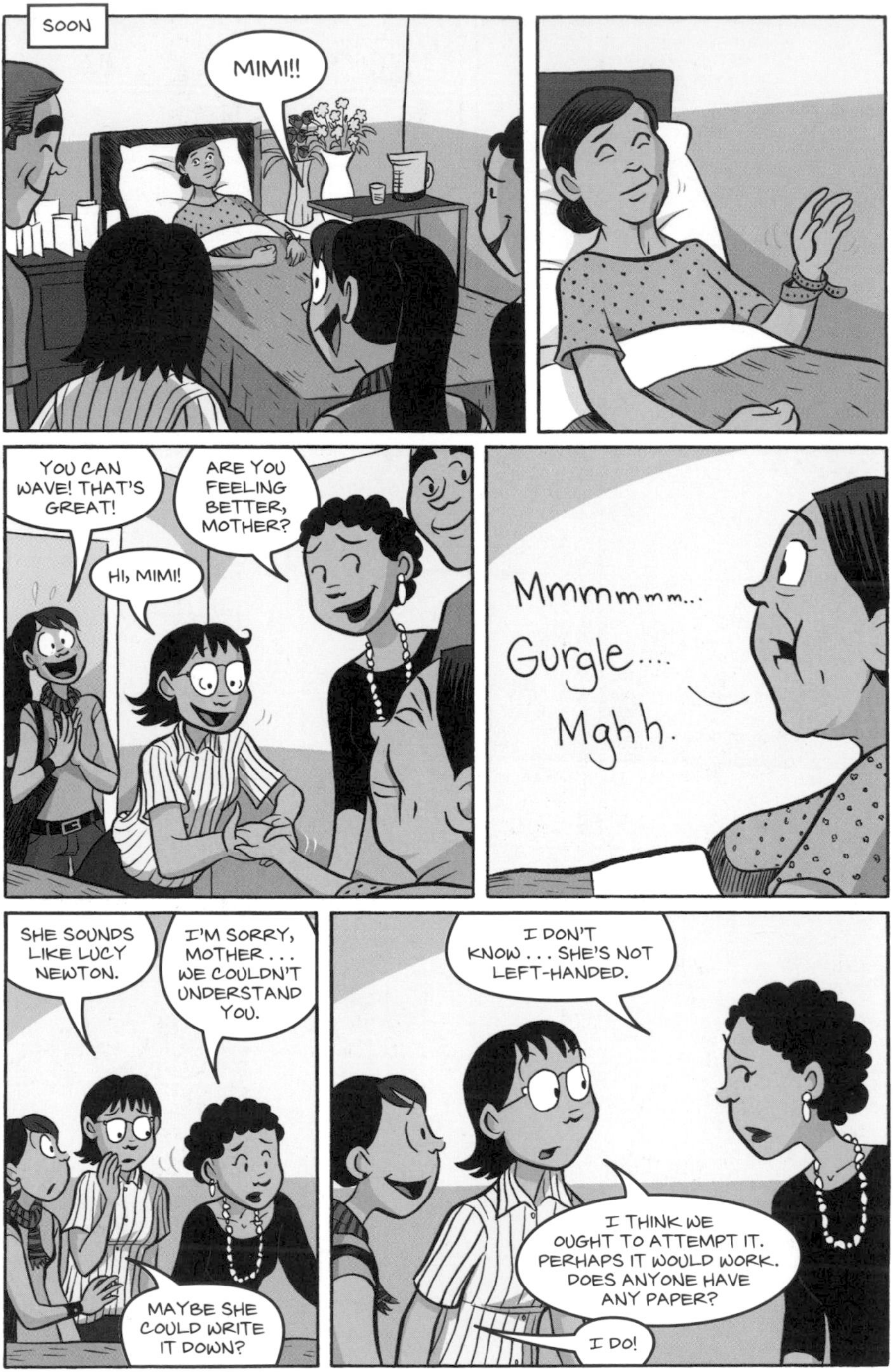
SOON
MIMI!!
YOU CAN WAVE! THAT'S GREAT!
ARE YOU FEELING BETTER, MOTHER?
HI, MIMI!
Mmmmmm...
Gurgle....
Mghh.
SHE SOUNDS LIKE LUCY NEWTON.
I'M SORRY, MOTHER . . . WE COULDN'T UNDERSTAND YOU.
MAYBE SHE COULD WRITE IT DOWN?
I DON'T KNOW . . . SHE'S NOT LEFT-HANDED.
I THINK WE OUGHT TO ATTEMPT IT. PERHAPS IT WOULD WORK. DOES ANYONE HAVE ANY PAPER?
I DO!

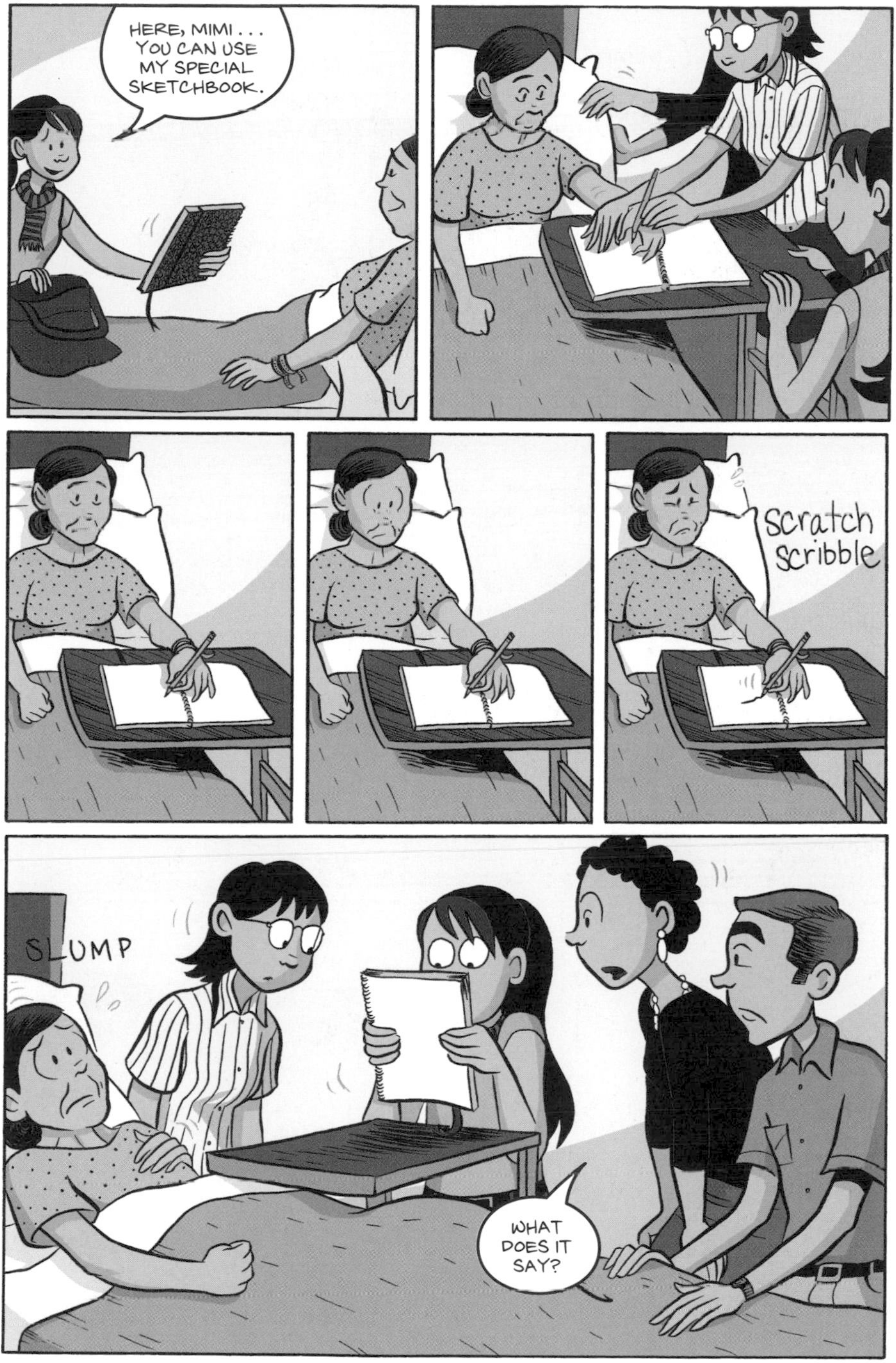
HERE, MIMI . . .
YOU CAN USE
MY SPECIAL
SKETCHBOOK.
Scratch
scribble
SLUMP
WHAT
DOES IT
SAY?

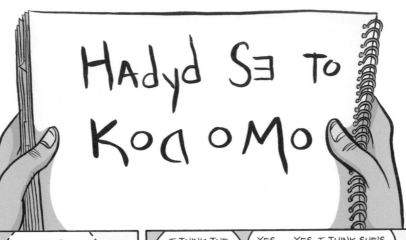

MOM? SOMETHING'S WRONG. WHY IS EVERYTHING ALL MIXED UP AND UPSIDE-DOWN?

I THINK THE FIRST WORD IS "HAPPY."

YES... YES, I THINK SHE'S SAYING SHE'S HAPPY TO SEE YOU GIRLS.

KODOMO IS JAPANESE FOR "CHILD" OR "CHILDREN."

BUT WHY DIDN'T SHE JUST SAY "CHILDREN"? OR USE OUR NAMES?

I DON'T KNOW, HONEY.

WELL! WHAT'S GOING ON IN HERE?

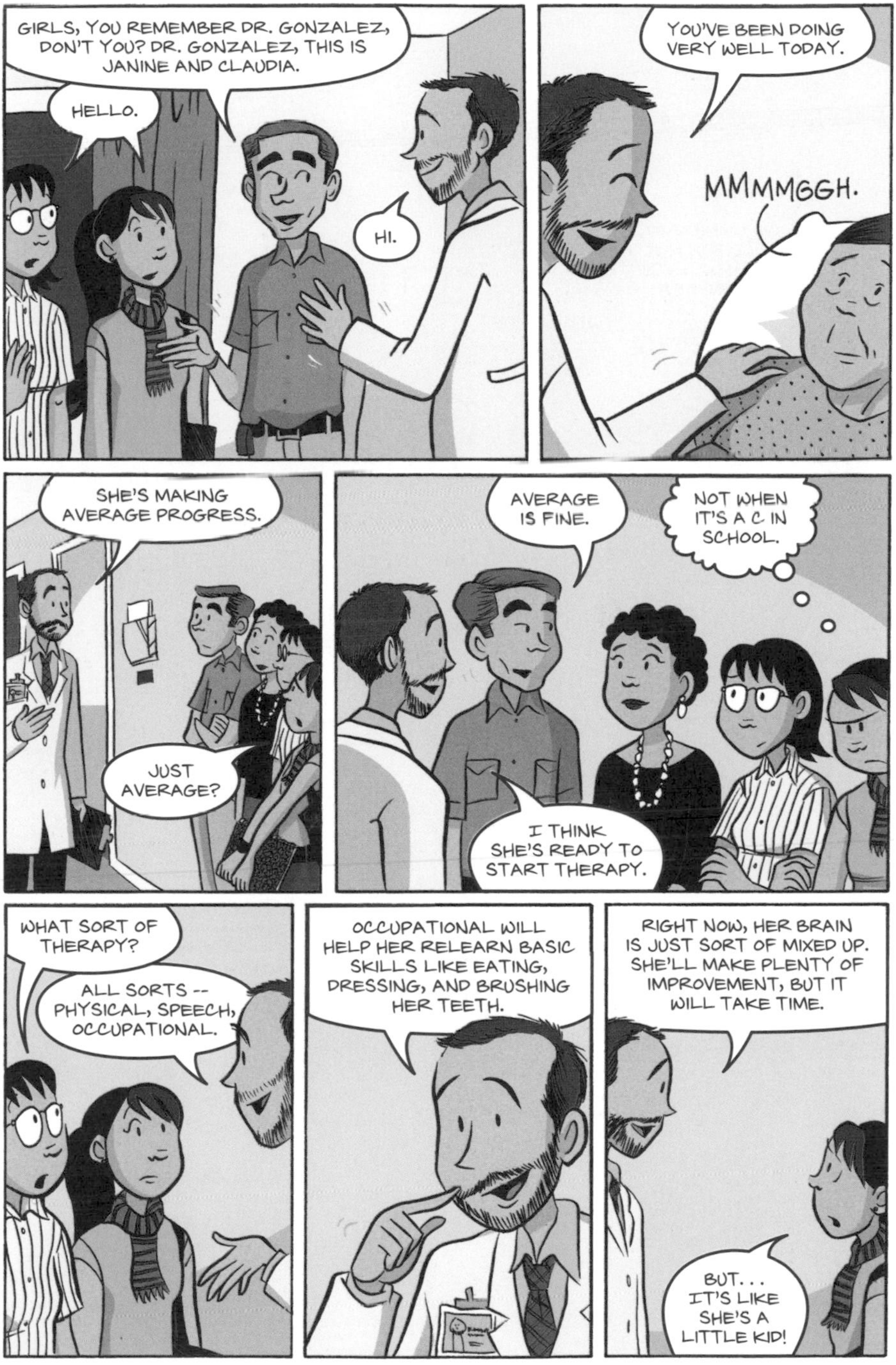
GIRLS, YOU REMEMBER DR. GONZALEZ, DON'T YOU? DR. GONZALEZ, THIS IS JANINE AND CLAUDIA.
HELLO.
HI.
YOU'VE BEEN DOING VERY WELL TODAY.
MMMMGGH.
SHE'S MAKING AVERAGE PROGRESS.
JUST AVERAGE?
AVERAGE IS FINE.
NOT WHEN IT'S A C IN SCHOOL.
I THINK SHE'S READY TO START THERAPY.
WHAT SORT OF THERAPY?
ALL SORTS -- PHYSICAL, SPEECH, OCCUPATIONAL.
OCCUPATIONAL WILL HELP HER RELEARN BASIC SKILLS LIKE EATING, DRESSING, AND BRUSHING HER TEETH.
RIGHT NOW, HER BRAIN IS JUST SORT OF MIXED UP. SHE'LL MAKE PLENTY OF IMPROVEMENT, BUT IT WILL TAKE TIME.
BUT. . . IT'S LIKE SHE'S A LITTLE KID!

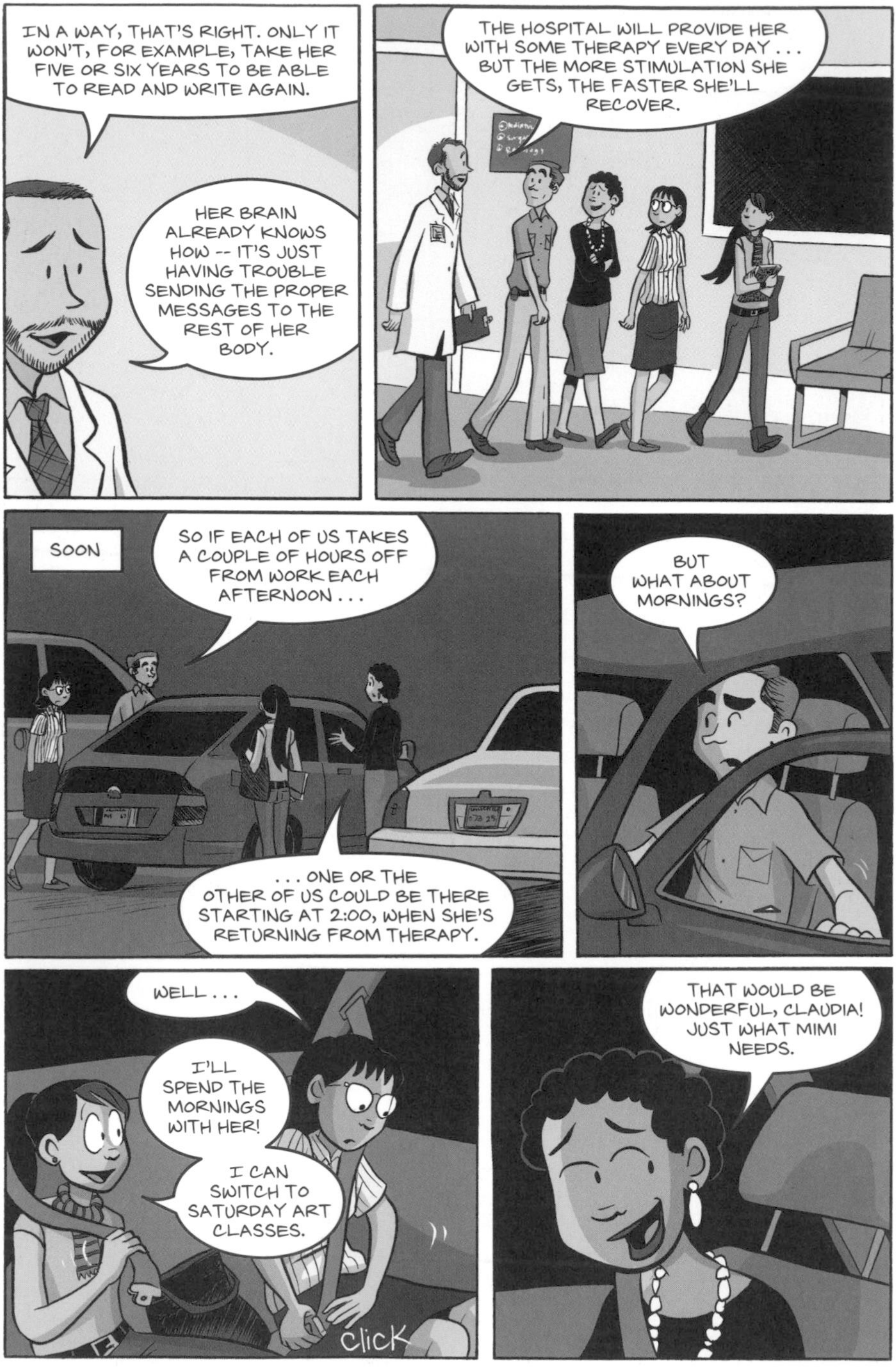
IN A WAY, THAT'S RIGHT. ONLY IT WON'T, FOR EXAMPLE, TAKE HER FIVE OR SIX YEARS TO BE ABLE TO READ AND WRITE AGAIN.
HER BRAIN ALREADY KNOWS HOW -- IT'S JUST HAVING TROUBLE SENDING THE PROPER MESSAGES TO THE REST OF HER BODY.
THE HOSPITAL WILL PROVIDE HER WITH SOME THERAPY EVERY DAY . . . BUT THE MORE STIMULATION SHE GETS, THE FASTER SHE'LL RECOVER.
SOON
SO IF EACH OF US TAKES A COUPLE OF HOURS OFF FROM WORK EACH AFTERNOON . . .
. . . ONE OR THE OTHER OF US COULD BE THERE STARTING AT 2:00, WHEN SHE'S RETURNING FROM THERAPY.
BUT WHAT ABOUT MORNINGS?
WELL . . .
I'LL SPEND THE MORNINGS WITH HER!
I CAN SWITCH TO SATURDAY ART CLASSES.
CLICK
THAT WOULD BE WONDERFUL, CLAUDIA! JUST WHAT MIMI NEEDS.

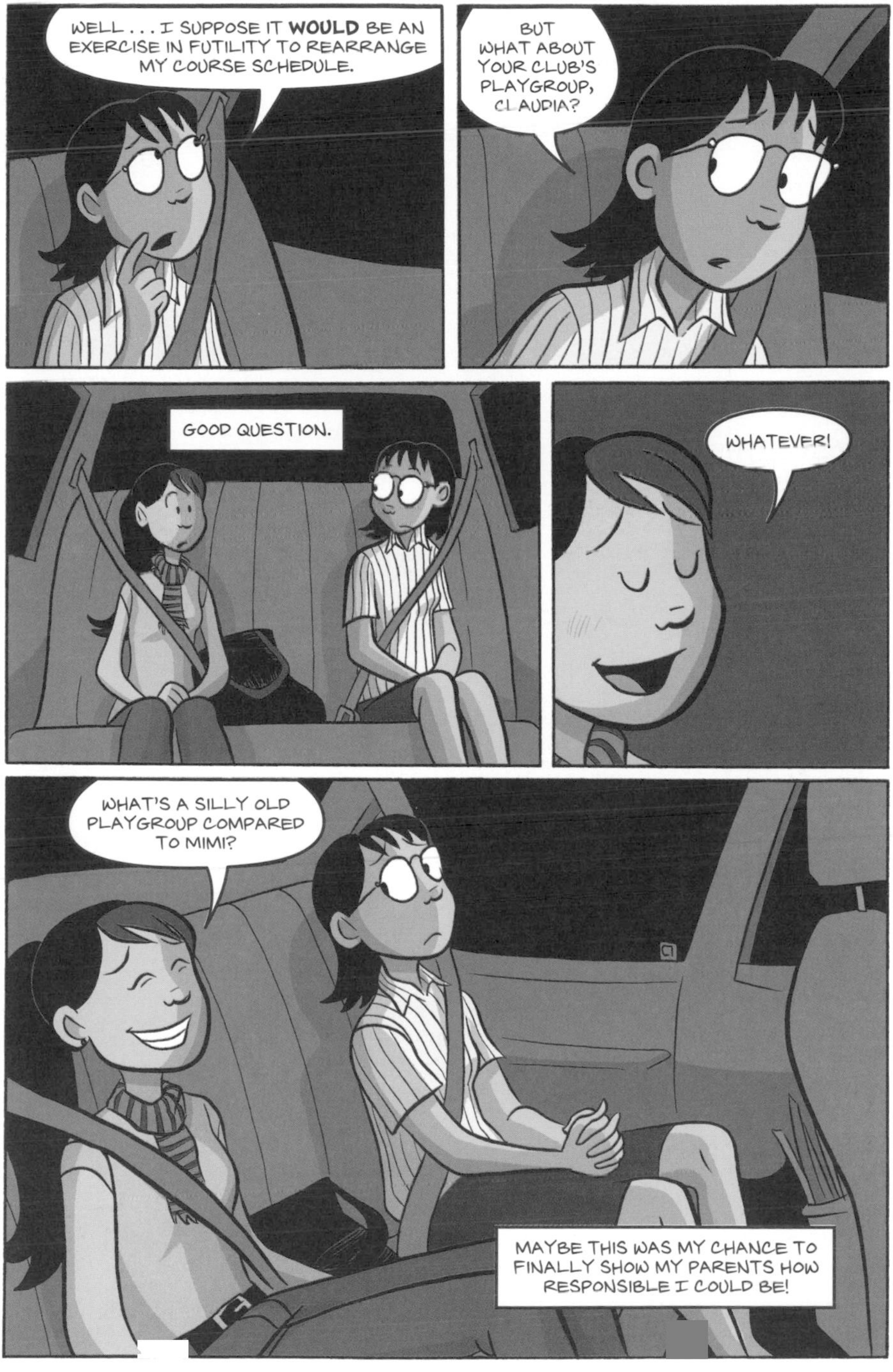
WELL . . . I SUPPOSE IT **WOULD** BE AN EXERCISE IN FUTILITY TO REARRANGE MY COURSE SCHEDULE.
BUT WHAT ABOUT YOUR CLUB'S PLAYGROUP, CLAUDIA?
GOOD QUESTION.
WHATEVER!
WHAT'S A SILLY OLD PLAYGROUP COMPARED TO MIMI?
MAYBE THIS WAS MY CHANCE TO FINALLY SHOW MY PARENTS HOW RESPONSIBLE I COULD BE!

Wednesday, June 23

Today's playgroup ended hours ago and I'm still laughing about what went on. Now this is an example of something hilarious that probably could never have happened in New York City. . . . It started when David Michael brought Louie to the playgroup. Just to set things off on the wrong foot, it turns out that Jenny is afraid (and I mean terrified) of dogs. Remember that for the future, you guys.

Then Kristy decided we needed to give Louie a bath. That's when the trouble really began. When the morning was over, Louie was the only one who was both clean and dry. Thank goodness Jenny was wearing her smock.

Claudia - we miss you!

Stacey

CHAPTER 12

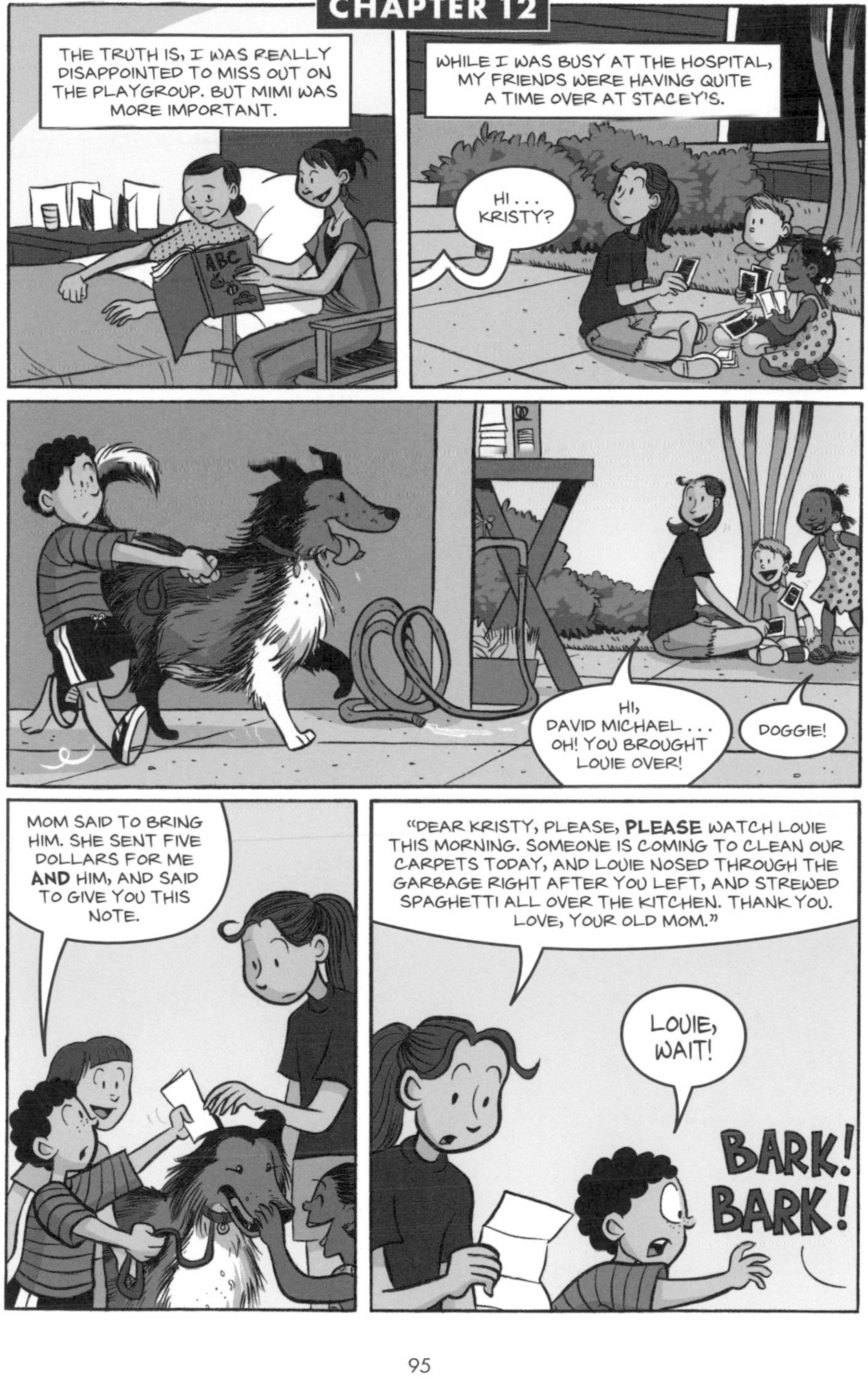
THE TRUTH IS, I WAS REALLY DISAPPOINTED TO MISS OUT ON THE PLAYGROUP. BUT MIMI WAS MORE IMPORTANT.
ABC
WHILE I WAS BUSY AT THE HOSPITAL, MY FRIENDS WERE HAVING QUITE A TIME OVER AT STACEY'S.
HI . . . KRISTY?
HI, DAVID MICHAEL . . . OH! YOU BROUGHT LOUIE OVER!
DOGGIE!
MOM SAID TO BRING HIM. SHE SENT FIVE DOLLARS FOR ME **AND** HIM, AND SAID TO GIVE YOU THIS NOTE.
"DEAR KRISTY, PLEASE, **PLEASE** WATCH LOUIE THIS MORNING. SOMEONE IS COMING TO CLEAN OUR CARPETS TODAY, AND LOUIE NOSED THROUGH THE GARBAGE RIGHT AFTER YOU LEFT, AND STREWED SPAGHETTI ALL OVER THE KITCHEN. THANK YOU. LOVE, YOUR OLD MOM."
LOUIE, WAIT!
BARK! BARK!

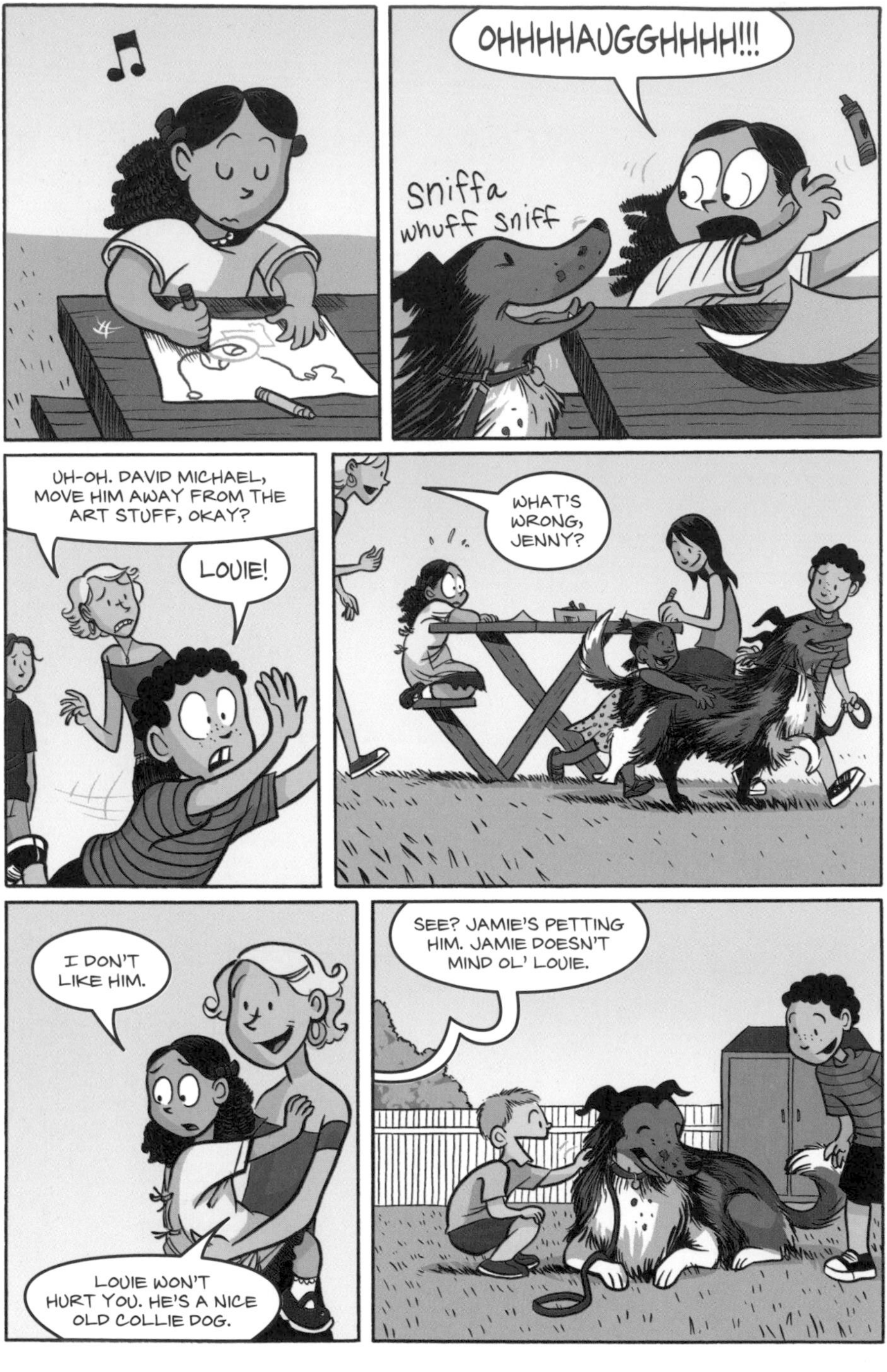
OHHHHAUGGHHHH!!!
sniffa
whuff sniff
UH-OH. DAVID MICHAEL, MOVE HIM AWAY FROM THE ART STUFF, OKAY?
LOUIE!
WHAT'S WRONG, JENNY?
I DON'T LIKE HIM.
LOUIE WON'T HURT YOU. HE'S A NICE OLD COLLIE DOG.
SEE? JAMIE'S PETTING HIM. JAMIE DOESN'T MIND OL' LOUIE.

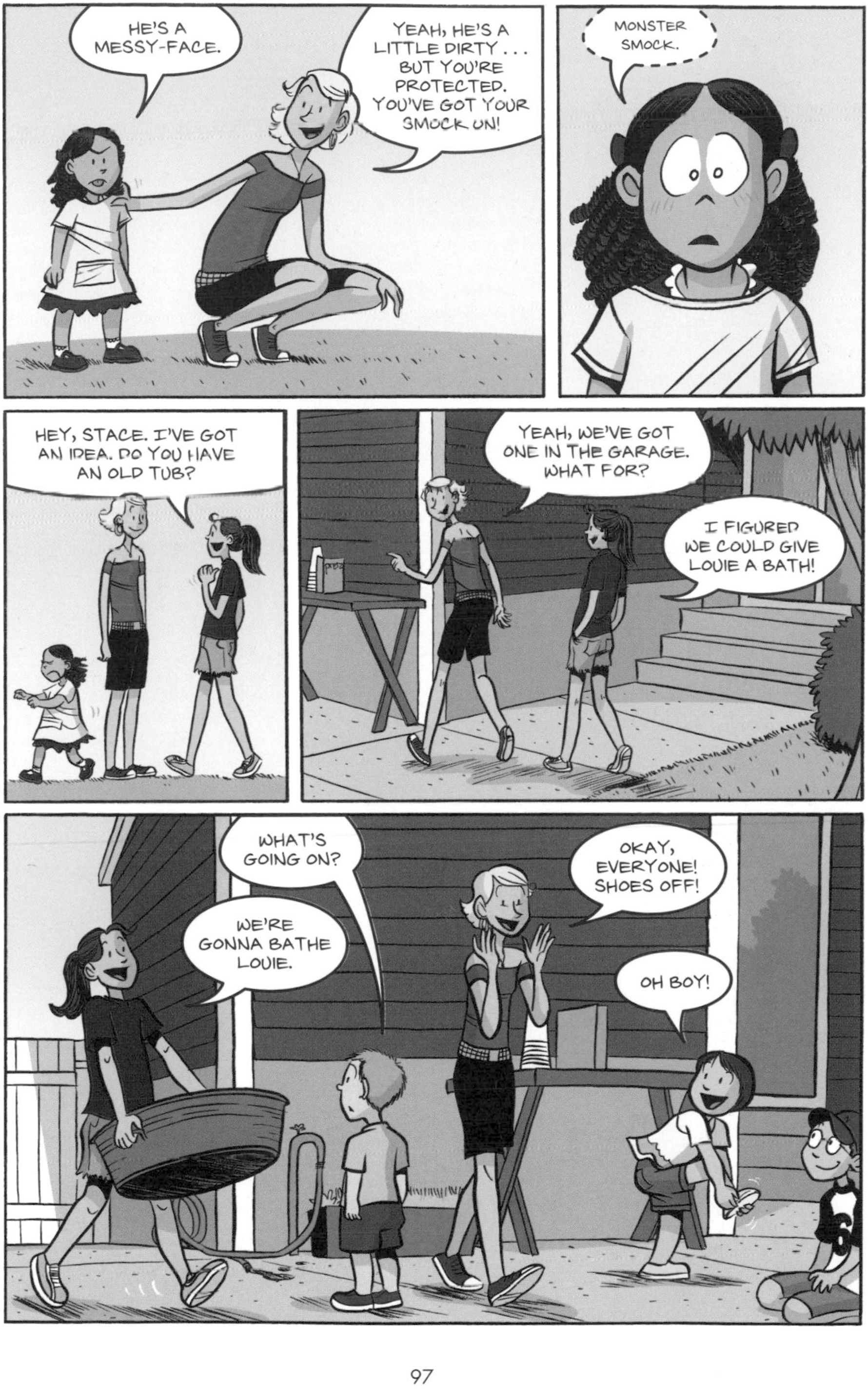
HE'S A MESSY-FACE.
YEAH, HE'S A LITTLE DIRTY . . . BUT YOU'RE PROTECTED. YOU'VE GOT YOUR SMOCK ON!
MONSTER SMOCK.
HEY, STACE. I'VE GOT AN IDEA. DO YOU HAVE AN OLD TUB?
YEAH, WE'VE GOT ONE IN THE GARAGE. WHAT FOR?
I FIGURED WE COULD GIVE LOUIE A BATH!
WHAT'S GOING ON?
WE'RE GONNA BATHE LOUIE.
OKAY, EVERYONE! SHOES OFF!
OH BOY!

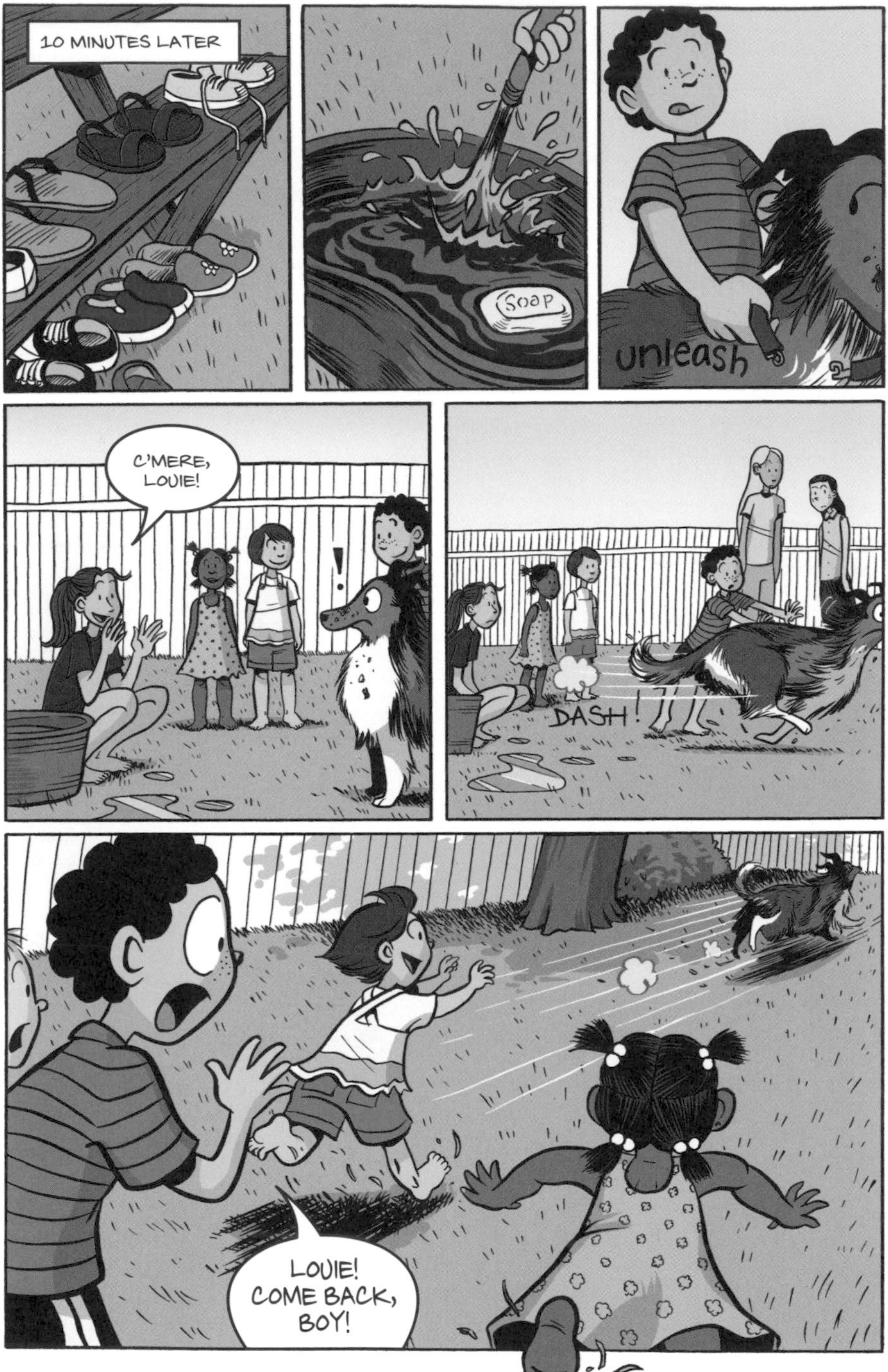

10 MINUTES LATER
Soap
unleash
C'MERE, LOUIE!
!
DASH!
LOUIE! COME BACK, BOY!

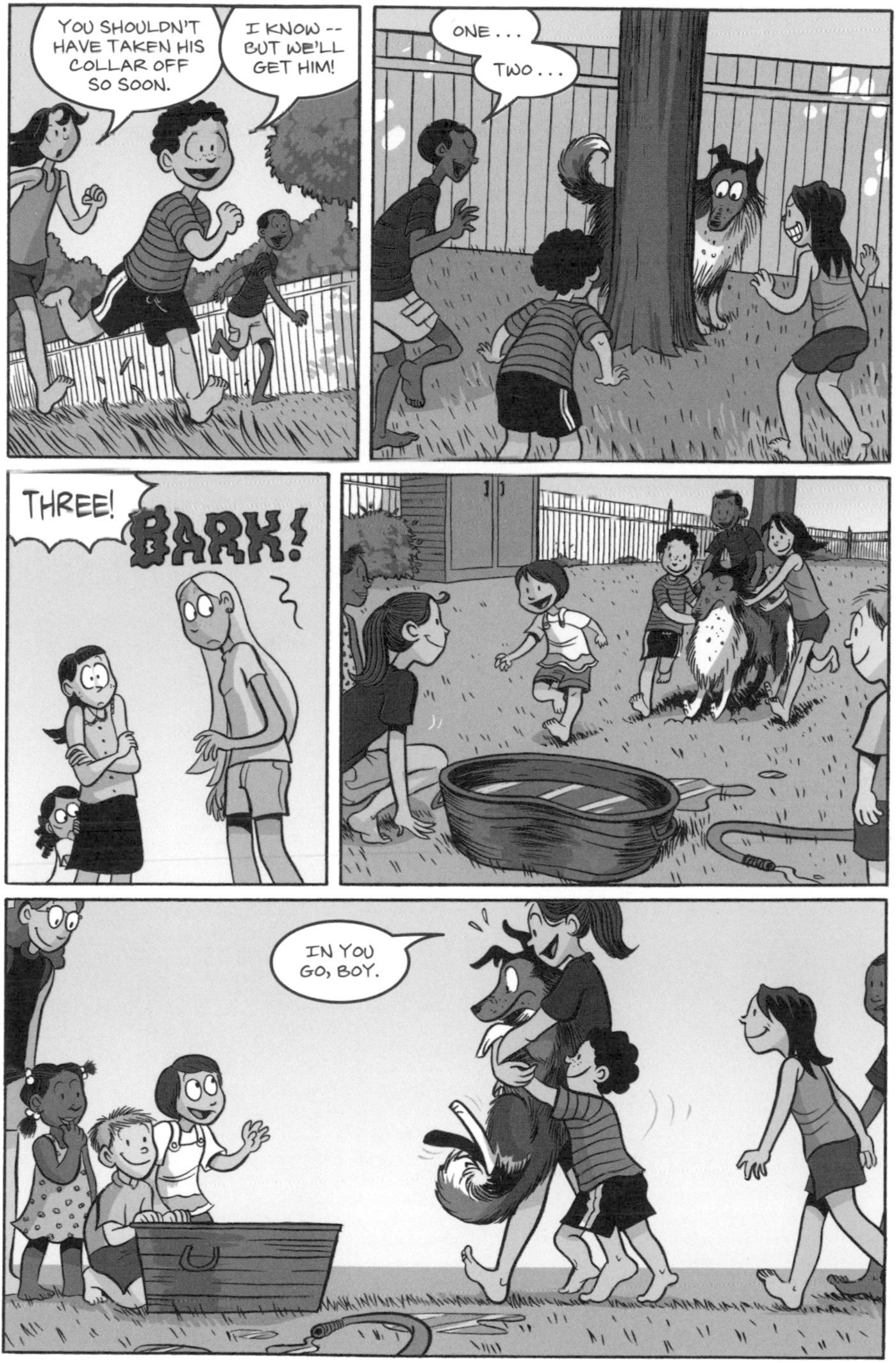
YOU SHOULDN'T HAVE TAKEN HIS COLLAR OFF SO SOON.
I KNOW -- BUT WE'LL GET HIM!
ONE . . .
TWO . . .
THREE!
BARK!
IN YOU GO, BOY.

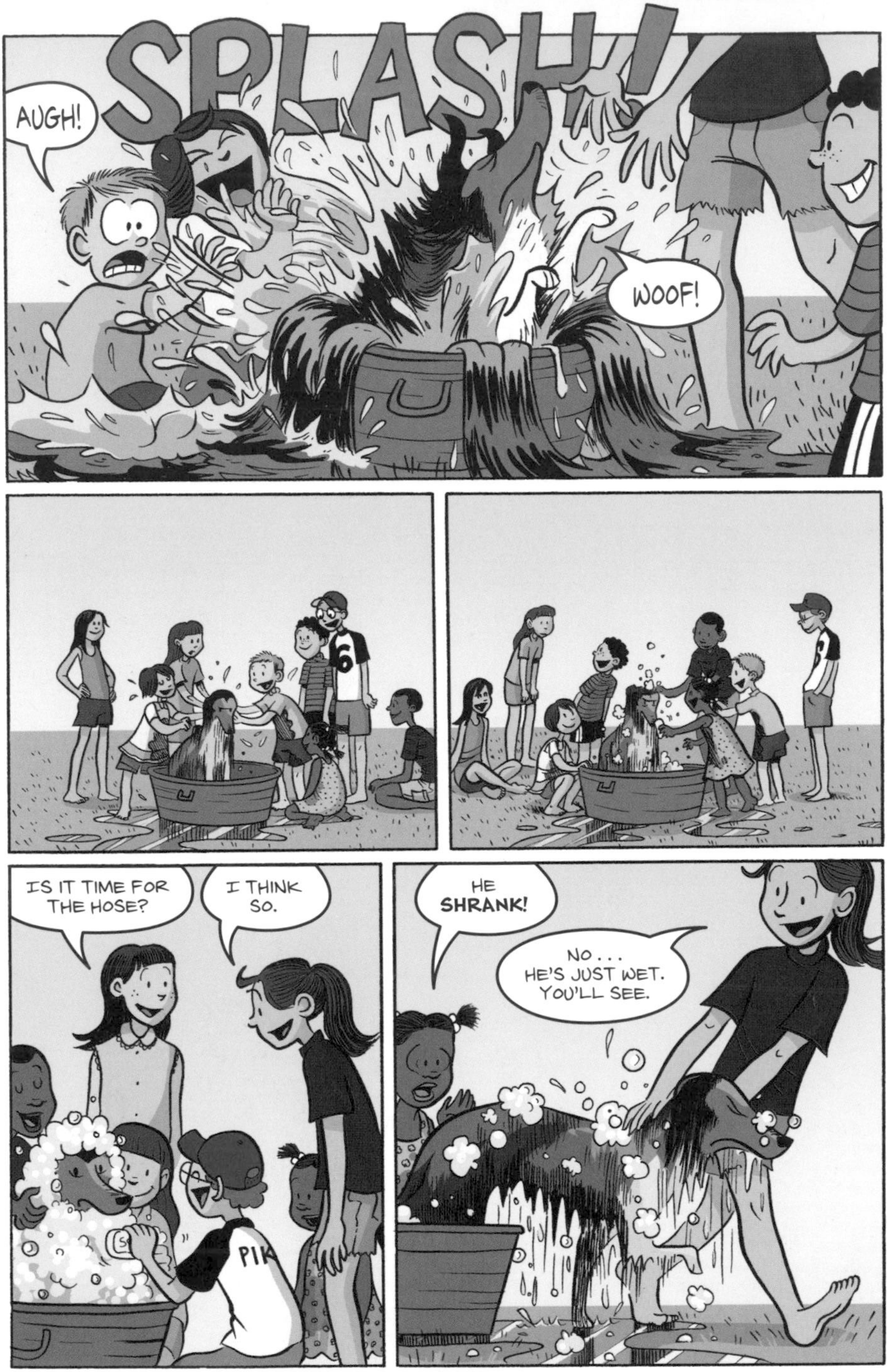
SPLASH!
AUGH!
WOOF!
IS IT TIME FOR THE HOSE?
I THINK SO.
PIK
HE **SHRANK!**
NO . . . HE'S JUST WET. YOU'LL SEE.

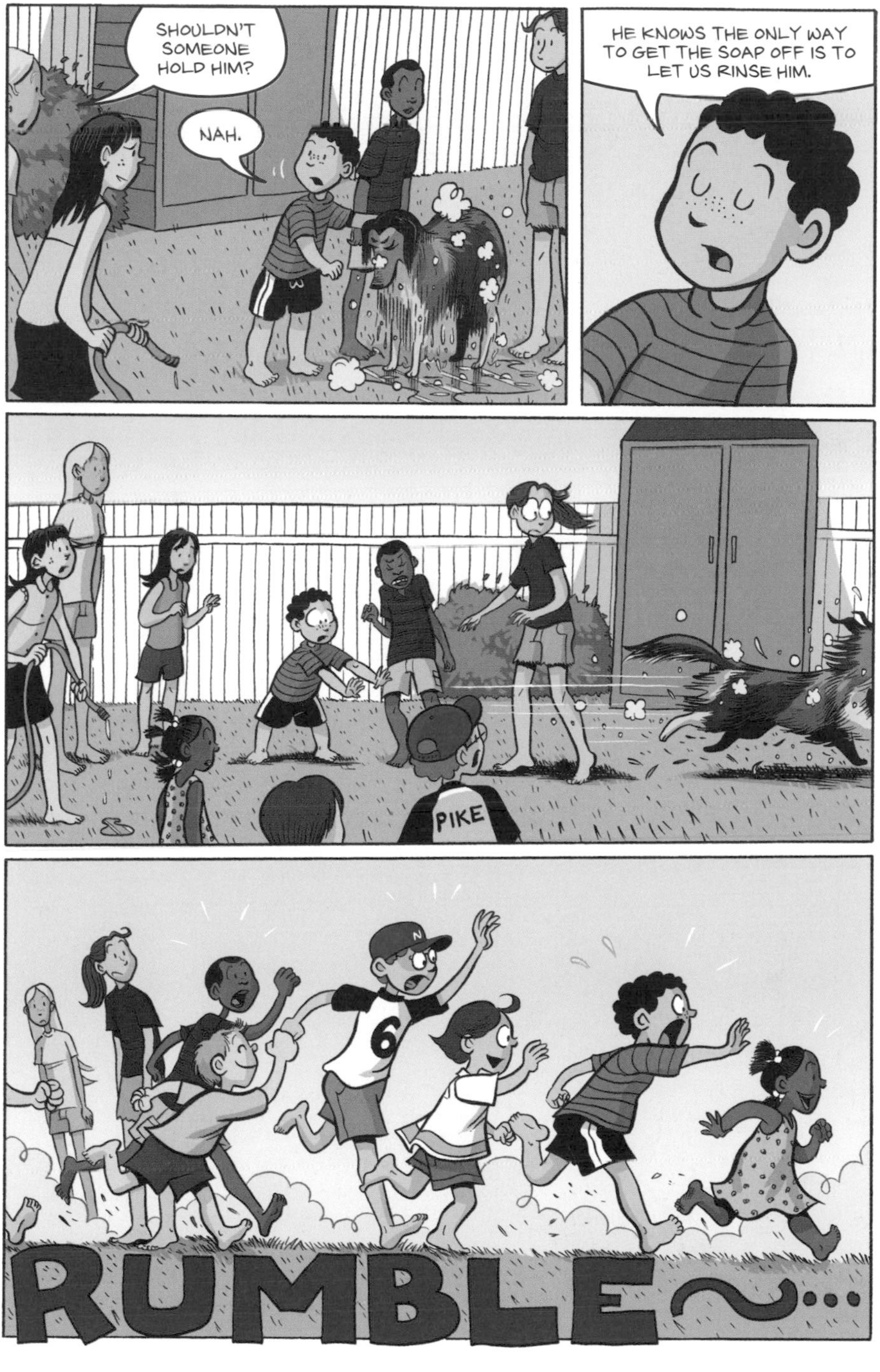
SHOULDN'T SOMEONE HOLD HIM?
NAH.
HE KNOWS THE ONLY WAY TO GET THE SOAP OFF IS TO LET US RINSE HIM.
PIKE
N
6
RUMBLE~...

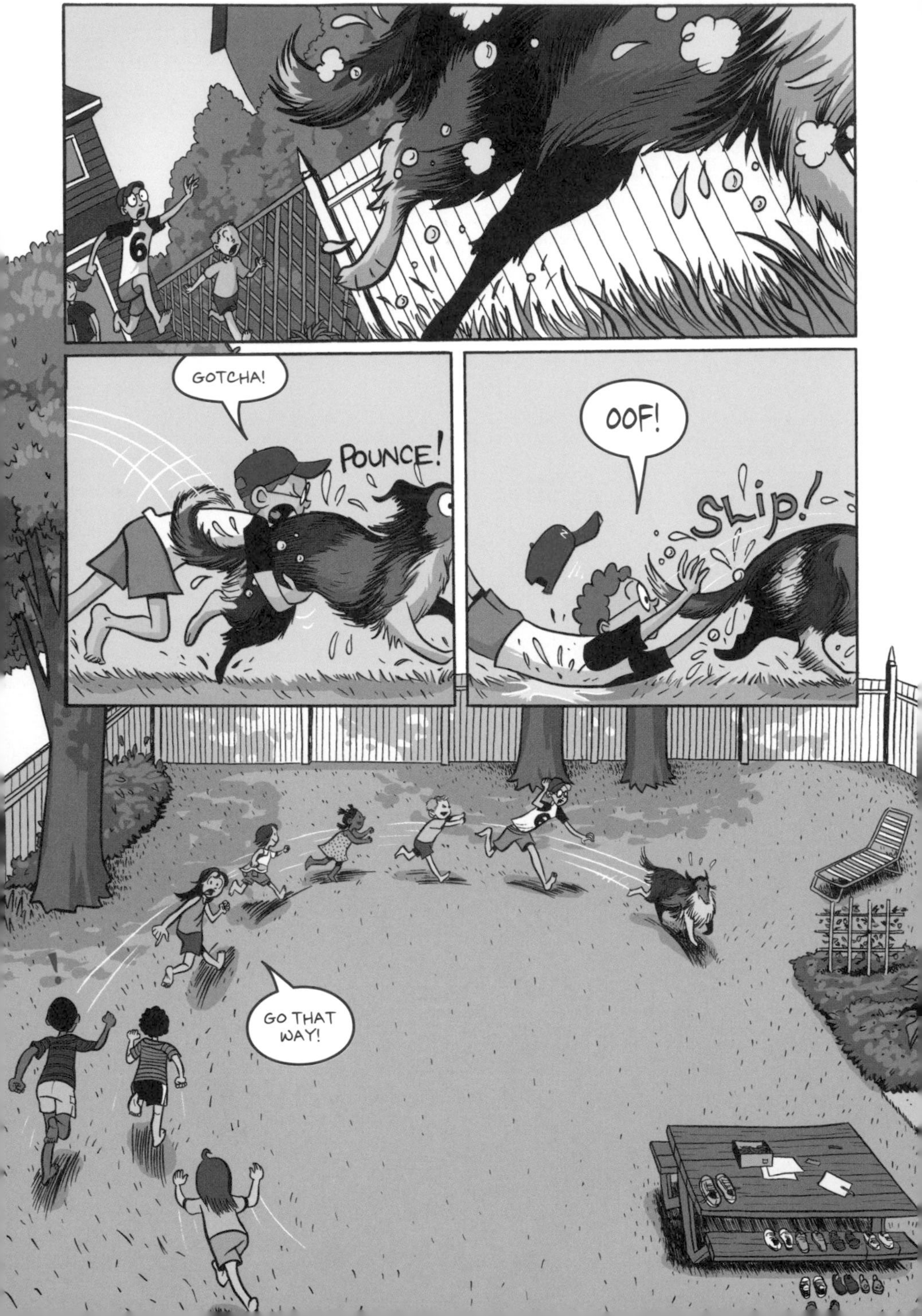
GOTCHA!
POUNCE!
OOF!
SLIP!
GO THAT WAY!

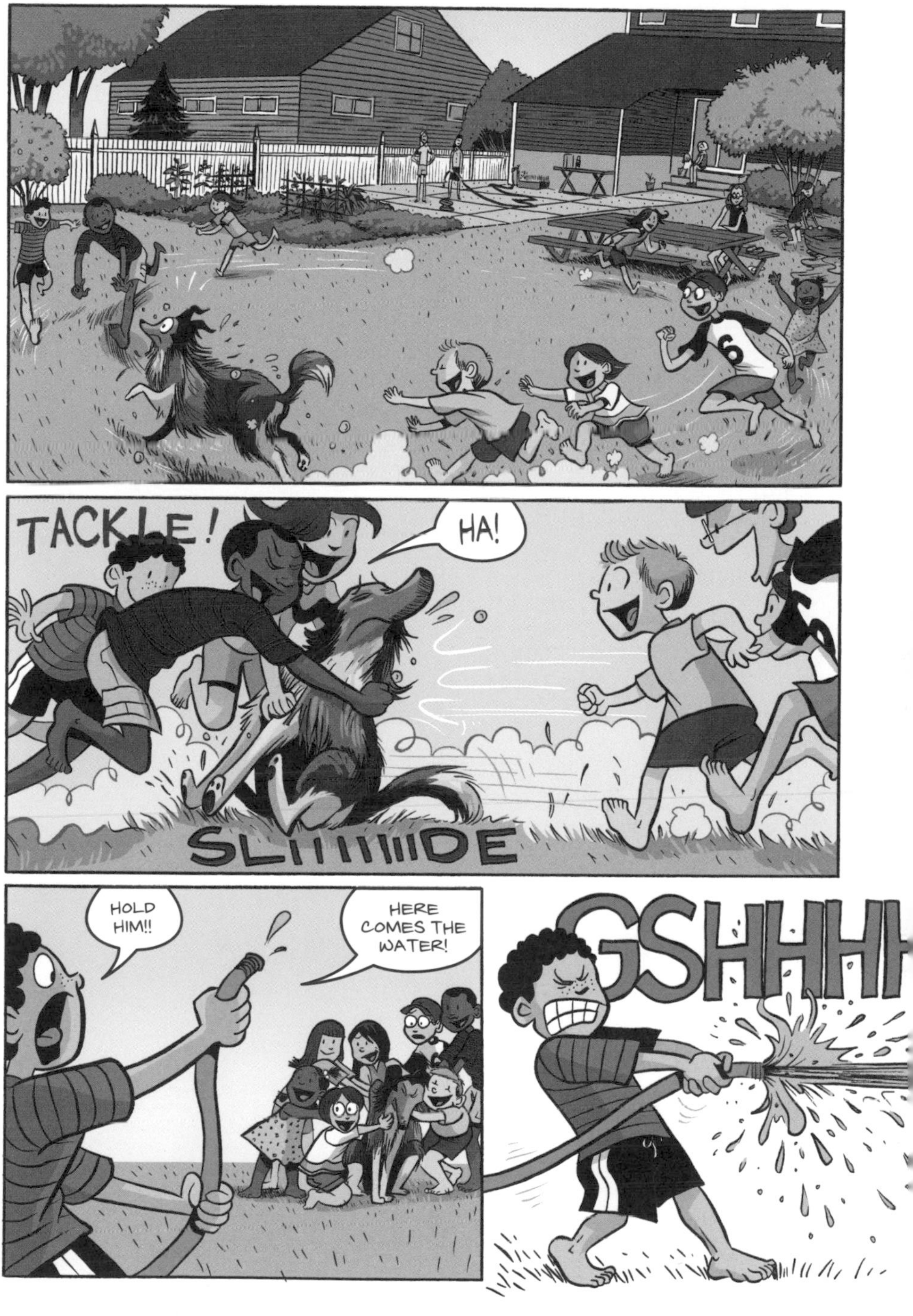
TACKLE!
HA!
SLIIIIIIDE
HOLD HIM!!
HERE COMES THE WATER!
GSHHH

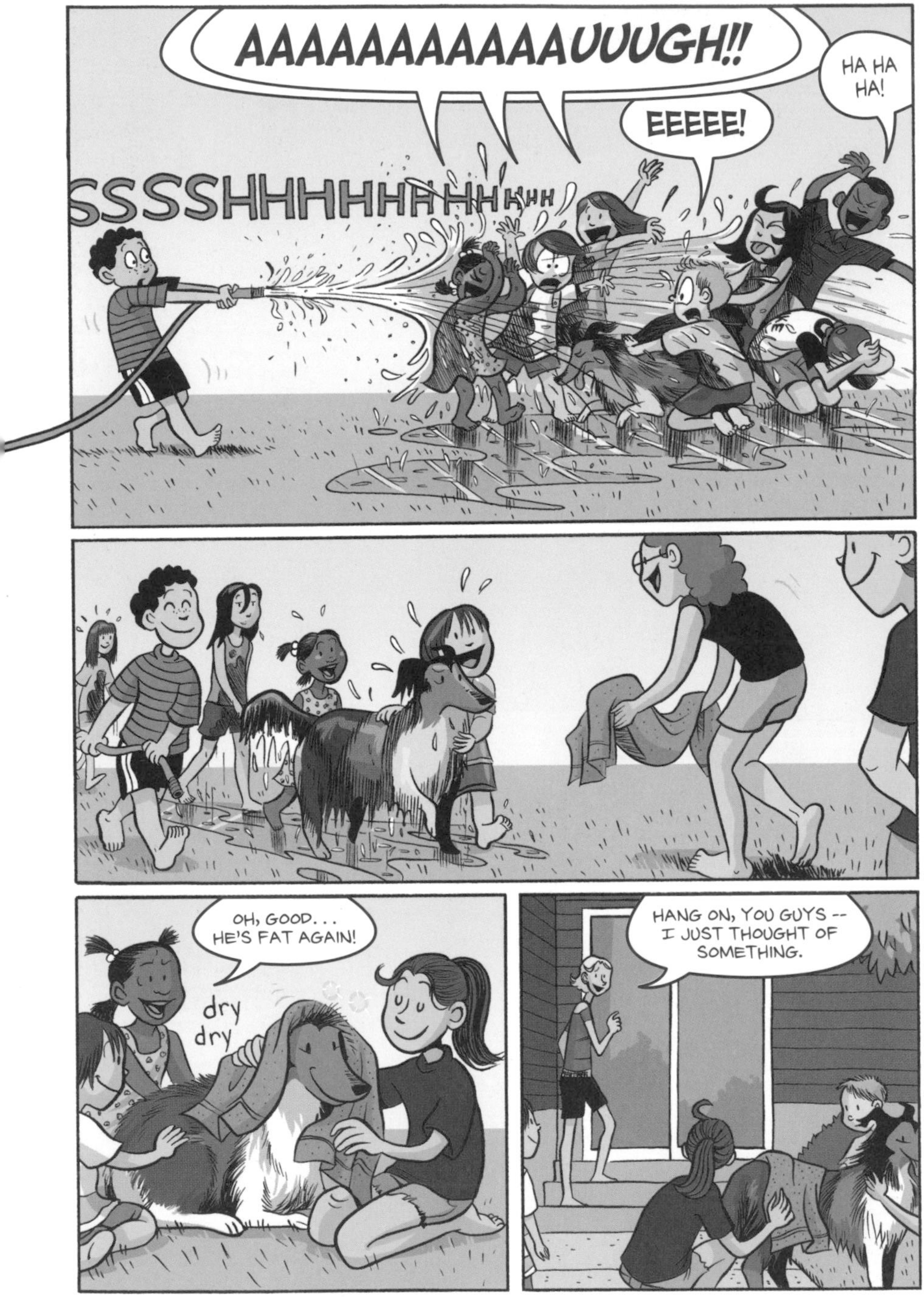
AAAAAAAAAAAAUUUGH!!
HA HA HA!
EEEEE!
SSSSHHHHHHHHHHH
OH, GOOD...
HE'S FAT AGAIN!
dry
dry
HANG ON, YOU GUYS --
I JUST THOUGHT OF SOMETHING.

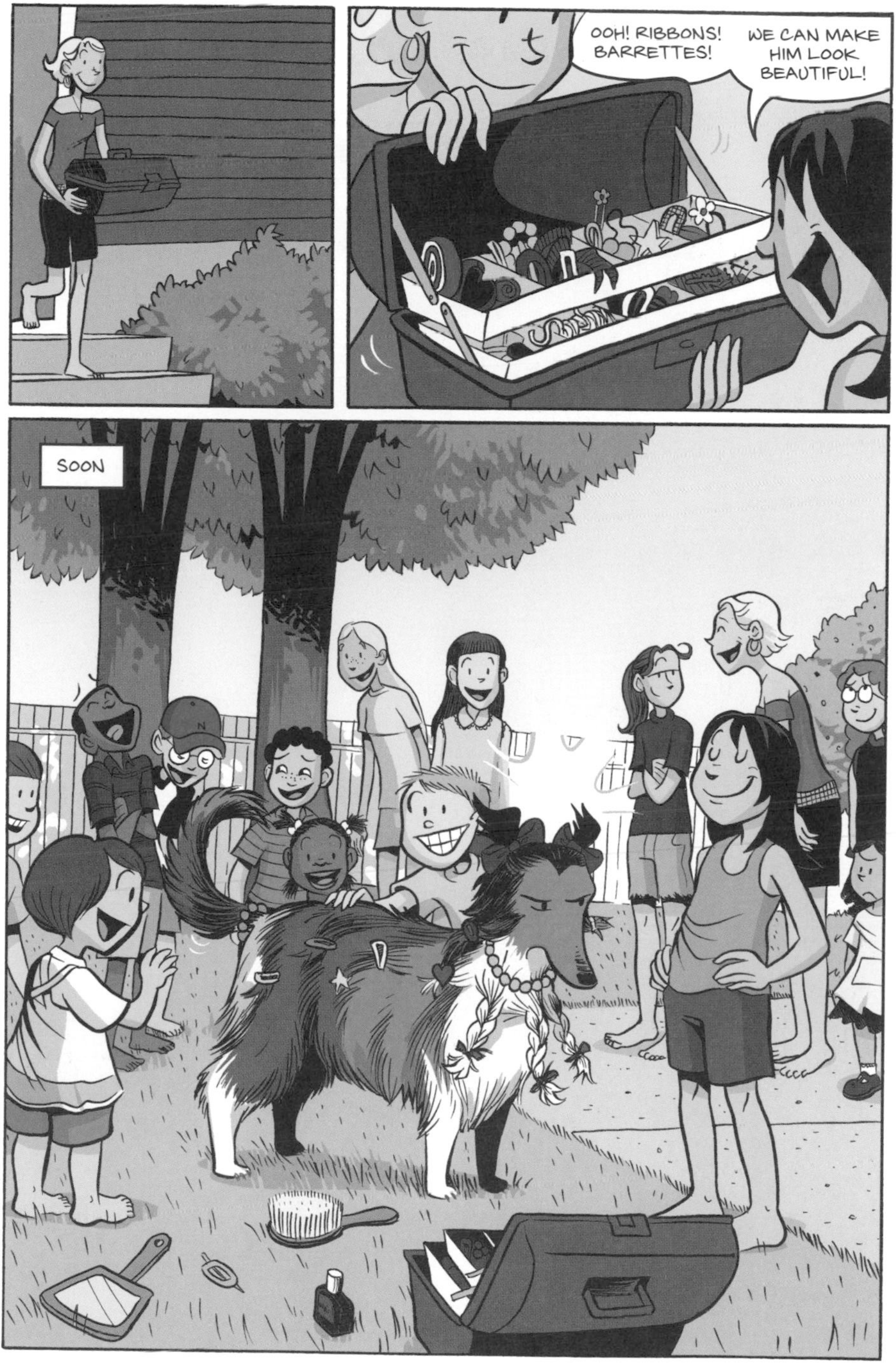
OOH! RIBBONS! BARRETTES!
WE CAN MAKE HIM LOOK BEAUTIFUL!
SOON

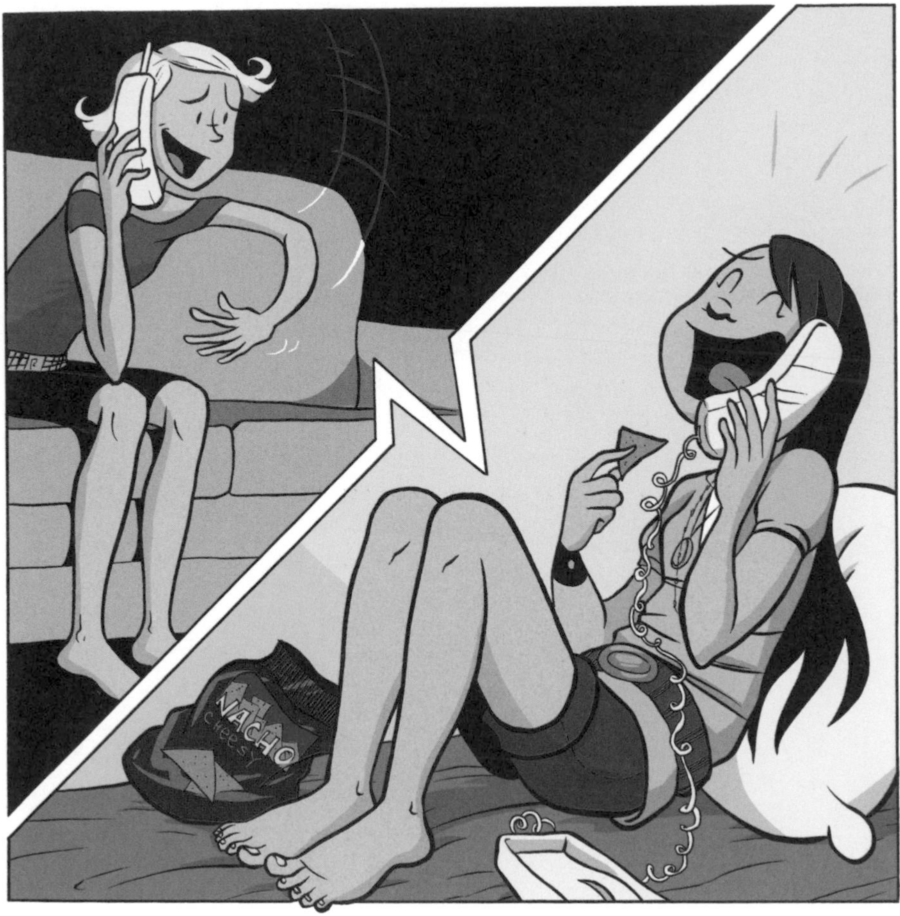
NACHO
cheesy

CHAPTER 13

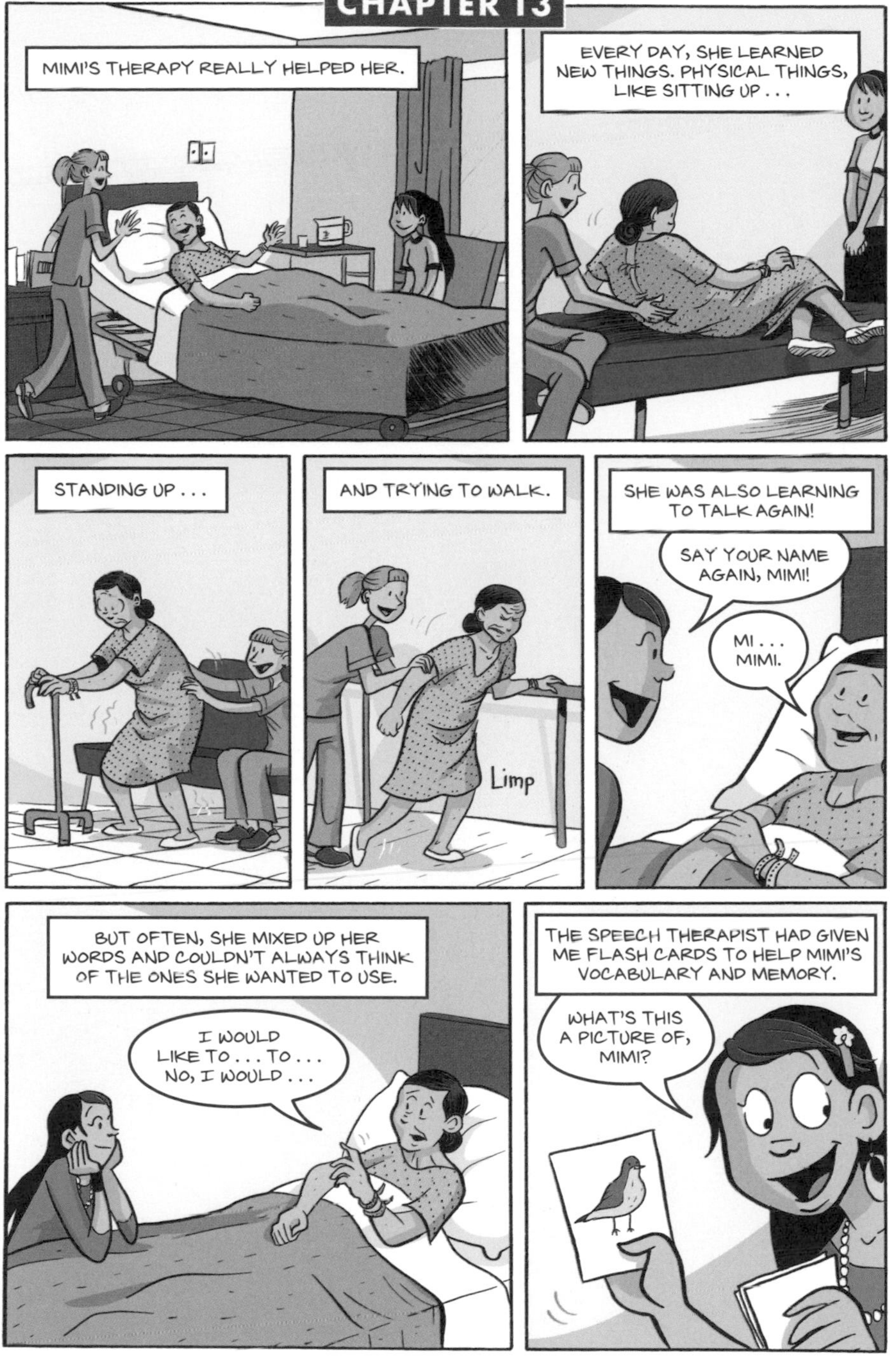
MIMI'S THERAPY REALLY HELPED HER.
EVERY DAY, SHE LEARNED NEW THINGS. PHYSICAL THINGS, LIKE SITTING UP . . .
STANDING UP . . .
AND TRYING TO WALK.
Limp
SHE WAS ALSO LEARNING TO TALK AGAIN!
SAY YOUR NAME AGAIN, MIMI!
MI . . . MIMI.
BUT OFTEN, SHE MIXED UP HER WORDS AND COULDN'T ALWAYS THINK OF THE ONES SHE WANTED TO USE.
I WOULD LIKE TO . . . TO . . . NO, I WOULD . . .
THE SPEECH THERAPIST HAD GIVEN ME FLASH CARDS TO HELP MIMI'S VOCABULARY AND MEMORY.
WHAT'S THIS A PICTURE OF, MIMI?

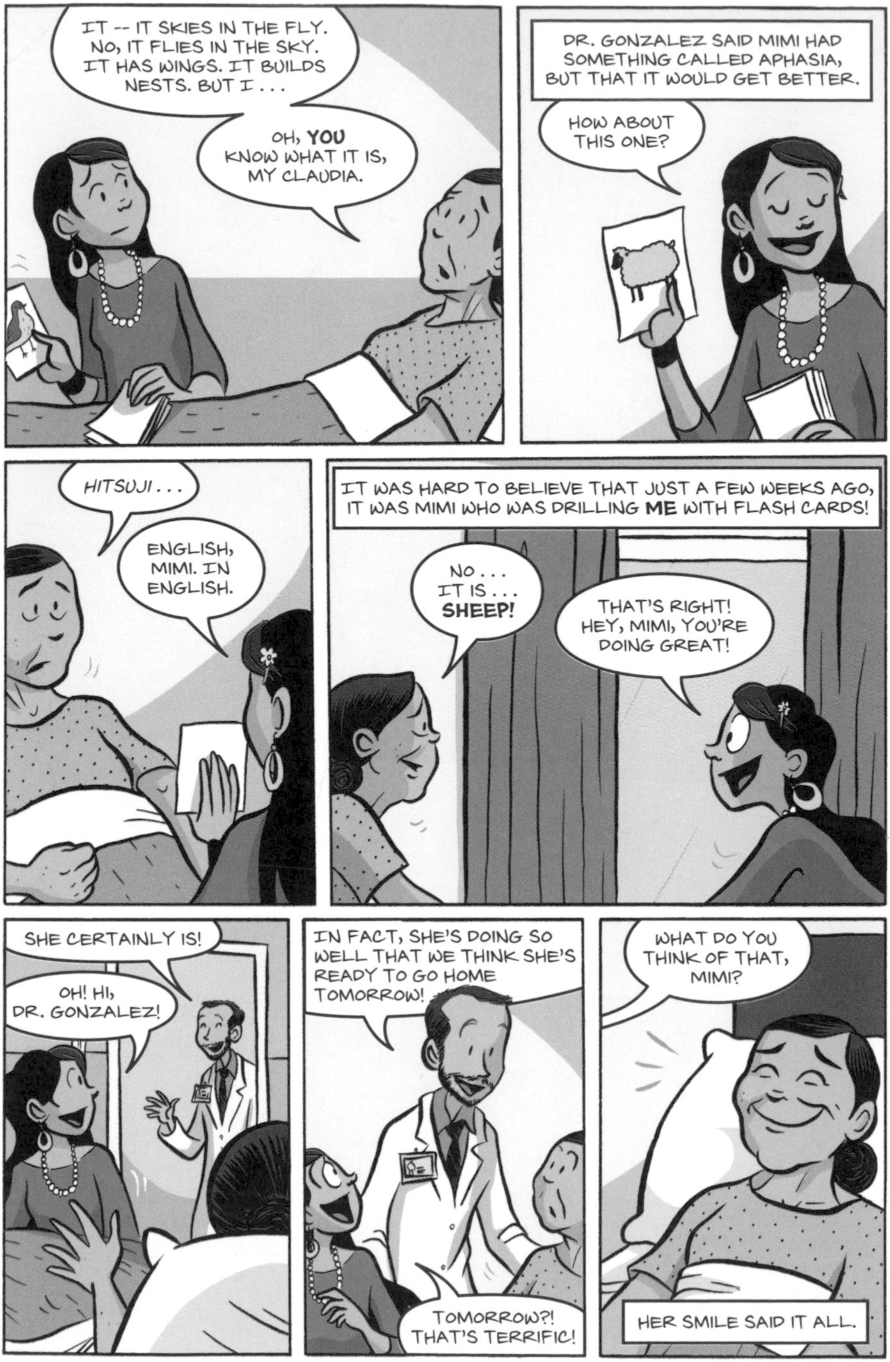
IT -- IT SKIES IN THE FLY. NO, IT FLIES IN THE SKY. IT HAS WINGS. IT BUILDS NESTS. BUT I . . .
OH, **YOU** KNOW WHAT IT IS, MY CLAUDIA.
DR. GONZALEZ SAID MIMI HAD SOMETHING CALLED APHASIA, BUT THAT IT WOULD GET BETTER.
HOW ABOUT THIS ONE?
HITSUJI . . .
ENGLISH, MIMI. IN ENGLISH.
IT WAS HARD TO BELIEVE THAT JUST A FEW WEEKS AGO, IT WAS MIMI WHO WAS DRILLING **ME** WITH FLASH CARDS!
NO . . . IT IS . . . **SHEEP!**
THAT'S RIGHT! HEY, MIMI, YOU'RE DOING GREAT!
SHE CERTAINLY IS!
OH! HI, DR. GONZALEZ!
IN FACT, SHE'S DOING SO WELL THAT WE THINK SHE'S READY TO GO HOME TOMORROW!
TOMORROW?! THAT'S TERRIFIC!
WHAT DO YOU THINK OF THAT, MIMI?
HER SMILE SAID IT ALL.

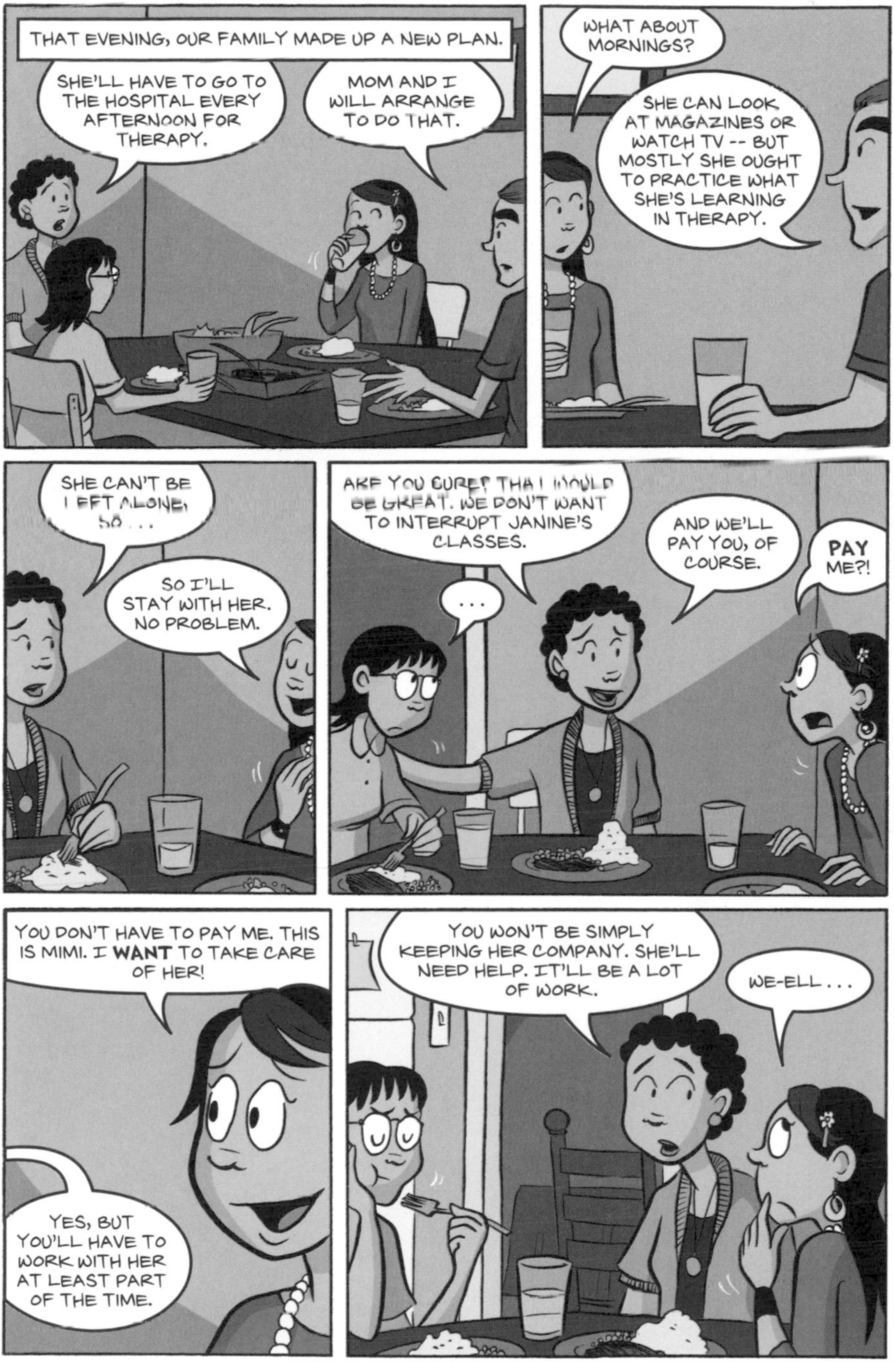
THAT EVENING, OUR FAMILY MADE UP A NEW PLAN.
SHE'LL HAVE TO GO TO THE HOSPITAL EVERY AFTERNOON FOR THERAPY.
MOM AND I WILL ARRANGE TO DO THAT.
WHAT ABOUT MORNINGS?
SHE CAN LOOK AT MAGAZINES OR WATCH TV -- BUT MOSTLY SHE OUGHT TO PRACTICE WHAT SHE'S LEARNING IN THERAPY.
SHE CAN'T BE LEFT ALONE, SO . . .
SO I'LL STAY WITH HER. NO PROBLEM.
ARE YOU SURE? THAT WOULD BE GREAT. WE DON'T WANT TO INTERRUPT JANINE'S CLASSES.
. . .
AND WE'LL PAY YOU, OF COURSE.
PAY ME?!
YOU DON'T HAVE TO PAY ME. THIS IS MIMI. I WANT TO TAKE CARE OF HER!
YES, BUT YOU'LL HAVE TO WORK WITH HER AT LEAST PART OF THE TIME.
YOU WON'T BE SIMPLY KEEPING HER COMPANY. SHE'LL NEED HELP. IT'LL BE A LOT OF WORK.
WE-ELL . . .

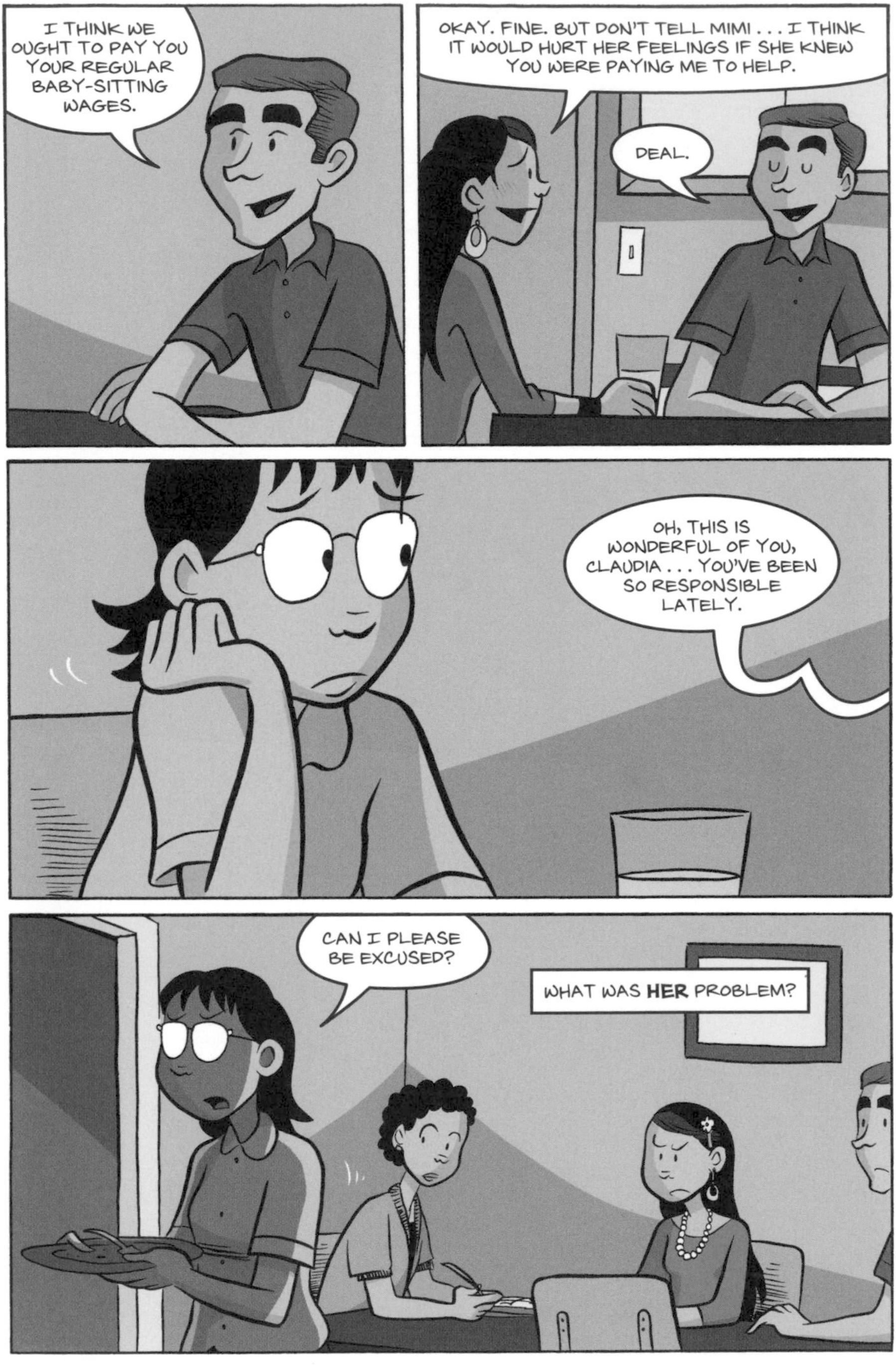
I THINK WE OUGHT TO PAY YOU YOUR REGULAR BABY-SITTING WAGES.
OKAY. FINE. BUT DON'T TELL MIMI . . . I THINK IT WOULD HURT HER FEELINGS IF SHE KNEW YOU WERE PAYING ME TO HELP.
DEAL.
OH, THIS IS WONDERFUL OF YOU, CLAUDIA . . . YOU'VE BEEN SO RESPONSIBLE LATELY.
CAN I PLEASE BE EXCUSED?
WHAT WAS **HER** PROBLEM?

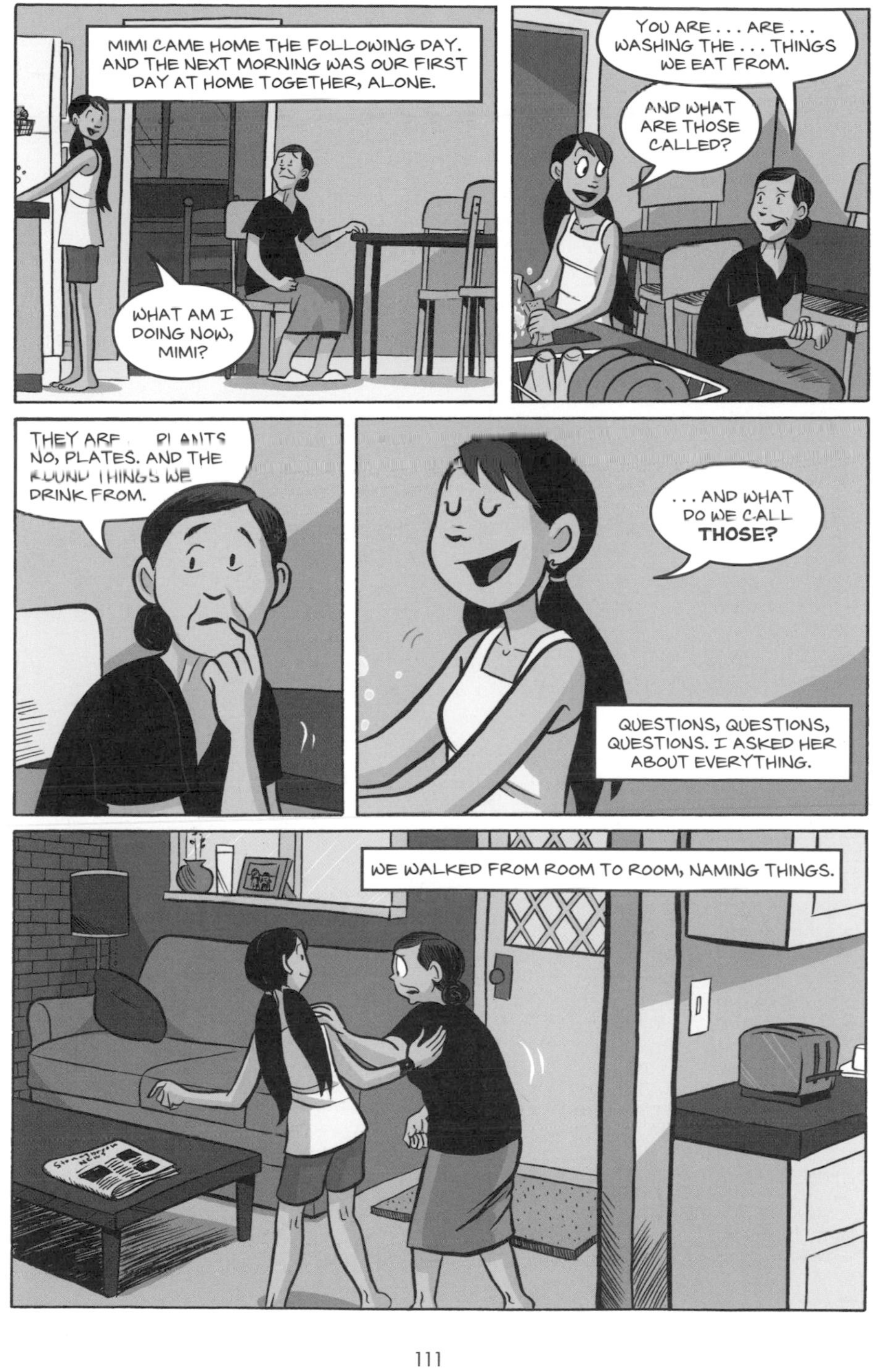
MIMI CAME HOME THE FOLLOWING DAY. AND THE NEXT MORNING WAS OUR FIRST DAY AT HOME TOGETHER, ALONE.
WHAT AM I DOING NOW, MIMI?
YOU ARE . . . ARE . . . WASHING THE . . . THINGS WE EAT FROM.
AND WHAT ARE THOSE CALLED?
THEY ARE PLANTS NO, PLATES. AND THE ROUND THINGS WE DRINK FROM.
. . . AND WHAT DO WE CALL **THOSE?**
QUESTIONS, QUESTIONS, QUESTIONS. I ASKED HER ABOUT EVERYTHING.
WE WALKED FROM ROOM TO ROOM, NAMING THINGS.

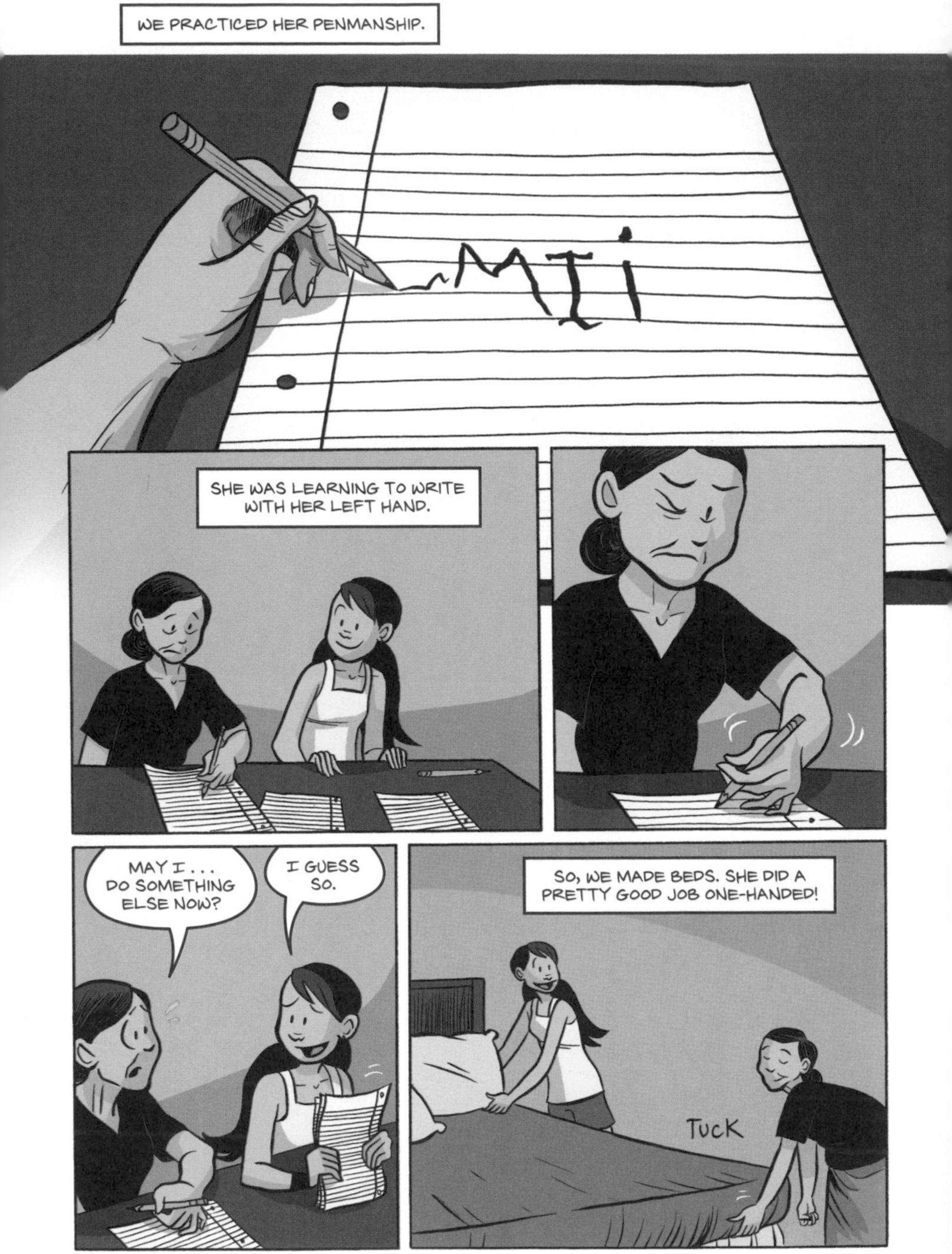
WE PRACTICED HER PENMANSHIP.
SHE WAS LEARNING TO WRITE WITH HER LEFT HAND.
MAY I . . . DO SOMETHING ELSE NOW?
I GUESS SO.
SO, WE MADE BEDS. SHE DID A PRETTY GOOD JOB ONE-HANDED!
TUCK

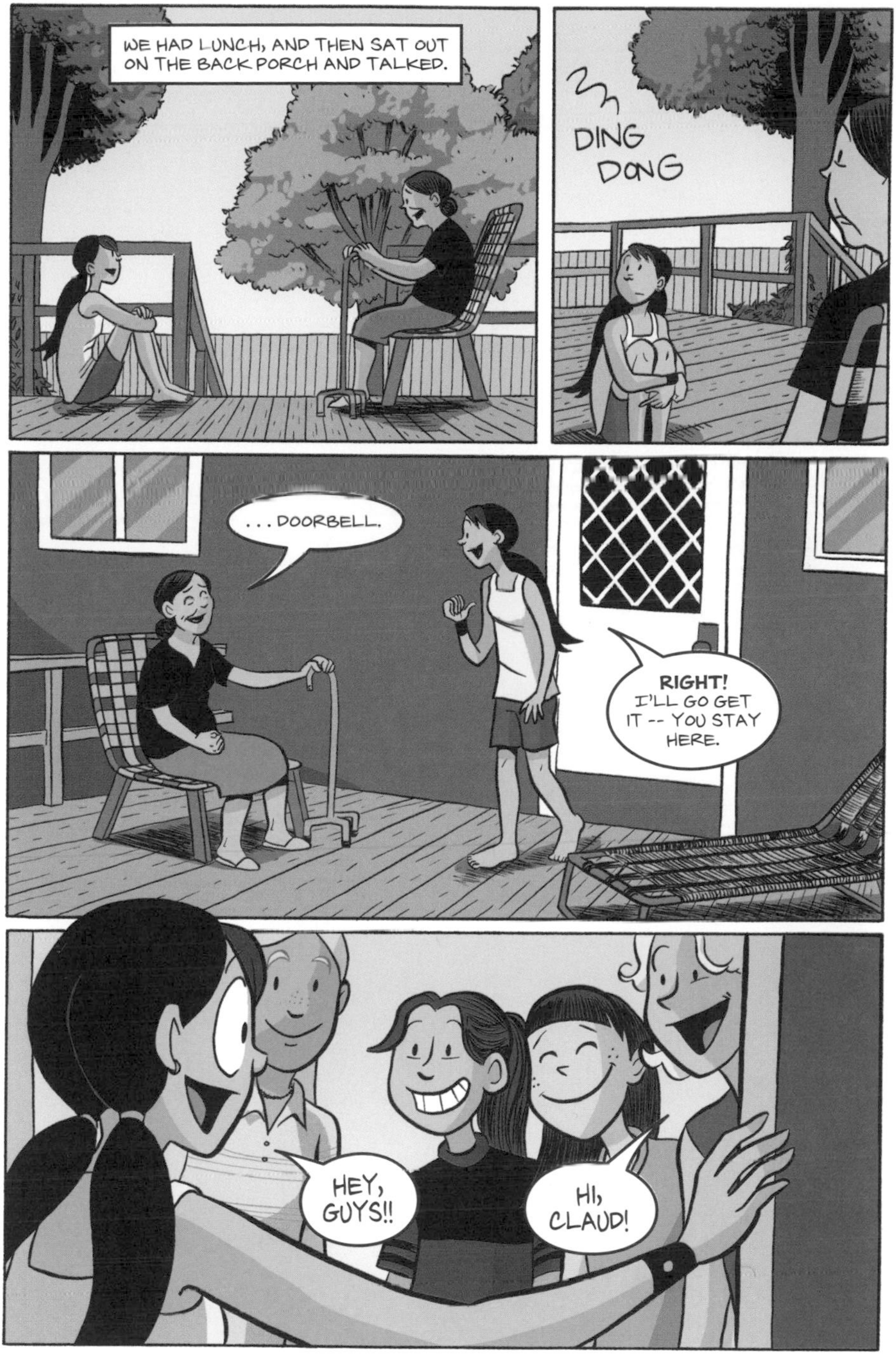
WE HAD LUNCH, AND THEN SAT OUT ON THE BACK PORCH AND TALKED.
DING DONG
. . . DOORBELL.
RIGHT! I'LL GO GET IT -- YOU STAY HERE.
HEY, GUYS!!
HI, CLAUD!

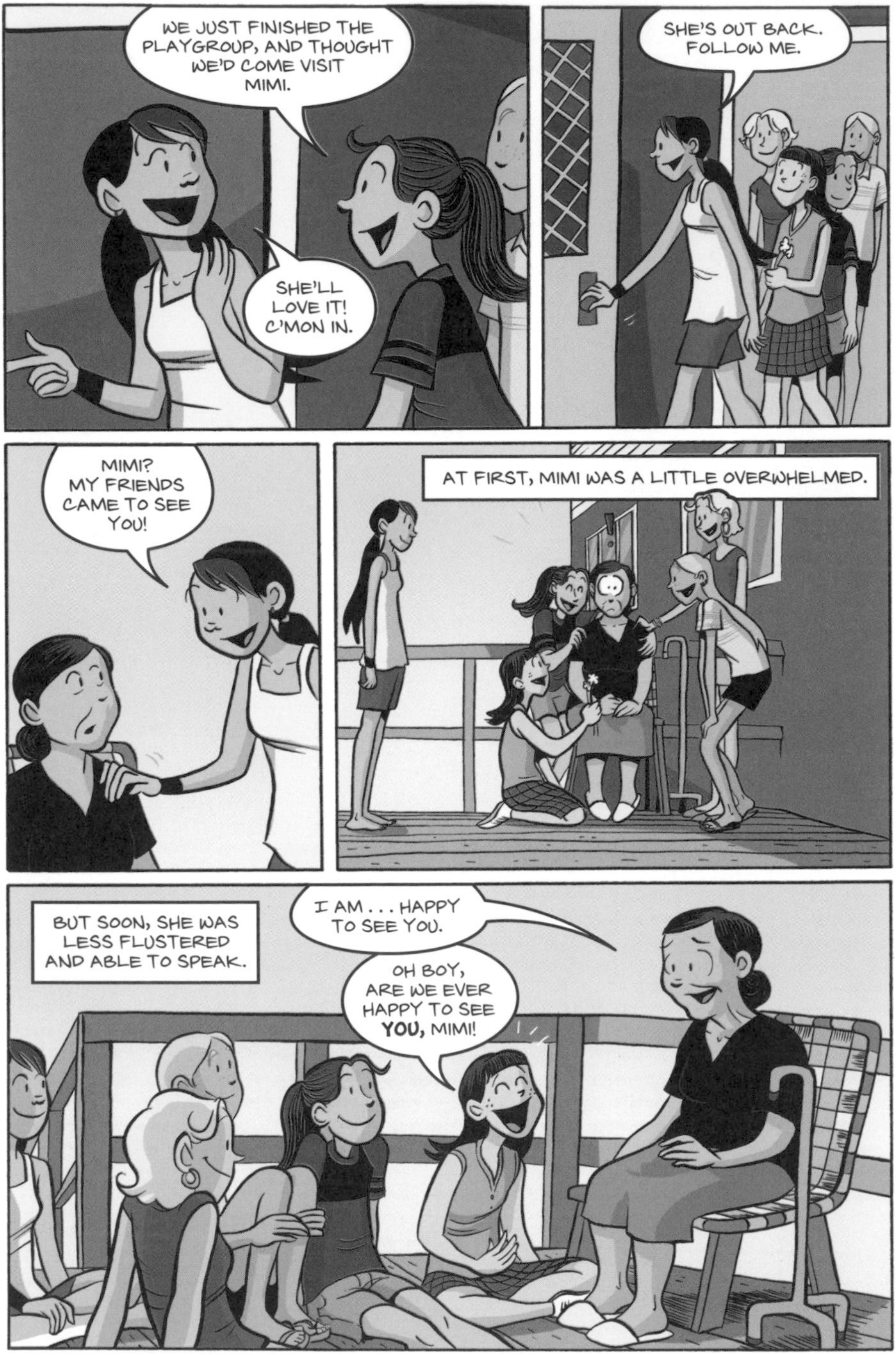
WE JUST FINISHED THE PLAYGROUP, AND THOUGHT WE'D COME VISIT MIMI.
SHE'LL LOVE IT! C'MON IN.
SHE'S OUT BACK. FOLLOW ME.
MIMI? MY FRIENDS CAME TO SEE YOU!
AT FIRST, MIMI WAS A LITTLE OVERWHELMED.
BUT SOON, SHE WAS LESS FLUSTERED AND ABLE TO SPEAK.
I AM . . . HAPPY TO SEE YOU.
OH BOY, ARE WE EVER HAPPY TO SEE **YOU,** MIMI!

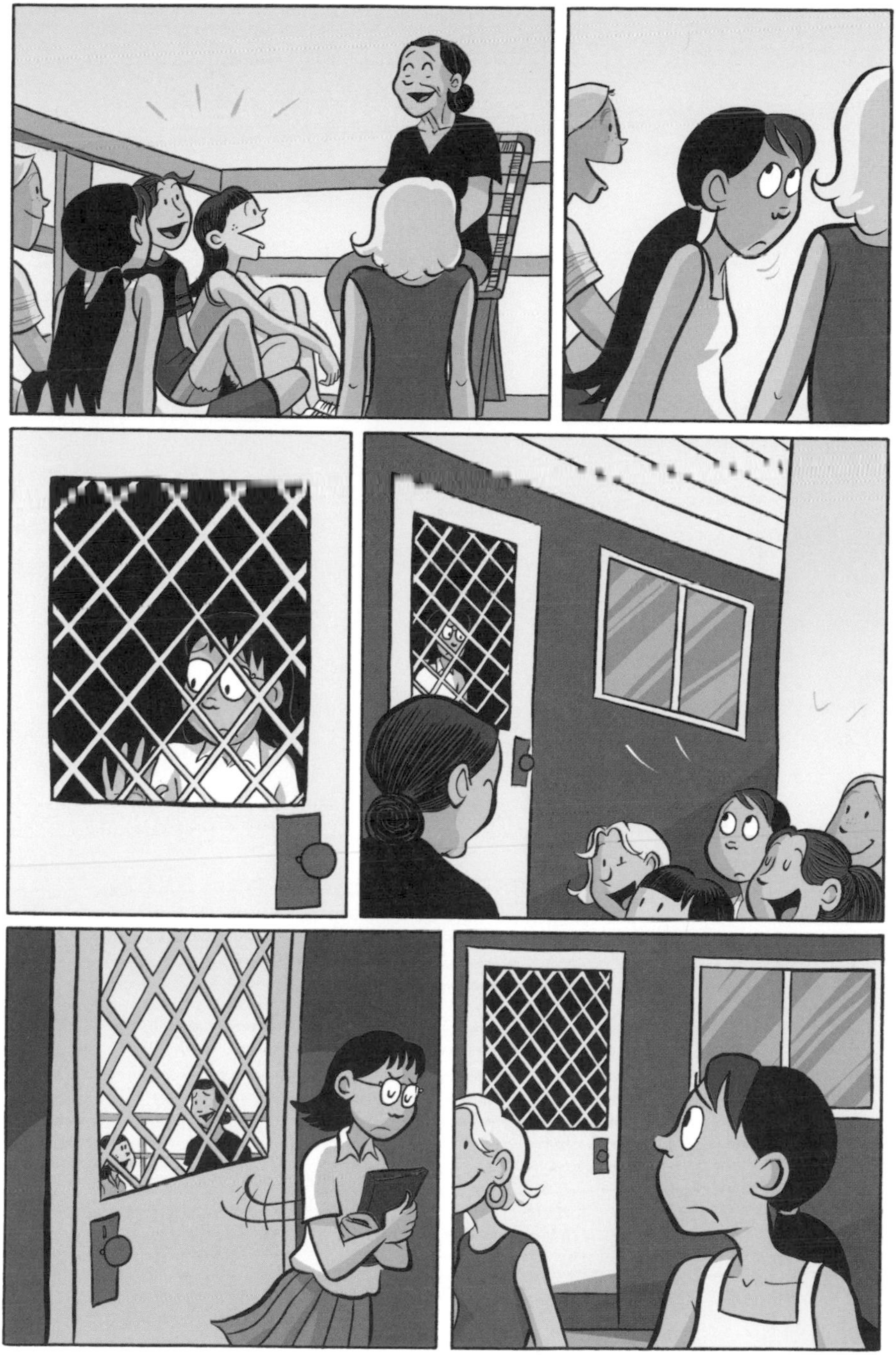

Friday, July 18

This morning I didn't baby-sit . . .

I Mimi-sat!

Claudia was helping out at the Newtons' all day, so Mrs. Kishi asked if I could stay with Mimi. I was happy to, of course, but I wasn't expecting Mimi to be so different. She can't even remember the simplest things sometimes.

In case any of you stays with Mimi while she's getting better, you should know that she gets upset easily. Frustrated, I guess. She yelled at me and Mimi has never, ever yelled at me. In fact, Claudia told me later that Mimi has never yelled at anyone in their family, so I assume Mimi was embarrassed about needing a sitter in the first place.

Mary Anne

CHAPTER 14

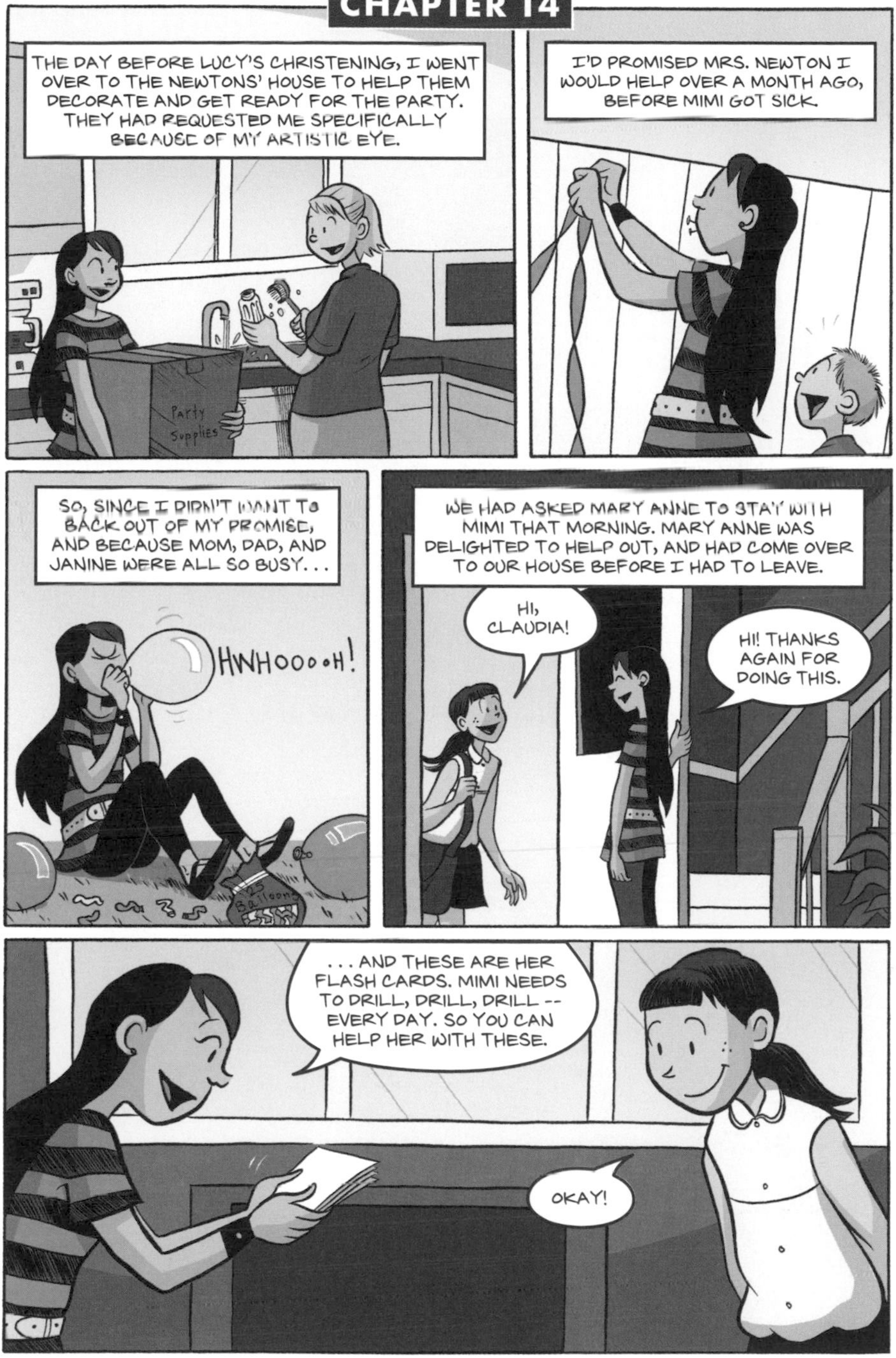

THE DAY BEFORE LUCY'S CHRISTENING, I WENT OVER TO THE NEWTONS' HOUSE TO HELP THEM DECORATE AND GET READY FOR THE PARTY. THEY HAD REQUESTED ME SPECIFICALLY BECAUSE OF MY ARTISTIC EYE.
Party Supplies
I'D PROMISED MRS. NEWTON I WOULD HELP OVER A MONTH AGO, BEFORE MIMI GOT SICK.
SO, SINCE I DIDN'T WANT TO BACK OUT OF MY PROMISE, AND BECAUSE MOM, DAD, AND JANINE WERE ALL SO BUSY. . .
HWHOOOoH!
25 Balloons
WE HAD ASKED MARY ANNE TO STAY WITH MIMI THAT MORNING. MARY ANNE WAS DELIGHTED TO HELP OUT, AND HAD COME OVER TO OUR HOUSE BEFORE I HAD TO LEAVE.
HI, CLAUDIA!
HI! THANKS AGAIN FOR DOING THIS.
. . . AND THESE ARE HER FLASH CARDS. MIMI NEEDS TO DRILL, DRILL, DRILL -- EVERY DAY. SO YOU CAN HELP HER WITH THESE.
OKAY!

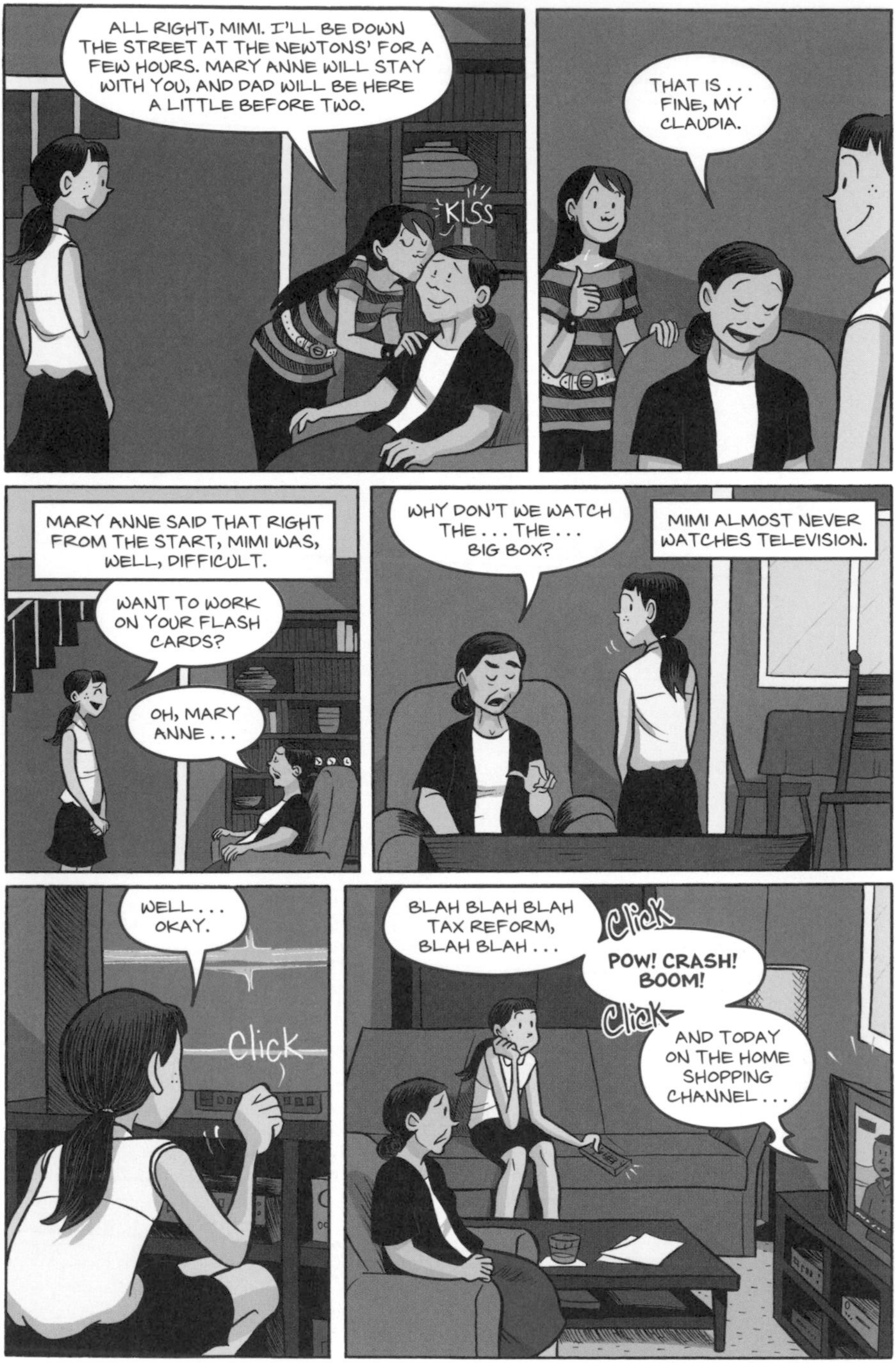
ALL RIGHT, MIMI. I'LL BE DOWN THE STREET AT THE NEWTONS' FOR A FEW HOURS. MARY ANNE WILL STAY WITH YOU, AND DAD WILL BE HERE A LITTLE BEFORE TWO.
KISS
THAT IS . . . FINE, MY CLAUDIA.
MARY ANNE SAID THAT RIGHT FROM THE START, MIMI WAS, WELL, DIFFICULT.
WANT TO WORK ON YOUR FLASH CARDS?
OH, MARY ANNE . . .
WHY DON'T WE WATCH THE . . . THE . . . BIG BOX?
MIMI ALMOST NEVER WATCHES TELEVISION.
WELL . . . OKAY.
Click
BLAH BLAH BLAH TAX REFORM, BLAH BLAH . . .
Click
POW! CRASH! BOOM!
Click
AND TODAY ON THE HOME SHOPPING CHANNEL . . .

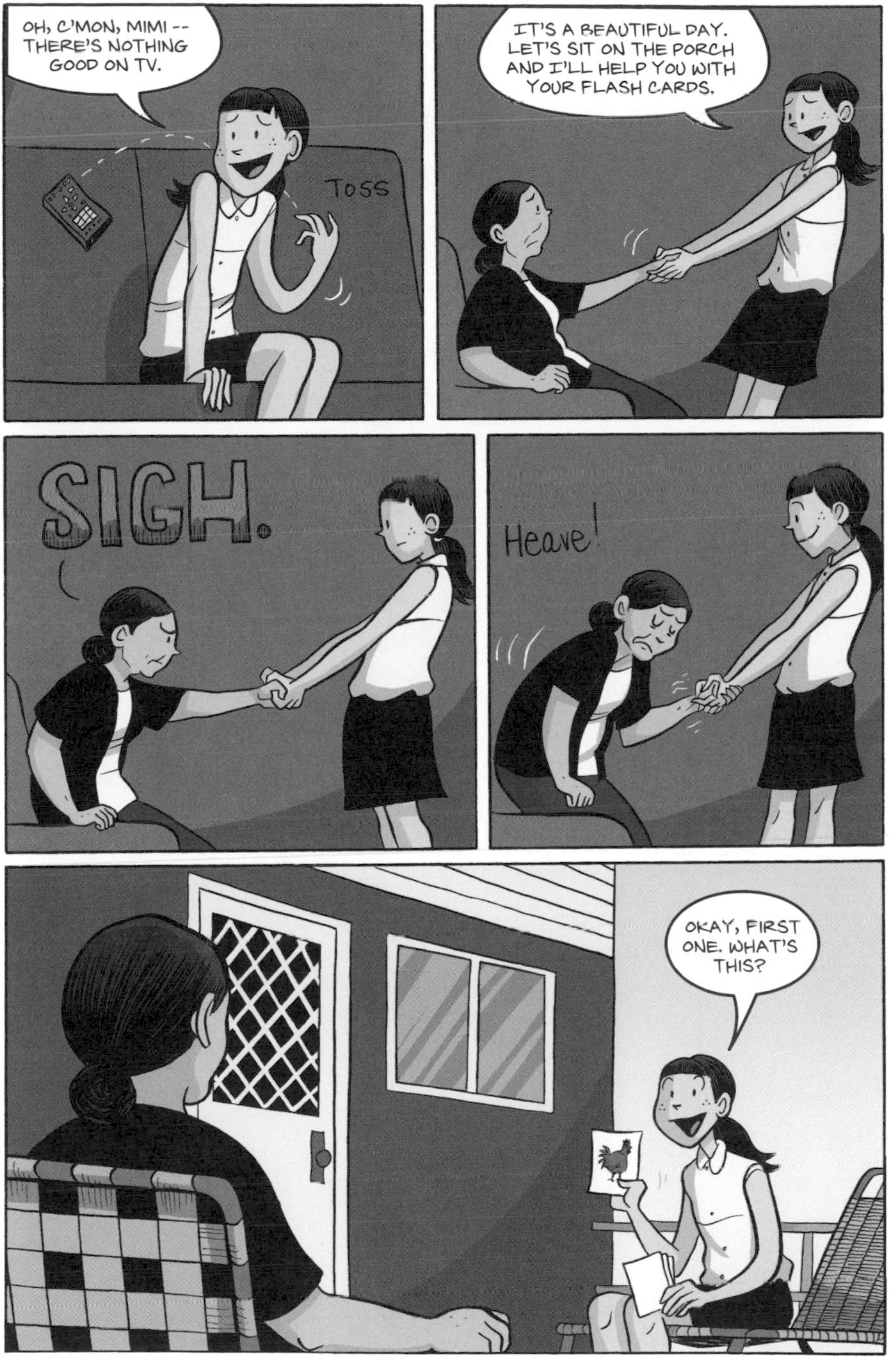
OH, C'MON, MIMI -- THERE'S NOTHING GOOD ON TV.
TOSS
IT'S A BEAUTIFUL DAY. LET'S SIT ON THE PORCH AND I'LL HELP YOU WITH YOUR FLASH CARDS.
SIGH.
Heave!
OKAY, FIRST ONE. WHAT'S THIS?

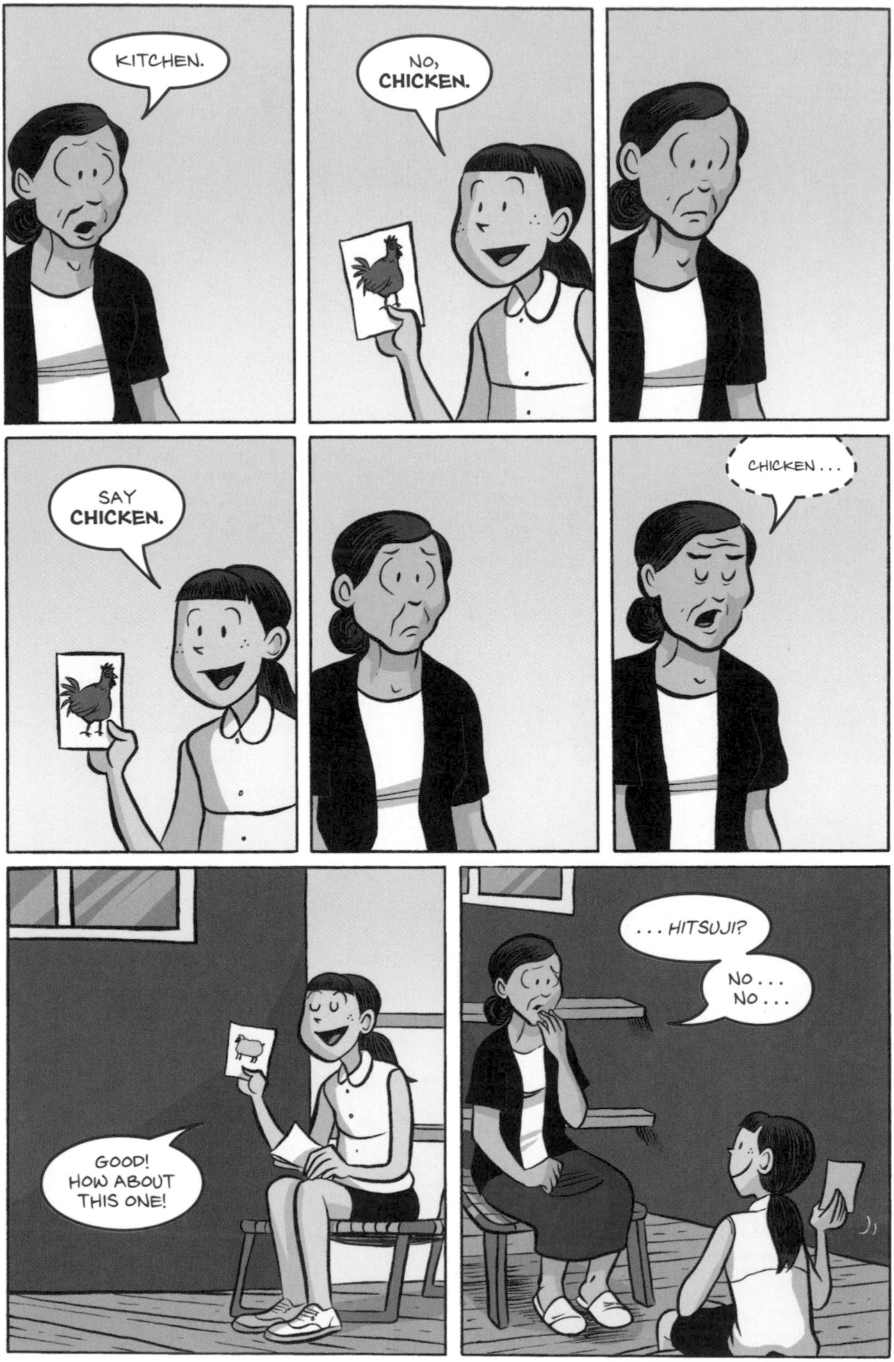
KITCHEN.
NO, **CHICKEN.**
SAY **CHICKEN.**
CHICKEN . . .
GOOD! HOW ABOUT THIS ONE!
. . . HITSUJI?
NO . . . NO . . .

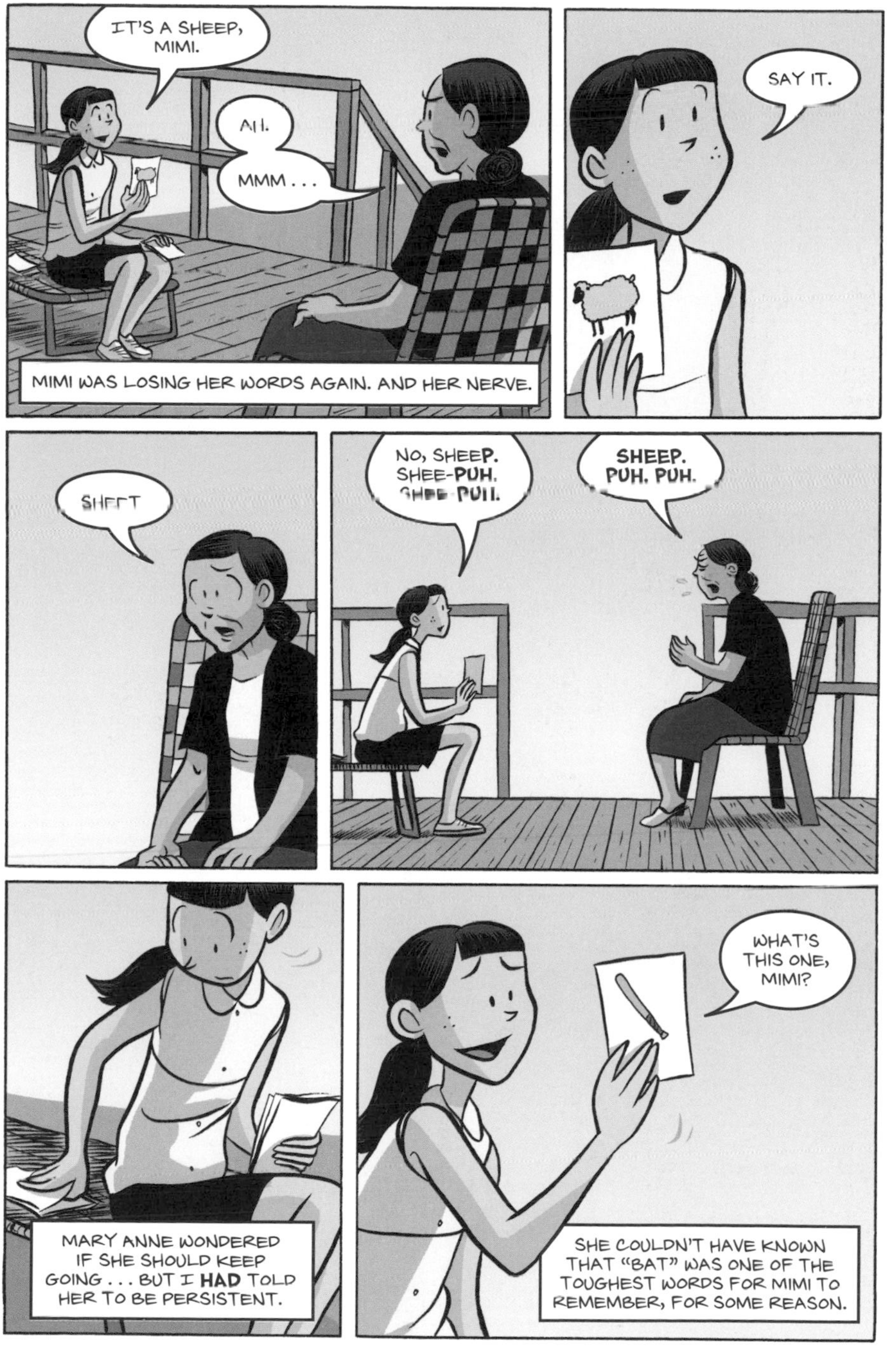

IT'S A SHEEP, MIMI.
AH.
MMM . . .
MIMI WAS LOSING HER WORDS AGAIN. AND HER NERVE.
SAY IT.
NO, SHEEP. SHEE-PUH. SHEE-PUH.
SHEEP. PUH. PUH.
MARY ANNE WONDERED IF SHE SHOULD KEEP GOING . . . BUT I **HAD** TOLD HER TO BE PERSISTENT.
WHAT'S THIS ONE, MIMI?
SHE COULDN'T HAVE KNOWN THAT "BAT" WAS ONE OF THE TOUGHEST WORDS FOR MIMI TO REMEMBER, FOR SOME REASON.

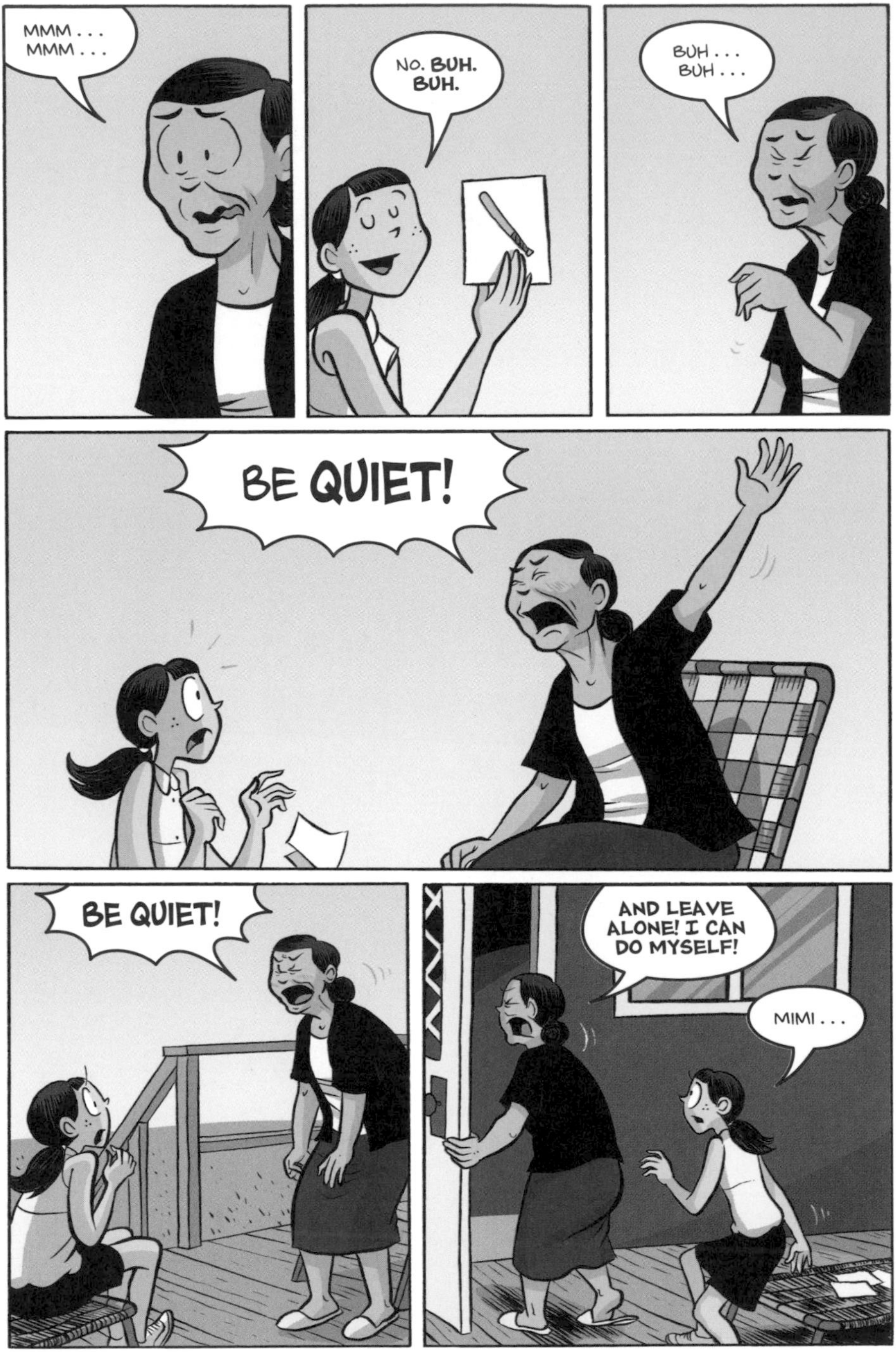
MMM . . .
MMM . . .
NO. BUH.
BUH.
BUH . . .
BUH . . .
BE QUIET!
BE QUIET!
AND LEAVE
ALONE! I CAN
DO MYSELF!
MIMI . . .

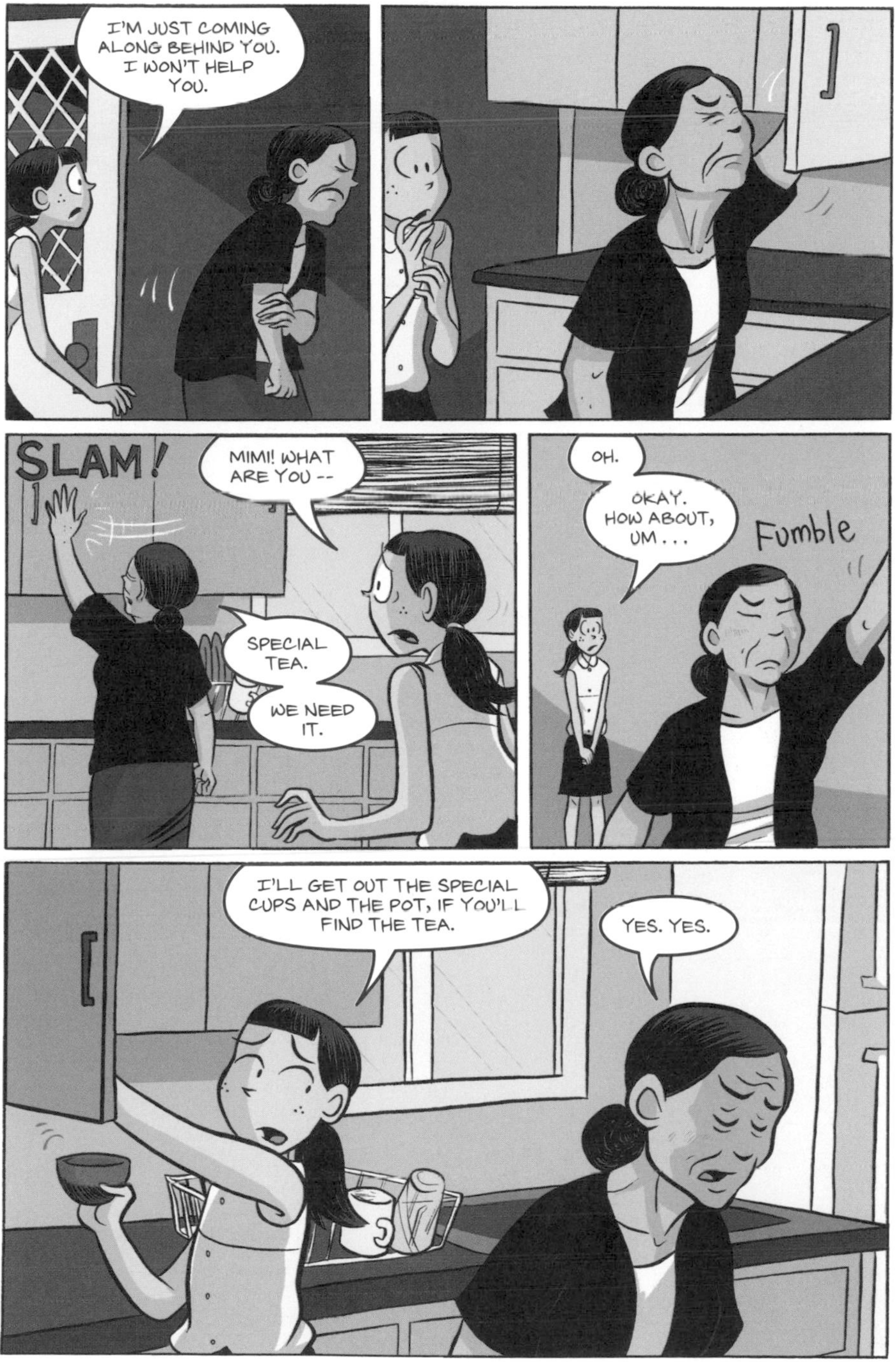
I'M JUST COMING ALONG BEHIND YOU. I WON'T HELP YOU.
SLAM!
MIMI! WHAT ARE YOU --
SPECIAL TEA.
WE NEED IT.
OH.
OKAY. HOW ABOUT, UM...
Fumble
I'LL GET OUT THE SPECIAL CUPS AND THE POT, IF YOU'LL FIND THE TEA.
YES. YES.

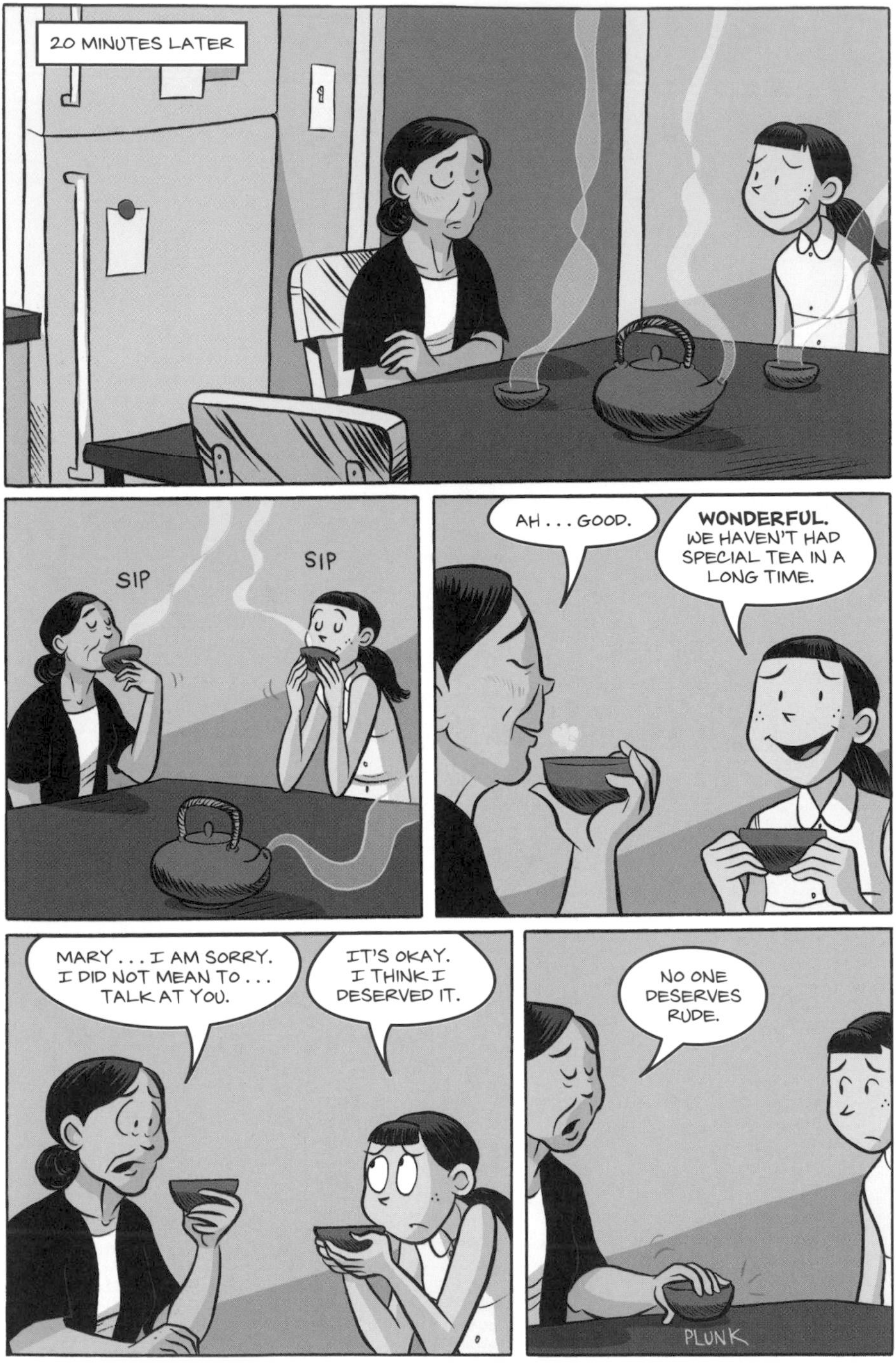
20 MINUTES LATER
SIP
SIP
AH . . . GOOD.
WONDERFUL. WE HAVEN'T HAD SPECIAL TEA IN A LONG TIME.
MARY . . . I AM SORRY. I DID NOT MEAN TO . . . TALK AT YOU.
IT'S OKAY. I THINK I DESERVED IT.
NO ONE DESERVES RUDE.
PLUNK

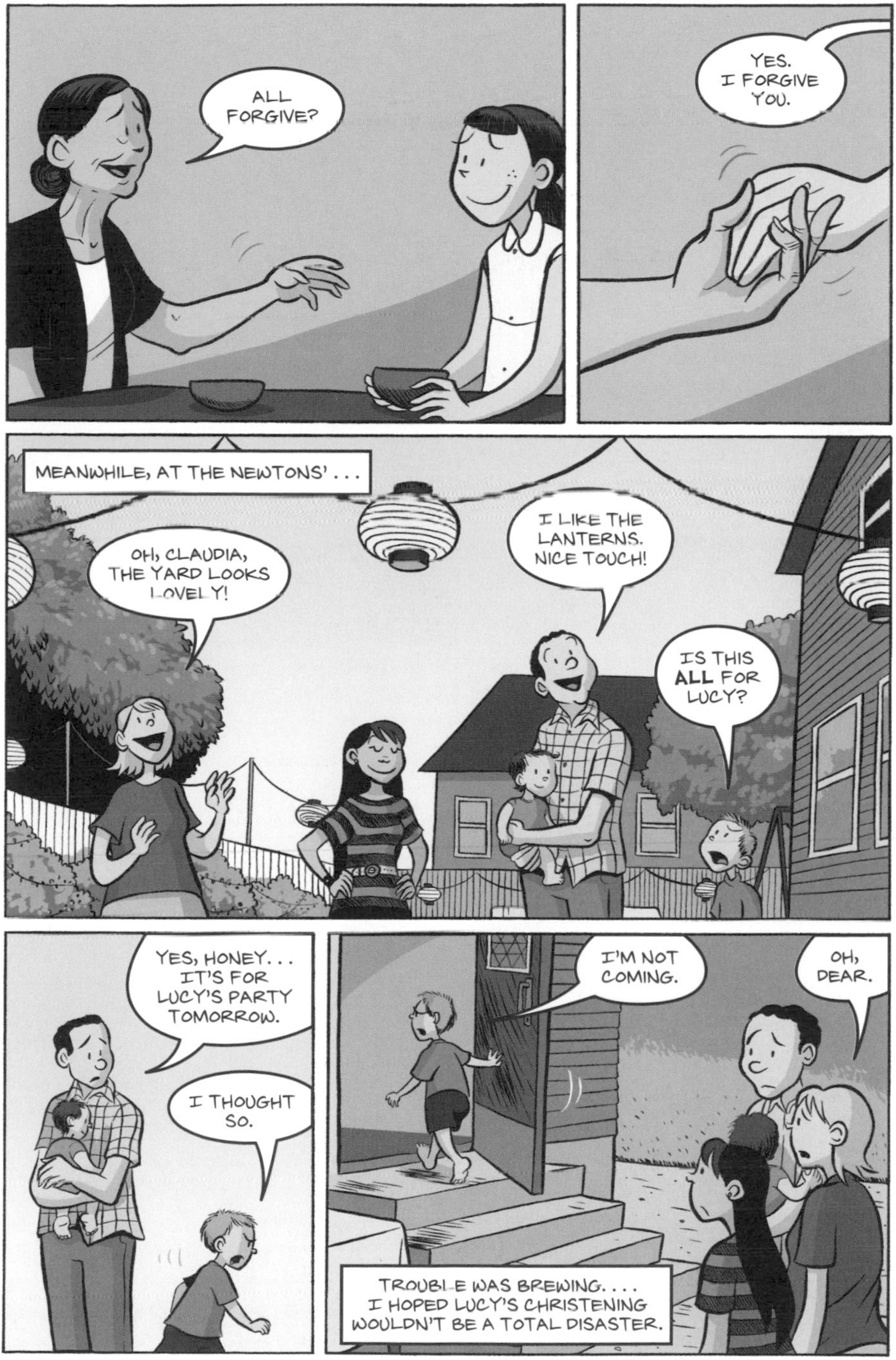

ALL FORGIVE?
YES. I FORGIVE YOU.
MEANWHILE, AT THE NEWTONS' . . .
OH, CLAUDIA, THE YARD LOOKS LOVELY!
I LIKE THE LANTERNS. NICE TOUCH!
IS THIS **ALL** FOR LUCY?
YES, HONEY . . . IT'S FOR LUCY'S PARTY TOMORROW.
I THOUGHT SO.
I'M NOT COMING.
OH, DEAR.
TROUBLE WAS BREWING. . . . I HOPED LUCY'S CHRISTENING WOULDN'T BE A TOTAL DISASTER.

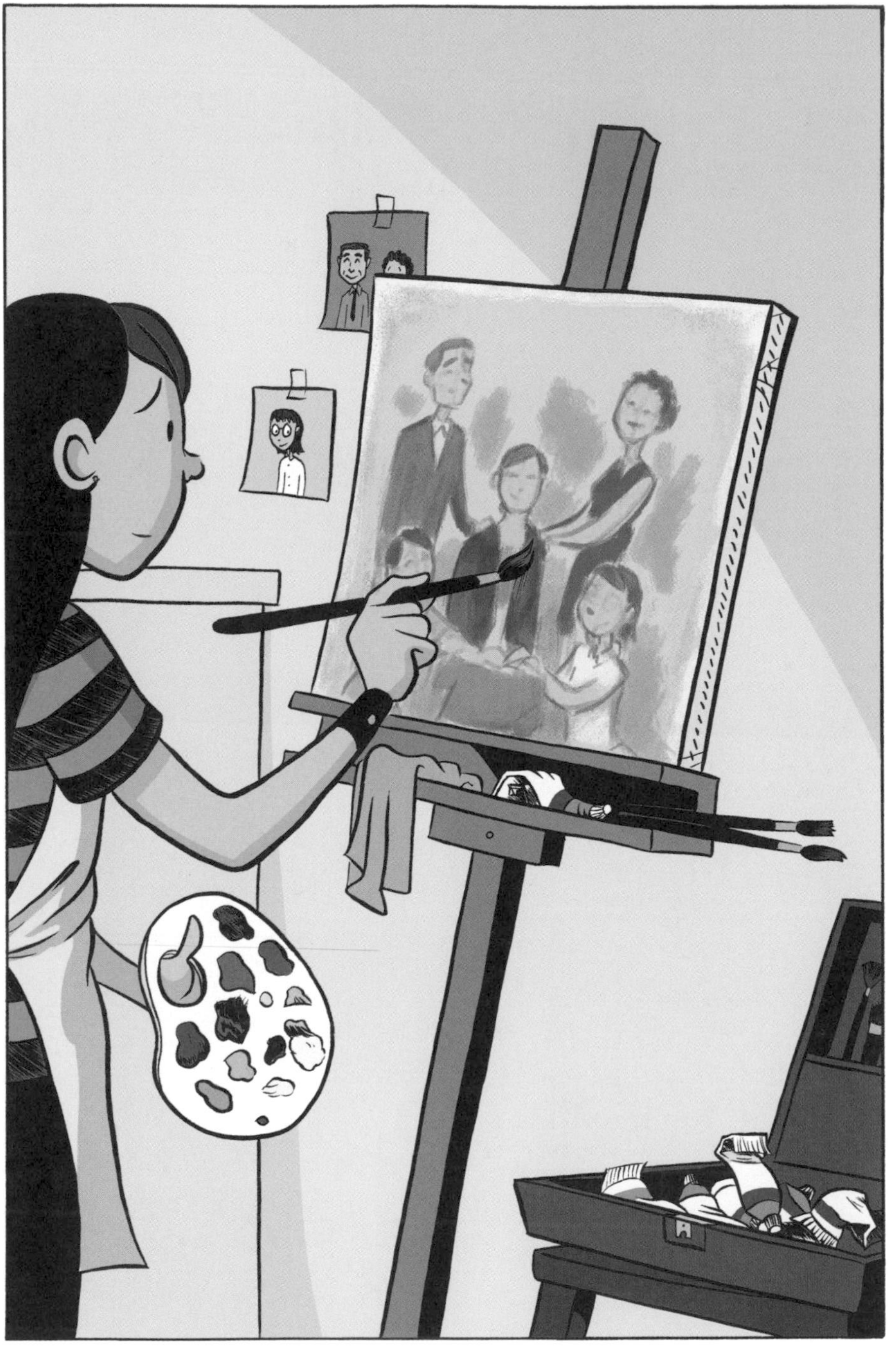

CHAPTER 15

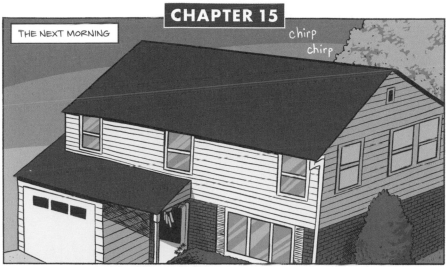

THE NEXT MORNING

chirp chirp

THE WEATHER WAS GORGEOUS. I FELT CHEERED AS I MADE MY WAY TO THE NEWTONS', A BIT EARLY.

BUT THINGS WEREN'T VERY CHEERFUL AT THEIR HOUSE.

I ALMOST FORGOT THE CAKE! CLAUDIA, WILL YOU HELP JAMIE GET DRESSED?

HEY, JAMIE! TIME TO GET DRESSED.

FOR THE PARTY?

YUP.

NOPE.

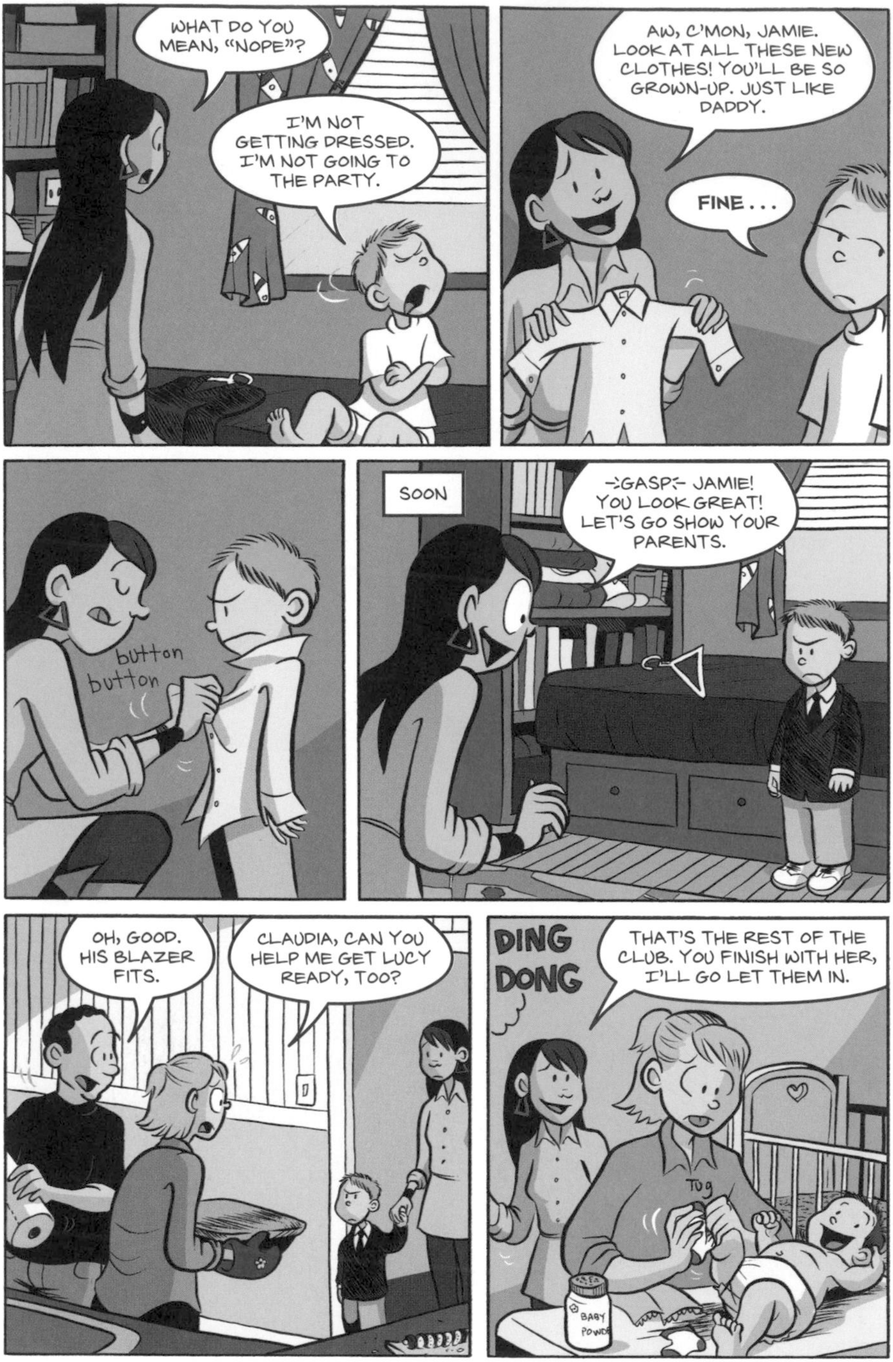

WHAT DO YOU MEAN, "NOPE"?
I'M NOT GETTING DRESSED. I'M NOT GOING TO THE PARTY.
AW, C'MON, JAMIE. LOOK AT ALL THESE NEW CLOTHES! YOU'LL BE SO GROWN-UP. JUST LIKE DADDY.
FINE . . .
button
button
SOON
-GASP- JAMIE! YOU LOOK GREAT! LET'S GO SHOW YOUR PARENTS.
OH, GOOD. HIS BLAZER FITS.
CLAUDIA, CAN YOU HELP ME GET LUCY READY, TOO?
DING DONG
THAT'S THE REST OF THE CLUB. YOU FINISH WITH HER, I'LL GO LET THEM IN.
TUG
BABY POWD

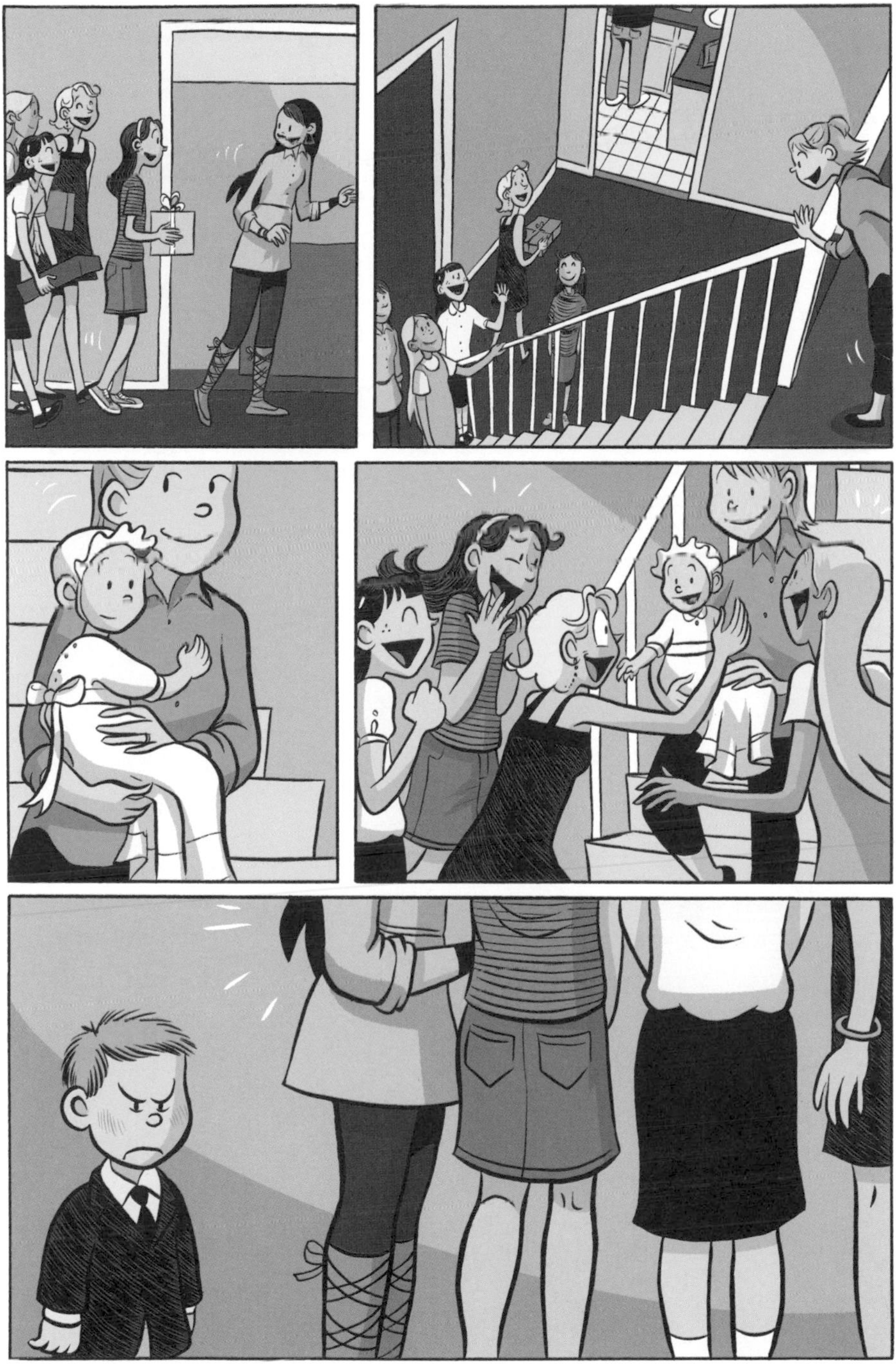

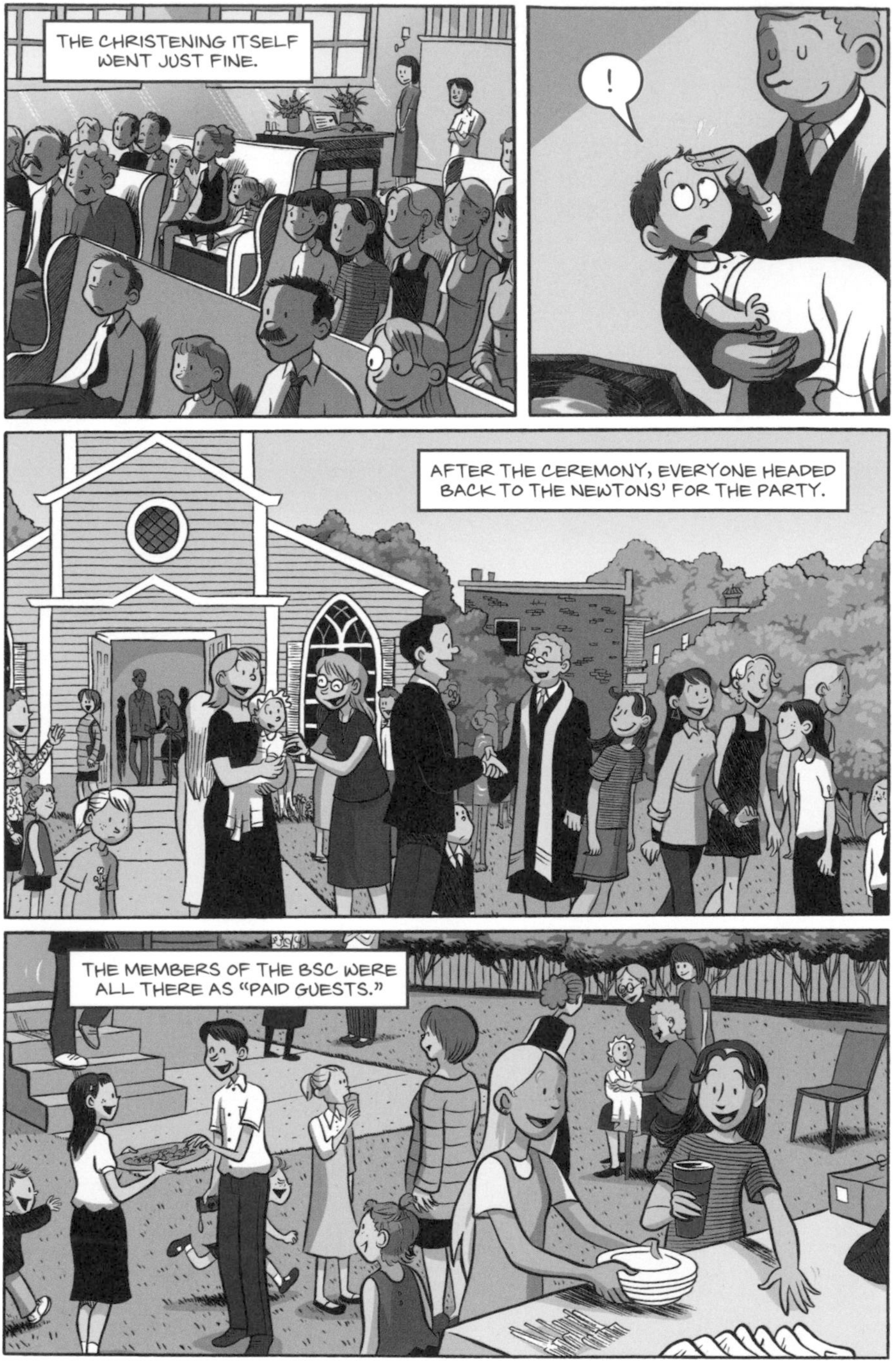
THE CHRISTENING ITSELF WENT JUST FINE.
!
AFTER THE CEREMONY, EVERYONE HEADED BACK TO THE NEWTONS' FOR THE PARTY.
THE MEMBERS OF THE BSC WERE ALL THERE AS "PAID GUESTS."

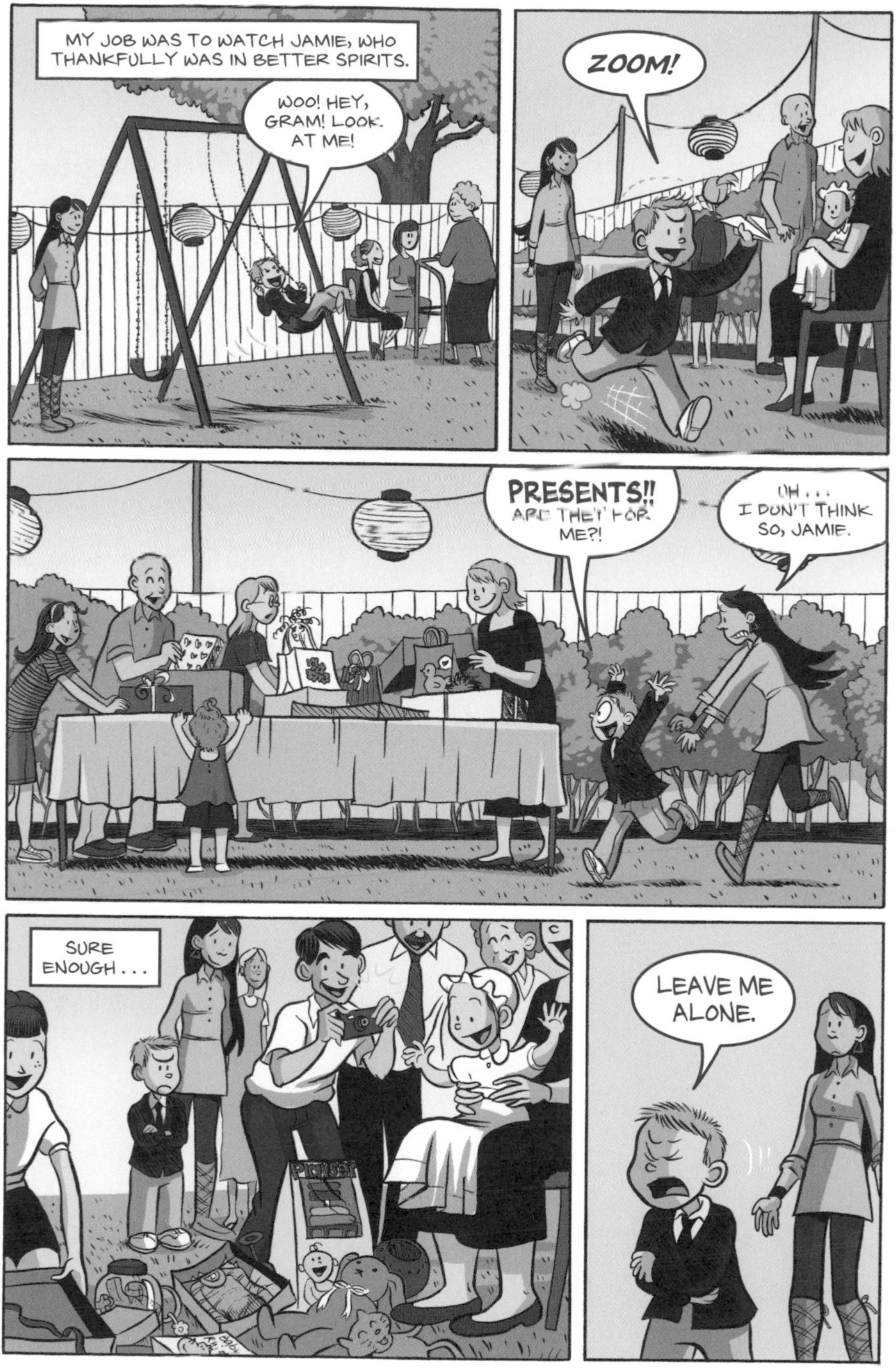
MY JOB WAS TO WATCH JAMIE, WHO THANKFULLY WAS IN BETTER SPIRITS.
WOO! HEY, GRAM! LOOK. AT ME!
ZOOM!
PRESENTS!! ARE THEY FOR ME?!
UH . . . I DON'T THINK SO, JAMIE.
SURE ENOUGH . . .
LEAVE ME ALONE.

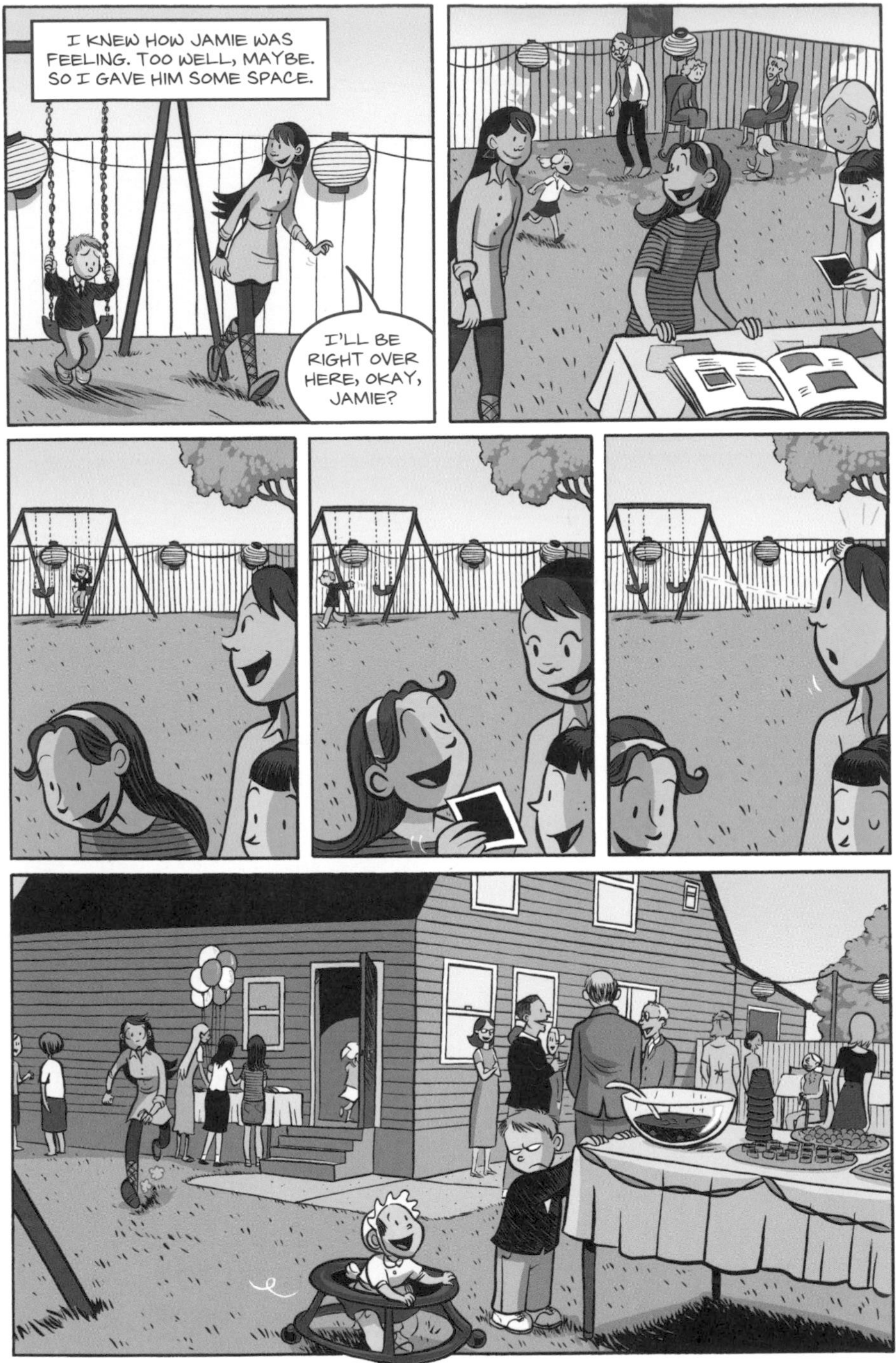
I KNEW HOW JAMIE WAS FEELING. TOO WELL, MAYBE. SO I GAVE HIM SOME SPACE.
I'LL BE RIGHT OVER HERE, OKAY, JAMIE?

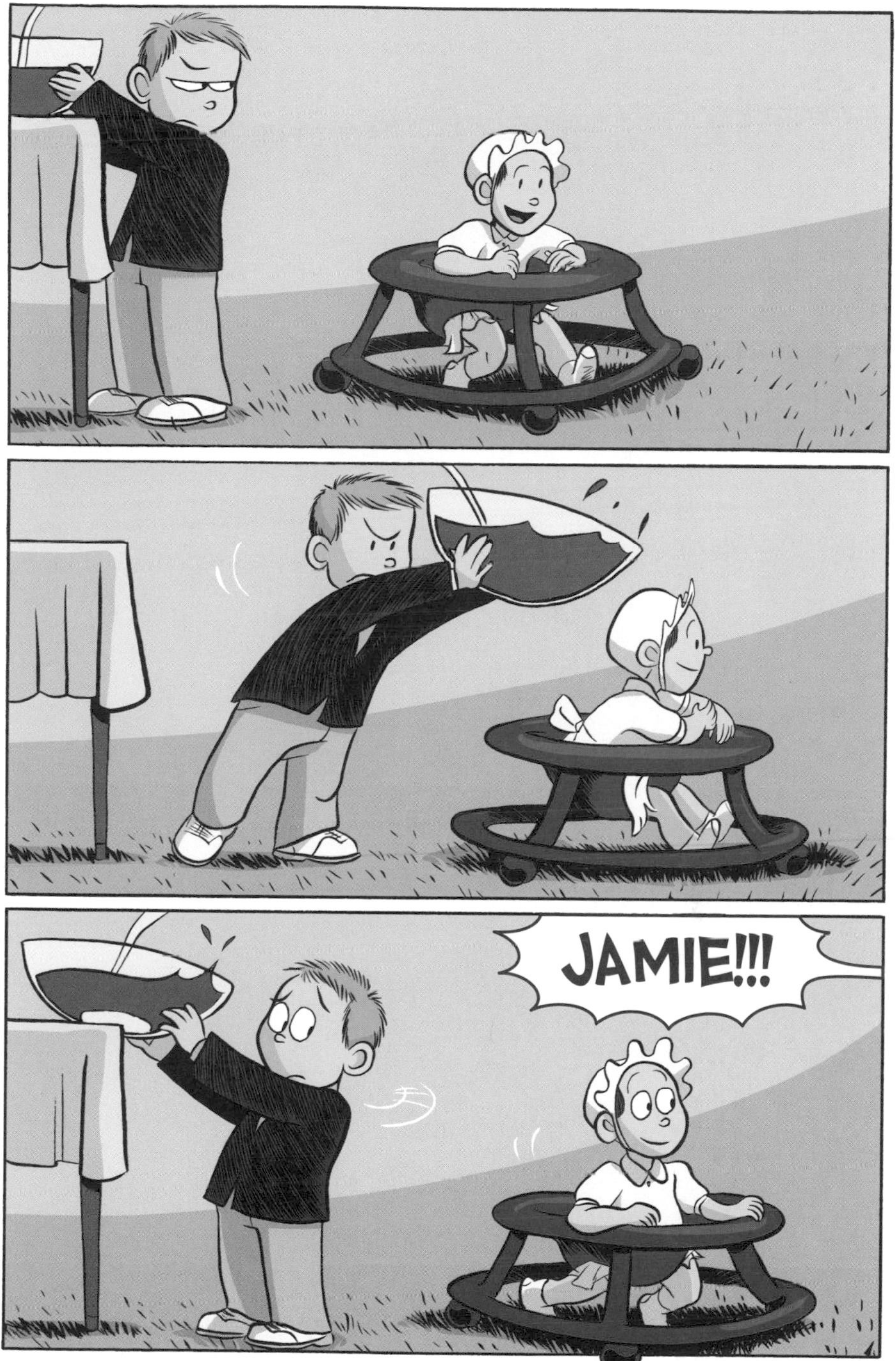
JAMIE!!!

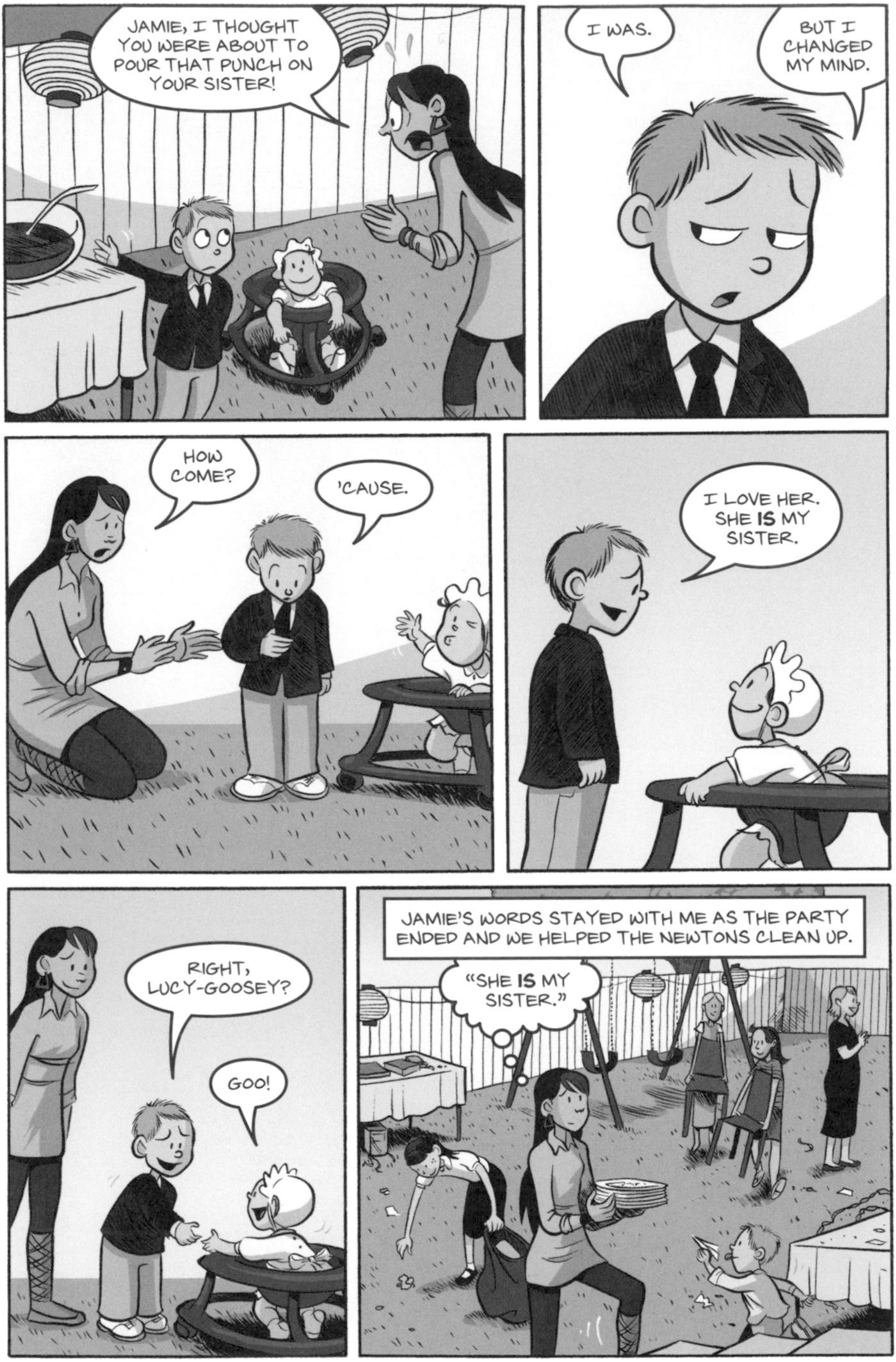
JAMIE, I THOUGHT YOU WERE ABOUT TO POUR THAT PUNCH ON YOUR SISTER!
I WAS.
BUT I CHANGED MY MIND.
HOW COME?
'CAUSE.
I LOVE HER. SHE **IS** MY SISTER.
RIGHT, LUCY-GOOSEY?
GOO!
JAMIE'S WORDS STAYED WITH ME AS THE PARTY ENDED AND WE HELPED THE NEWTONS CLEAN UP.
"SHE **IS** MY SISTER."

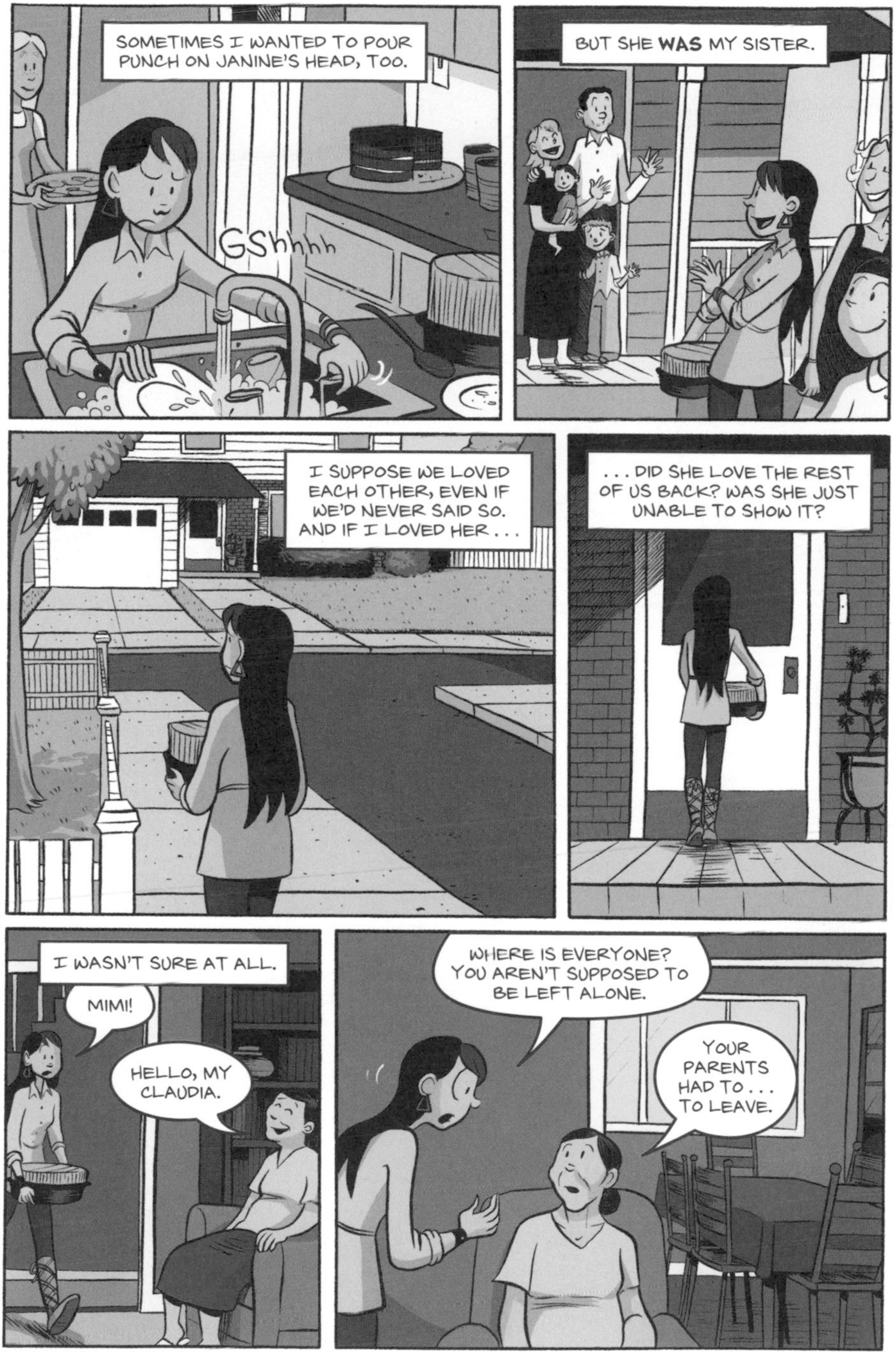
SOMETIMES I WANTED TO POUR PUNCH ON JANINE'S HEAD, TOO.
GShhhh
BUT SHE **WAS** MY SISTER.
I SUPPOSE WE LOVED EACH OTHER, EVEN IF WE'D NEVER SAID SO. AND IF I LOVED HER . . .
. . . DID SHE LOVE THE REST OF US BACK? WAS SHE JUST UNABLE TO SHOW IT?
I WASN'T SURE AT ALL.
MIMI!
HELLO, MY CLAUDIA.
WHERE IS EVERYONE? YOU AREN'T SUPPOSED TO BE LEFT ALONE.
YOUR PARENTS HAD TO . . . TO LEAVE.

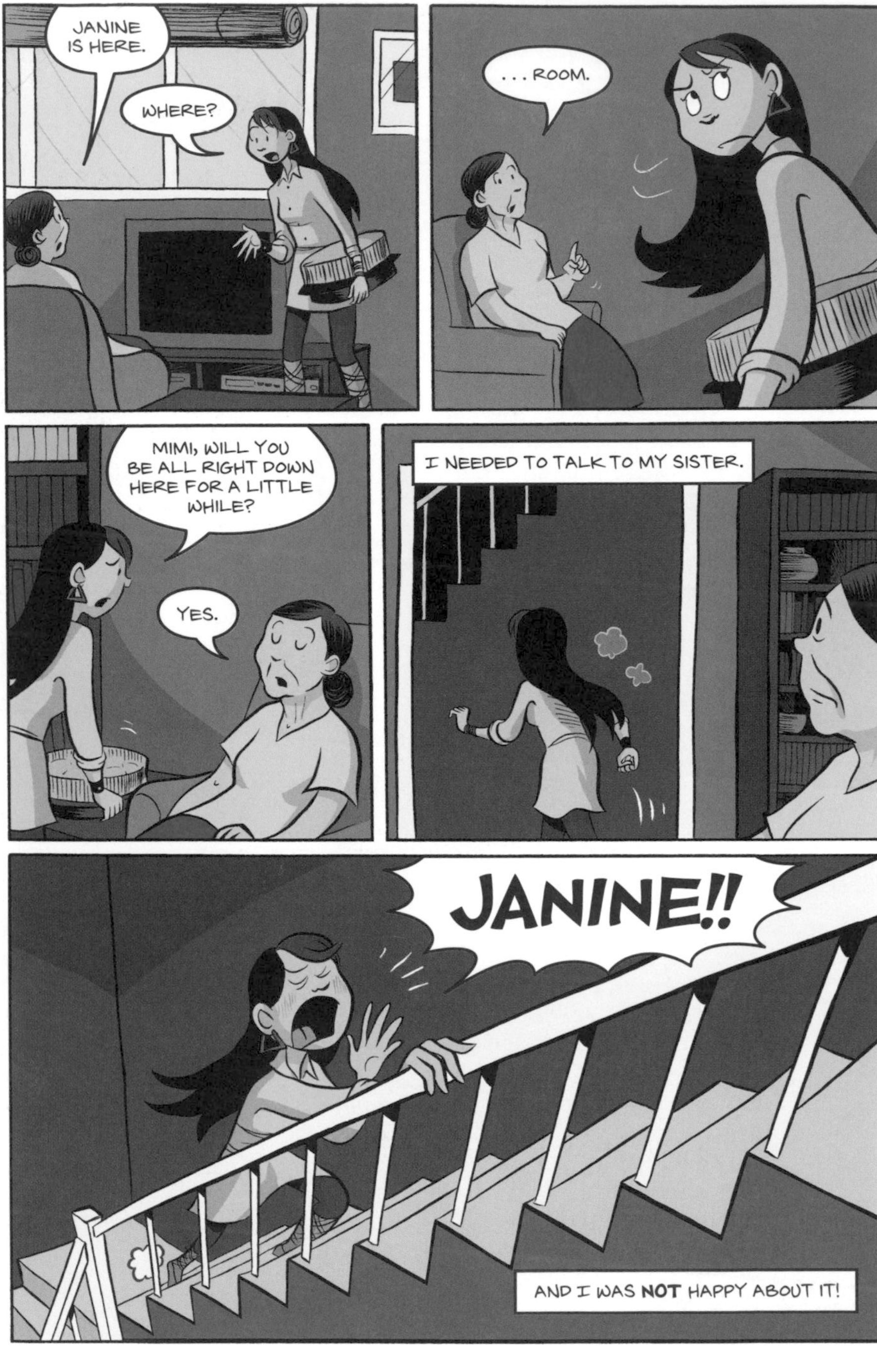
JANINE IS HERE.
WHERE?
. . . ROOM.
MIMI, WILL YOU BE ALL RIGHT DOWN HERE FOR A LITTLE WHILE?
YES.
I NEEDED TO TALK TO MY SISTER.
JANINE!!
AND I WAS NOT HAPPY ABOUT IT!

CHAPTER 16

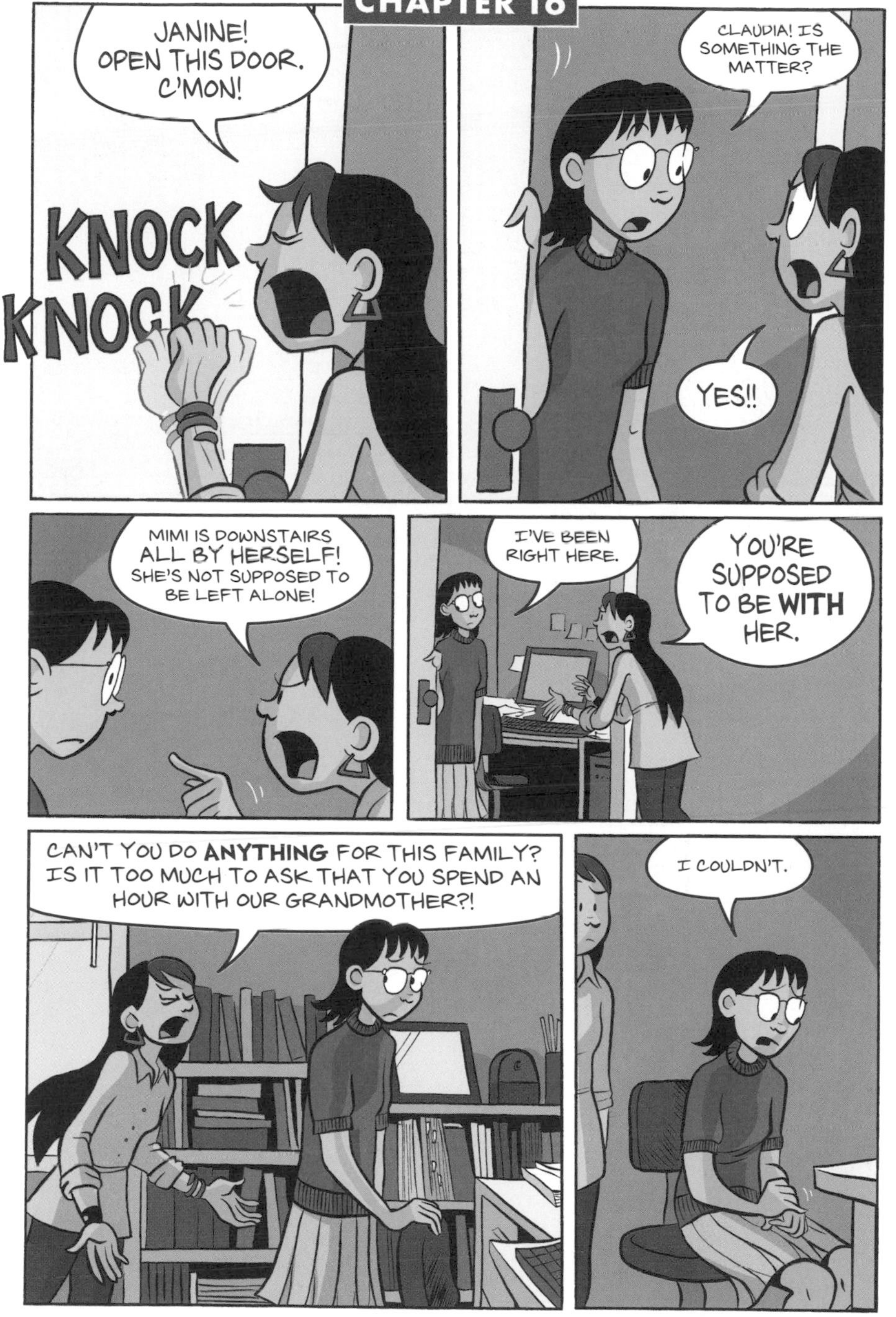
JANINE! OPEN THIS DOOR. C'MON!
KNOCK KNOCK
CLAUDIA! IS SOMETHING THE MATTER?
YES!!
MIMI IS DOWNSTAIRS ALL BY HERSELF! SHE'S NOT SUPPOSED TO BE LEFT ALONE!
I'VE BEEN RIGHT HERE.
YOU'RE SUPPOSED TO BE WITH HER.
CAN'T YOU DO ANYTHING FOR THIS FAMILY? IS IT TOO MUCH TO ASK THAT YOU SPEND AN HOUR WITH OUR GRANDMOTHER?!
I COULDN'T.

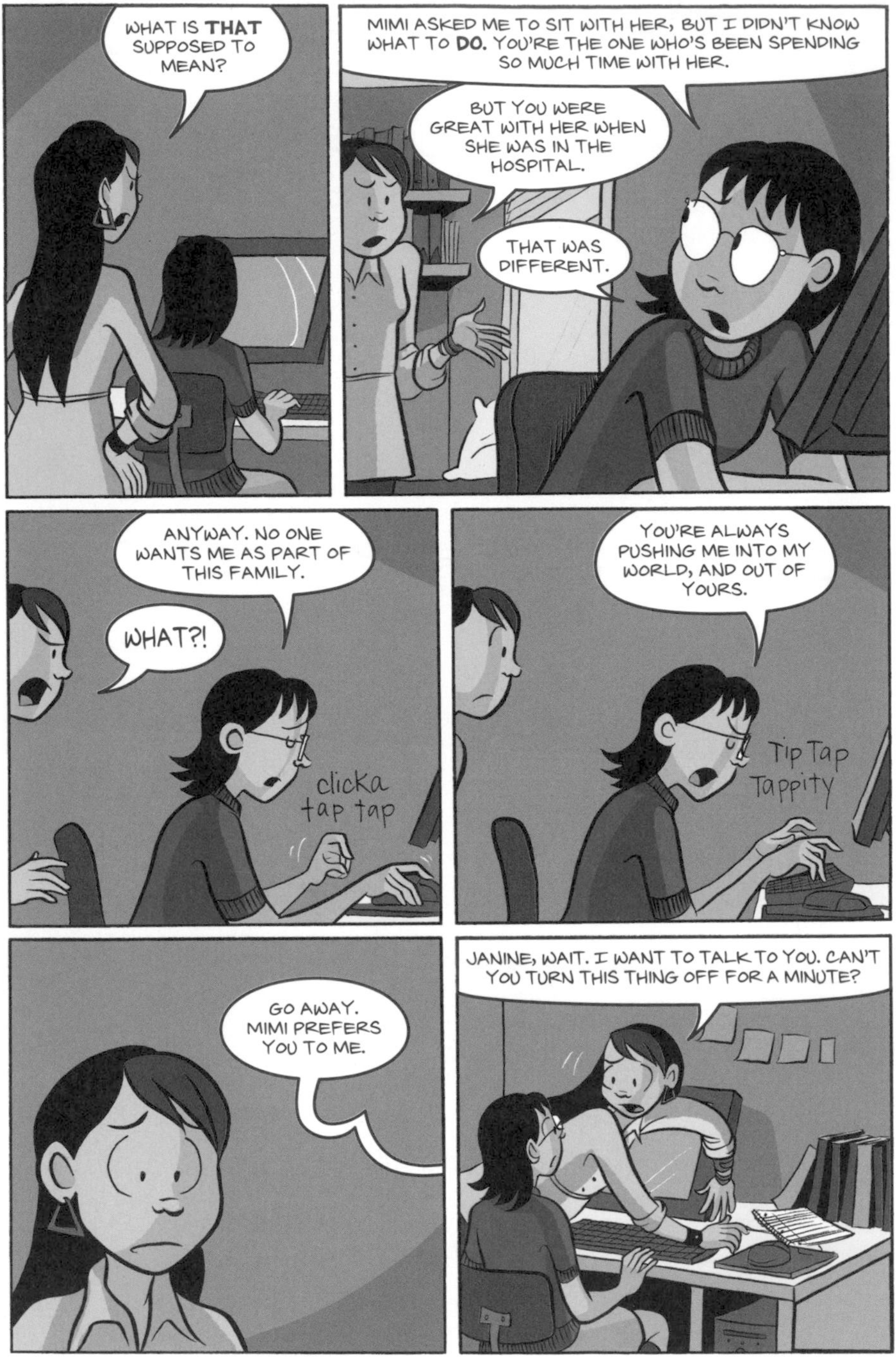
WHAT IS **THAT** SUPPOSED TO MEAN?
MIMI ASKED ME TO SIT WITH HER, BUT I DIDN'T KNOW WHAT TO **DO.** YOU'RE THE ONE WHO'S BEEN SPENDING SO MUCH TIME WITH HER.
BUT YOU WERE GREAT WITH HER WHEN SHE WAS IN THE HOSPITAL.
THAT WAS DIFFERENT.
ANYWAY. NO ONE WANTS ME AS PART OF THIS FAMILY.
WHAT?!
clicka tap tap
YOU'RE ALWAYS PUSHING ME INTO MY WORLD, AND OUT OF YOURS.
Tip Tap Tappity
GO AWAY. MIMI PREFERS YOU TO ME.
JANINE, WAIT. I WANT TO TALK TO YOU. CAN'T YOU TURN THIS THING OFF FOR A MINUTE?

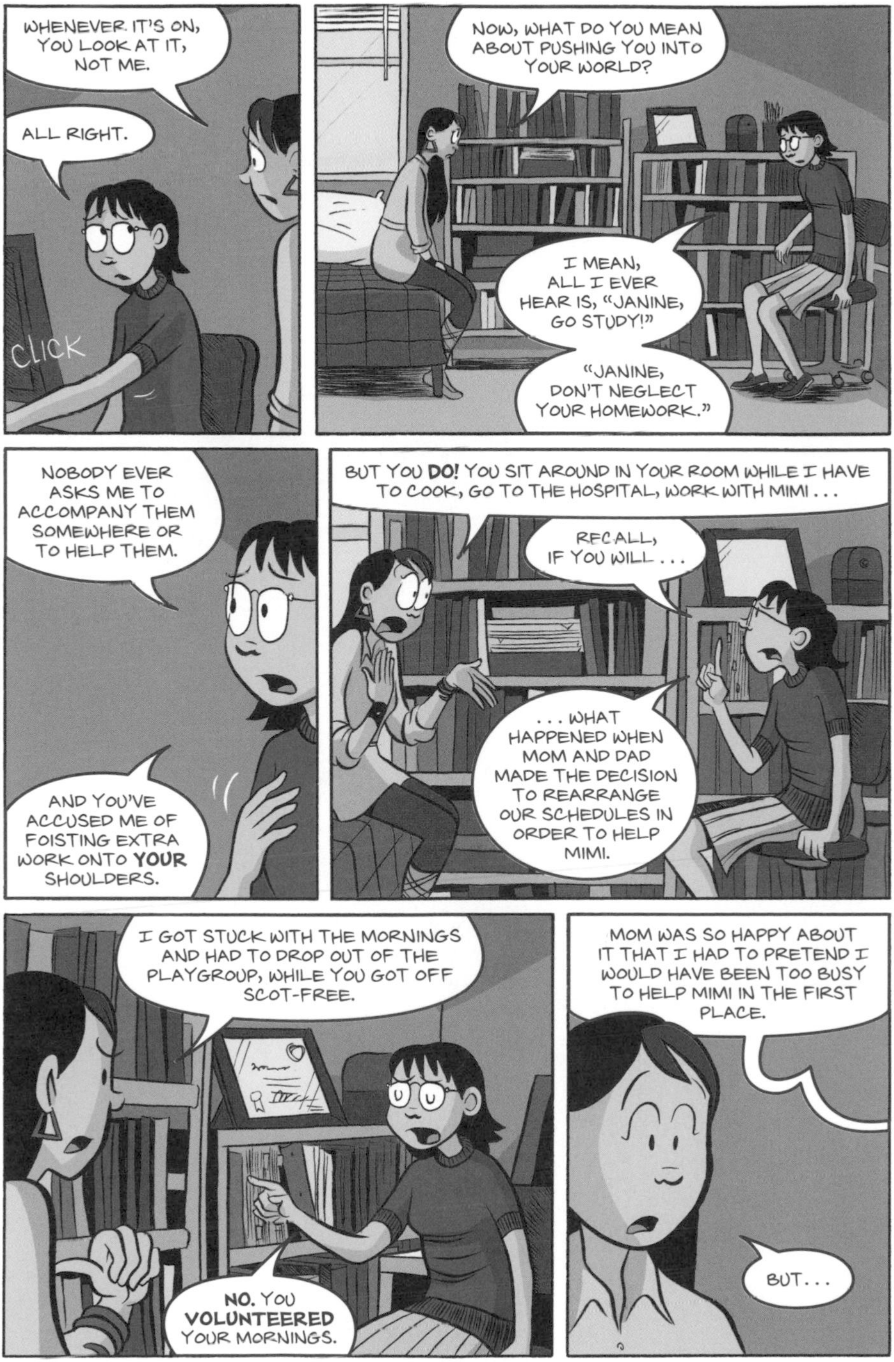
WHENEVER IT'S ON, YOU LOOK AT IT, NOT ME.
ALL RIGHT.
CLICK
NOW, WHAT DO YOU MEAN ABOUT PUSHING YOU INTO YOUR WORLD?
I MEAN, ALL I EVER HEAR IS, "JANINE, GO STUDY!"
"JANINE, DON'T NEGLECT YOUR HOMEWORK."
NOBODY EVER ASKS ME TO ACCOMPANY THEM SOMEWHERE OR TO HELP THEM.
AND YOU'VE ACCUSED ME OF FOISTING EXTRA WORK ONTO **YOUR** SHOULDERS.
BUT YOU **DO!** YOU SIT AROUND IN YOUR ROOM WHILE I HAVE TO COOK, GO TO THE HOSPITAL, WORK WITH MIMI . . .
RECALL, IF YOU WILL . . .
. . . WHAT HAPPENED WHEN MOM AND DAD MADE THE DECISION TO REARRANGE OUR SCHEDULES IN ORDER TO HELP MIMI.
I GOT STUCK WITH THE MORNINGS AND HAD TO DROP OUT OF THE PLAYGROUP, WHILE YOU GOT OFF SCOT-FREE.
NO. YOU **VOLUNTEERED** YOUR MORNINGS.
MOM WAS SO HAPPY ABOUT IT THAT I HAD TO PRETEND I WOULD HAVE BEEN TOO BUSY TO HELP MIMI IN THE FIRST PLACE.
BUT. . .

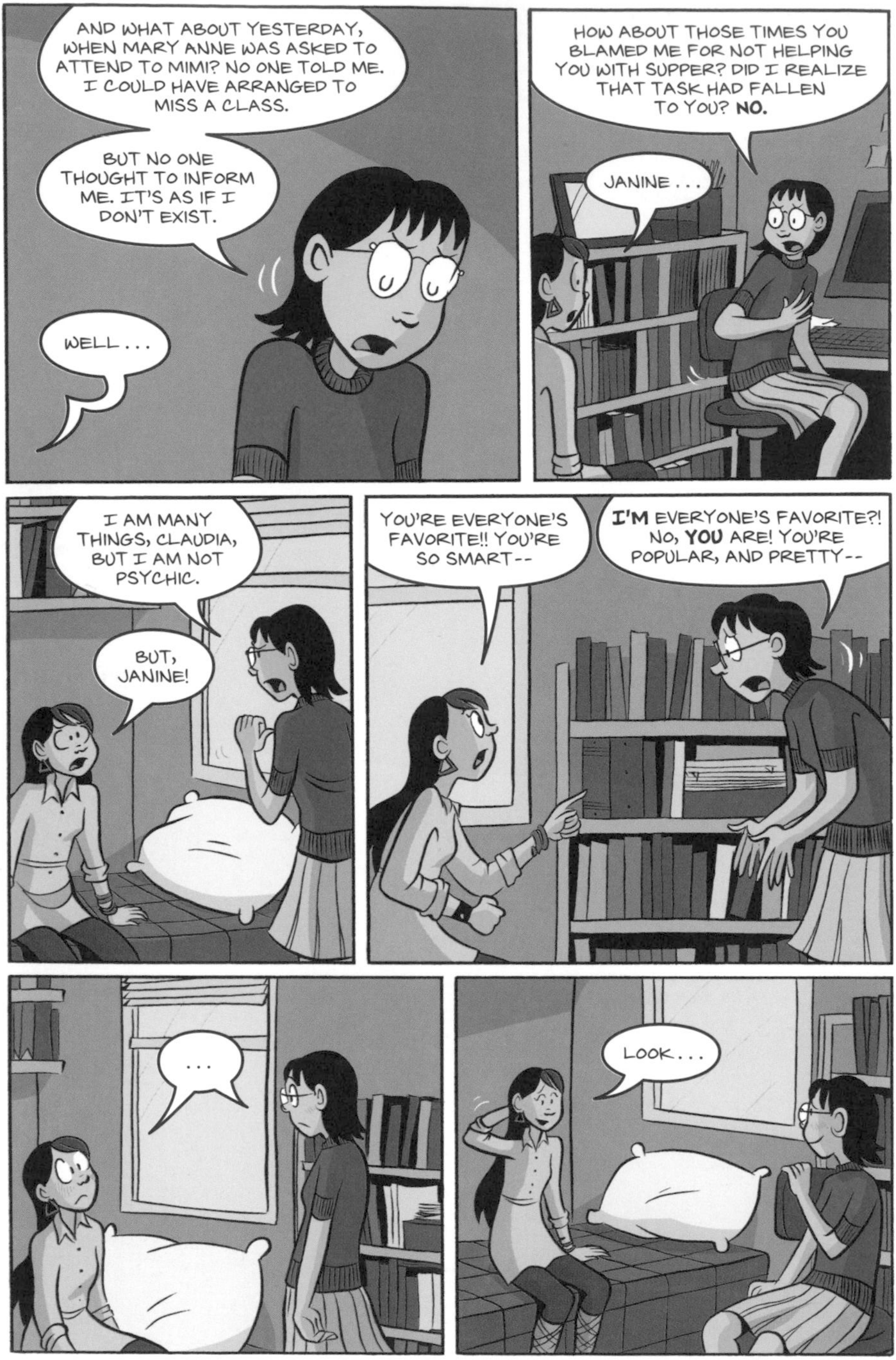
AND WHAT ABOUT YESTERDAY, WHEN MARY ANNE WAS ASKED TO ATTEND TO MIMI? NO ONE TOLD ME. I COULD HAVE ARRANGED TO MISS A CLASS.
BUT NO ONE THOUGHT TO INFORM ME. IT'S AS IF I DON'T EXIST.
WELL . . .
HOW ABOUT THOSE TIMES YOU BLAMED ME FOR NOT HELPING YOU WITH SUPPER? DID I REALIZE THAT TASK HAD FALLEN TO YOU? **NO.**
JANINE . . .
I AM MANY THINGS, CLAUDIA, BUT I AM NOT PSYCHIC.
BUT, JANINE!
YOU'RE EVERYONE'S FAVORITE!! YOU'RE SO SMART--
I'M EVERYONE'S FAVORITE?! NO, **YOU** ARE! YOU'RE POPULAR, AND PRETTY--
. . .
LOOK . . .

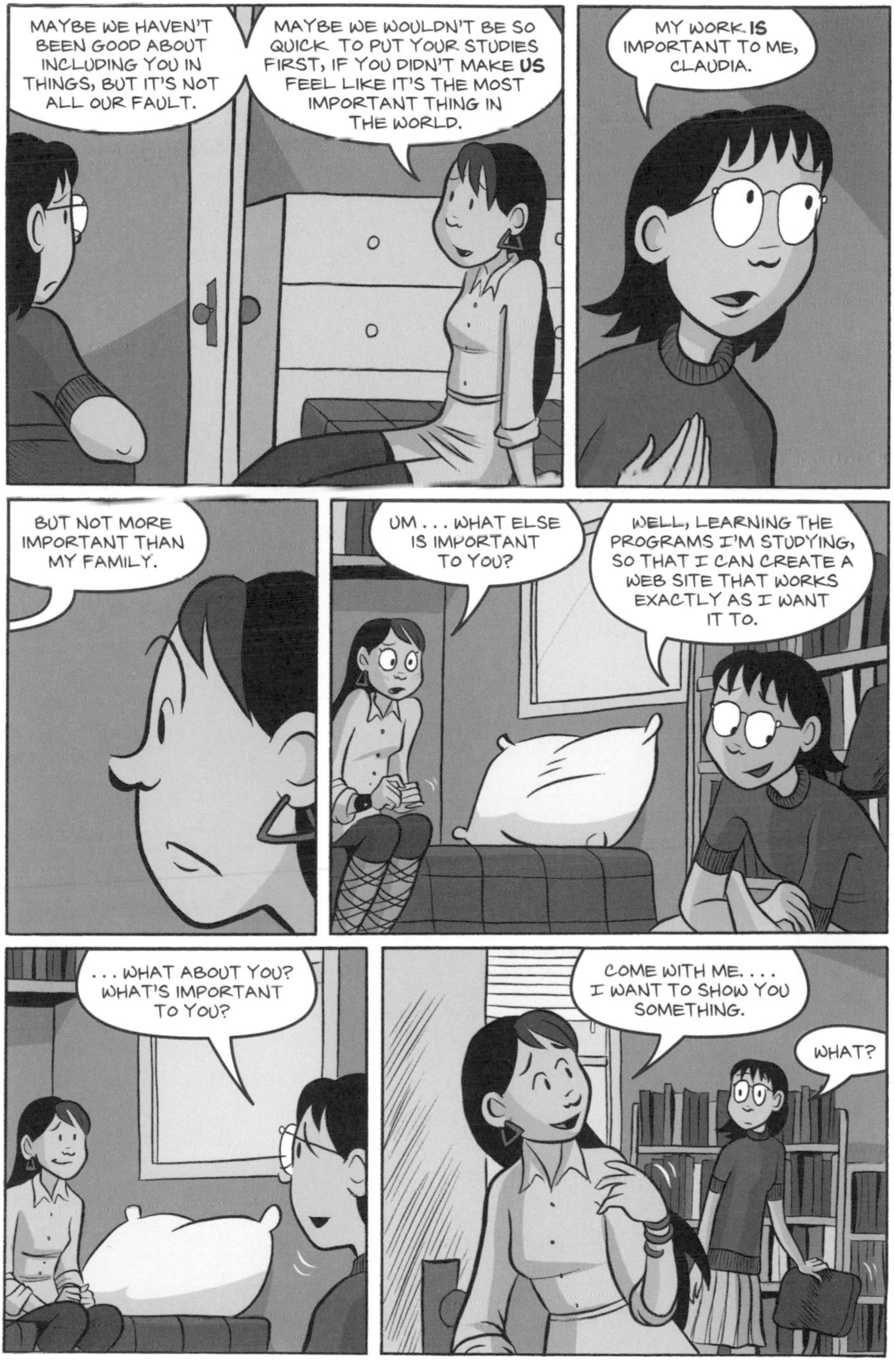
MAYBE WE HAVEN'T BEEN GOOD ABOUT INCLUDING YOU IN THINGS, BUT IT'S NOT ALL OUR FAULT.
MAYBE WE WOULDN'T BE SO QUICK TO PUT YOUR STUDIES FIRST, IF YOU DIDN'T MAKE US FEEL LIKE IT'S THE MOST IMPORTANT THING IN THE WORLD.
MY WORK IS IMPORTANT TO ME, CLAUDIA.
BUT NOT MORE IMPORTANT THAN MY FAMILY.
UM . . . WHAT ELSE IS IMPORTANT TO YOU?
WELL, LEARNING THE PROGRAMS I'M STUDYING, SO THAT I CAN CREATE A WEB SITE THAT WORKS EXACTLY AS I WANT IT TO.
. . . WHAT ABOUT YOU? WHAT'S IMPORTANT TO YOU?
COME WITH ME. . . . I WANT TO SHOW YOU SOMETHING.
WHAT?

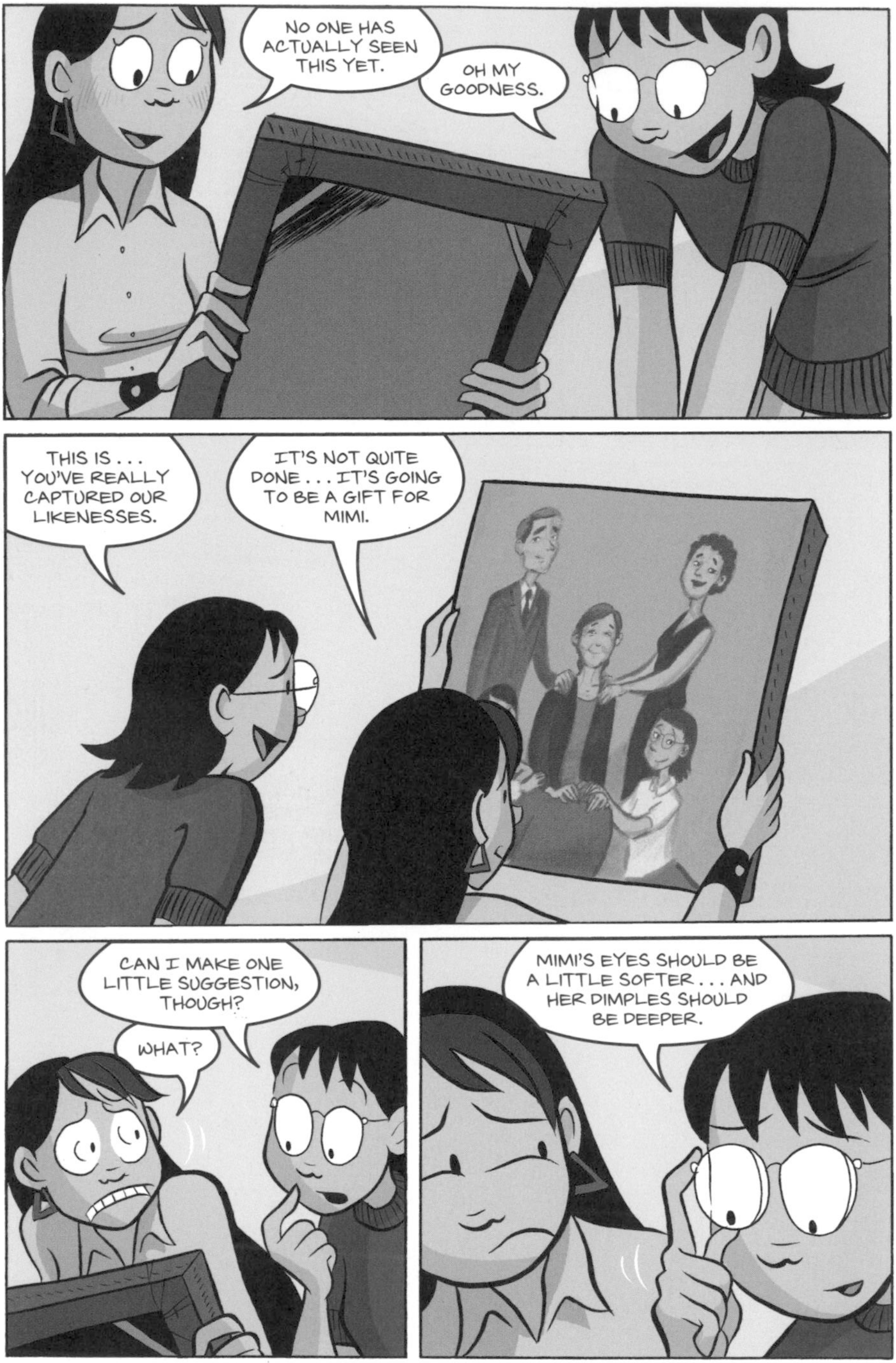
NO ONE HAS ACTUALLY SEEN THIS YET.
OH MY GOODNESS.
THIS IS . . . YOU'VE REALLY CAPTURED OUR LIKENESSES.
IT'S NOT QUITE DONE . . . IT'S GOING TO BE A GIFT FOR MIMI.
CAN I MAKE ONE LITTLE SUGGESTION, THOUGH?
WHAT?
MIMI'S EYES SHOULD BE A LITTLE SOFTER . . . AND HER DIMPLES SHOULD BE DEEPER.

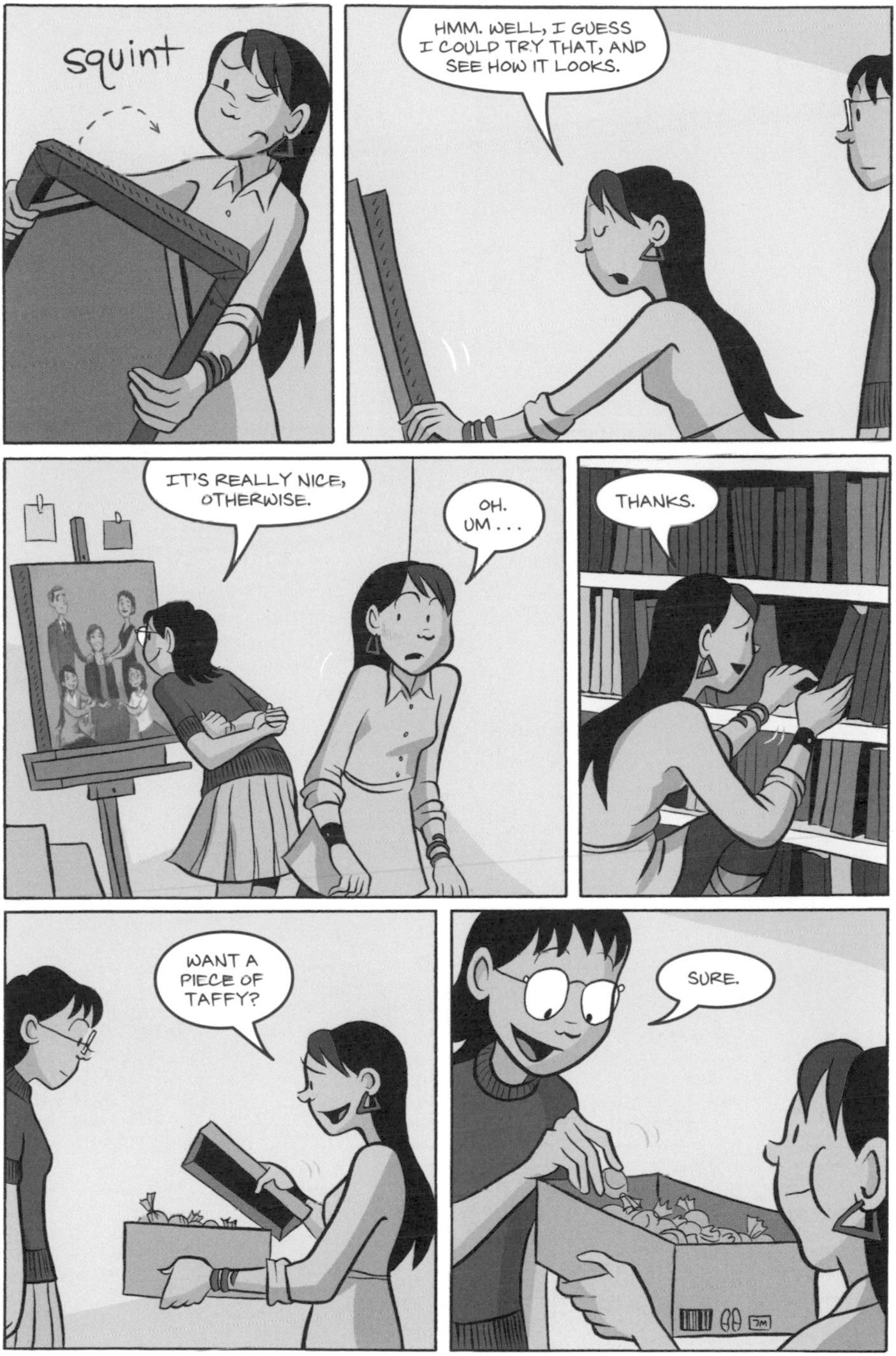
squint
HMM. WELL, I GUESS I COULD TRY THAT, AND SEE HOW IT LOOKS.
IT'S REALLY NICE, OTHERWISE.
OH. UM . . .
THANKS.
WANT A PIECE OF TAFFY?
SURE.

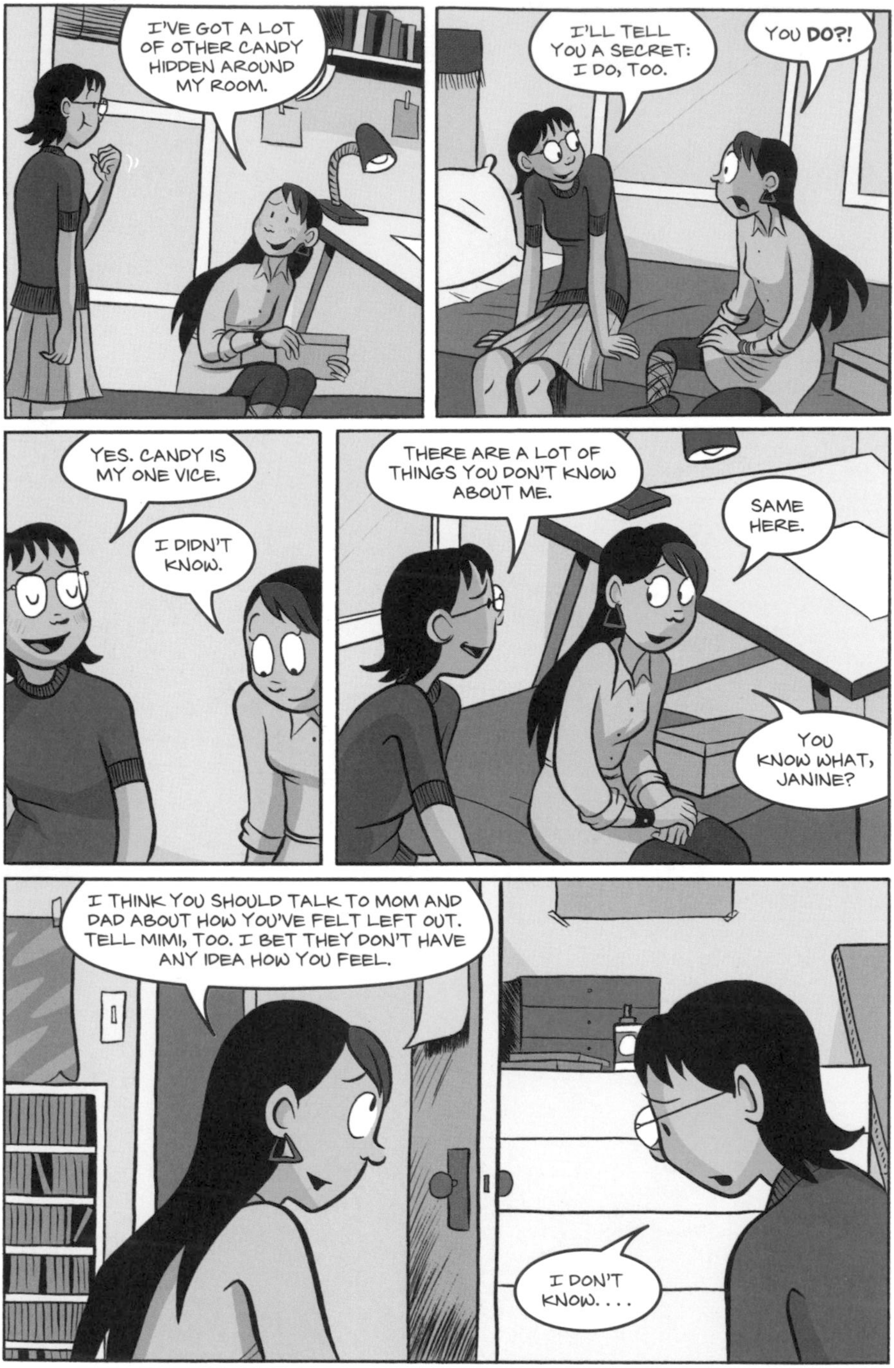
I'VE GOT A LOT OF OTHER CANDY HIDDEN AROUND MY ROOM.
I'LL TELL YOU A SECRET: I DO, TOO.
YOU **DO?!**
YES. CANDY IS MY ONE VICE.
I DIDN'T KNOW.
THERE ARE A LOT OF THINGS YOU DON'T KNOW ABOUT ME.
SAME HERE.
YOU KNOW WHAT, JANINE?
I THINK YOU SHOULD TALK TO MOM AND DAD ABOUT HOW YOU'VE FELT LEFT OUT. TELL MIMI, TOO. I BET THEY DON'T HAVE ANY IDEA HOW YOU FEEL.
I DON'T KNOW. . . .

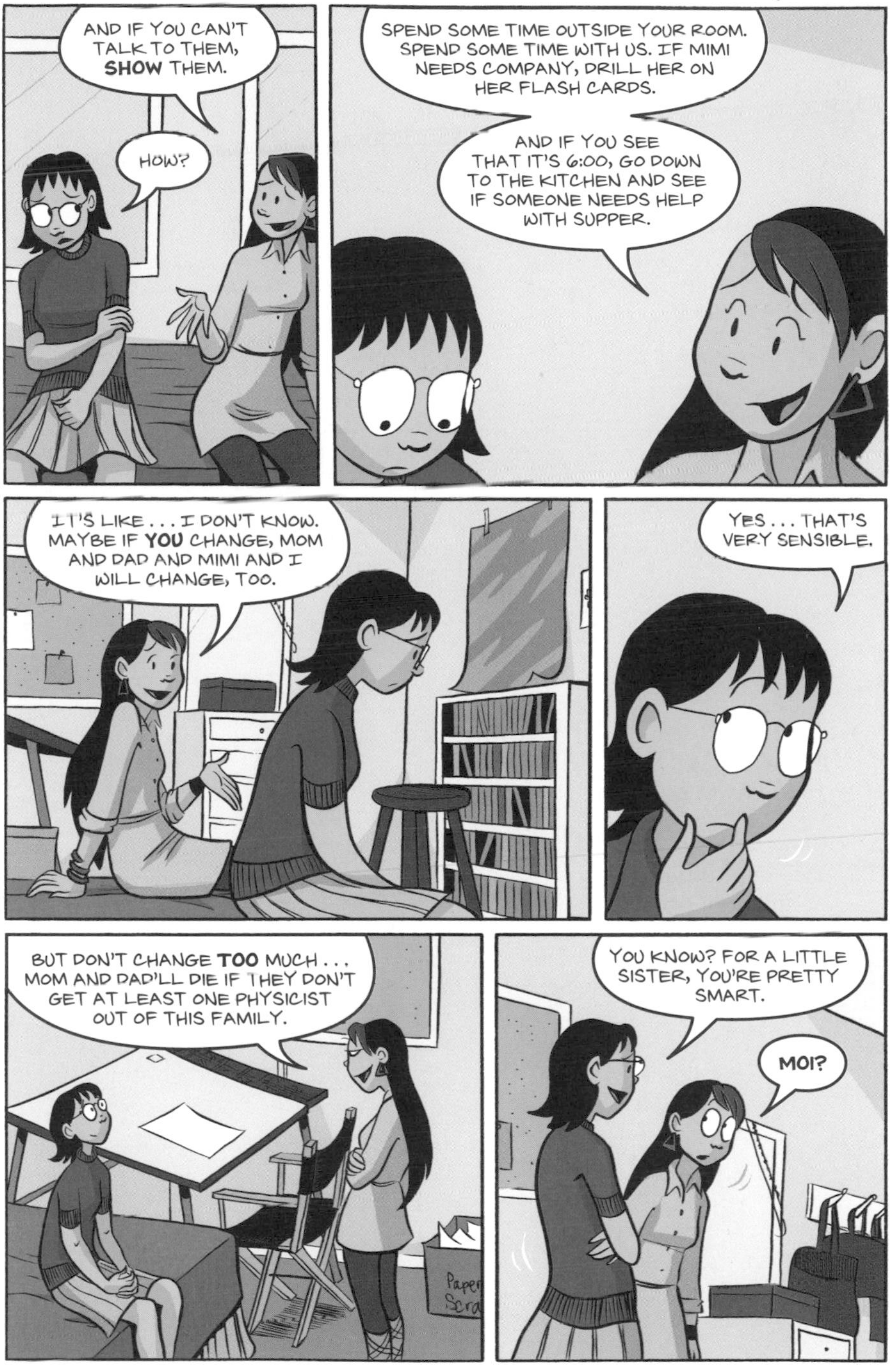
AND IF YOU CAN'T TALK TO THEM, **SHOW** THEM.
HOW?
SPEND SOME TIME OUTSIDE YOUR ROOM. SPEND SOME TIME WITH US. IF MIMI NEEDS COMPANY, DRILL HER ON HER FLASH CARDS.
AND IF YOU SEE THAT IT'S 6:00, GO DOWN TO THE KITCHEN AND SEE IF SOMEONE NEEDS HELP WITH SUPPER.
IT'S LIKE . . . I DON'T KNOW. MAYBE IF **YOU** CHANGE, MOM AND DAD AND MIMI AND I WILL CHANGE, TOO.
YES . . . THAT'S VERY SENSIBLE.
BUT DON'T CHANGE **TOO** MUCH . . . MOM AND DAD'LL DIE IF THEY DON'T GET AT LEAST ONE PHYSICIST OUT OF THIS FAMILY.
YOU KNOW? FOR A LITTLE SISTER, YOU'RE PRETTY SMART.
MOI?

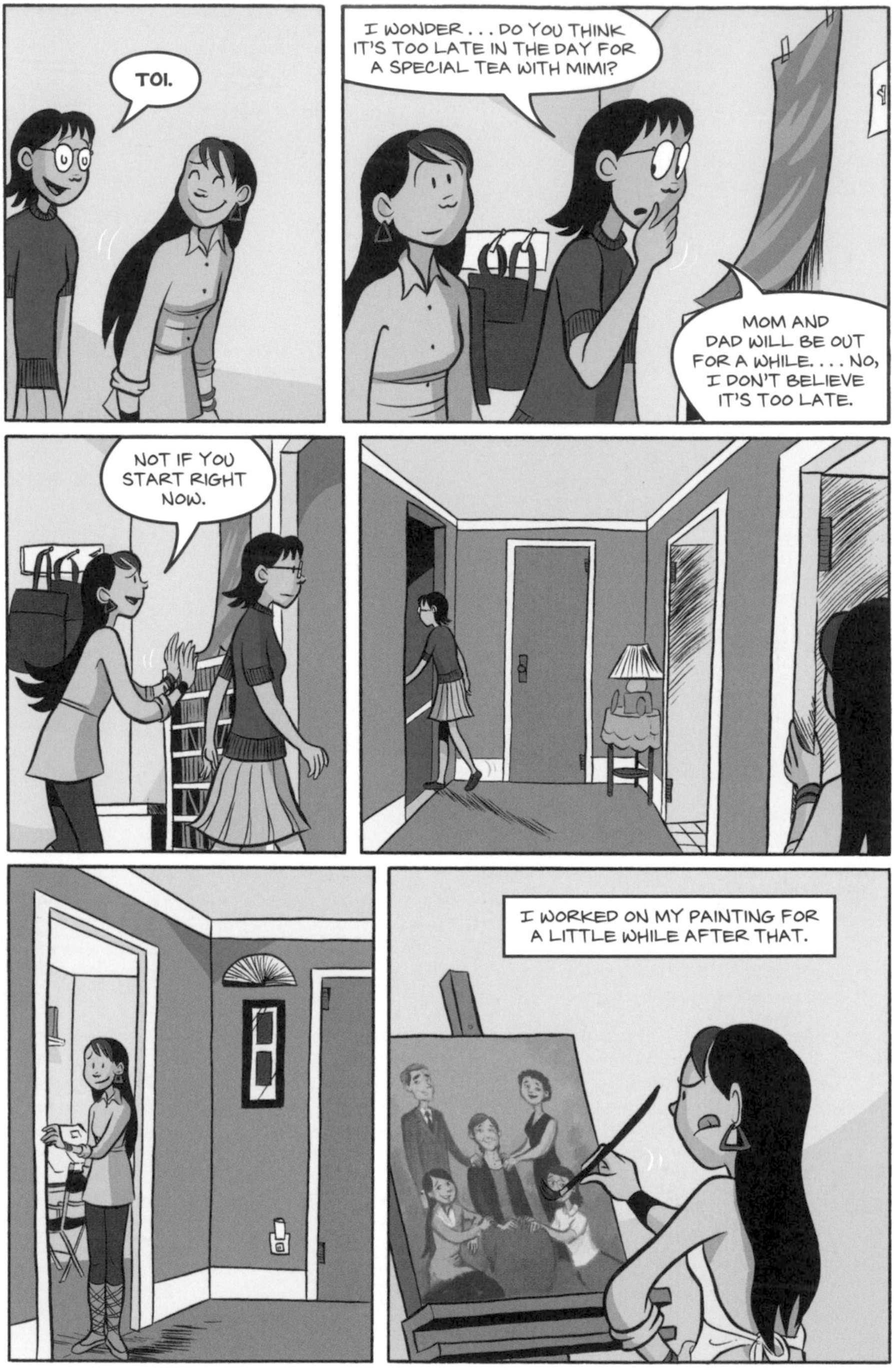
TOI.
I WONDER . . . DO YOU THINK IT'S TOO LATE IN THE DAY FOR A SPECIAL TEA WITH MIMI?
MOM AND DAD WILL BE OUT FOR A WHILE. . . . NO, I DON'T BELIEVE IT'S TOO LATE.
NOT IF YOU START RIGHT NOW.
I WORKED ON MY PAINTING FOR A LITTLE WHILE AFTER THAT.

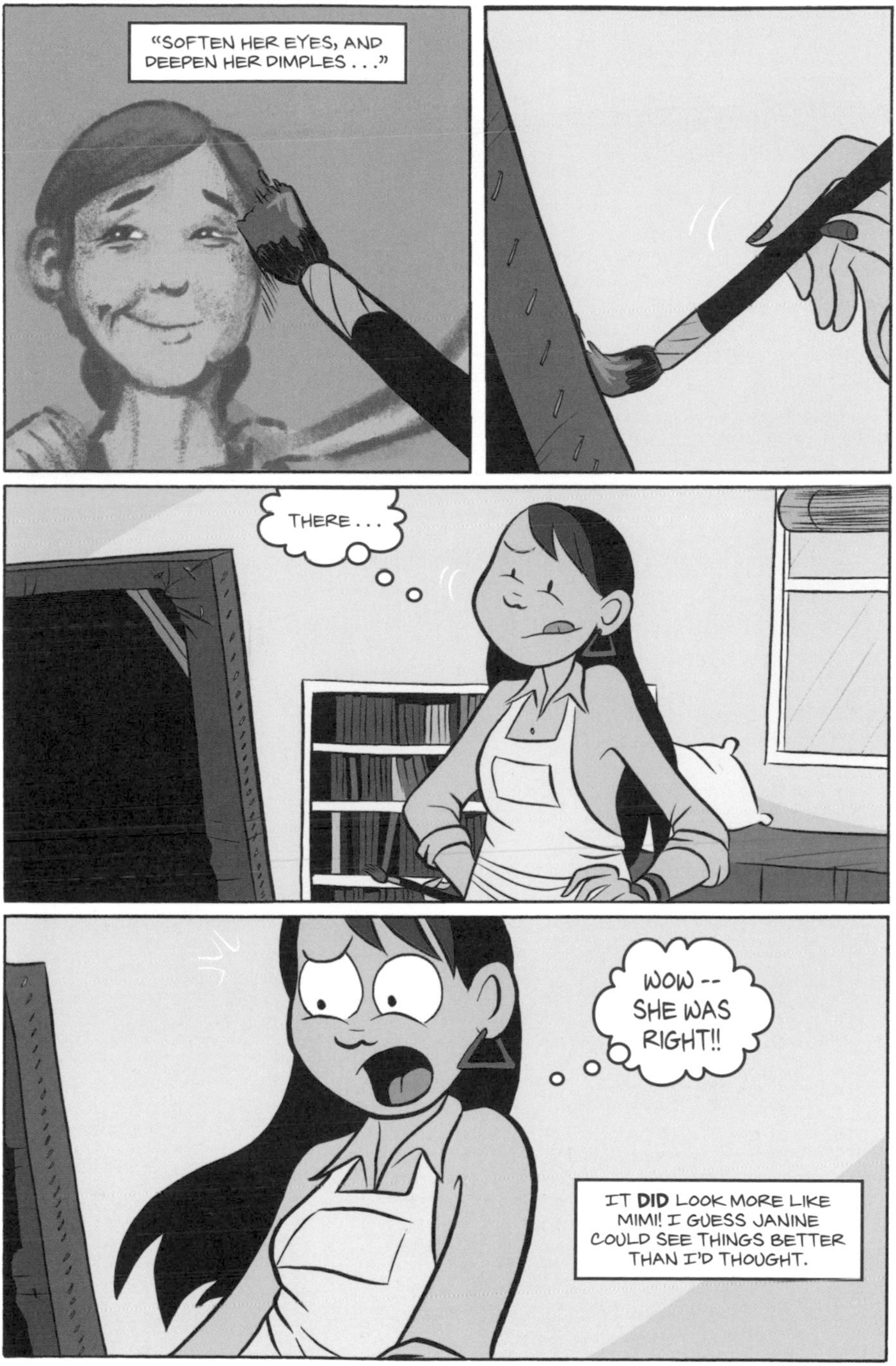
"SOFTEN HER EYES, AND DEEPEN HER DIMPLES . . ."
THERE . . .
WOW -- SHE WAS RIGHT!!
IT **DID** LOOK MORE LIKE MIMI! I GUESS JANINE COULD SEE THINGS BETTER THAN I'D THOUGHT.

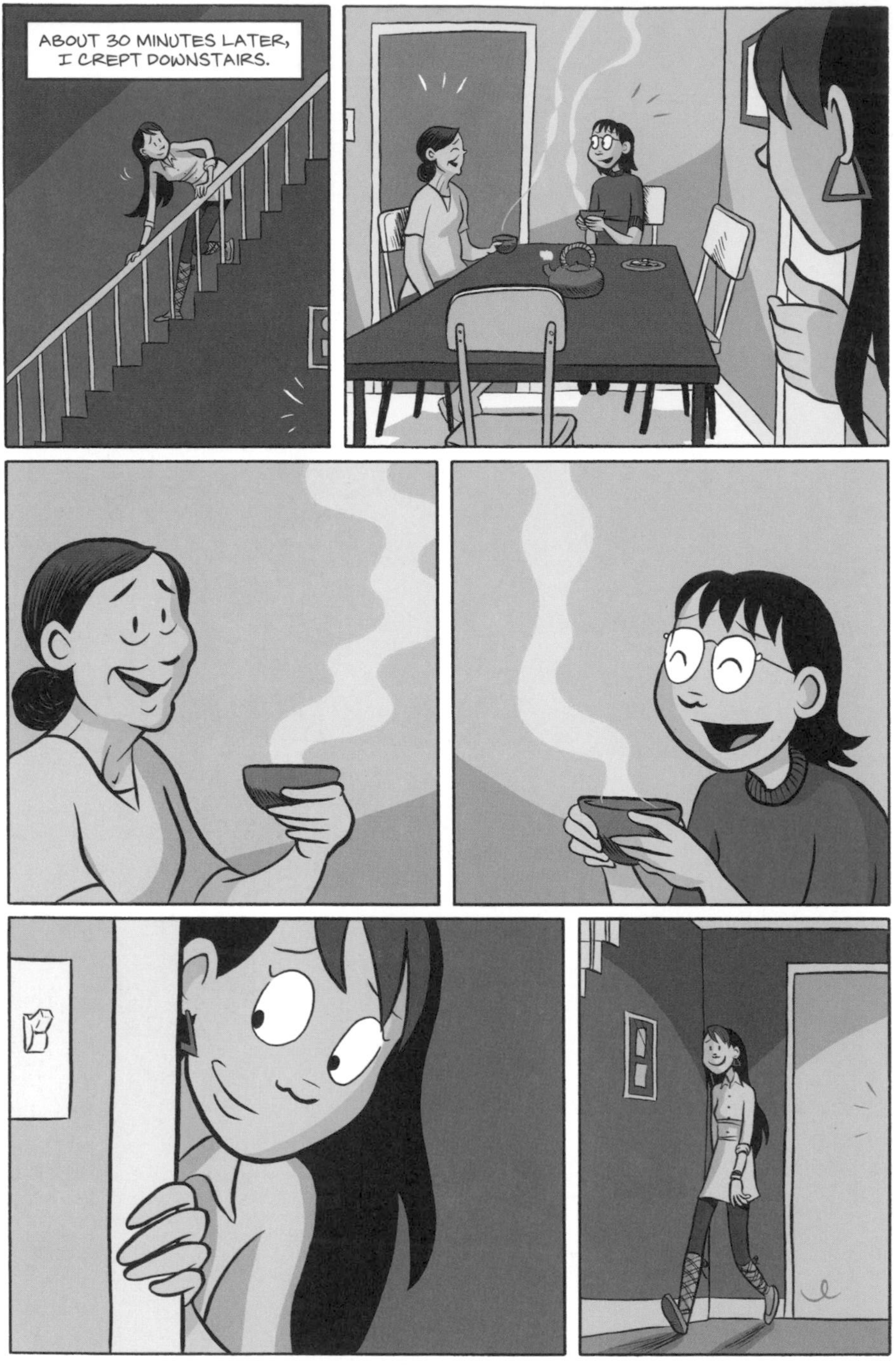
ABOUT 30 MINUTES LATER, I CREPT DOWNSTAIRS.

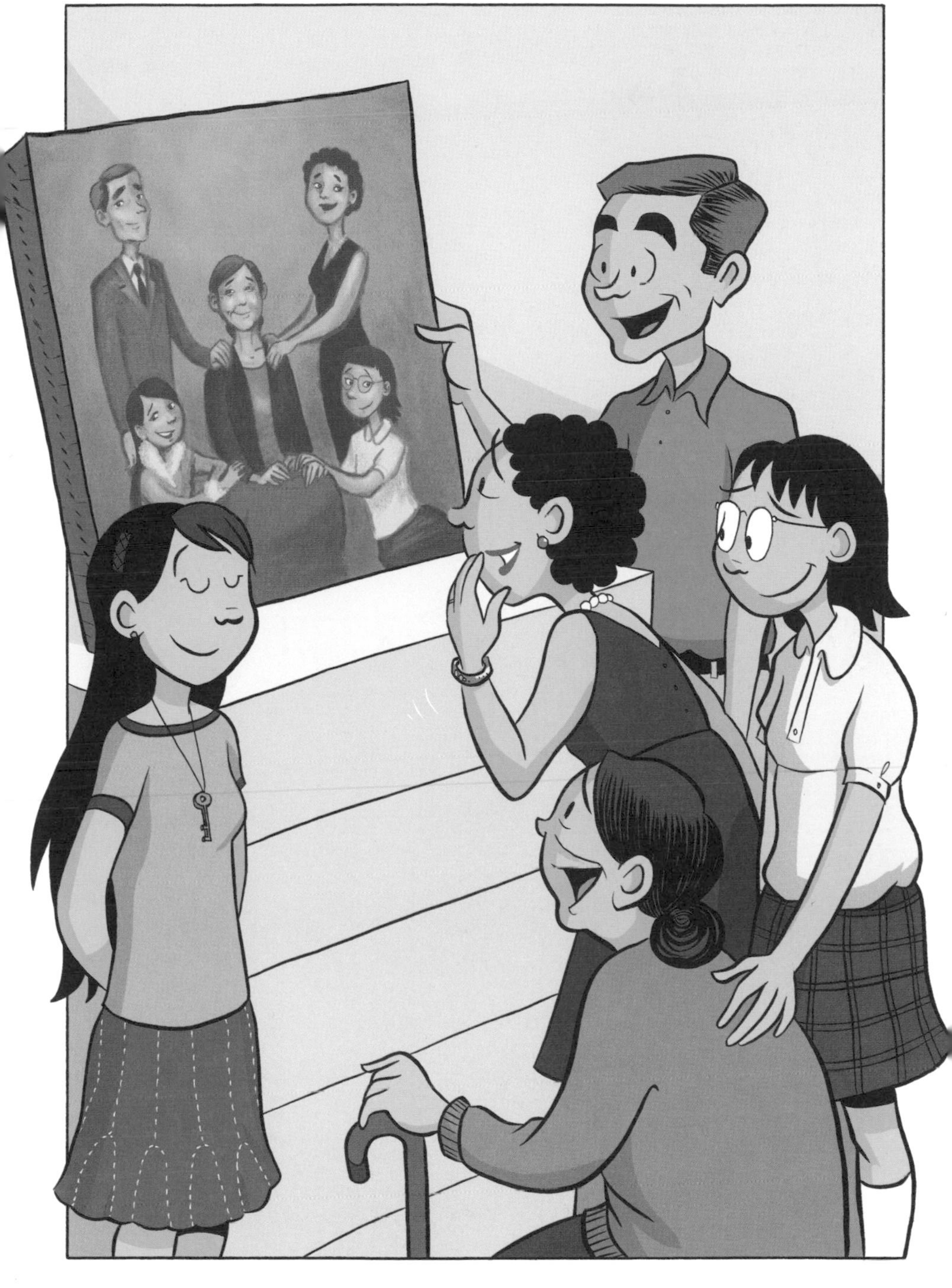

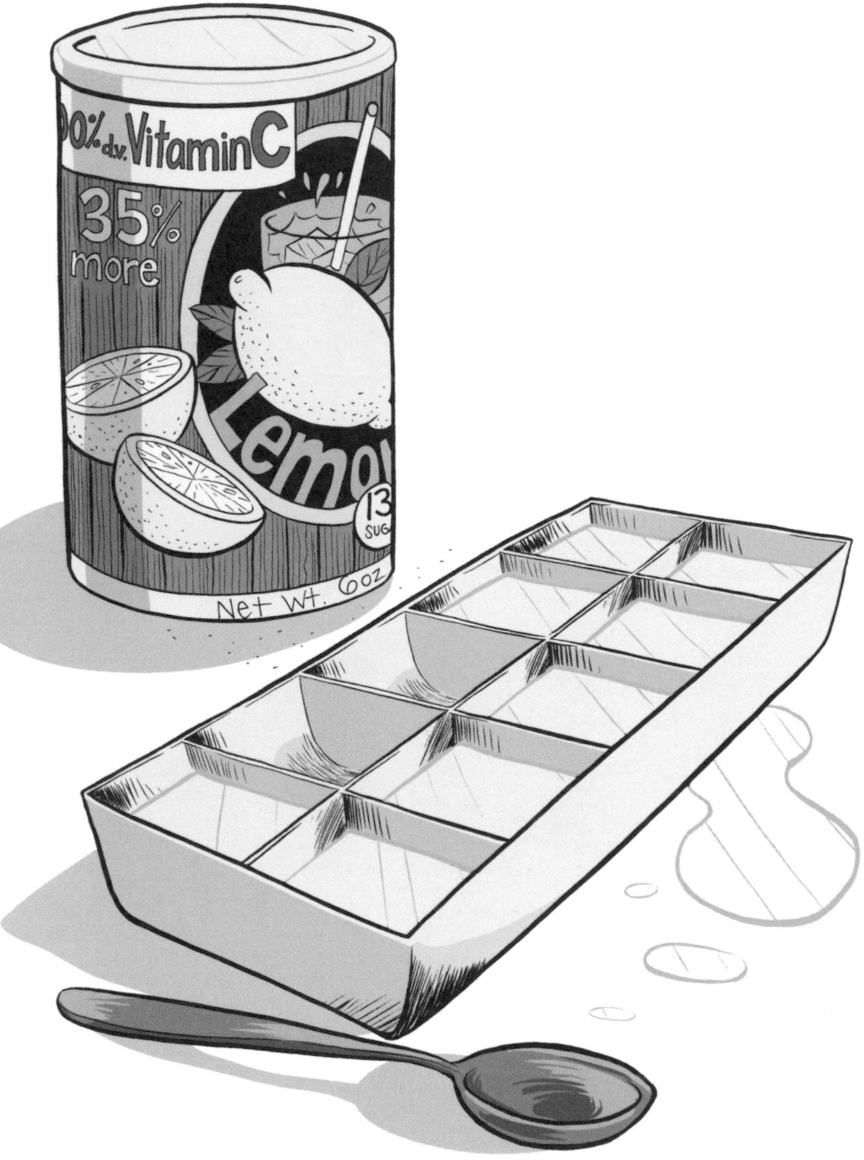
00% d.v. VitaminC
35% more
Lemo
Net Wt. 6oz

CHAPTER 17

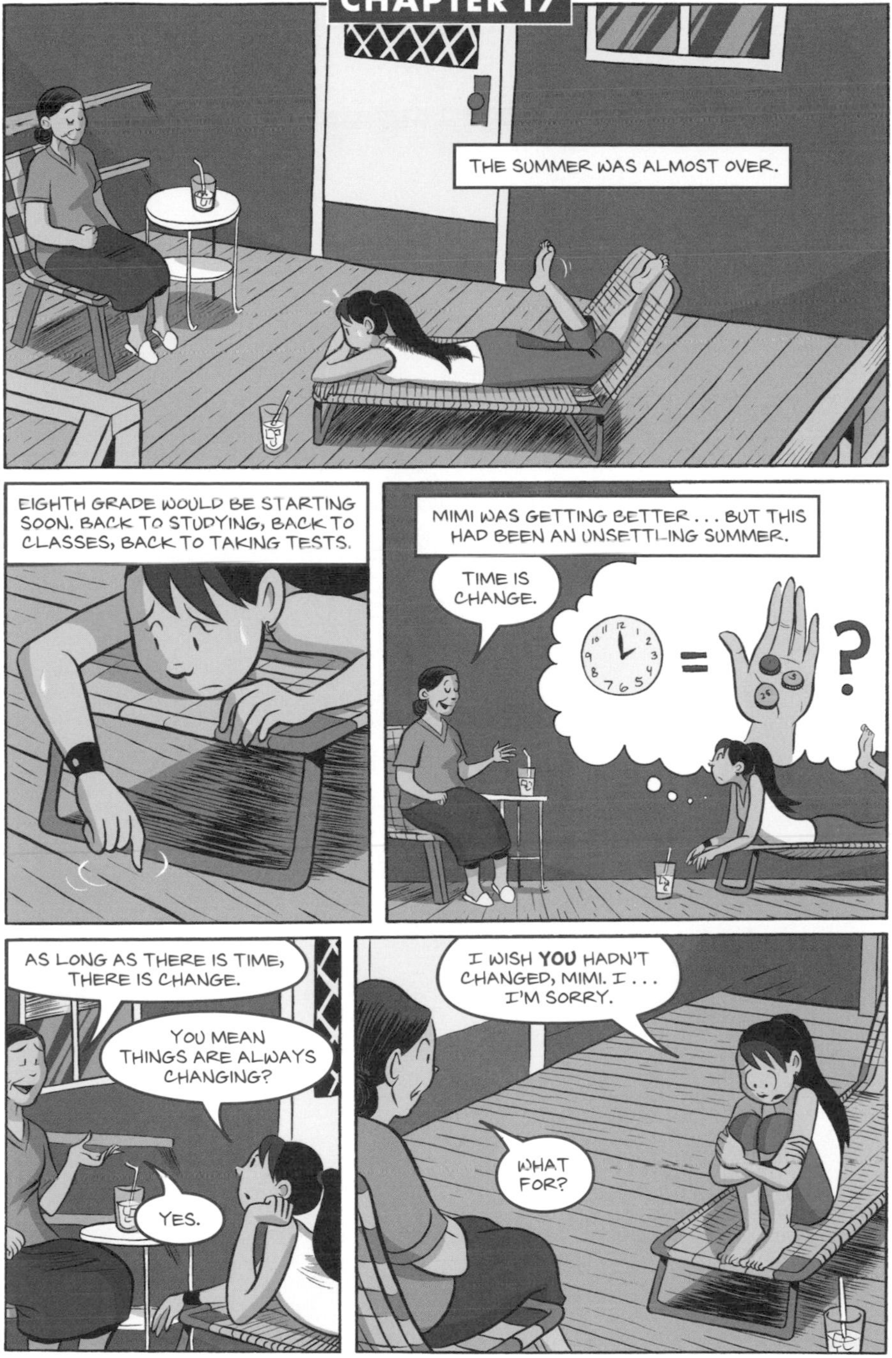
THE SUMMER WAS ALMOST OVER.
EIGHTH GRADE WOULD BE STARTING SOON. BACK TO STUDYING, BACK TO CLASSES, BACK TO TAKING TESTS.
MIMI WAS GETTING BETTER . . . BUT THIS HAD BEEN AN UNSETTLING SUMMER.
TIME IS CHANGE.
AS LONG AS THERE IS TIME, THERE IS CHANGE.
YOU MEAN THINGS ARE ALWAYS CHANGING?
YES.
I WISH YOU HADN'T CHANGED, MIMI. I . . . I'M SORRY.
WHAT FOR?

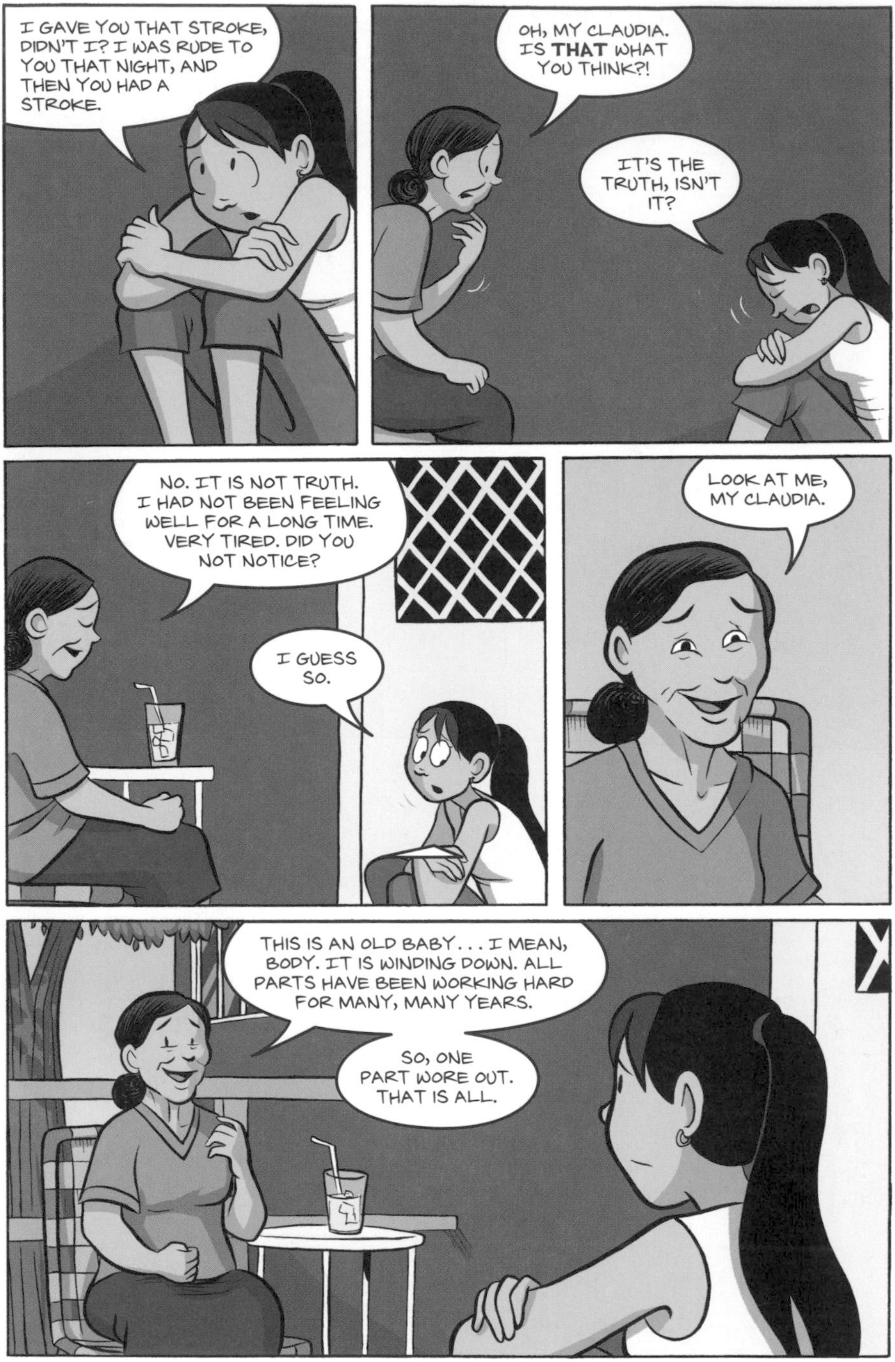

I GAVE YOU THAT STROKE, DIDN'T I? I WAS RUDE TO YOU THAT NIGHT, AND THEN YOU HAD A STROKE.
OH, MY CLAUDIA. IS **THAT** WHAT YOU THINK?!
IT'S THE TRUTH, ISN'T IT?
NO. IT IS NOT TRUTH. I HAD NOT BEEN FEELING WELL FOR A LONG TIME. VERY TIRED. DID YOU NOT NOTICE?
I GUESS SO.
LOOK AT ME, MY CLAUDIA.
THIS IS AN OLD BABY . . . I MEAN, BODY. IT IS WINDING DOWN. ALL PARTS HAVE BEEN WORKING HARD FOR MANY, MANY YEARS.
SO, ONE PART WORE OUT. THAT IS ALL.

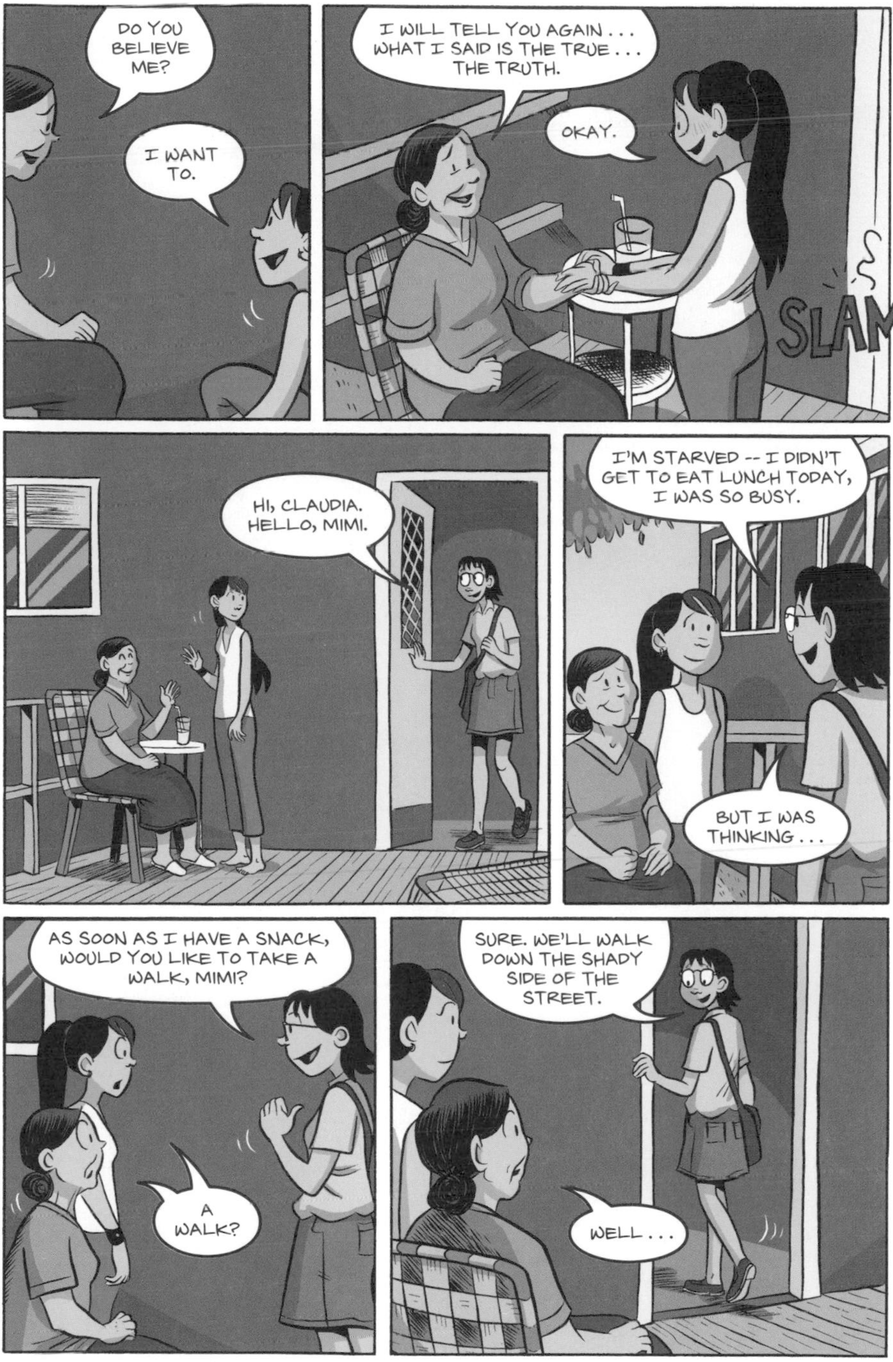
DO YOU BELIEVE ME?
I WANT TO.
I WILL TELL YOU AGAIN . . . WHAT I SAID IS THE TRUE . . . THE TRUTH.
OKAY.
SLAM
HI, CLAUDIA. HELLO, MIMI.
I'M STARVED -- I DIDN'T GET TO EAT LUNCH TODAY, I WAS SO BUSY.
BUT I WAS THINKING . . .
AS SOON AS I HAVE A SNACK, WOULD YOU LIKE TO TAKE A WALK, MIMI?
A WALK?
SURE. WE'LL WALK DOWN THE SHADY SIDE OF THE STREET.
WELL . . .

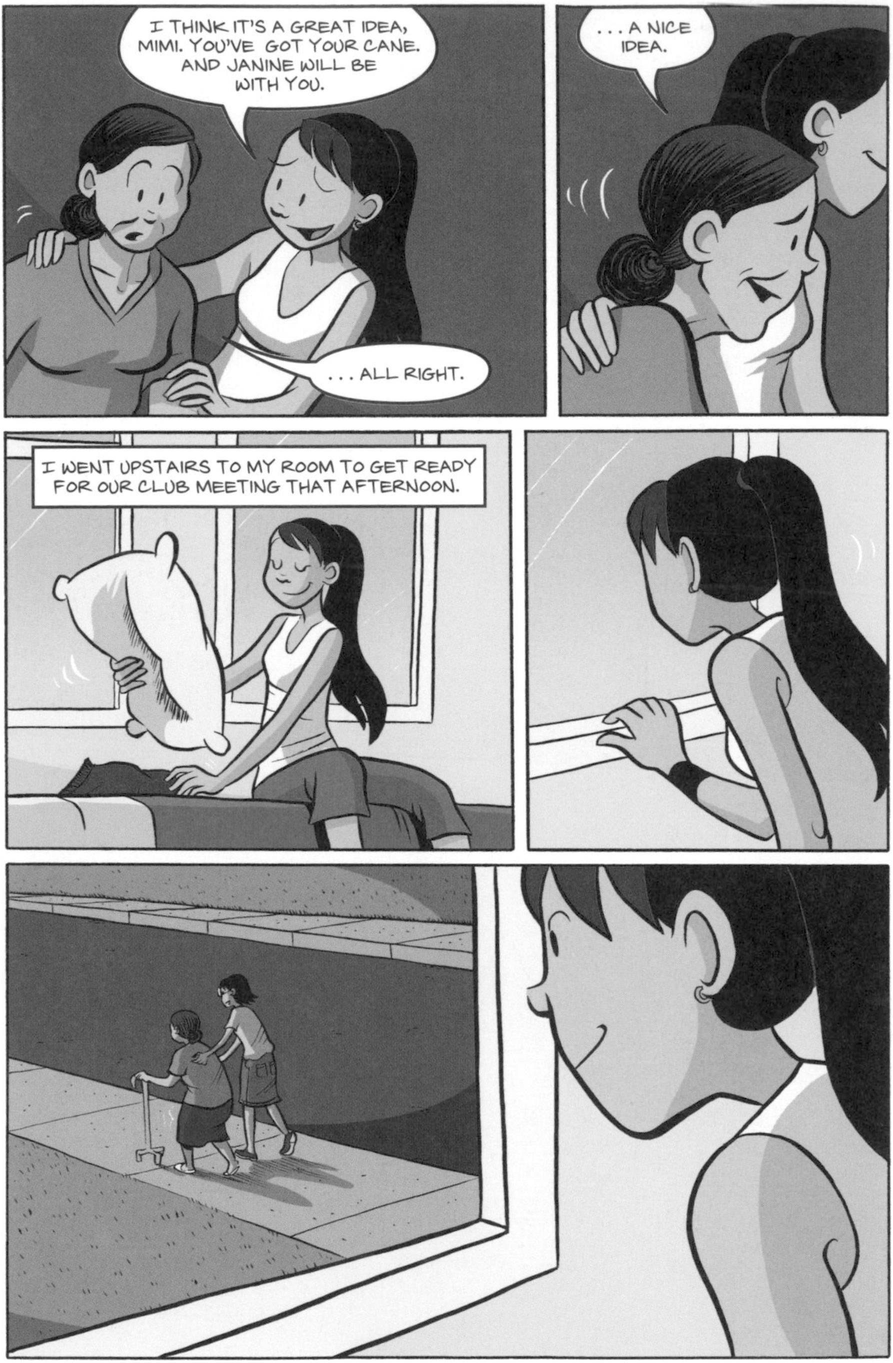
I THINK IT'S A GREAT IDEA, MIMI. YOU'VE GOT YOUR CANE. AND JANINE WILL BE WITH YOU.
. . . ALL RIGHT.
. . . A NICE IDEA.
I WENT UPSTAIRS TO MY ROOM TO GET READY FOR OUR CLUB MEETING THAT AFTERNOON.

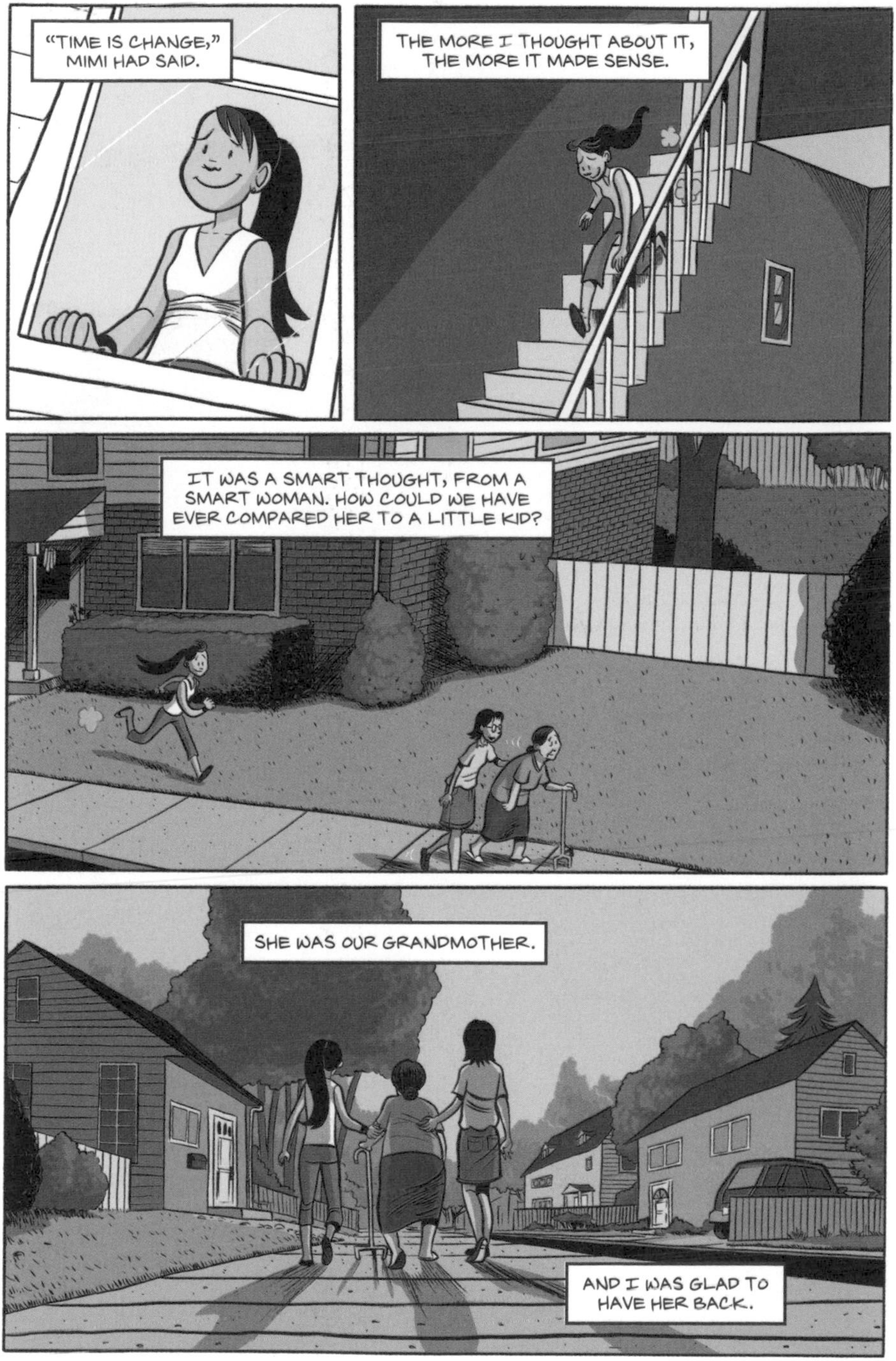
"TIME IS CHANGE,"
MIMI HAD SAID.
THE MORE I THOUGHT ABOUT IT, THE MORE IT MADE SENSE.
IT WAS A SMART THOUGHT, FROM A SMART WOMAN. HOW COULD WE HAVE EVER COMPARED HER TO A LITTLE KID?
SHE WAS OUR GRANDMOTHER.
AND I WAS GLAD TO HAVE HER BACK.

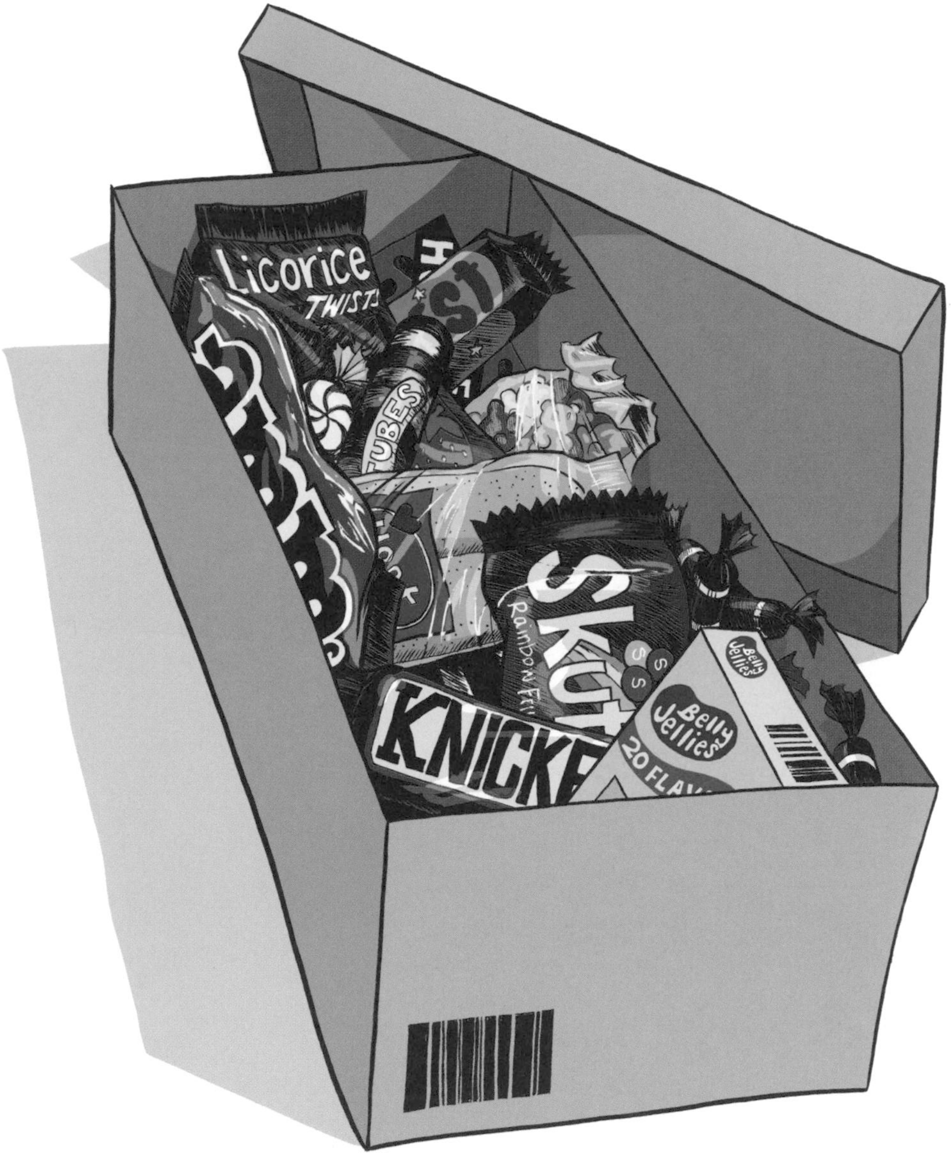
Licorice
TWISTS
TUBES
Belly Jellies
Belly Jellies

EPILOGUE

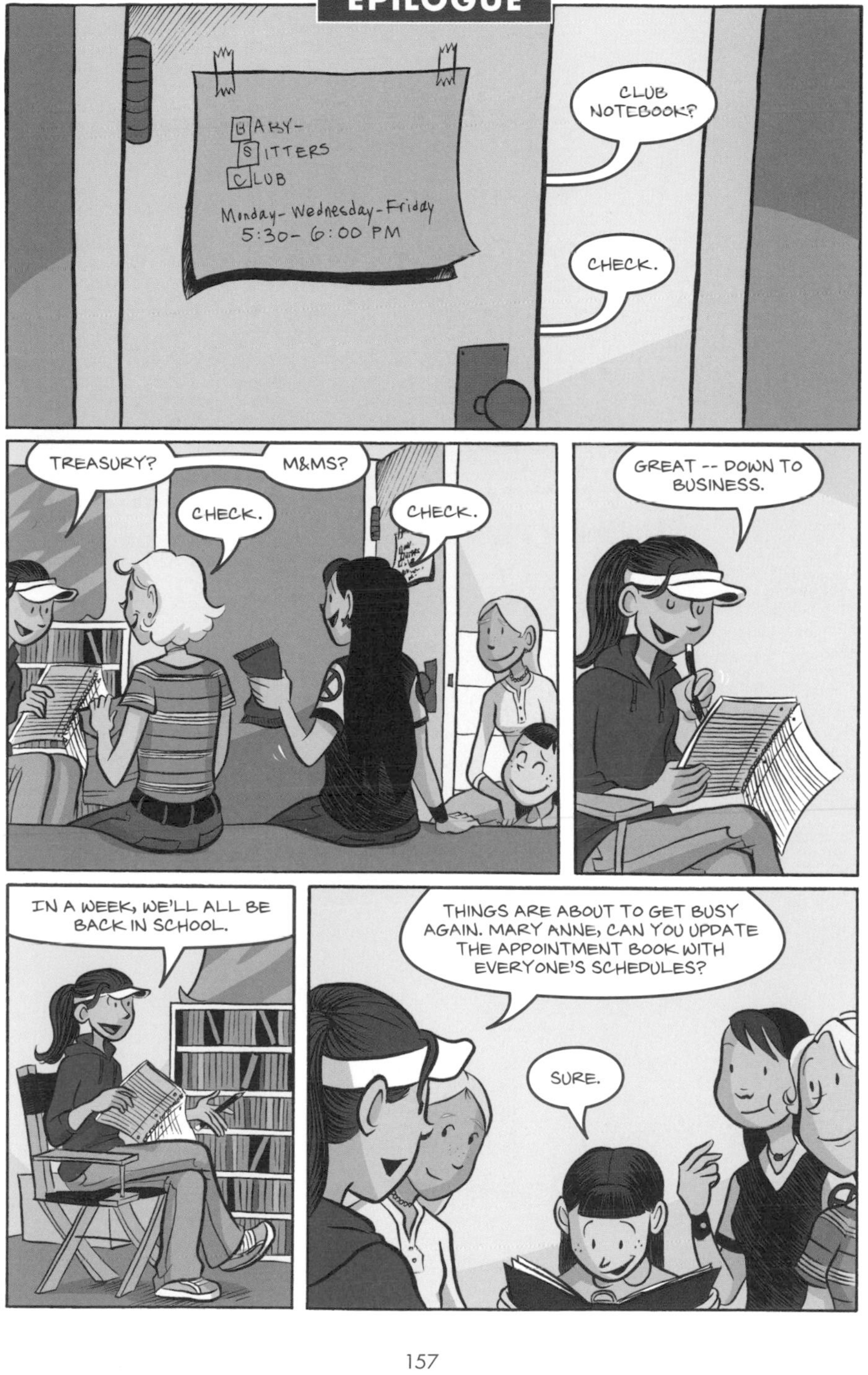
BABY-
SITTERS
CLUB
Monday-Wednesday-Friday
5:30-6:00 PM
CLUB NOTEBOOK?
CHECK.
TREASURY?
CHECK.
M&MS?
CHECK.
GREAT -- DOWN TO BUSINESS.
IN A WEEK, WE'LL ALL BE BACK IN SCHOOL.
THINGS ARE ABOUT TO GET BUSY AGAIN. MARY ANNE, CAN YOU UPDATE THE APPOINTMENT BOOK WITH EVERYONE'S SCHEDULES?
SURE.

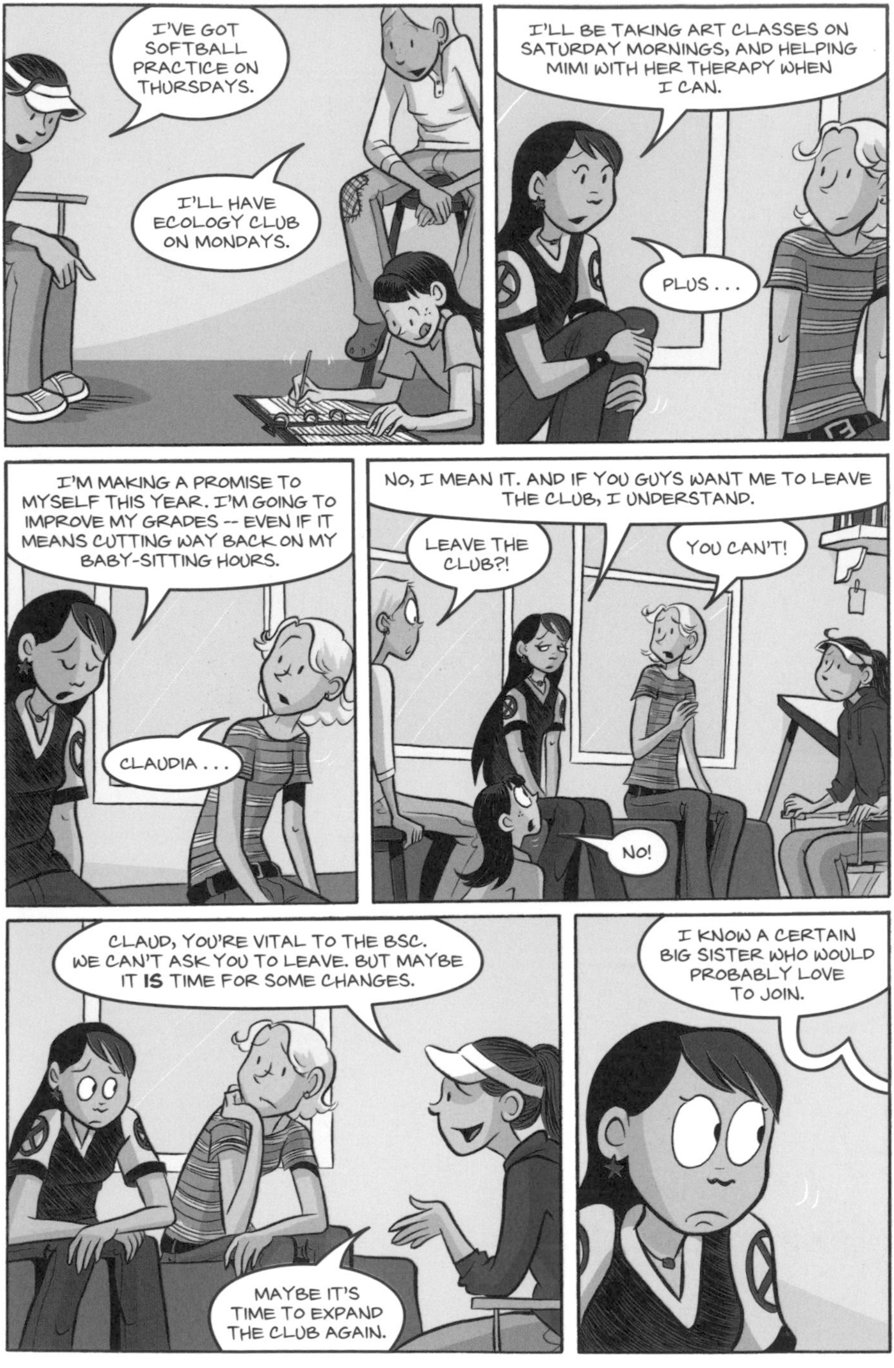
I'VE GOT SOFTBALL PRACTICE ON THURSDAYS.
I'LL HAVE ECOLOGY CLUB ON MONDAYS.
I'LL BE TAKING ART CLASSES ON SATURDAY MORNINGS, AND HELPING MIMI WITH HER THERAPY WHEN I CAN.
PLUS . . .
I'M MAKING A PROMISE TO MYSELF THIS YEAR. I'M GOING TO IMPROVE MY GRADES -- EVEN IF IT MEANS CUTTING WAY BACK ON MY BABY-SITTING HOURS.
CLAUDIA . . .
NO, I MEAN IT. AND IF YOU GUYS WANT ME TO LEAVE THE CLUB, I UNDERSTAND.
LEAVE THE CLUB?!
YOU CAN'T!
NO!
CLAUD, YOU'RE VITAL TO THE BSC. WE CAN'T ASK YOU TO LEAVE. BUT MAYBE IT **IS** TIME FOR SOME CHANGES.
MAYBE IT'S TIME TO EXPAND THE CLUB AGAIN.
I KNOW A CERTAIN BIG SISTER WHO WOULD PROBABLY LOVE TO JOIN.

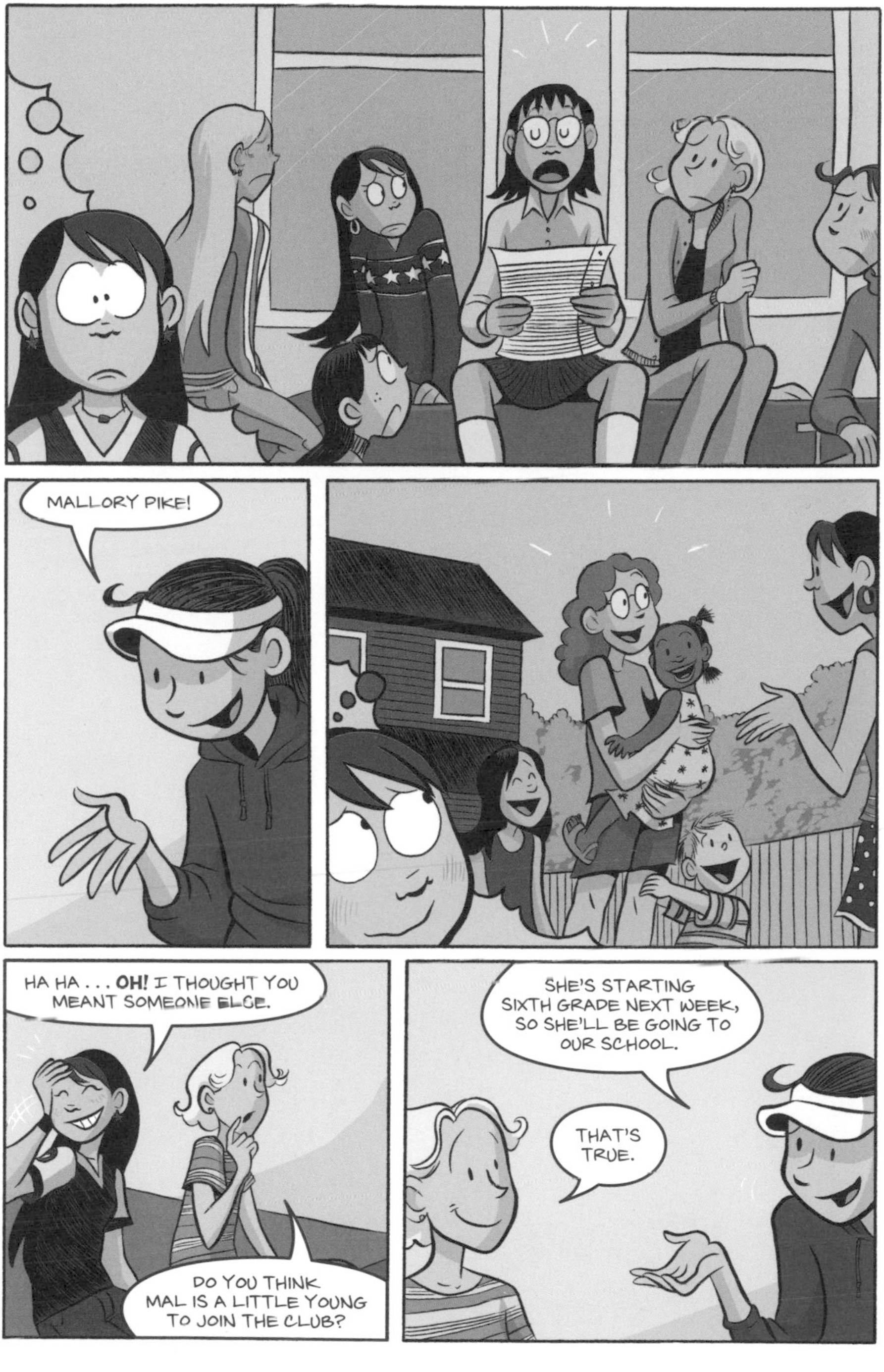
MALLORY PIKE!
HA HA . . . **OH!** I THOUGHT YOU MEANT SOMEONE ELSE.
DO YOU THINK MAL IS A LITTLE YOUNG TO JOIN THE CLUB?
SHE'S STARTING SIXTH GRADE NEXT WEEK, SO SHE'LL BE GOING TO OUR SCHOOL.
THAT'S TRUE.

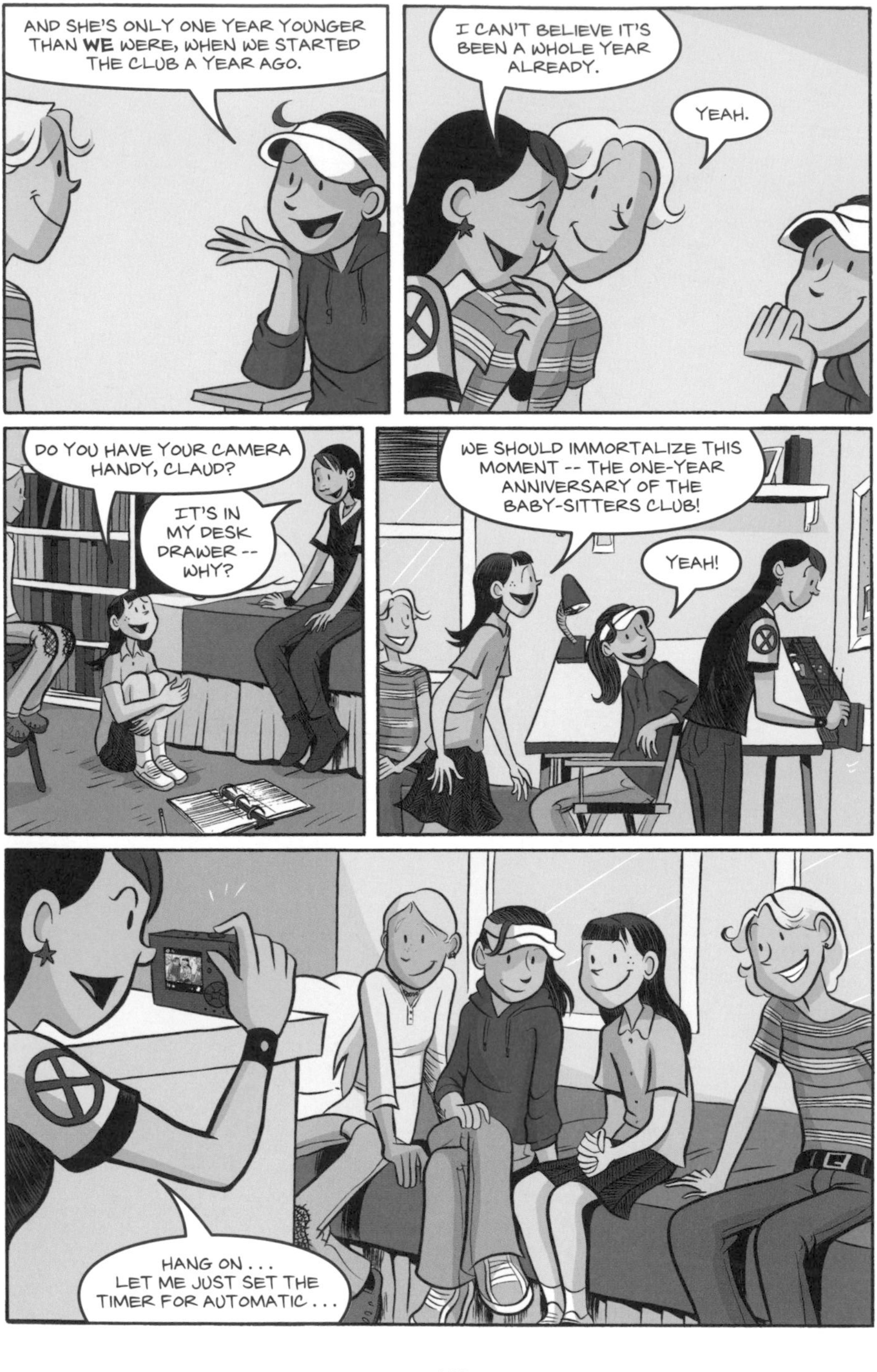
AND SHE'S ONLY ONE YEAR YOUNGER THAN **WE** WERE, WHEN WE STARTED THE CLUB A YEAR AGO.
I CAN'T BELIEVE IT'S BEEN A WHOLE YEAR ALREADY.
YEAH.
DO YOU HAVE YOUR CAMERA HANDY, CLAUD?
IT'S IN MY DESK DRAWER -- WHY?
WE SHOULD IMMORTALIZE THIS MOMENT -- THE ONE-YEAR ANNIVERSARY OF THE BABY-SITTERS CLUB!
YEAH!
HANG ON . . . LET ME JUST SET THE TIMER FOR AUTOMATIC . . .

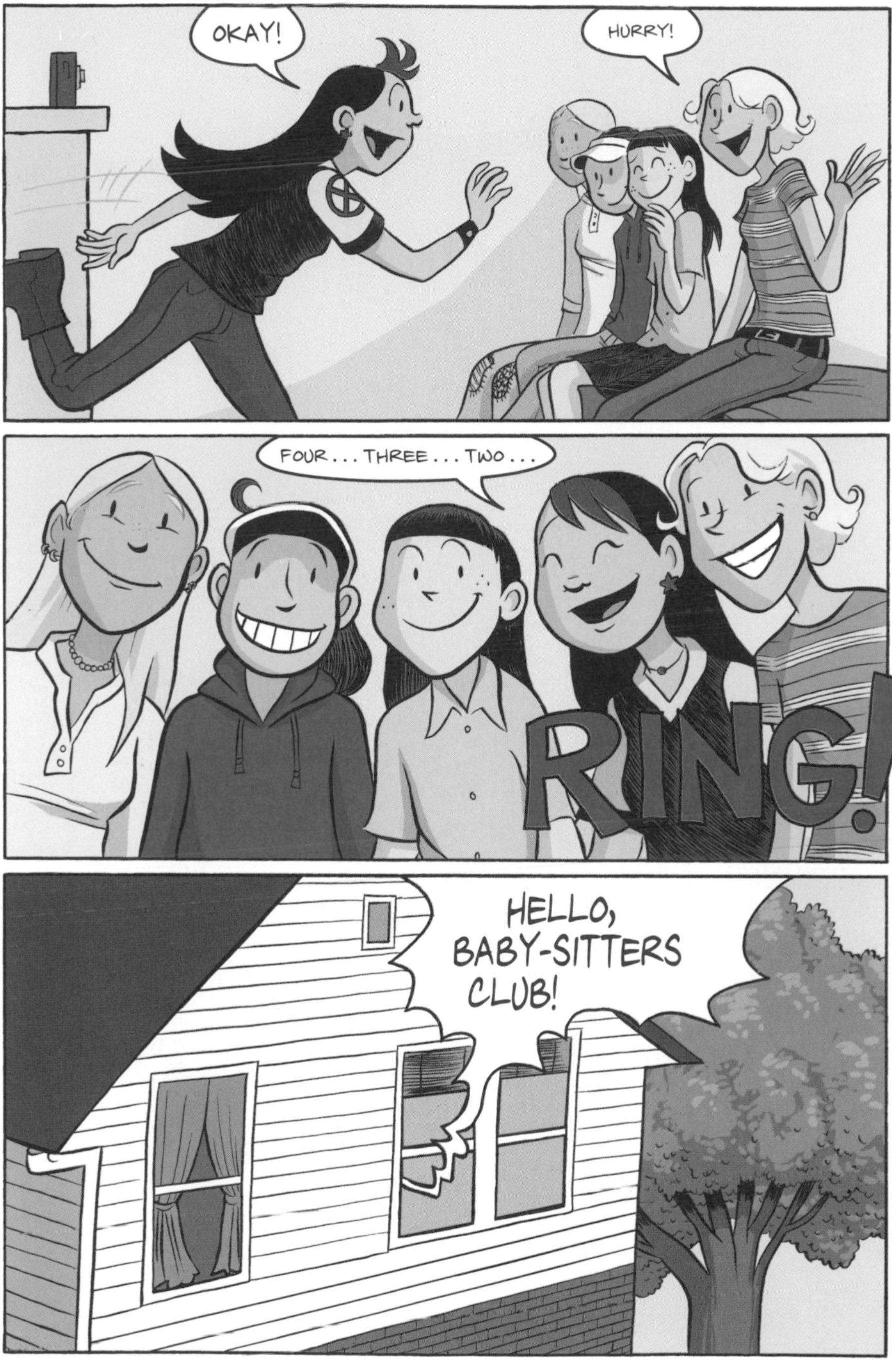
OKAY!
HURRY!
FOUR . . . THREE . . . TWO . . .
RING!
HELLO, BABY-SITTERS CLUB!

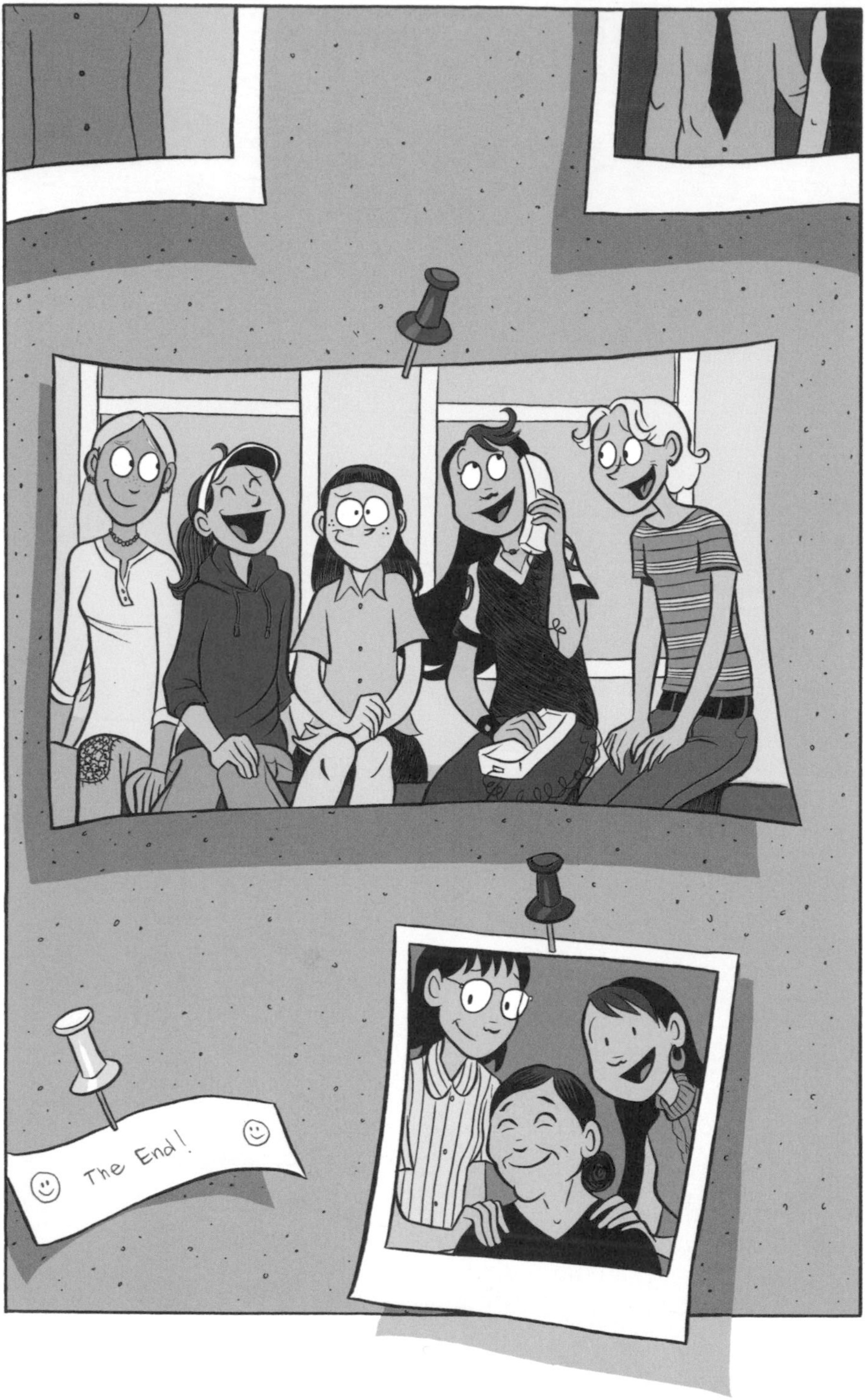
The End!

THE MAKING OF THE BABY-SITTERS CLUB®

(GRAPHIC NOVEL)

STEP 1

Raina reads the original Baby-sitters Club book she is about to adapt several times before she starts working on the graphic novel. She underlines parts she especially likes, writes notes, and draws sketches of any new characters. Raina was a big fan of the BSC books when she was young, and often remembers things about the stories from the very first time she read them!

"Nobody likes me," she wailed. She was sitting at a picnic table making a get-well card. She lowered her head onto her arm, the picture of despair.

A blue crayon rolled across the table, heading for her lap.

I dove for it and caught it before it landed on her dress.

"But Jenny, you said you didn't want to play with them," I pointed out.

"Well, I do now!"

"So go play."

"I can't. I'll get my dress dirty."

I rolled my eyes. Jenny was what Mimi would call "a trial." But apart from Jenny, the kids had fun at the play group that morning. And they made a total of nineteen cards for Mimi.

That
and his
ran erra
glad I h
kept my
I love
Newtor
of the
only litt
born. A
how Jar

Start w/ rainy summer night - right before school ends?

56

move to Ch. 4?

house. We were sure he'd be jealous. And he was a little bit, but only sometimes.

Now the Newtons were planning a big party for Lucy's christening. The party was coming up soon.

"Look at this stuff. Look at all this stuff," Jamie said to me after his mother had left. He led me into the dining room. "Mommy is getting ready to give a party, a big one. And it's all for *her*." Jamie nodded his head toward the second floor, where Lucy was taking her afternoon nap.

The Newtons did seem to be getting ready for a very large party. The dining room table was covered with boxes of crackers, cans of peanuts, tins of candies, stacks of napkins; plus glasses, silverware, plates, a punch bowl and cups, serving spoons, and more.

"You know what?" I said. "When you were Lucy's age, your parents gave a great big party after your christening."

"They did?" Jamie brightened. Then he frowned. "But I don't remember it!" he said loudly.

"Shh." I put a finger to my lips. "The baby —"

"I know," said Jamie sullenly. "The baby is sleeping."

Uh-oh, I thought. This doesn't look good.

57

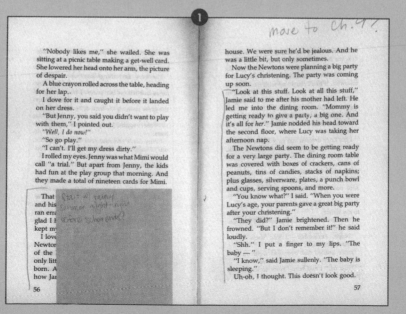

STEP 2

Then, she begins to create thumbnails. These are small, simple, quick pages created on pieces of computer paper. Using a No. 2 pencil, Raina sketches out where the action and dialogue and drawings will appear on every page. She does this for the entire book, so she can see if the whole story works as well in comic form as it did in written form. It's easy to edit, shift things around, re-sketch, and rewrite at this stage. She also shows this to her editors and Ann M. Martin, the BSC's original author!

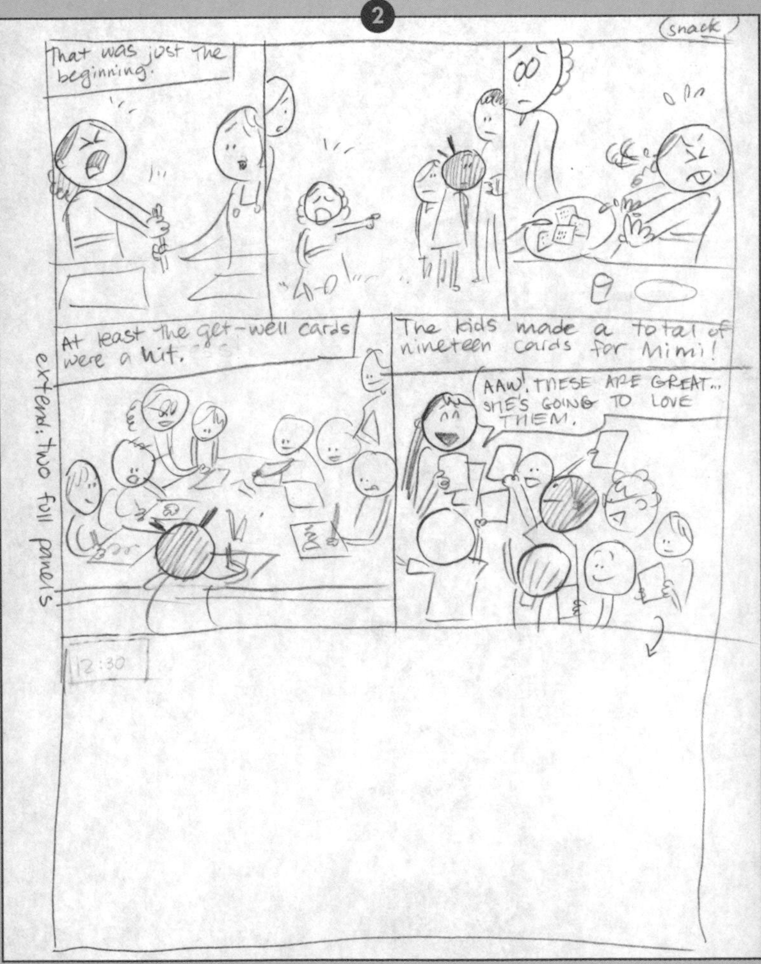
2
(snack)
That was just the beginning.
At least the get-well cards were a hit.
The kids made a total of nineteen cards for Mimi!
AAW! THESE ARE GREAT... SHE'S GOING TO LOVE THEM.
extend: two full panels
12:30

STEP 3

Once the thumbnails have been approved, Raina types up all the dialogue. This will be used when the book gets lettered (Step 8).

3

PAGE 46

PANEL 1
1. Caption: That was just the beginning.

PANEL 4
2. Caption: At least the get-well cards were a hit.

PANEL 5
3. Caption: The kids made a total of nineteen cards for Mimi!
4. Claudia: Aww! These are great. . . . She's going to love them.

STEP 4

Next, Raina uses a light blue pencil to do final layouts. She draws the panel borders and redraws her sketches onto large 11" x 14" Bristol board. It's a lot of work to redraw the sketches, even though they look very simple. This is where Raina works out perspective, composition, and general action in every panel. It also helps her see where the word balloons are going to go, so she can leave room for them. Being messy is no problem because blue pencil doesn't show up when the pages are scanned! See how this page changed between the thumbnail stage and the layout stage?

STEP 5

Now the real fun begins! Raina draws over her blue lines with a regular No. 2 pencil, this time going nice and slow and drawing in all the details. You can see how different the page is starting to look! The blue lines help guide the more finished art.

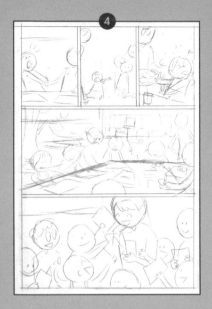

STEP 6

Raina's favorite stage is inking. She uses a Faber-Castell artist pen to draw the panel borders (using a ruler, of course!), and then a #2 Winsor & Newton watercolor brush and a bottle of waterproof India ink to ink the drawings. Little details like eyeballs and buttons are drawn with a tiny-tipped Micron pen, and are usually added last.

STEP 7

After the ink dries, Raina erases all the pencil lines. Each page is scanned into the computer at 64% its size, and then "cleaned up" in Photoshop. Instead of using Wite-Out, Raina just erases little mistakes digitally, which is faster. When each page file is clean, they are sent to the letterer!

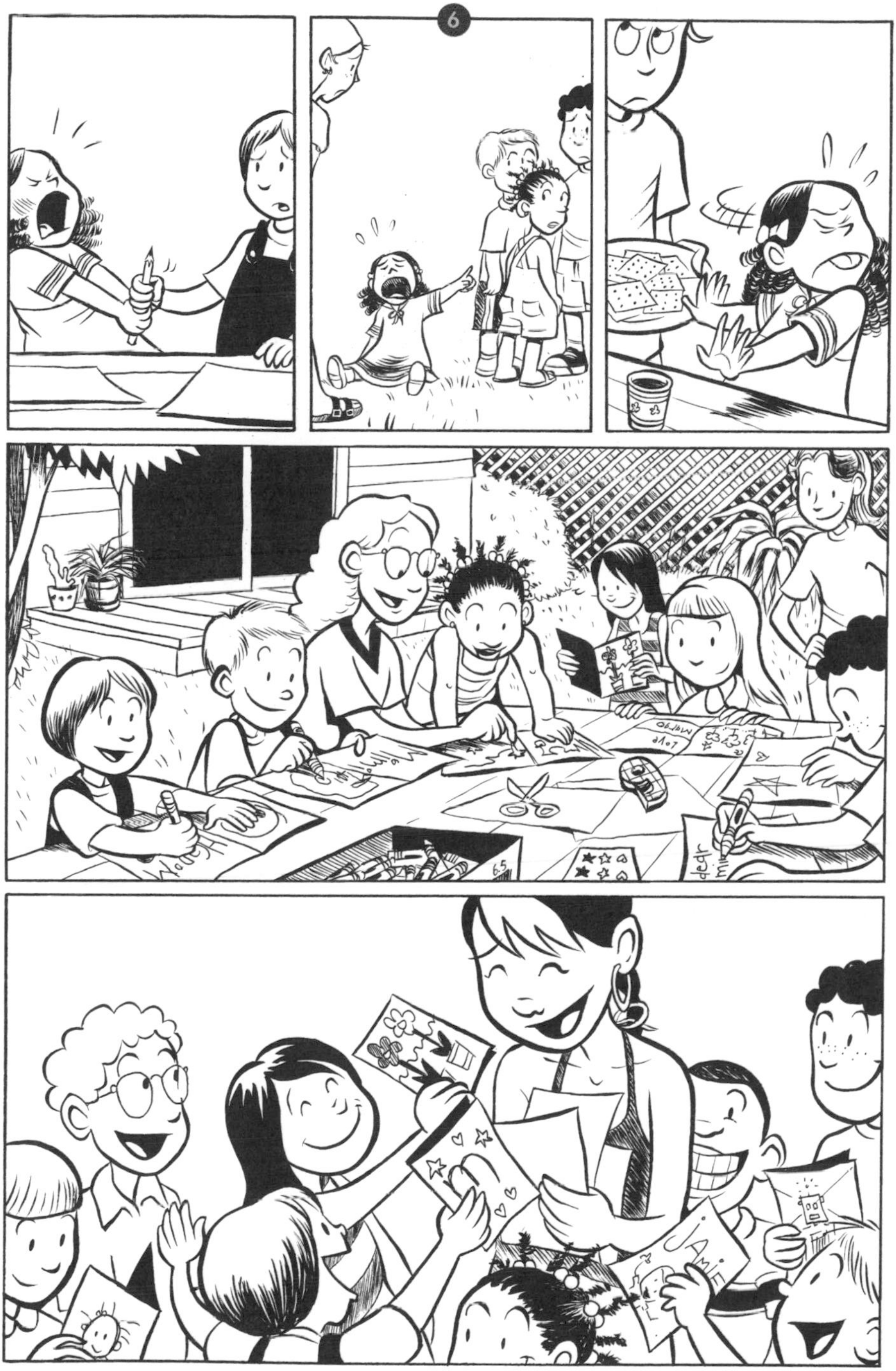
6
JAMIE

STEP 8

The letterer, John, creates word balloons in Adobe Illustrator, and then fills them in with the dialogue from the script that Raina typed up.

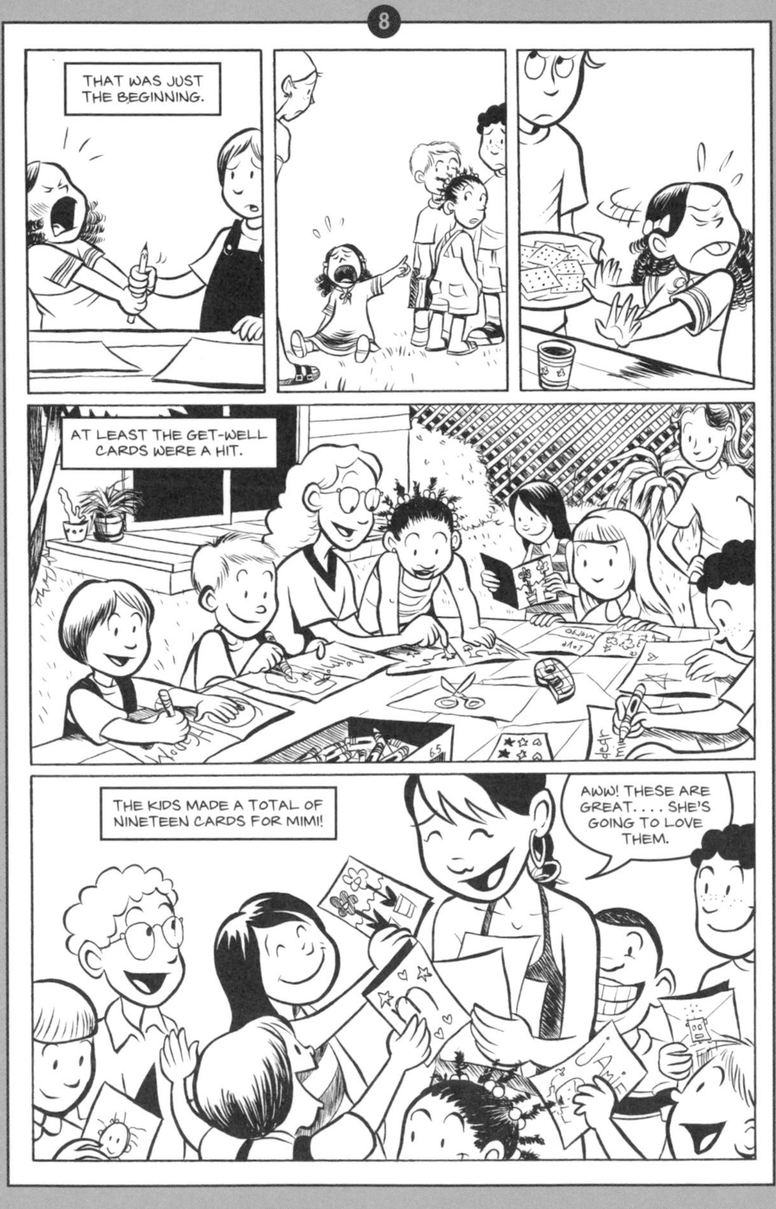
8
THAT WAS JUST THE BEGINNING.
AT LEAST THE GET-WELL CARDS WERE A HIT.
THE KIDS MADE A TOTAL OF NINETEEN CARDS FOR MIMI!
AWW! THESE ARE GREAT. . . . SHE'S GOING TO LOVE THEM.

STEP 9

In the final step, the colorist, Braden, uses Adobe Photoshop to add digital color to the black-and-white art. Now the finished pages are ready to go to the printer!

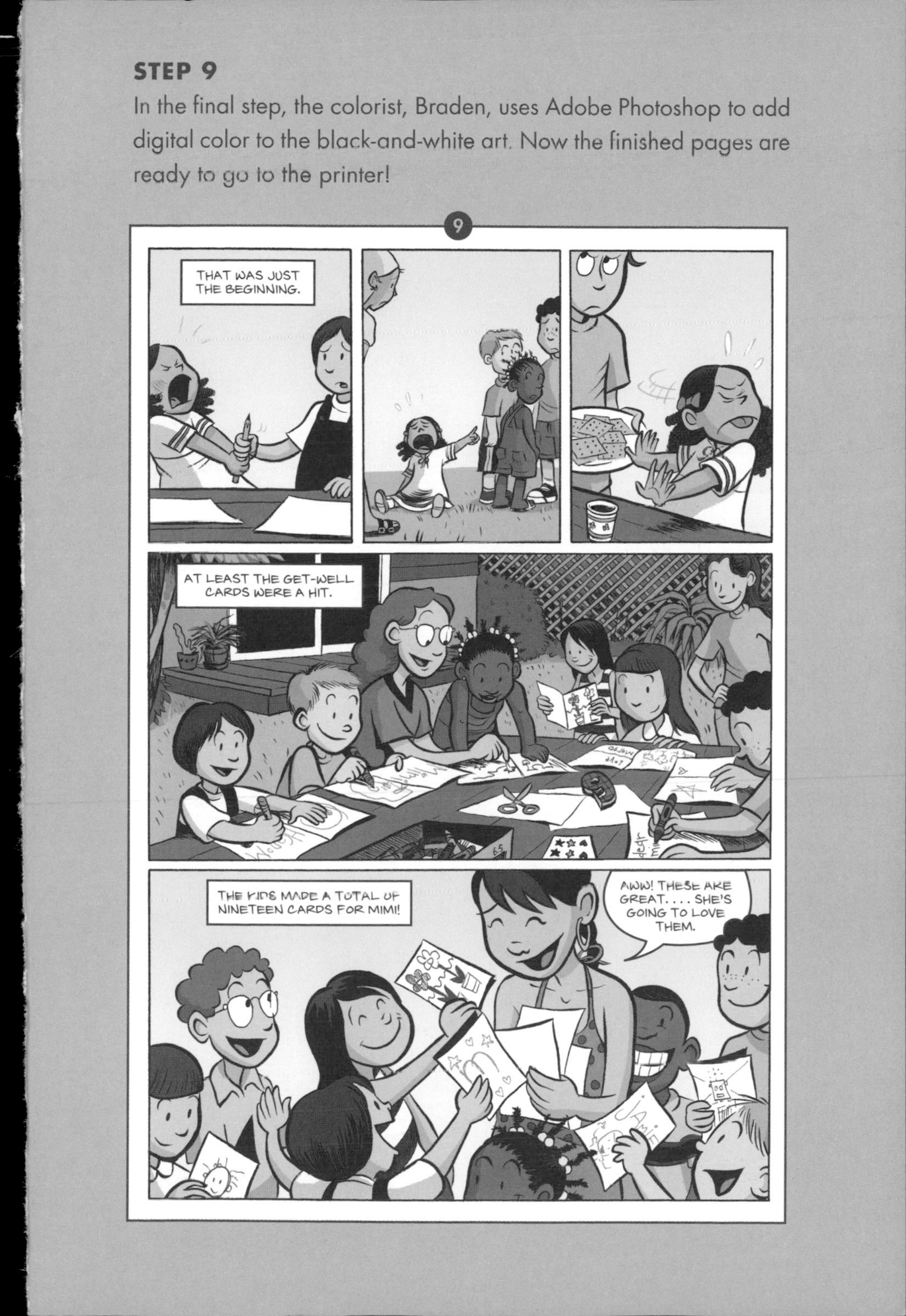
9
THAT WAS JUST THE BEGINNING.
AT LEAST THE GET-WELL CARDS WERE A HIT.
THE KIDS MADE A TOTAL OF NINETEEN CARDS FOR MIMI!
AWW! THESE ARE GREAT.... SHE'S GOING TO LOVE THEM.

ANN M. MARTIN'S The Baby-sitters Club is one of the most popular series in the history of publishing — with more than 176 million books in print worldwide — and inspired a generation of young readers. Her novels include *Belle Teal*, *A Corner of the Universe* (a Newbery Honor book), *Here Today*, *A Dog's Life*, and *On Christmas Eve*, as well as the much-loved collaborations, *P.S. Longer Letter Later* and *Snail Mail No More*, with Paula Danziger, and *The Doll People* and *The Meanest Doll in the World*, written with Laura Godwin and illustrated by Brian Selznick. She lives in upstate New York.

RAINA TELGEMEIER is the #1 *New York Times* bestselling, multiple Eisner Award–winning creator of *Smile* and *Sisters*, which are both graphic memoirs based on her childhood. She is also the creator of *Drama*, which was named a Stonewall Honor Book and was selected for YALSA's Top Ten Great Graphic Novels for Teens. Raina lives in the San Francisco Bay Area. To learn more, visit her online at www.goRaina.com.